UTHER AND IGRAINE

"PELLEAS WATCHED HER AS HER GREY GOWN WENT AMID THE GREEN AND RED"

UTHER AND IGRAINE

BY

WARWICK DEEPING

ILLUSTRATED BY W. BENDA

WILDSIDE PRESS

www.wildsidepress.com

Published October, 1903.
Reprinted November, 1903.
Reprinted January, 1904.
Reprinted April, 1904.

To

MAUDE MERRILL

WITH THE AUTHOR'S HOMAGE

CONTENTS

BOOK I

BOOK II

BOOK III

BOOK IV

BOOK I

THE WAY TO WINCHESTER

I

Beneath the dark cornices of a thicket of wind-stunted pines stood a small company of women looking out into the hastening night. The half light of evening lay over the scene, rolling wood and valley into a misty mass, while the horizon stood curbed by a belt of imminent clouds. In the western vault, a vast rent in the wall of grey gave out a blaze of transient gold that slanted like a spear-shaft to a sullen sea.

A wind cried restlessly amid the trees, gusty at intervals, but tuning its mood to a desolate and constant moan. There was an expression of despair on the face of the west. The woods were full of a vague woe, and of troubled breathing. The trees seemed to sway to one another, to fling strange words with a tossing of hair, and outstretched hands. The furze in the valley — swept and harrowed — undulated like a green lagoon.

The women upon the hill were garbed after the fashion of grey nuns. Their gowns stood out blankly against the ascetic trunks of the pines. They were huddled together in a group, like sheep under a thorn hedge when storms threaten. The dark ovals of their hoods were turned towards the south, where the white patch of a sail showed vaguely through the gathering grey.

Between the hill and the cliffs lay a valley, threaded by a meagre stream, that quavered through pastures. A mist hung there despite the wind. Folded by a circle of oaks rose the grey walls of an ecclesiastical building of no inconsiderable size, while the mournful clangour of a bell came up upon the wind, with a vague sound as of voices chanting.

Valley, stream, and abbey were rapidly melting into the indefinite background of the night.

Suddenly a snarling murmur seemed to swell the plaining of the bell. A dark mass that was moving through the meadows beneath like a herd of kine broke into a fringe of hurrying specks that dissolved into the shadows of the circle of oaks. The bell still continued to toll, while the women beneath the pines shivered and drew closer together as though for warmth and comfort. There was not one among them who had not grasped the full significance of the sinister sound that had come to them from the valley. A novice, taller than her sisters, stood forward from the group, as though eager to catch the first evidence of the deed that was to be done on that drear evening. She held up a hand to those behind her, in mute appeal to them to listen. The bell had ceased pulsing. In its stead sounded a faint eerie whimper, an occasional shrill cry that seemed to leap out of silence like a bubble from a pool where death has been.

The women were shaken from their strained vigilance as by a wind. The utter grey of the hour seemed to stifle them. Some were on their knees, praying and weeping; one had fainted, and lay huddled against the trunk of a pine. It was such a tragedy as was often played in those days of disruption and despair, for Rome — the decrepit Saturn of history — had fallen from empire to a tottering dotage. Her colonies — those Titans of the past — still quivered beneath the doom piled upon them by the Teuton. In Britain, the cry of a nation had gone out blindly into the night. Vortigern had perished in the flames of Genorium. Reculbuum, Rhutupiæ, and Durovernum had fallen. The fair fields of Kent were open to the pirate; while Aurelius, stout soldier-king, gathered spear and shield to remedy the need of Britain.

The women upon the hill were but the creatures of destiny. Realism had touched them with cynical finger. The barbarians had come shorewards that day in their ships, and at the first breathing of the news the abbey dependants had fled, leaving nun and novice to the mercies of the moment. It had become a matter of flight or martyrdom. Certain fervent women had chosen to remain beside their abbess in the abbey chapel, to await with vesper chant and bell the coming of sword and saexe. Those more frail of spirit had fled with the novices from the valley, and now knelt numb with a tense terror on the brow of that wind-swept hill, watching fearfully for the abbey's doom. They could imagine what was passing in the shadowy chapel where they had so often worshipped. The face of the Madonna would be gazing placidly on death — and on more than death. It was all very swift — very terrible. Thenceforward cloister and garden were theirs no more.

A red gleam started suddenly from the black mass in the valley. The nuns gripped hands and watched, while the gleam became a glare that poured steadily above the dark outline of the oaks. A long flame leapt up like a red finger above the trees. The belfry of the chapel rose blackly from a circlet of fire, and gilded smoke rolled away nebulously into the night. The barbarians had set torch to the place. The abbey of Avangel went up in flame.

The tall novice who had been kneeling in advance of the main company rose to her feet, and turned to those who still watched and prayed under the pines. The girl's hood had fallen back; the hair that should have been primly coifed rolled down in billowy bronze upon her shoulders. There was infinite pride on the wistful face — a certain scorn for the frailer folk who wept and found sustenance in prayer. The girl's eyes shone largely even in the meagre light under the trees, and there was a straight courage about her lips. She approached and spoke to the women who knelt and watched the burning abbey in a cataleptic stupor.

"Will you kneel all night?" she said.

The words were scourges in their purpose. Several of the nuns looked up from the flames in the valley.

"Shame on you, worldling!" said one of thin and thankless

visage; "down on your knees, brat, and pray for the dead."

The novice gave a curt, low laugh. The reproofs of a year rankled in her like bitter herbs.

"Let the dead bury their dead," quoth she. "I am for life and the living."

"Shame, shame!" came the ready response. "May the Mother of Mercy melt your proud heart, and punish you for your sins. You are bad to the core."

"Shame or no shame," said the girl, "my heart can grieve for death as well as thine, Sister Claudia; and now the abbey's burnt, you may couch here and scold till dawn if you will. You may scold the heathen when they come to butcher you all. I warrant they will give such a beauty short shrift."

The lean nun ventured no answer. She had been worsted before by this rebellious tongue, and had discovered expediency in silence. Several of the women had risen, and were thronging round the novice Igraine, querulous and fearful. Implicit faith, though pious and admirable in the extreme, neither pointed a path nor provided a lantern. Southwards lay the sea and the barbarians; the purlieus of Andredswold came down to touch the ocean. There was night in the sky; no refuge within miles, and wild folk enough in the world to make travelling sufficiently perilous. Moreover, the day's deed had harried the women's emotions into a condition of vibrating panic. The unknown seemed to hem them in, to smother as with a cloak. They were like children who fear to stir in the dark, and shrink from impalpable nothingness as though a strange hand waited to grip them to some spiritual torture. As it was, they were fluttering among the pines like birds who fear the falcon.

"It grows dark," said one.

"Let Claudia pray for us."

"Igraine, you are wiser in the world than we!"

"Truth," said the girl, "you may bide and snivel with Claudia if you will. I am for Anderida through the woods."

"But the woods," said a child with wide, dark eyes, "the woods are fearful at night."

"They are kinder than the heathen," said Igraine, taking the girl's hand. "Come with me; I will mother you."

Even as she spoke the novice saw a point of fire disjoint itself from the dark circle of the oaks below. Another and another followed it, and began to jerk hither and thither in the meadows. The dashes of flame gradually took a northern trend, as though the torch-bearers were for ascending the long slope that idled up to the ragged thicket of pines. She turned without further vigil, and made the most of her tidings in an appeal to the women under the trees.

"Look yonder," she said, pointing into the valley. "Let Sister Claudia say whether she will wait till those torches come over the hill."

There was instant hubbub among the nuns. Cooped as they had been within the mothering arms of the Church, peril found them utterly impotent when self-reliance and natural instinct were needed to shepherd them from danger. The night seemed to sweep like a wheel with the burning pyre in the meadows for axle. The torches were moving hither and thither in fantastic fashion, as though the men who bore them were doubling right and left in the dark, like hounds casting about for a scent. The sight was sinister, and stirred the women to renewed panic.

"Igraine, help us," came the cry.

Even tyranny is welcome in times of peril. Witless, resourceless, they gathered about her in a dumb stupor. Even Claudia lost her greed for martyrdom and became human. They were all eager enough for the forest now, and hungry for a leader. Igraine stood up among them like a tall figure of hope. Her eyes were on the east, where a weird glow above the tree tops told her that the moon was rising.

"See," she said, "we shall have light upon our way. There is a bridle-path through the wold here that goes north, and touches the road from Durovernum. I am going by that path, follow who will."

"We will follow Igraine," came the answer.

North, east, and west lay Andredswold, sinister as a sea at night. The hill, tangled with gorse and bracken, and sapped by burrows, dipped to it gradually like an outjutting of the land. To the east they could see a wide tangle of pines latticing the light of the moon. It was dark, and the ground more than dubious to the feet. The women, nine in all, herded close on Igraine, who walked like an Eastern shepherdess with the sheep following in her track. First came Claudia, who had held sway over the linen, with Malt, the stout cellaress, next Elaine and Lily, twin sisters, two nuns, and two novices. There was much stumbling, much clutching at one another in the dark; but, thanks to holy terror, their progress was in measure ungracefully speedy.

The girl Igraine led with a keen gleam in her eyes and a queer cheerfulness upon her face, as she stepped out blithely for the dark mass where the wold began. Her sojourn in the abbey had been brief and stormy, a curt attempt at discipline that had failed most nobly. One might as well have sought to hem in spring with winter as to curb desire that leapt towards greenness and the dawn like joy. She had ever thought more of a net for her hair than of her rosary. The little pool in the pleasaunce had served her as her mirror, casting back a full face set with amber shadowed eyes, and a bosom more attuned to passion than to dreams of quiet sanctity. She had been the wayward child of the abbey flock, flooded with homilies, surrendered to eternal penances, yet holding her own in a fair worldly fashion that left the good women of the place wholly to leeward.

Thrust out into the world again she took to the wild like a fox to the woodland, while her more tractable comrades were like caged doves baffled by unaccustomed freedom. Matins, complines, vespers were no more. Cold stone arched no more to tomb her fancies. Above stretched the free dome of the sky; around, the wilderness free and untainted; in lieu of psalms she heard the gathering cry of the wind, and the great voice of the forest at night.

In due course they came to where a dark mass betokened the rampart thickets of the wold, rising like a wall across the sky. Igraine hoped for the track, and found it running like a white fillet about the brow of a wood. They followed till it thrust into the trees, a thin thread in the shadows. As they went, great oaks overreached them with sinuous limbs. The vault was fretted innumerably with the faint overdome of the sky. Now and again a solitary star glimmered through. To the women that place seemed like an interminable cavern, where grotto on grotto dwindled away into oblivious gloom. But for the track's narrow comfort, Igraine and her company would have been impotent indeed.

The prospect was sad for these folk who had lived for peace, and had tuned their lives to placid chants and the balm of prayer. In Britain Christ was worshipped and the Cross adored, yet abbeys were burnt, and children martyred, and strong towns given over to sack and fire. Truth seemed to taunt them with the apparent impotence of their creed. The abbess Gratia had often said that Britain, for its sloth and sin, deserved to meet the scourge of war, and here were her words exampled by her own stark death. The nuns talked of the state of the land, as they plodded on through the night. There was no soul among them that had not been grossly stirred by the fate that had overtaken Avangel, Gratia, and her more zealous nuns. It was but natural that a cry for vengeance should have gained voice in the hearts of these outcast women, and that a certain querulous bitterness should have found tongue against those in power.

Igraine, walking in the van, listened to their words, and laughed with some scorn in her heart.

"You are very wise, all of you," she said presently over

her shoulder. "You speak of war and disruption as though the whole kingdom were in the dust. True, Kent is lost, the heathen have burnt defenceless places on the coast, and have stormed a few towns. The abbey of Avangel is not all Britain. Have we not Aurelius and the great Uther? Our folk will gather head anon, and push these whelps into the sea."

"God grant it," said Claudia, with a smirk heavenward.

"We need a man," quoth Igraine.

"Perhaps you will find him, pert one."

"Peril will," said the girl; "there is no hero when there is no dragon or giant in need of the sword. Britain will find her knight ere long."

"Lud," said Malt, the cellaress, "I wish I could find my supper."

Thereat they all laughed, Igraine as heartily as any.

"Perhaps Claudia will pray for manna dew," she said.

"Scoffer!"

"It will be cranberries, and bread and water, till better seasons come. I have heard that there are wild grapes in the wold."

"Bread!" quoth Malt; "did some kind soul say bread?"

"I have a small loaf here under my habit."

"Ah, Igraine, girl, I would chant twenty psalms for a morsel of that loaf."

"Chant away, sister. Begin on the 'Attendite, popule.' I believe it is one of the longest."

"Don't trifle with a hungry wretch."

"The psalms, Malt, or not a crust."

"Keep it yourself, greedy hussy; I can go without."

"We will share it, all of us, presently," said the girl, "unless Malt wants to eat the whole."

They held on under the ban of night, following the track like Theseus did his thread. At times the path struck out into a patch of open ground, covered with scrub and bracken, or bristling thick with furze. Igraine had never seen such timid folk as these nuns from Avangel. If a stick cracked they would start, huddle together, and vow they heard footsteps. They mistook an owl's hoot for a heathen cry, and a night-jar's creaking note made them swear they caught the chafe of steel. Once they suffered a most shrewd fright. They drove a herd of red deer from cover, and the rush and tumultuous sound of their galloping created a most holy panic among the women. It was some time before Igraine could get them on the march again.

As the night wore on they began to lag from sheer weariness. Two or three were feeble as sickly children, and the abbey life had done little for the body, though it had done much to deform the mind. Igraine had to turn tyrant in very earnest. She knew the women looked to her for courage and guidance, and that they would be hopeless without her stronger mind to lead them. She put this knowledge to effect, and held it like a lash over their weakly spirits.

Igraine found abundant scope for her ingenuity. When they voted a halt for rest, she vowed she would hold on alone and leave them. The threat made the whole company trail after her like sheep. When they grumbled, she told tales of the savagery and lust of the heathen, and made their fears ache more lustily than did their feet. By such devices she kept them to it for the greater portion of the night, knowing that the shrewdest kindness lay in seeming harshness, and that to humour them was but mistaken pity.

At last — heathen or no heathen — they would go no further. It was some hours before dawn. The trees had thinned, and through more open colonnades they looked out on what appeared to be a grass-grown valley sleeping peacefully under the moon. A great cedar grew near, a pyramid of gloom. Malt, the cellaress, grumbling and groaning, crept under its shadows, and commended Igraine to purgatorial fire. The rest, limp and spiritless, vowed they would rather die than take another step. Huddling together under the branches, they were soon half of them asleep in an ecstasy of weariness. Igraine, seeing further effort useless, surrendered to the inevitable, and lay down herself to sleep under the tree.

II

DAY came with an essential stealth. The great trees stood without a rustling leaf, in a stupor of silence. A vast hush held as though the wold knelt at orisons. Soon ripple on ripple of light surged from the hymning east, and the night was not.

The sleep of the women from Avangel had proved but brief and fitful, couched as they had been under so strange a roof. They were all awake under the cedar. Igraine, standing under its green ledges, listened to their monotonous talk as they rehearsed their plight dismally under the shade. The nun Claudia's voice was still raised weakly in pious fashion; she had learnt to ape saintliness all her life, and it was a mere habit with her. The cellaress's red face was in no measure placid; hunger had dissipated her patience like an ague, and she found comfort in grumbling. The younger women were less voluble, as age and custom behoved them to be. Unnaturally bred, they were like images of wax, capable only of receiving the impress of the minds about them. Such a woman as Malt owed her individuality solely to the superlative cravings of the flesh.

About them rose the slopes of a valley, set tier on tier with trees, nebulous, silent in the now hurrying light. Grassland, moist and spangled, lay dew-heavy in the lap of the valley, with the track curling drearily into a further tunnel of green.

Igraine, scanning the trees and the stretch of grassland, found on a sudden something to hold her gaze. On the southern side of the valley the walls of a building showed vaguely through the trees. It was so well screened that a transient glance would have passed over the line of foliage without discovering the white glimmer of stone. She pointed it out to her companions, who were quickly up from under the cedar at the thought of the meal and the material comforts such a forest habitation might provide. They were soon deep in the tall grass, their habits wet to the knee with dew, as they held across the valley for the manor amid the trees.

The place gathered distinctness as they approached. Two horns of woodland jutted out — enclosing and holding it jealously from the track through the valley. There were outhouses packed away under the trees. A garden held it on the north. The building itself was modelled somewhat after the fashion of a Roman villa, with a porch — whitely pillared — leading from a terrace fringed with flowers.

The silence of the place impressed itself upon Igraine and the women as they drew near from the meadowlands. The manor seemed lifeless as the woods that circled it. There were no cattle — no servants to be seen, not even a hound to bay warning on the threshold. Passing over a small stone bridge, they went up an avenue of cypresses that led primly to the garden and the terrace. They halted at the steps leading to the portico. The garden, broken in places, and somewhat unkempt, glistened with colour in the early sun; terrace and portico were void and silent; the whole manor seemed utterly asleep.

The women halted by the stairway, and looked dubiously into one another's faces. There was something sinister about the place — a prophetic hush that seemed to stand with finger on lip and bid the curious forbear. After their march over the meadows, and considering the hungry plight they were in, it seemed more than unreasonable to turn away without a word. None the less, they all hesitated, beckoning each to her fellow to set foot first in this house of silence. Igraine, seeing their indecision, took the initiative as usual, and began to climb the steps that led to the portico. Claudia and the rest followed her in a body.

Within the portico the carved doors were wide. The sun streamed down through a latticed roof into a peristylum, where flowers grew, and a pool shone silverly. There were statues at the angles; one had been thrown down, and lay half buried in a mass of flowers. The place looked wholly deserted, though, by the orderly mood of court and garden, it could not have been long since human hands had tended it.

The women gathered together about the little font in the centre of the peristylum, and debated together in low tones. They were still but half at ease with the place, and quite ready to suspect some sudden development. The house had a scent of tragedy about it that was far from comforting.

Said Malt, "I should judge, sisters, that the folk have fled, and that we are to be sustained by the hand of grace. Come and search."

Claudia demurred a moment.

"Is it lawful," quoth she, "to possess one's self of food and raiment in a strange and empty house?"

"Nonsense," said the cellaress with a sniff.

"But, Malt, I never stole a crust in my life."

"Better learn the craft, then. King David stole the shewbread."

"It was given him of the priests."

"Tut, sister, then are we wiser than David; we can thieve with our own hands. I say this house is God-sent for our need. May I stifle if I err."

"Malt is right," said Igraine, laughing; "let us deprive the barbarians of a pie or a crucifix."

"Aye," chimed Malt, "want makes thieving honest. *Jubilate Deo.* I'm for the pantry."

A colonnade enclosed the peristylum on every quarter. Beneath the shadows cast by the architrave and roof, showed the portals of the various chambers. Igraine led the way. The first room that they essayed appeared to have been a sleeping apartment, for there were beds in it, the bedding lying disordered and fallen upon the floor as though there had been a struggle, or a sudden wild flight. It was a woman's chamber, judging by its mirror of steel, and the articles that were scattered on floor and table. The next room proved to be a species of parlour or living-room. A meal had been spread upon the table, and left untouched. Platter and drinking cups were there, a dish of cakes, a joint on a great charger, bread, olives, fruit, and wine. Armour hung on the walls, with mirrors of steel, and paintings upon panels of wood.

The women made themselves speedily welcome after the trials of the night. Each was enticed by some special object, and character leaked out queerly in the choosing. Malt ran for a beaker of wine; the cakes were pilfered by the younger folk; Claudia—whispering of Saxon desecration—possessed herself with an obeisance of a little silver cross that hung upon the wall. Igraine took down a bow, a quiver of arrows, and a sheathed hunting knife; she slung the quiver over her shoulder, and strapped the knife to her girdle. The clear kiss of morning had sharpened the hunger of a night, and the meal spread in that woodland manor proved very comforting to the fugitives from Avangel.

Satisfied, they passed out to explore the rooms as yet unvisited. A fine curiosity led them, for they were like children who probe the dark places of a ruin. The eastern chambers gave no greater revealings than did those upon the west. The kitchen quarters were empty and soundless, though there was a joint upon the spit that hung over the ashes of a spent fire. It seemed more than likely that the inmates had fled in fear of the barbarians, leaving the house in the early hours of some previous dawn.

As yet they had not visited a room whose door opened upon the southern quarter of the peristyle. Judging by its portal, it promised to be a greater chamber than any of the preceding, probably the banqueting or guest room. The door stood ajar, giving view of a frescoed wall within.

Malt, who had waxed jovial since her communion with the tankard, pushed the door open, and went frankly into the half light of a great chamber. She came to an abrupt halt on the threshold, with a fat hand quavering the symbol of a cross in the air. The women crowded the doorway, and looked in over the cellaress's stout shoulders.

In a gilded chair in the centre of the room sat the figure of a man. His hands were clenched upon the lion-headed arms of the siege, and his chin bowed down upon his breast. He was clad in purple; there were rings upon his fingers, and his brow was bound with a band of gold. At his feet crouched a great wolf-hound, motionless, dead.

The women in the doorway stared on the scene in silence. The man in the chair might have been thought asleep save for a certain stark look — a bleak immobility that contradicted the possibility of life. Here they had stumbled on tragedy with a vengeance. The mute face of death lurked in the shadows, and the vast mystery of life seemed about them like a cold vapour. It was a sudden change from sunlight into shade.

Igraine pushed past Malt, and ventured close to the crouching hound. Bending down, she looked into the dead man's face. It was pinched and grey, but young, none the less, and bearing even in death a certain sensuous haughtiness and dissolute beauty. The man had been dark, with hair turbulent and lustrous. In his bosom glinted the silver pommel of a knife, and there were stains upon cloak and tessellated pavement. Clasped in one hand was a small cross of gold that looked as though it had been plucked from a chain or necklet, and held gripped in the death agony. The wolf-hound had been thrust through the body with a sword.

"Hum," said Malt, with a sniff, — "Christian work here. And a comely fellow, too — more's the pity. Look at the rings on his fingers; I wonder whether I might take one for prayer money? It would buy candles."

Igraine was still looking at the dead man with strange awe in her heart.

"Keep off," she said, thrusting off Malt; "the man has been stabbed."

"Well, haven't I eyes too, hussy?"

Claudia came in, white and quavering, with her crucifix up.

"Poor wretch!" said she; "can't we bury him?"

"Bury him!" cried Malt.

"Yes, sister."

"Thanks, no. It would spoil my dinner."

Claudia gave a sudden scream, and jumped back, holding her skirts up.

"There's blood on the floor! Holy mother! did the dog move?"

"Move!" quoth Malt, giving the brute a kick; "what a mouse you are, Claudia."

"Are you sure the man's dead?"

"Dead, and cold," said Igraine, touching his cheek, and drawing away with a shiver. "Come away, the place makes my flesh creep. Shut the door, Malt. Let us leave him so."

The women from Avangel had seen enough of the manor in the forest. Certainly, it held nothing more perilous than a corpse, perched stiffly in a gilded chair; but the dead man seemed to exert a sinister influence upon the spirits of the company, and to stifle any desire for a further sojourn in the place. Folk with murder fresh upon their hands might still be within the purlieus of the valley. The women thought of the glooms of the forest, and of the strong walls of Anderida, and discovered a very lively desire to be free of Andredswold, and the threats of the unknown.

They left the man sitting in his chair, with the hound at his feet, and went to gather food for the day's journey. Bread they took, and meat, and bound them in a sheet, while Malt filled a flask with wine, and bestowed it at her girdle. Igraine still had her bow, shafts, and hunting knife. Before sallying, they remembered the dead. It was Igraine's thought. They went and stood before the door of the great chamber, sang a hymn, and said a prayer. Then they left the place, and held on into the forest.

Nothing befell them on their way that morning. It was noon before they struck the road from Durovernum to Anderida, a straight and serious highway that went whitely amid wastes of scrub, thickets, and dark knolls of trees. The women were glad of its honest comfort, and blessed the Romans who had wrought the road of old. Later in the day they neared the sea again. Between masses of trees, and over the slopes, they caught glimpses of the blue plain that touched the sky. From a little hill that gave broader view, they saw the white sails of ships that were ploughing westward with a temperate wind. They took them for the galleys of the Saxons, and the thought hurried them on their way the more.

Presently they came to a mild declivity, with a broken toll-house standing by the roadside, and two horsemen on the watch there, as the distant galleys swept over the sea towards the west. The men belonged to the royal forces in Anderida. They were reticent in measure, and in no optimistic mood. They told how the heathen had swept the coast, how their ships had ventured even to Vectis, to burn, slay, and martyr. The women learnt that Andred's town was some ten miles distant. There was little likelihood, so the men said, of their getting within the walls that night, for the place was in dread of siege, and was shut up like a rock after dusk.

Igraine and the nuns elected, none the less, to hold upon their way. Despite their weariness, the women preferred to push on and gain ground, rather than to lag and lose courage. For all they knew, the Saxons might be soon ashore, ready to raid and slay in their very path. They left the soldiers at the toll-house, and went downhill into a long valley.

Possibly they had gone a mile or more when they heard the sound of galloping coming in their wake. On the slope of the hill they had left, they could see a distant wave of dust curling down the road like smoke. The two men from Andred's town were coming on at a gallop. They were very soon within bowshot, but gave no hint of halting. Thundering on, they drew level with the women, shouted as they went by, and held on fast,—dust and spume flying.

"God's curse upon the cravens," said Malt, the cellaress.

Cravens they were in sense; yet the men had reason on their side, and the women were left staring at the diminishing fringe of dust. There was much frankness in the phenomenon, a curt hint that carried emphasis, and advised action. "To the woods," it said; "to the woods, good souls, and that quickly."

The road ran through the flats at that place, with marsh and meadowland on either hand. Further westward, the wold thrust forth a finger from the north to touch the highway. Southward, scrub and grassland swept away to the sea. It was when looking southwards that the nuns from Avangel discovered the stark truth of the soldier's warning. Against the skyline could be seen a number of jerking specks, moving fast over the open land, and holding north-west as though to touch the road. They were the figures of men riding.

The outjutting of woodland that rolled down to edge the highway was a quarter of a mile from where the women stood. A bleak line of roadway parted them from the mazy refuge of the wold. They started away at a run; Igraine and another novice dragging the nun Claudia between them. The display was neither Olympic nor graceful; it would have been ridiculous but for the stern need that inspired it. Igraine and her fellows made the best of the highway. In the west, the wold seemed to stretch an arm to them like a mother.

The heathen raiders were coming fast over the marshes. Igraine, dragging the panting Claudia by the hand, looked back and took measure of the chase. There were some score at the gallop three furlongs or more away, with others on foot, holding on to stirrups, running and leaping like madmen. The girl caught their wild, burly look even at that distance. They were hallooing one to another, tossing axe and spear — making a race of it, like huntsmen at full pelt. Possibly there was sport in hounding a company of women, with the chance of spoil and something more brutish to entice.

Igraine and her flock were struggling on for very life. Their feet seemed weighted with the shackles of an impotent fear, while every yard of the white road appeared three to them as they ran. How they anguished and prayed for the shadows of the wood. A frail nun, winded and lagging, began to scream like a hare when the hounds are hard on her haunches. Another minute, and the trees seemed to stride down to them with green-bosomed kindness. A wild scramble through a shallow dyke brought them to bracken and a tangled barrier about the hem of the wood. Then they were amid the sleek, solemn trunks of a beech wood, scurrying up a shadowed aisle with the dull thudding of the nearing gallop in their ears.

It was borne in upon Igraine's reason as she ran that the trees would barely save them from the purpose of pursuit. The women — limp, witless, dazed by danger — could hardly hold on fast enough to gain the deeper mazes of the place, and the sanctuary the wold could give. Unless the pursuit could be broken for a season, the whole company would fall to the net of the heathen, and only the Virgin knew what might befall them in that solitary place. Sacrifice flashed into the girl's vision — a sudden ecstasy of courage, like hot flame. These abbey folk had been none too gentle with her. None the less she would essay to save them.

She cast Claudia's hand aside, and turned away abruptly from the rest. They wavered, looking at her as though for guidance, too flurried for sane measures. Igraine waved them on, with a certain pride in her that seemed to chant the triumph song of death.

"What will you do, girl? Are you mad?"

"Go!" was all she said. "Perhaps you will pray for me as for Gratia the abbess."

"They will kill you!"

"Better one than all."

They wavered, unwilling to be wholly selfish despite their fear and the sounding of pursuit. There shone a fine light on the girl's face as they beheld her — tyrannical even in heroism. Her look awed them and made them ashamed; yet they obeyed her, and like so many winging birds they fled away into the green shadows.

Igraine watched them a moment, saw the grey flicker of their gowns go amid the trees, and then turned to front her fortune. Pursing her lips into a queer smile, she took post behind a tree bole, and waited with an arrow fitted to her string. She heard a sluthering babel as the men reined in, with much shouting, on the forest's margin. They were very near now. Even as she peered round her tree trunk a figure on foot flashed into the grass ride, and came on at the trot. The bow snapped, the arrow streaked the shadows, and hummed cheerily into the man's thigh. Igraine had not hunted for nothing. A second fellow edged into view, and took the point in his shoulder. Igraine darted back some forty paces and waited for more.

In this fashion — slipping from tree to tree, and edging north-west — she held them for a furlong or more. The end came soon with an empty quiver. The wood seemed full of armed men; they were too speedy for her, too near to her for flight. She threw the empty quiver at her feet, with the bow athwart it, put a hand in the breast of her habit, and waited. It was not for long. A man ran out from behind a tree and came to a curt halt fronting her.

He was young, burly, with a great tangle of hair, and a yellow beard that bristled like a hound's collar. A naked sword was in his hand, a buckler strapped between his shoulders. He laughed when he saw the girl — the coarse laugh of a Teuton — and came some paces nearer to her, staring in her face. She was very rich and comely in a way foreign to the fellow's fancy. There was that in his eyes that said as much. He laughed again, with a guttural oath, and stretched out a hand to grip the girl's shoulder.

An instant shimmer of steel, and Igraine had smitten him above the golden torque that ringed his throat. Life rushed out in a red fountain. He went back from her with a stagger, clutching at the place, and cursing. As the blood ebbed he dropped to his knees, and thence fell slantwise against a tree. He had found death in that stroke.

A hand closed on the girl's wrist. The knife that had been turned towards her own heart was smitten away and spurned to a distance. There were men all about her — ogrish folk, moustachioed, jerkined in skins, bare armed, bare legged. Igraine stood like a statue — impotent — frozen into a species of apathy. The bearded faces thronged her, gaped at her with a gross solemnity. She had no glance for them, but thought only of the man twitching in the death trance. The wood seemed full of gruff voices, of grotesque words mouthed through hair.

Then the barbaric circle rippled and parted. A rugged-faced old man with white hair and beard came forward slowly. There was a tense silence over the throng as the old man stood and looked at the figure at his feet. There were shadows on the earl's face, and his hands shook, for the smitten man was his son.

Out of silence grew clamour. Hands were raised, fingers pointed, a sword was poised tentatively above the girl's head. The wood seemed full of bearded and grotesque wrath, and the hollow aisles rang with the clash of sword on buckler. But age was not for sudden violence, though the blood of youth ebbed on the grass. The old man pointed to a tree, spoke briefly, quietly, and the rough warriors obeyed him.

They stripped Igraine, cast her clothes at her feet, and bound her to the trunk of the tree with their girdles. Then they took up the body of the dead man, and so departed into the forest.

III

It was well towards evening when the men disappeared into the wood, leaving the girl bound naked to the tree. The day was calm and tranquil, with the mood of June on the wind, and a benign sky above. Igraine's hair had fallen from its band, and now hung in bronze masses well-nigh to her knees, covering her as with a cloak. Her habit, shift, and sandals lay close beside her on the grass. The barbarians had robbed her of nothing, according to their old earl's wishes. She was simply bound there, and left unscathed.

When the men were gone, and she began to realise what had passed, she felt a flush spread from face to ankle, a glow of shame that was keen as fire. Her whole body seemed rosily flaked with blushes. The very trees had eyes, and the wind seemed to whisper mischief. There were none to see, none to wonder, and yet she felt like Eve in Eden when knowledge had smitten the pure flesh with gradual shame. Though the place was solitary as a dry planet, her aspen fancy peopled it with life. She could still see the heavy-jowled barbaric faces staring at her like the malign masks of a dream.

The west was already prophetic of night. There was the golden glow of the decline through the billowy foliage of the trees, and the shadows were very still and reverent, for the day was passing. A beam of gold slanted down upon Igraine's breast, and slowly died there amid her hair. The west flamed and faded, the east grew blind. Soon the day was not.

Igraine watched the light faint above the trees, wondering in her heart what might befall her before another sun could set. She had tried her bonds, and had found them lacking sympathy in that they were staunch as strength could make them. She was cramped, too, and began to long for the hated habit that had trailed the galleries of Avangel, and had brought such scorn into her discontented heart. There was no hope for it. She was pilloried there, bound body, wrist, and ankle. Philosophy alone remained to her, a poor enough cloak to the soul, still worse for things tangible.

Her plight gave her ample time for meditation. There were many chances open to her, and even in mere possibilities fate had her at a vantage. In the first place, she might starve, or other unsavoury folk find her, and her second state be worse than her first. Then there were wolves in the wold; or country people might find and release her, or even Claudia and the women might return and see how she had fared. There was little comfort in this last thought. She shrewdly guessed that the abbey folk would not stop till they happened on a stone wall, or the heathen took them. Lastly, the road was at no very great distance, and she might hear perchance if any one passed that way.

Presently the moon rose upon Andredswold with a stupendous splendour. The veil of night seemed dusted with silver as it swept from her tiar of stars. Innumerable glimmering eyes starred the foliage of the beeches. Vague lights streamed down and netted the shadows with mysterious magic. Here and there a tree trunk stood like a ghost, splashed with a phosphor tunic.

The wilderness was soundless, the billowy bastions of the trees unruffled by a breath. The hush seemed vast, irrefutable, supreme. Not a leaf sighed, not a wind wandered in its sleep. The great trees stood in a silver stupor, and dreamt of the moon. The solemn aisles were still as Thebes at midnight; the smooth boles of the beeches like ebony beneath canopies of jet.

The scene held Igraine in wonder. There was a mystery about a moonlit forest that never lessened for her. The vasty void of the night, untainted by a sound, seemed like eternity unfolded above her ken. She forgot her plight for the time, and took to dreaming, such dreams as the warm fancy of the young heart loves to remember. Perhaps beneath such a benediction she thought of a pavilion set amid water lilies, and a boy who had looked at her with boyish eyes. Yet these were childish things. They lost substance before the chafing of the cords that bound her to the tree.

Presently she began to sing softly to herself for the cheating of monotony. She was growing cold and hungry, too, despite all the magic of the place, and the hours seemed to drag like a homily. Then with a gradual stealthiness the creeping fear of death and the unknown began to steal in and cramp even her buoyant courage. It was vain for her to put the peril from her, and to trust to day and the succour that she vowed in her heart must come. Dread smote into her more cynically than did the night air. What might be her end? To hang there parched, starved, delirious till life left her; to hang there still, a loathsome, livid thing, rotting like a cloak. To be torn and fed upon by birds. She knew the region was as solitary as death, and that the heathen had emptied it of the living. The picture grew upon her distraught imagination till she feared to look on it lest it should be the lurid truth.

It was about midnight, and she was beginning to quake with cold, when a sound stumbled suddenly out of silence, and set her listening. It dwindled and grew again, came nearer, became rhythmic, and ringing in the keen air. Igraine soon had no doubts as to its nature. It was the steady smite of hoofs on the high-road, the rhythm of a horse walking.

Now was her chance if she dared risk the character of the rider. Doubts flashed before her a moment, hovered, and then merged into decision. Better to risk the unknown, she thought, than tempt starvation tied to the tree. She made her choice and acted.

"Help, there! Help!"

The words went like silver through the woods. Igraine, listening hungrily, strained forward at her bonds to catch the answer that might come to her. The sound of hoofs ceased, and gave place to silence. Possibly the rider was in doubt as to the testimony of his own hearing. Igraine called again, and again waited.

Stillness held. Then there was a stir, and a crackling as of trampled brushwood, followed by the snort of a horse and the thrill of steel. The sounds came nearer, with the deadened tramp of hoofs for an underchant. Igraine, full of hope and fear, of doubt and gratitude, kept calling for his guidance. Presently a cry came back to her in turn.

"By the holy cross, who are you that calls?"

"A woman," she cried in turn, "bound here by the heathen."

"Where?"

"Here, in a grass ride, tied to a tree."

The words that had come to her were very welcome, heralding, as they did, a friend, at least in race, and there was a manly depth in the voice, too, that gave her comfort. She saw a glimmer of steel in the shadows of the wood as man and horse drew into being from the darkness. Moonlight played fitfully upon them, weaving silver gleams amid a smoke of gloom, making a white mist about the man's great horse. A single ray burnt and blazed like a halo about the rider's casque, and his spear-point flickered like a star beneath the vaultings of the trees. He had halted, a solitary figure wrapped round with night, and rendered grand and wizard by the misty web of the moon.

The sight was pathetic enough, yet infinitely fair. Light streamed through, and fell full upon the tree where Igraine stood. The girl's limbs were white and luminous against the dark bosom of the beech, and her rich hair fell about her like mist. As for the strange rider, he could at least claim the inspiration accorded to a Christian. The servant of the Galilean has, like Constantine, a symbol in the sky, prophetic in all need, generous of all guidance. The Cross is a perpetual Delphi oracular on trivial matters as on the destinies of kingdoms. The man dismounted, knelt for a moment with sword held before him, and then rose and strode to the tree with shield held before his face.

Igraine was looking at the figure in armour, kindly,

redly, from amid the masses of her hair. The small noblenesses of his bearing towards her had won her trust with a flush of gratitude. The man saw only the white feet like marble amid the moss as he cut the thongs where they circled the tree. The bands fell, he saw the white feet flicker, a trail of hair waving under his shield. Then he turned on his heel without a word, and went to tether his horse.

The interlude was as considerate as courtesy had intended. Igraine darted for her habit with a rapturous sigh. When the man turned leisurely again, a tall girl met him, cloaked in grey, with her hair still hanging about her, and sandals on her feet.

"Mother Virgin, a nun!"

The words seemed sudden as an echo. Igraine bent her head to hide the half-abashed, half-smiling look upon her face. It had been thus at Avangel. Nun and novice had worn like habits, and there had been nothing to distinguish them save the final solemn vow. The man's notions were plainly celibate, and, with a sudden twinkling inspiration, she fancied they should bide so. It would make matters smoother for them both, she thought.

"My prayers are yours, daily, for this service," she said.

The man bent his head to her.

"I am thankful, madame," he answered, "that I should have been so good fortuned as to be able to befriend you. How came you by such evil hazard?"

"I was of Avangel," she said.

"You speak as of the past," quoth he, with a keen look.

"Avangel was burnt and sacked but yesterday," she said. "Many of the nuns were martyred; some few escaped. I was made captive here, and bound to this tree by the heathen."

Igraine could see the man's face darken even in the moonlight, as though pain and wrath held mute confederacy there. He crossed himself, and then stood with both hands on the pommel of his sword, stately and statuesque.

"And the Lady Gratia?" he said.

"Dead, I fear."

A half-heard groan seemed to come from the man's helmet. He bent his head into the shadows and stood stiff and silent as though smitten into thought. Presently he seemed to remember himself, Igraine, and the occasion.

"And yourself, madame?" he said, with a twinge of tenderness in his voice.

The girl blushed, and nearly stammered.

"I am unscathed," she hastened to say, "thanks to heaven. I am safe and whole as if I had spent the day in a convent cell. My name is Igraine, if you would know it. I fear I have told you heavy tidings."

The man turned his face to the sky like one who looks into other worlds.

"It is nothing," he said, gazing into the night; "nothing but what we must look for in these stark days. Our altars smoke, our blood is spilt, and yet we still pray. Yet may I be cursed, and cursed again, if I do not dye my sword for this."

There was a sudden bleak fierceness in his voice that betrayed his fibre and the strong thoughts that were stirring in his heart that moment. His face looked almost fanatical in the cold gloom, gaunt, heavy-jawed, lion-like. Igraine watched this thunder-cloud of thought and passion in silence, thinking she would meet the man in the wrack of life rather as friend than as foe. The brief mood seemed to pass, or at least to lose expression. Again, there was that in the kindness of his face that made the girl feel beneath the eye of a brother.

"You will ride with me?" he asked.

Igraine hesitated a moment.

"I was for Anderida," she said, "and it is only three leagues distant. Now that I am free I can go through the wold alone, for I am no child."

"An insult to my manhood," said the stranger.

"But the heathen are everywhere, and I should but cumber you."

"Madame, you talk like a fool."

There was a sheer sincerity about the speech that pleased Igraine. His spirit seemed to overtop hers, and to silence argument. Proud heart! yet without thought of debate she gave way in the most placid manner, and was content to be shepherded.

"I might walk at your stirrup," she said meekly.

The man seemed to ponder. He merely looked at her with dark, solemn eyes, showing a quiet disregard for her humility.

"Listen to me," he said, "you, a woman, must not attempt Anderida alone. The town will be beleaguered, or I am no prophet. To Anderida I cannot go, for I have folk at Winchester who wait my coming. If you can put trust in me, and will ride with me to Winchester, you will find harbour there."

She considered a moment.

"Winchester," she said, "yes, and most certainly I trust you."

The man stretched out a hand to her with a smile.

"God willing," he said, "I will bear you safe to the place. As for your frocks and vows, they must follow necessity, and pocket their pride. It will not damn you to ride before a man."

"I trow not," she said, with a little laugh that seemed to make the leaves quiver. So they took horse together, and rode out from the beech wood into the moonlight.

IV

WHEN they were clear of the solemn beeches, and saw the road white as white before them, Igraine began to tell the man of the doom of Avangel, and the great end made by

Gratia the abbess. The knight had folded his red cloak and spread it for her comfort. Her tale seemed very welcome to him despite its grievous humour, and he questioned her much concerning Gratia, her goodness and her charity. Now it had been well known in Avangel that Gratia had come of noble and excellent descent, and seeing that this stranger had been familiar with her in the past, Igraine guessed shrewdly that he himself was of some ancient and goodly stock. To tell the truth, she was very curious concerning him, and it was not long before she found a speech ready to her tongue likely to draw some confession from his lips.

"I have promised to pray for you," she said, "and pray for you I will, seeing that you have done me so great a blessing to-night. When I bow to the Virgin and the Saints, what name may I remember?"

The man did not look at her, for her face was in the shadow of her hood and his clear and white in the light of the moon.

"To some I am known as Sir Pelleas," he said.

"And to me?"

"As Sir Pelleas, if it please you, madame."

Igraine understood that she was to be pleased with the name, whether she liked it or not.

"Then for Sir Pelleas I will pray," she said, "and may my gratitude avail him."

There was silence for a space, broken by the rhythmic play of hoofs upon the road, and the dull jar of steel. Igraine was meditating further catechism, adapting her questions for the knowledge she wished for.

"You ride errant," she said presently.

"I ride alone, madame."

"The wold is a rude region set thick with perils."

"Very true," quoth the man.

"Perhaps you are a venturesome spirit."

"I believe that I am often as careful as death."

Igraine made her culminating suggestion.

"Some high deed must have been in your heart," she said, "or probably you would not have risked so much.'

The man Pelleas did not even look at her. She felt the bridle-arm that half held her tighten unconsciously, as though he were steeling himself against her curiosity.

"Madame," he said very gravely, "every man's business should be for his own heart, and I do not know that I have any need to share the right or wrong of mine with others. It is a grand thing to be able to keep one's own counsel. It is enough for you to know my name."

Igraine none the less was not a bit abashed.

"There is one thing I would hear," she said, "and that is how you came to know of the abbess Gratia."

For the moment the man looked black, and his lips were stern —

"You may know if you wish," he said.

"Well?"

"Madame, the Lady Gratia was my mother."

Igraine felt a flood of sudden shame burst redly into her heart. Gratia was the man's mother, and she had been plying him with questions, cruelly curious. She caught a short, shallow breath, and hung her head, shrinking like a prodigal.

"Set me down," she said. "I am not worthy to ride with you."

"Pardon me," quoth the man; "you did not think, not knowing I was in pain."

"Set me down," was all she said; "set me down — set me down."

The man Pelleas changed his tone.

"Madame," he said, with a sudden gentleness that made her desire to weep, "I have forgiven you. What, then, does it matter?"

Igraine hung her head.

"I am altogether ashamed," she said.

She drew her hood well over her face, and took her

reproof to heart like a veritable penitent. Even religious solemnities make little change in the notorious weaknesses of woman. Igraine was angry, not only for having blundered clumsily against the man's sorrow, but also because of the somewhat graceless part she seemed to have played after the deliverance he had vouchsafed her. As yet her character seemed to have lost honour fast by mere brief contrast with the man's.

Pelleas meanwhile rode with eyes watching the wan stretch of road to the west. On either hand the woods rose up like nebulous hills bowelled by tunnelled mysteries of gloom. He had turned his horse to the grass beside the roadway, so that the tramp of hoofs should fall muffled on the air. Igraine, close against his steeled breast, with his bridle-arm about her, looked into his face from the shadows of her hood, and found much to initiate her liking.

If she loved strength, it was there. If she desired the grand reserve of silent vigour, it was there also. The deeply caverned eyes watching through the night seemed dark with a quiet destiny. The large, finely moulded face, gaunt and white in its meditative repose, seemed fit to front the ruins of a stricken land. It was the face of a man who had watched and striven, who had followed truth like a shadow, and had found the light of life in the heavens. There was bitterness there, pain, and the ghost of a sad desire that had pleaded with death. The face would have seemed morose, but for a certain something that made its shadows kind.

Instinctively, as she watched the mask of thought beneath the dark arch of his open casque, she felt that he had memories in his heart at that moment. His thoughts were not for her, however much she pitied him or longed to tell him of her shame and sympathy. Nothing could come into that sad session of remembrances, save the soul of the man and the memories of his mother. That he was grieving deeply Igraine knew well. His was a strong nature that brooded in silence, and felt the more; it must be a terrible thing, she thought, to have the martyrdom of a mother haunting the heart like a fell dream at night.

Slipping from such a reverie, the turmoil and weariness of the past days returned to take their tribute. Despite the strangeness of the night, Igraine began to feel sleepy as a tired child. The magnetic calm of the man beside her seemed to lull to slumber, while the motion of the ride cradled her the more. The noise of hoofs, the dull clink of scabbard against spur or harness, grew faint and faint. The woods seemed to swim into a mist of silver. She saw, as in a dream, the strong face above her staring calmly into the night, the long spear poised heavenwards. Her head was on the man's shoulder. With scarcely a thought she was asleep.

It was then that Pelleas discovered the girl heavy in his arms, and looked down to find her sleeping, with hood fallen and a white face turned peacefully to his. Strangely enough, the sorrow that had taken him seemed to make his senses vibrate strongly to the more human things of life. The supple warmth of the girl's slim body crept up the sinews of his arm like a subtle flame. From her half-parted lips the sigh of her breathing came into his bosom. Over his harness clouded her hair, and her two hands had fastened themselves upon his sword-belt with a restful trust.

The man bent his head and watched her in some awe. Her lips were like autumn fruit fed wistfully on moonlight. To Pelleas, woman was still wonderful, a creature to be touched with reverence and soft delight. The drab, the scold, and the harlot had failed to debase the ideals of a staunch spirit, and the fair flesh at his breast was as full of mystery as a woman could be.

He took his fill of gazing, feeling half ashamed of the deed, and half dreading lest Igraine should wake suddenly and look deeply into his eyes. He felt his flesh creep with magic when she stirred or sighed, or when the hands upon his belt twitched in their slumber. Pelleas had seen stark things of late, burnt hamlets, priests slaughtered and churches in flames, children dead in the trampled places of the slain. He had ridden where smoke ebbed heavenwards, and blood clotted the green grass. Now this ride beneath the quiet eyes of night, with the bosomed silence of the woods around, and this lily plucked from death in his arms, seemed like a passage of calm after a page of tempest. Little wonder that he looked long into the girl's face, and thrilled to the soft sway of her bosom. He thanked God in his heart that he had plucked her blemishless from gradual death. It was even thus, he thought, that a good soldier should ride into Paradise bearing the soul of the woman he loved.

Igraine stirred little in her sleep. "Poor child," thought Pelleas, "she has suffered much, has feared death, and is weary. Let her sleep the night through if she can." So he drew the cloak gently about her, said his prayers in his heart, and, holding as much as possible under the shadows of the trees, kept watch patiently on the track before him.

All that night Pelleas rode, thinking of his mother, with the girl sleeping in his arms. He saw the moon go down in the west, while the grey mist of the hour before dawn made the forest gaunt like an abode of the dead. He heard the birds wake in brake and thicket. He saw the red deer scamper, frightened into the glooms, and the rabbits scurrying amid the bracken. When the east mellowed he found himself in fair meadowlands lying locked in the depths of the wold, where flowers were thick as on some rich tapestry, and where the scent of dawn was as the incense of many temples. With a calm sorrow for the dead he rode on, threading the meadowland, till the girl woke and looked up into his face with a little sigh. Then he smiled at her half sadly, and wished her good-morning.

Igraine, wide-eyed, looked round in a daze.

"Day?" she said, "and meadows? It was moonlight when I fell asleep."

"It has dawned an hour or more."

"Then I have slept the night through? You must be tired to death, and stiff with holding me."

"Not so," said Pelleas.

"I am sorry that I have been selfish," she said. "I was asleep before I could think. Have you ridden all night?"

"Of course," quoth he, with a smile, "and not a soul have I seen. I have been watching your face and the moon."

Igraine coloured slightly, and looked sideways at him from under her long lashes. Her sleep had chastened her, and she felt blithe as a bird, and ready to sing. Putting the man's scarlet cloak from her, she shook her hair from her shoulders, and sprang lightly from her seat to the grass.

"I will run at your side awhile," she said, "and so rest you. Perhaps you will halt presently, and sleep an hour or two under a tree. I can watch and keep guard with your sword."

Pelleas smiled down at her like the sun from behind a cloud.

"Not yet," he said; "a soldier needs no sleep for a week, and I feel lusty as Christopher. We will go awhile before breakfast, if it please you. There is a stream near where I can water my horse, and we can make a meal from such stuff as I have. When you are tired, tell me, and I will mount you here again."

She nodded at him gravely. Grass and flowers were well-nigh to her waist. Her gown shook showers of dew from the feathery hay. Foxgloves rose like purple rods amid the snow webs of the wild daisy. Tangled domes of dogrose and honeysuckle lined the white track, and there were countless harebells lying like a deep blue haze under the green shadows of the grass.

Presently they came to where red poppies grew thickly in the golden meads. Igraine ran in among them, and began to make a great posy, while Pelleas watched her as her grey gown went amid the green and red. In due course she came back to him holding her flowers in her bosom.

"Scarlet is your colour," she said, "and these are the flowers of sleep and of dreams for those that grieve. Hold them in the hollow of your shield for me."

Pelleas obeyed her mutely. She began to sing a soft slumberous dirge while she walked beside the great black horse and plaited the flowers into its mane. The man watched her with a kind of wondering pain. The song seemed to wake echoes in him, like sea surges wake in the caverns of a cliff. He understood Igraine's grace to him, and was grateful in his heart.

"How long were you mewed in Avangel?" he said, presently.

"Long enough," quoth she, betwixt her singing, "to learn to love life."

"So I should judge," said Pelleas, curtly.

His tone disenchanted her. She threw the rest of the flowers aside, and walked quietly beside him, looking up with a frank seriousness into his face.

"I was placed there by my parents," she said, by way of explanation, "and against my will, for I had no hope in me to be a nun. But the times were wild, and my father — a solemn soul — thought for the best."

"But your novitiate. You had your choice."

"I had my choice," she answered vaguely. "Did ever a woman choose for the best? Avangel was no place for me."

Pelleas eyed her somewhat sadly from his higher vantage. "The nun's is a sorry life," he said, "when her thoughts fly over the convent walls."

A level kindness in the words seemed to loose her tongue like magic. Twelve long months had her sympathies been outraged, and her young desires crushed by the heel of a so-called godliness. Never had so kind a chance for the outpouring of her discontent come to her. Women love an honest grumble. In a moment all her bitterness found ready flight into the man's ears.

"I hated it!" she said, "I hated it! Avangel had no hold on me. What were vigils, penitences, and long prayers to a girl? They made us kneel on stone, and sleep on boards. The chapel bell seemed to ring every minute of the day; we had vile food, and no liberty. It was Saint This, Saint

That, from morning till night. We saw no men. We might never dress our hair; and, believe me, there were no mirrors. I had to go to a little pool in the garden to see my face.

"And they were so dull,—so dismal. No one ever laughed; no one ever told romances; all our legends were of pious things in petticoats. And what was the use of it all? Was any one ever a jot the better? I used to get into my cell and stamp. I felt like a corpse in a charnel-house, and the whole world seemed dead."

Pelleas scanned her half smilingly, half sadly.

"I am sorry for your heart," he said.

"Sorry! You needs must be when you are a soldier, with life in your ears like a clarion cry."

"Life is a sorry ballad, Sister Igraine, unless we remember the Cross."

"Ah, yes, I have all the saints in mind—dear souls; but then, Sir Pelleas, one cannot live on one's knees. I was made to laugh and twinkle, and if such is sin, then a sorry nun am I."

"You misunderstand me," said the man. "I would that a Christian held his course over the world, with a great cross set in the west to lead him. He can laugh and joy as he goes, sleep like the good, and take the fruits of life in his time. Yet ever above him should be the glory of the cross, to chasten, purge, and purify. There is no sin in living merrily if we live well, but to plot for pleasure is to lose it. Look at the sun; there is no need for us to be ever on our knees to him, yet we know well it would be a sorry world without his comfort."

"Ah," she said, with a little gesture. "I see you are too devout for me, despite my habit. Take me up again, Sir Pelleas, and I will ride with you, though I may not argue."

Pelleas halted his horse, and she was soon in the saddle before him, somewhat subdued and pensive in contrast to her former vivacity. The man believed her a nun, and she had a character to play. Well, when she wearied of it, which would probably be soon, she could tell him and so end the matter. It was not long before they came to the ford across the stream Pelleas had spoken of. It was a green spot shut in by thorn trees, and here they made a halt as the knight had purposed.

Before the meal Pelleas knelt by the stream and prayed. Igraine, seeing him so devout, did likewise, though her eyes were more on the man than on heaven. Her thoughts never got above the clouds. When they were at their meal of meat and bread, with a horn of water from the stream, she talked yet further of her life at Avangel, and the meagre blessing it had been to her. It was while she talked thus that she saw something about the man's person that fired her memory, and set her thinking of the journey of yesterday.

Pelleas was wearing a gold chain that bore a cross hanging above the left breast, but with no cross over the right. Looking more keenly, Igraine saw a broken link still hanging from the right portion of the chain. Instinctively her thoughts fled back to the silent manor in the wood, and the dead man seated stiffly in the great carved chair.

Without duly weighing the possible gravity of her words, she began to tell Pelleas of the incident.

"Yesterday," she said, "I saw a strange thing as we fled through the wold. We came to a villa, and, seeking food there, found it deserted, save for a dead man seated in a chair, and stricken in the breast. The dead man had a small gold cross clutched in his fingers, and there was a dead hound at his feet."

The man gave her a keen look from the depths of his dark eyes, and then glanced at the broken chain.

"You see that I have lost a cross," he said.

Igraine nodded.

"Your reason can read the rest."

She nodded again.

"There is nothing like the truth."

Igraine stared at the man in some astonishment. He was cold as a frost, and there was no shadow of discomfort on his strong face. Knowledge had come to her so sharply that she had no answer for him at the moment. Yet there stood a sublime certainty in her heart that this violent deed was deserving of absolute approval, so soon had her faith in him become like steel.

"The man deserved death," she said presently, with a curt and ingenuous confidence.

Pelleas eyed her curiously.

"How should you know?" he asked.

"I have faith in you," was all she said.

Pelleas smiled, despite the subject.

"No man deserved death better."

"And so you slew him."

He nodded without looking at her, and she could see still the embers of wrath in his eyes.

"I slew him in his own manor, finding him alone, and ready to justify himself with lies. Honour does not love such deeds; but what would you?—Britain is free of a viper."

"And you have blood on your hand."

He winced slightly, and glanced at his fingers as though she had not spoken in metaphor.

"All is blood in these days," he said.

"And what think you of such laws?" she ventured, with a supreme reaching after the requirements of her Order. "What of the Cross?"

"There was blood upon it."

"But the blood of self-sacrifice."

Her words moved him more than she had purposed. His dark face flushed, and light kindled in his eyes as though the basal tenets of his life had been called in question. He glowed like a man whose very creed is threatened. Igraine watched the fire rising in him with a secret pleasure,—the love of a woman for the hot courage of a man.

"Listen to me," he said strongly; "which think you is the worthier life: to dream in a stone cell mewed from the world like a weak weed in a cellar, or to go forth with a red heart and a mellow honour; to strive and smite for the weak and the wounded; to right the wrong; to avenge the fatherless? Choose and declare."

"Choose," she said, with a shrill laugh and a kindling colour, "truth, and I will. Away with the rosary; give me the sword."

Like a wild echo to her human choice came the distant cry of a horn borne hollowly over the sleeping meadows. Both heard it and started. The great war-horse, grazing near by, tossed his head, snorted, and stood listening with ears twitching and head to the east. Pelleas rose up and scanned the road from under his hand, with the girl Igraine beside him.

"A Saxon horn," he said laconically; "the heathen are in the woods."

V

As they watched, looking down betwixt two thorn trees, a faint puff of dust rose on the road far to the east, and hung like a diminutive cloud over the meadows. This danger signal counselled the pair. Pelleas caught his horse and sprang to selle; Igraine clambered by his stirrup, and was lifted to her seat before him. Pelleas slung his shield forward, and loosened his sword.

"If it comes to battle," he said, "I will set you down, and you must hide in the meadows or woods, while I fight. You would but cumber me, and be in great peril here. Rest assured, though, that I shall not desert you while I live."

With that he turned his horse to the road, and halted, gazing down amid the placid fields to where the little cloud of dust had hinted at life. It was there still, only larger, and sounded on by the distant triple canter of horses at the gallop. Pelleas and Igraine could see three mounted figures coming up the road amid a white haze, moving fast, as though pressed by some as yet unseen enemy. It was soon evident to Pelleas and the girl that one of the fugitives was a woman.

"We will abide them," said the man, "and learn their peril. We shall be stronger, too, for company, and may succour one another if it comes to smiting. Look! yonder comes the heathen pack."

A second and larger cloud of dust had appeared, a mile or less beyond the first. Pelleas watched it awhile, and then turned and began riding at a trot towards the west, so that the three fugitives should overtake him. He bade Igraine keep watch over his shoulder while he scanned the meadows before them for sign of peril or of friendly harbour.

"Have no fear, child," he said; "I could vow, by these fields, that there is a manor near. I trust confidently that we shall find refuge."

Igraine smiled at him.

"I am no coward," she said.

"That is well spoken."

"I would, though, that you would give me your dagger, so that, if things come to an evil pass, I shall know how to quit myself."

"My dagger!" he said, with a sudden stare. "I left it in the man's heart in Andredswold."

"Ah!" said Igraine; "then I must do without."

The dull thunder of the nearing gallop came up to them—a stirring sound, full of terse life and eager hazard. Pelleas spurred to a canter, while Igraine's hair blew about his face and helmet as they began to meet the kiss of the wind. She clung fast to him with both hands, and told what was passing on the road in their rear.

"How they ride," she said; "a tangle of dust and whirling hoofs. There is a lady in blue on a white horse, with an armed man on either flank. They are very near now. I can see the heathen far away over the meadows. They are galloping, too, in a smoke of dust. Our folk will be with us soon."

In a minute the lady and her men were hurtling close in Pelleas's wake. He spurred to a gallop in turn, and bade Igraine wave them on to his side. The three were soon with them, stride for stride. The girl on the white horse drew up on Pelleas's right flank. She was habited in blue and silver — a flaxen-haired damosel, with the round face of a child. Seemingly she was possessed of little hardihood, for her mouth was a red streak in a waste of white, and her blue eyes so full of fear that Igraine pitied her. She cried shrilly to Pelleas, her voice rising above the din like the cry of a frightened bird.

"The heathen!" she cried.

"Many?" shouted the man.

"Two score or more. There is a strong manor near. If we gain it we may live."

"How far?"

"Not a mile over the meadows."

"Lead on," said Pelleas; "we will follow as we may."

The damosel on the white horse turned from the road, and headed southwards over the meadows, with her men galloping beside her. The long grass swayed, water-like, before them, its summer seed flying like a mist of dew. Wood and pasture slid back on either hand. The ground seemed to rise and fall before them as a sea, while rocks here and there thrust up bluff noses in the grass like great lizards stirred by the hurtling thunder of the gallop.

On they went, with white spume on breast and bridle; leaping, swerving where rough ground showed. To Igraine the ride was life indeed, bringing back many a whistling gallop from the past. She felt her heart in her leaping to the horse's stride. Now and again she took a sly look at Pelleas's face, finding it calm and vigilant — the face of a man whose thought ran a silent course unruffled by the breeze of peril. She felt his bridle-arm staunchly about her like a girdle of steel. Although she could see the dust gathering thickly on the distant road, she felt blithe as a new bride in the man's company, and there was no fear at all in her thought.

The grassland began to slope gradually towards the south. A quavering screech of joy came back to them from the woman riding in the van. Pelleas spoke his first word during the gallop.

"Courage," he said. "Southwards lies our refuge."

Igraine looked over his shoulder, and saw how their flight tended down the flank of a gentle hill into the lap of a fair valley. The grass stretch was broken by great trees — oaks, beeches, and huge, corniced cedars. Down in the green hollow below them a mere shone with the soul of the sky steeped in its quiet waters. It was ringed with trailing willows, and an island held its centre, piled with green shadows and the grey shape of a fair manor. The place looked as peaceful as sleep in the eye of the morning.

The woman on the white horse bade one of her men take his bugle-horn and blow a summons thereon to rouse the folk upon the island. Twice the summons sounded down over the water, but there was no answering stir to be marked about the house or garden. The place was smokeless, lifeless, silent. Like many another home, its hearths were cold for fear of the barbarian sword.

As they held downhill, Igraine wove the matter through her thought like swift silk through a shuttle.

"Should there be no boat," she said, giving voice to her misgivings, "what can you do for us?"

"We must swim for it," said Pelleas, keenly.

"It is a broad, fair water, and the horse cannot bear us both."

"He shall, if needs be."

She felt that the brute would, after Pelleas had spoken so. She patted the arched black neck, and smiled at the sky as they came down to the mere's edge at a canter. The water was lapping softly at the sedges amid a blaze of marsh marigolds and purple flags, the surface gleaming like glass in the sun. Half a score water-hens went winging from the reeds, and skimming low and fast towards the island. A heron rose from the shallows, and laboured heavenwards with legs trailing.

Riding round the margin, they found to their joy a barge grounded in a little bay, with sweeps ready upon the thwarts, and a horse-board fitted at the prow. A purple cloak hung over one bulwark, trailing in the water; a small crucifix and a few trinkets were scattered on the poop, as though those who had used the ferry last had fled in fear, forgetful of everything save flight.

Then came the embarkation. The barge would but hold three horses at one voyage, so Pelleas ordered Igraine and the rest into the boat, and bade the men row over and return. Igraine demurred a moment.

"Leave your horse," she said; "they may come before the boat can take you."

Pelleas refused her with a smile, running his fingers through the brute's black mane.

"I have a truer heart than that," he said.

The men launched away, and pulled at the sweeps with a will, Igraine helping, and doing her devoir for the man Pelleas's sake. The barge slid away, with ripples playing from the prow, and a gush of foam leaping from each smile of the blades. It was a hundred yards or more to the island, and the craft was ponderous enough to make the crossing slow.

Pelleas sat still and watched the meadows. Suddenly — bleakly — a figure on horseback topped the low hill on the north, and held motionless on the summit, scanning the valley. A second joined the first. Pelleas caught a shout, muffled by the wind, as the two plunged down at full gallop for the mere, sleeping in its bed of green. Here were two gentlemen who had outstripped their fellows, and were as keen as could be to catch Pelleas before the barge could recross, and set the mere betwixt them. Pelleas saw his hazard in a moment. Even if the barge came before the heathen, there would be some peril of its capture in the shallows.

He would have to fight for it, unless he cared to swim the mere. Provided he could deal with these two outriders before the main company came up, well and good, the raiders would find clear water between the quarry and their swords. He thought of Avangel, and grew iron of heart. Then there was the nun, Igraine, with the wonderful eyes, and hair warm as the dun woods in autumn. He was her sworn knight as far as Winchester. God helping him, he thought, he would yet see her face again. So he rode out grimly to get fair field for horsecraft, and waited for the two who swept the meadows.

Igraine, standing on the wooden stage at the water's edge, saw Pelleas taking ground and preparing for a tussle. The barge had put off again and had already half spanned the water. She was alone with the woman of the white horse, who stood beside her still quaking like a reed, and almost voiceless from the fulsome terror of an unshrived death. Igraine had no heed for her at the moment. Her whole thought lurked with the red shield and the black horse in the meadows. Worldly heart! her desire burnt redly in her own bosom, and found no flutter for the powers above.

She saw Pelleas gathering for the course, while the heathen slackened so as not to override their mark. A crescent of steel flashed as the foremost man launched his axe at the knight's head. The red shield caught and turned it. In a trice Pelleas's spear had picked the rogue from the saddle, despite his crouching low and seeking to shun it. The second fellow came in like a whirlwind. His horse caught the black destrier cross counter and rolled him down like a rammed wall. Pelleas avoided, and was up with bleak sword. Smiting low, he caught the man's thigh, and broke the bone like a lath. The Saxon lost his seat, and came down with a snarling yell. The rest was easy as beating down a maimed wolf.

The main company had just topped the hill. Pelleas, with the skirmish ended to his credit, shook his sword at them, and led his horse into the shallows. The barge swept in, took its burden from the bank, and held back for the island, where Igraine stood watching on the stage, ready with her welcome. She was glad of Pelleas in her heart, as though the comradeship of half a day had given her the right to share his honour, and to chime her joy with his. The woman in her swamped the assumed sanctity of the nun. As the water stretch lessened between them, Pelleas, silent and dark-browed as was his wont, found himself beneath the beck of eyes that gazed like the half-born wonder of the sky at dawn. It was neither joy nor great light in them, but a kind of quiet musing, as though there were strange new music in her soul.

"Are you hurt?" she asked, as he sprang from the barge and stood beside her, with head thrown back and his great shoulders squared.

"Not a graze."

"Two to one, and a fair field," quoth she, with a quaver of triumph; "my heart sang when those men went down. That was a great spear thrust."

"Less and less of the rosary!"

She caught his deep smile, and laughed.

"I am a greater heathen than either," she said. "God rest their souls."

Meanwhile the lady in the blue tunic had somewhat recovered her squandered wits and courage. She came forward with a simpering dignity, walking daintily, with her gown gathered in her right hand, and her left laid over her heart. Her eyes were very big and blue, their brightness giving her an eager, sanguine look that was upheld the more by an assumed simpleness of manner. Her childish bearing, winsomely studied, exercised its subtleties with a lavish embellishment of smiles and blushes. Looked at more closely, and in repose, her face belied in measure the perspicuous personality she had adopted. A sensual boldness lurked in mouth and nostrils, and there was more carnal wisdom there than a pretended child should possess.

"Courtesy fails me, sir," she said, letting her shoulders fall into a graceful stoop, and turning her large eyes to Pelleas's face; "courtesy fails me when I would most praise you for your knightly deed in yonder meadows. I am so frightened that I cannot speak as I would. My heart is quite tired with its fear and flutter. Think you — you can save us from these wolves?"

Pelleas had neither the desire nor the leisure to stand juggling courtesies with the woman.

"Madame," he said, "we shall fight. Leave the rest to Providence. I can give you no better comfort."

"No," she said, "no" — as in a daze.

Pelleas, reading her misery, repented somewhat of his abrupt truthfulness.

"Come," he said, with a kind strength and a hand on her shoulder; "go to the house and rest there with Sister Igraine. I see you are too much shaken. Go in and pray if you can, while we hold the island."

The girl looked at him unreservedly for a moment. Then she gave a little laugh that was half a sob, and, bending to him, kissed his hand before he could prevent her. Giving him yet another glance from her tumbled hair, she stepped aside to Igraine, and they turned together towards the manor, and the trees and gardens that ringed it. The girl had set her hand in Igraine's with a little gesture that was intended to be indicative of confidence in the supposed nun's greater intelligence.

"Let us go and sit under that yew tree," she suggested. "I cannot stifle within walls now. You are named Igraine. I am called Morgan — Morgan la Blanche, — and I am a lord's daughter. I almost envy you your frock now, for death cannot frighten you as it frightens me. Of course you are very good, and the Saints guard and watch over you. As for me, I have always been very thoughtless."

"Not more than I," said Igraine, with a smile. "I have often hummed romances when I should have praised Paul or Peter."

"But doesn't the fear of death blight you like a frost?"

"I never think of death."

"It seems so near us now that I can hardly breathe. Do you think we are tortured in the other world, if there be one?"

"How should I know, simple one?"

"I wish the mere were a league broad. I should feel further from the pit."

"Is your conscience so unkind?"

"Conscience, sister? It is self-love, not conscience. I only want to live. Look!—the heathen are coming down to the mere. How their axes shine. Holy Mother!—I wish I could pray."

Igraine, catching the girl's pinched face, with lips drawn and twitching, pitied her from her very heart.

"Come then, I will pray with you," she said.

"No, no, my prayers would blacken heaven. I cannot, I cannot."

The wild company had swept down between the great trees in disorderly array. Their weapons shone in the sunlight, their round bucklers blickered. They were soon at the place where Pelleas had slain his men in fair and open field. Dismounting, they gathered about their dead fellows, and sent up, after their custom, a vicious, dismal ululation, a sound like the howling of wolves, drear enough to make the flesh tingle under the stoutest steel. Lining the bank among the willows, they shook buckler and axe, gesticulating, threatening, their long hair blowing wild, their skin-clad bodies giving them a wolfin look not pleasant to behold. Round the margin they paddled—searching—casting about for a boat. They seemed like beasts behind the gates of some Roman amphitheatre—caged from the slaughter. The girl Morgan looked at them, screamed, and hid her face in her tunic.

Igraine found the girl's quaking hand, and held it fast in hers.

"Courage, courage," she said; "there is no boat, and, even if they swim, Sir Pelleas is a great knight."

"What can he do against fifty?" whined the girl, with her face still covered.

"Fifty? There are but a score. I have numbered them myself."

"I would give all the jewels in the world to be in Winchester."

"Ah! girl, I have no jewels to give; but this, I promise you, is better than a convent."

The barbarians had gathered in a group beneath a great willow. Plainly they were in debate as to what should be done. Some, by their gestures, their tossing weapons, and their bombast, were for swimming the mere. Their councils were palpably divided. Possibly the sager folk among them did not think the venture worth the loss to them it might entail, seeing that one of those cooped upon the island had already given proof of no mean prowess. They could see the three armed men waiting grimly by the water's edge, ready to strike down the swimmer who should crawl half-naked from the water weeds and mire. Gradually, but surely, the elder tongues held the argument, and the balance went down solemnly for those upon the island.

Pelleas and the two men, watching keenly for any movement, saw the circle of figures break and melt towards the horses. They saw them pick up the bodies of their two dead fellows, and lay them across the saddle. In a minute the whole troop turned, and held away southwards at a trot, flinging back a last wild cry over the water. The meadows rolled away behind them; the gradual trees hid them from moment to moment. Pelleas and the two servants stood and watched till the black line had gone southwards into the thickening woods.

Under the yew tree Morgan la Blanche had uncased her white face, and was smiling feebly.

"I am glad I did not pray," she said; "it would have been so weak. Look! I have torn my tunic, and my belt's awry. Bind my hair for me, sister, quickly,—before Sir Pelleas comes."

VI

With the heathen lost in the distant woods, Pelleas and the women essayed the house, leaving the two servants to sentinel the island.

The great gates of the porch were ajar. Pushing in, they crossed into the atrium, and found it sleepy as solitude. The water in the impluvium gleamed with the gold flanks of the fish that moved through its shadows. Lilies were there, white and wonderful, swooning to their own images in the pool. The tiled floor was rich with colour. Venturing further, they found the triclinium untouched, rich couches and flaming curtains everywhere, gilded chairs, and deep-lustred mirrors, urns, and flowers. In the chapel candles were guttered on the altar; dim lights came down upon a wealth of solemn beauty—saints, censers, crosses, frescoed walls all green and azure, gold and scarlet. The viridarium, set betwixt chapel and tablinum, held them dazed with a glowing paradise of flowers. Here were dreamy palms, orange trees like mounts of gold, roses that slept in a deep delight of green. Over all was silence, untainted even by the silken purr of a bird's wing.

Gynœcium and bower were void of them in turn. Everywhere they found the relics of a swift desertion. The manor folk had gone, as if to the ferry of death, taking no worldly store or sumptuous baggage with them. Not a living thing did they discover, save the fish darting in the water. The cubicula were empty, their couches tumbled; the culina fireless, and its hearth cold.

Pelleas and the women marvelled much at the beauty of the place; its solitude seemed but a ghostly charm to them.

As for the girl Morgan, she had taken Pelleas into her immediate and especial favour, holding at his side everywhere, a-bubble with delight. The luxury of the place pleased her at every glance; her vanity ran riot like a bee among flowers. She eyed herself furtively in mirrors, and put a rose daintily in her hair while Pelleas was not looking. She had already rifled a cabinet, strung a chain of amethysts about her neck, and poked her fingers into numberless rings. Then she would try the couches, queen it for a moment in some stately chair, or smother her face sensuously in the flowers growing from the urns. All these pretty vapourings were carried through with a most mischievous grace. Igraine, who had seen the girl white and whimpering an hour before and in deadly horror of the pit, wondered at her, and hated her liberally in her heart.

Nor was Pelleas glad of the change her presence had wrought; for her childish subtleties had no hold on him, and even her thieving seemed insipid. With solemn and shadowy thoughts in his heart, her frivolous worldliness came like some tinkling discord. Igraine seemed to have dimmed her eyes from him beneath the shadow of her hood. Her face was set like the face of a statue, and there was no play of thought upon it. She walked proudly behind the pair — not with them — like one elbowed out of companionship by a vapouring rival.

In the women's bower Morgan found a lute, and pounced upon it.

"One's whole desire seems here," she chattered. "This bower suits my fancy like a dream, and I could lodge here a month for love of it. What think you, Knight Pelleas? I never set foot in a fairer manor. I warrant you there are meat and wine in the cellars. We will feast and have music anon."

Pelleas's face looked more suited to a burial. Igraine pitied him, for his eyes looked tired and sad. Morgan ran on like a jay. In the chapel she found Igraine a share.

"Here is your portion, holy Sister," she said; "mine the bower, yours the altar. So you see we are all well suited. Come, though, is it not very horrible having to look solemn all day, and to wear a grey gown? I should fade in a week inside such a hood; besides, it makes you look such a colour."

Igraine could certainly boast a colour at that moment that might have warned the woman of her rising fume. Pelleas broke in and took up the argument.

"Men do not consider dress," he said; "everything is fair to the comely. I look into a woman's face and into her eyes, and take the measure of her heart. Such is my catechism."

"But you like to see rich silks and a smile, and to hear a laugh at times. What is a girl if she is not gay? No discourtesy to you, sister; but you seem so far set from Sir Pelleas and myself."

Igraine, lacking patience, flared up like a torch. "Ha! mark you," she said, "my habit makes me no coward, nor do I thieve. No discourtesy to you, my dear lady."

Morgan set up a thrill of laughter.

"How true a woman is a nun," quoth she; "but you are too severe, too careful. Thieving, too; why, I may as well have a trinket or so before the place is rifled, even if I take a single ring. And what is more, I have been turned from my own house with hardly a bracelet or a bodkin. Come, Sir Pelleas, let us be going; the Sister would be at her prayers. I see we but hinder her."

Pelleas had lost both pity and patience in the last minute. Partisanship is inevitable even in the most trivial differences, and Pelleas's frown was strongly for Morgan la Blanche.

"Perhaps it would be well, madame," said he, "if we all went on our knees for the day's deliverance. I cannot see that there is any shame in gratitude."

"Gratitude!" chirped the girl. "Gratitude to whom?"

"To the Lord Saviour, madame, and the Mother Virgin."

She half laughed in his face, but his eyes sobered her.

For a moment she fronted him with an incredulous smirk, then her glance wavered, and lowered to his breast. It held there with a tense stare, while her whole face hardened. Pelleas saw her pupils darken, her cheeks flush and pale in a moment. He thought nothing of it, or ascribed her distraught and strange look to some sudden shame or shock of penitence. In a trice the smile was back again, and she seemed pert and pleased as ever.

"I see you are too devout for me," she said with a glib laugh, "and that I am too wicked a thing for the moment. I will leave you to Sister Igraine till you both have prayed your fill." Here she laughed again, a laugh that made Igraine's cheeks burn. "Remember me to St. Anthony if you may. If I recollect rightly he was a nice old gentleman, who cured 'the fire' for a miracle, and nearly fell in love with a devil. Till you have done, I will go and gather flowers."

Pelleas and Igraine looked at one another.

"A devout child," said the man.

"And not bred in a nunnery."

"The world's convent, I should say."

For the moment Igraine was almost for telling him of her own hypocrisy, but the thought found her more troubled on that score than she could have guessed. She had acted a lie to the man, and feared his true eyes despite her courage. "Another day I will tell him," she thought; "it is not so great a sin after all." So they turned and knelt at their devotions.

Morgan la Blanche went away like the wind. She ran through atrium and porch with hate free in her eyes, and her child's face twisted into a scowl of temper. In the garden she idled up and down awhile in a restless fume, like one whose thoughts bubble bodingly. Sometimes she would smite a lily peevishly with her open hand, or pluck a flower and trample it under her feet as though it had wronged her. Then she would take something from her bosom and stare at it while her lips worked, or while she bit her fingers as though galled by some inward barb. Presently she found her way by a laurel walk to the orchard, and thence by a wicket-gate to the island's rim, where one of her men kept watch on the further meadows.

She stood under an apple tree, called to him, and beckoned. He came to her — a short, burly fellow with the look of a bull, and brute writ large on his visage. Morgan drew him under the swooping dome of the tree, plucked something that shone from her bosom, and dangled it before his eyes.

"The cross," she said, almost in a whisper. "Galerius, the cross."

The man stared at her stupidly. Morgan lifted a finger, ran this way and that peering into the green glooms and listening. Then she came back to the man, soft-footed, glib as a cat, with the cross of gold gripped in her fingers. She smiled at him, a smile that was almost a leer.

"Galerius," she said, "the knight in the house yonder wears a chain with one cross missing, and the fellow cross matches this. Moreover, his poniard sheath is empty. I marked all this as I stood by him a moment ago. This is the man who slew my lord."

The servant's heavy face showed that he understood her well enough now.

"To-night," she said, almost skipping under the trees with the intensity of her malice, "it shall be with his own poniard. I have it here. Galerius, you have always been a good fellow."

The man grinned.

"Keep silence and leave all to me. I shall need your hand and no more."

"Nor shall he," said Galerius curtly.

Morgan grew suddenly bleak and quiet, with the thought of murder harboured in her heart.

"Look for yourself, Galerius," she said; "see that my eyes have not deceived me. The man must have come upon Lord Madan when he was alone, after our hirelings had deserted the house. He slew him in the winter room —this whelp sent by Aurelius the king. You and I, Galerius, found the cross in my lord's dead hand, and the poniard in his bosom. I warrant you we will level this deed before we hold again for Winchester."

"Trust my hand, Madame Morgan," quoth the man; "if you can have the fellow sleeping, so much the better, one need not strike in a hurry."

"Leave it to me," she said; "I will give you your knife and your chance to-night."

With that she sent the fellow back to his watching, and threaded the orchard to the manor garden. Pelleas and Igraine had long ended their prayers in the chapel. Morgan found them in the atrium, watching the fish in the water and their own reflections in the pool. The girl had quite smothered the bleak look that had held her features in the orchard. She was the same ingenuous, self-pleased little woman whose blue eyes seemed as clear and honest as a sleeping sea in summer. Before, she had flown in Pelleas's face for vanity's sake; now she seemed no less his woman —ready with smiles and childish flattery, and all the pleasantness she could gather. She was at his side again—quick with her eyes and tongue. Probably she guessed that the man despised her, but then that was of no moment now, seeing that it made the secret in her heart more bitter.

At noon they dined in the triclinium, with man Galerius to serve. He had ransacked kitchen and pantry, and from the ample store discovered, had spread a sufficient meal. His eyes were ever on Pelleas as he waited. There was no doubt about cross or poniard sheath; and Galerius found pleasure in scanning the knight's armour and looking for the place where he might strike.

The afternoon proved sultry, and Pelleas took his turn in keeping watch by the bank. Cool and placid lay the water in the sun, while vapoury heat hung over the meadows and the distant woods. There was still fear lest the heathen might return, thinking to catch the islanders napping. The very abruptness of their retreat had been in itself suspicious; and Pelleas was all for caution. Igraine's face seemed to make him more careful of peril. He thought much of her as he paced the green bank for three hours or more, before leaving the duty to Galerius and his fellow.

Returning to the manor he found Igraine cushioned on the tiled floor beside the impluvium, fingering the lute that Morgan la Blanche had found. The latter lady was still in the tablinum, so Igraine said, pilfering and admiring at her leisure, with fruit and a cup of spiced wine ready at her hand. Pelleas took post on the opposite side of the pool to Igraine, unarmed himself at his leisure, and began to clean his harness. No task could have pleased Igraine better. She put the lute away, took his helmet on her lap, and burnished it with the corner of her gown. Pelleas had sword, breast-plate, greaves and shoulder pieces beside him. Their eyes often met over the pool as they sat with the scent of lilies in the air, and talked little — but thought the more.

Igraine felt queerly happy. There seemed a warm fire in her bosom, a stealthy, happy heat that crept through every atom of her frame like the sap into the fibres of some rich rose. Her heart seemed to unfold itself like a flower in the sun. She looked often at Pelleas, and her eyes were very soft and bright.

"A fair place, this," she said presently, as the man furbished his sword.

"Fair indeed," said he; "a rich manor."

"It is strange to me after Avangel."

"Perhaps more beautiful."

"Ah," she said, with a sudden kindling; "I think my whole soul was made for beauty, my whole desire born for fair and lovely things. You will smile at me for a dreamer, but often my thoughts seem to fly through forests — marvellous green glooms all drowned in moonlight. I love to hear the wind, to watch the great oaks battling, to see the sea one laugh of gold. Every sunset harrows me into a moan of woe. I can sing to the stars at night—songs such as the woods weave from the voice of a gentle wind, dew-ladened, green and lovely. Sometimes I feel faint for sheer love of this fair earth."

Pelleas's eyes were on her with a strange deep look. His dark face was aglow with a new wonder, as though his soul had flashed to hers. The great sword lay naked and idle in his hands.

"Often have I felt thus," he said, "but my lips could never say it. Thoughts are given to some without words."

"But the joy is there," she answered, with a quiet smile.

"Joy in beauty?"

"Yes."

"Ah, girl, a beautiful face, or a blaze of gold and scarlet over the western hills, are like strange wine to my heart."

"Yes, yes, it is grand to live," said Igraine.

Pelleas's head went down over his sword as though in thought.

"It would seem," he said presently, "that beauty is a closed book, save to the few. It is good to find a heart that understands."

"Ah, that know I well," she chimed; "in Avangel they had souls like clay; they saw nothing, understood nothing. I think I would rather die than be soul blind."

"So many folk," said the man, "seem to live as though they were ever scanning the bottom of a pot. They never get beyond reflections on appetite."

As they talked, Morgan la Blanche came in from behind the looped curtains, with silks, samites, siclatons, and sarcanets in her arms. She had found some rich chest in the bower accomplice to her fingers, and had revelled gloriously. She sat herself down near Pelleas, and began to laugh and chatter like a pleased child. The dainty stuffs were tossed this way and that, gathered into scarves or frills, spread over her lap and eyed critically as to colour, before being bound in a bale for her journey. Vain and vapid as her behaviour seemed, there was more in this little woman's heart than either Pelleas or Igraine could have guessed. Her whole mood was false. Foolish as she seemed on the surface, she was more keen, more subtle by far than Igraine, whose whole soul spelt fire and courage.

As the day drew towards evening, Morgan became more stiff and silent. Her eyes were bright as the jewels round her neck; they would flash and waver, or fall at times into long, sidelong stares. More than once Igraine caught the girl's face in hard thought, the pert lips straight and cruel, the eyes hungry and very shallow. It reminded her of Morgan's look in the morning, when she was in such stark fear of the heathen and of death. Yet while she watched her, smiles and glib vivacity would sweep back again as though there had been but a transient cloud of thought over the girl's face.

With the shadows lengthening, they turned, all three of them, into the garden, and found ease on a grass bank beneath the black boughs of a great cedar. The arch of the dark foliage cut the sky into a semicircle of azure. All about them the grass seemed dusted with dim flowers — blue, white, and violet. A rich company of tiger lilies bowed to the west. Dense banks of laurels and cypresses stood like screens of blackest marble, for the sun was sinking. As they lay under the tree, they could look down upon the water, sheeny and glorious in the evening peace. Further still, the willows slept like a mist of green, with the fields Elysian and full of sweet stupors, the woods beyond standing solemn and still at the beck of night.

Morgan, who had brought the lute with her, began to touch the strings, and to sing softly in a thin, elfin voice —

My heart is open at the hour of night
When lilies swoon
And roses kiss in bed.

When all the dreams of sad-lipped passion rise
From sleep's blue bowers
To die in lover's eyes.
  Come flame,
  Come fire,
A woman's bosom
Is but life's desire.
So, all my treasures are but held for love
In scarlet silks
And tapestries of snow.
I long, white-bosomed like the stars that sigh
A bed in heaven
For love's ecstasy.
  Come flame,
  Come fire,
A woman's bosom
Is all man's desire.

The birds were nestling and gossiping in the laurel bushes, taking lodging for the night. From the topmost pinnacle of the cedar, a thrush, a feathered muezzin, had called the world to prayer. From the mere came the cries of water-fowl; the eerie wail of the lapwing rose in the meadows. Presently, all was still and breathless; a vast hush seemed to hold the world. The west was fast dying.

Under the cedar the light lurked dim and magic. Morgan's fingers were still hovering on the strings, and she was singing to herself in a whisper, as though she had care for nothing, save for that which was in her heart. Pelleas and Igraine were quite near each other in the shadow. They had looked into each other's eyes — one long, deep look. Each had turned away troubled, yet with a sudden glory of quick anguish in their hearts. The night seemed very subtle to them, and the whole world sweet.

VII

IGRAINE'S thoughts were to music when she went to bed that night. Pelleas's eyes stayed with her, darkly, sadly;

his tragic face seemed to look out of the night, like the face of one dead. And he more than liked her. She felt sure of that, even if she did not dream of kinder things sprung from long looks and quiet sighings. She sat on her bed, and smiled the whole strange day over to herself again. She had the man before her in all his looks and poses; how he sat his horse, the habit he had of looking deeply into nothingness, his strength and quiet knightliness, and above all his devout soul. He seemed to please her at every point in a way that set her thrilling within herself with a delicious wonder. Last, she thought of the weird twilight under the grand old tree — rare climax to a day of deeds and memories. She felt her heart leap as she remembered the great wistful look that had shone out on her from Pelleas's eyes.

The manor house seemed still as the night itself. Morgan la Blanche had taken herself to a couch in the triclinium, choosing it rather than one of the cubicles leading from the atrium. Galerius was on guard, pacing the mere's bank, while his comrade slept in the kitchen. Pelleas, armed, with sword and shield beside him, had quartered himself on cushions in the great porch, with the doors open.

It was about ten o'clock. Igraine, full of sweet broodings, crept into bed, and settled herself for sleep. The night was wonderfully peaceful. The window of the room was overgrown with a tangle of roses, the flowers seeming to mellow the air as it came softly in, and there was a faint shimmer into the shadows that hinted at moonlight. Igraine lay long awake, with her eyes on the few stars that peeped through between the jambs. There was too much in her heart to let sleep in for the while, and her thoughts were a' dance within her brain like wild, fleet-footed things. As she lay in a happy fever of thought, her face grew hot upon the pillow, and her tumbled hair was like a lustrous lava flow over the bed. In course, despite her tossing, she fell into a shallow, fitful sleep that verged between wakefulness and dreams.

It was well past midnight when she started, wide awake,

with the half-dreamt memory of some eerie sound in her ears. She sat up in bed, and listened, shivering. There were footfalls, swift and light, on the pavement of the atrium. From somewhere came a gruff voice, speaking tersely and in bated tones. Next, there was something that sounded like a groan, and then silence.

Igraine crept out of bed, hurried on her habit, opened the door gently, and looked out. Moonlight streamed in through the square aperture in the roof of the hall, but all else lay in darkness. The porch gates were ajar, with a band of light slanting through upon the tiles. Eager, tremulous, she fancied as she stood that she heard the beat of oars. Then the low, groaning cough that she had heard before thrilled her into action like a trumpet cry.

She was across the court in a second, and into the darkened porch. The doors swung back to her hands, and the night streamed in. Clear before her, lit with a silver emphasis, lay the water, and on it she saw the dark outline of the barge, moving with foaming oars towards the further bank. For the moment her heart seemed to halt within her.

"Pelleas!" she cried. "Pelleas!"

A stifled sound answered her from a dark corner of the porch. With a sudden frost in her bosom she saw a black rill trickling over the tiles in the moonlight, even touching her feet. Great fear came upon her, but left her power to think. In the triclinium she had seen a lamp, with tinder, steel, and flint in a tray beside it, and in her fear she ran thither, tore her fingers in her haste with stone and steel, but had the lamp lit with such speed as she had never learnt at Avangel. Then she went back trembling into the porch.

The knight Pelleas lay in the corner, half propped against the wall. His head was bowed down upon his chest, and he had both hands clasped upon the neck-band of his tunic. Blood was trickling from his mouth, and he seemed to be hardly breathing, while under the left arm-pit shone the silver hilt of the knife that had been thrust there by Galerius's hand. To the thought of the girl it seemed as if the man were in his death agony.

The utter realism of the moment drove all fear from her. She set the lamp on the tiles, and kneeling by Pelleas, pulled the knife slowly from his side. A gush of blood followed. She strove to staunch it with a corner of her gown. The man was quite unconscious, and never heeded her, though he was still breathing jerkily and feebly, with a rattling stridor in his throat. She lifted his head and rested it upon her shoulder, while she knelt and pressed her hand over the wound, dreading to see him die each moment.

For an hour she knelt, cold and almost bare-kneed, on the stone floor, holding the man to her, watching his breathing with a tense fear, pressing upon the wound as though ethereal life would ebb and mock her fingers. Little by little she felt the warm flow cease, felt her fingers stiffened at their task, while the minutes dragged like æons, and the lamp flickered low in the night. At last she knew that the issue was stayed, and that Pelleas bled no more. Gradually, fearfully, lest life should fall away like a poised wand, she laid the man down, and again watched with her hand over the stricken side. He was breathing more noticeably now, with less of the look of death about him. Encouraged thus, she dared to meditate leaving him to find wine, and sheets to cover him there. When she essayed to move she found her habit clotted to the wound where she had held it. It took her minutes to cut the cloth through with the knife that had stabbed Pelleas, for she was palsied lest the wound should break again and lose her her love's labour.

Free at last, she fled into her room, tore the clothes in which she had lain from the bed, and carried them trailing into the porch. Then, lamp in hand, she spoiled the triclinium of rugs and cushions, and found there the chalice of wine that Morgan had sipped from. Ladened, she struggled back across the hall, fearing all the while to find the man parted. No such foul fortune, however. He was breathing better and better.

Then she set to to make a bed. She spread cushions and rugs; and then, so slowly, so gently, that she seemed hardly to move, she had the man laid upon the couch, with two cushions under his head. Next she covered him with the clothes taken from her own bed. Thus much completed without mishap, she washed his lips and face with water taken from the pool, trickled some wine down his throat, and set the doors wide to watch for dawn.

So pressed had she been by the man's peril, that even the right of thought had been denied her. Now, seated by the lamp, she began to sift matters as well as her meagre knowledge would suffer, keeping constant watch on wounded Pelleas the while. She knew that Morgan and her men were gone in the barge, but as to who gave Pelleas his wound, she could come to no clear understanding in her heart. There must have been some deep feud for such a stroke, though she could find no reason for the deed. Still, she could believe anything of that chit Morgan la Blanche, and there the riddle rested for a season.

Before long she saw the summer dawn stealing silently and mysteriously into the east. The face of the sky grew grey with waking light, and the hold of the moon and night relaxed on wood and meadow. Then the birds began in the garden, till she thought their shrill piping must wake Pelleas from his swoon, so blithe and lusty were they. The east was forging day fast in its furnace of gold. The glare touched the clouds and rolled them into wreaths of amber fire.

A sigh from the couch brought her to her feet like magic. She went and knelt by the bed in quite a tumult of expectation. Pelleas's hands were groping feebly over the coverlet like weak, blind things. Igraine caught them in hers, thrilled as they closed upon her fingers, and, bending low, she waited with her lips almost on the man's, her hair on his forehead, her eyes fixed on his closed lids. All her soul seemed to droop above him like a lily over a grave. Presently he sighed again, stirred and opened his eyes full on Igraine's, as she knelt and mingled her breath with his.

"Pelleas," she whispered. "Pelleas."

He looked at her for a moment with a dazed stare that dawned into a smile that made her long to sing.

"It is Igraine," she said.

Pelleas caught a deep breath, and groaned as his stricken side twinged to the quick.

Igraine put two fingers on his lips.

"Lie still," she said, "lie still if you love earth. You must not speak, no, not one little word. I must have you quiet as a child, Pelleas. You have been so near death."

She felt the man's hand answer hers. He did not speak or move, but lay and looked at her as a little child in a cradle looks at its mother, or as a dog eyes his master. Igraine put his hands gently down upon the coverlet, and smiled at him.

"Lie so, Pelleas," she said; "be very quiet, for I am to leave you, for a minute and no more. You must not move a finger, or I shall scold."

She beamed at him, started up and ran straight to the chapel, her heart a-whimper with a joy that was not mute. She went full length on the altar steps with her face turned to the cross above — the cross whose golden arms were aglow with the sun through the eastern window. In her mood, the white Christ's face seemed to smile on her with equal joy. She learnt more in that moment than Avangel had taught her in a year.

Hardly five minutes had passed before she was with Pelleas again, bearing fruit and olives, bread and oil. She made a sweet dish of bread and berries, with some wine in it for his heart's sake, and then knelt at his side to feed him. She would not let him lift a finger, but served him herself with silver spoon and platter, smiling to give him courage as he obeyed her like a babe. It seemed very pitiful to her that so much strength and manliness should have been smitten so low in one brief night. None the less, the man's feebleness brought her more joy than ever his courage had done, and his peril had discovered clear wells of ruth in her that might have been months hidden but for the hand of Galerius. When Pelleas had finished the bread and fruit, she gave him more wine, and then set to to bathe his hands and face with scented water taken from the tablinum. Pelleas's eyes, with deep shadows under them now, watched her all the while with a kind of wondering calm. The sunlight flooded in, and lit her hair like red gold, and made her neck to shine like alabaster. Meeting his look, she reddened, and turned to hide her face for a moment, that he might not see all that was writ there in letters of flame.

"Now you must sleep, Pelleas," she said, crossing his hands upon the quilt.

He shook his head feebly.

"I am going to leave you," she persisted, "so you must not flout me, Pelleas. I shall be here, ready, when you wake."

She smiled at him, and closed his lids gently with her finger tips.

"Sleep," she said, brushing her hand softly over his forehead, "for sleep will give you strength again. You may need it."

She left him there, and taking bread and olives with her, she closed the porch gates to shade him, and went herself into the garden. After a meal under the old cedar, she went down to the water's edge and washed her feet from the stains of Pelleas's blood, and bathed her hands and face. She saw the barge amid the reeds and rushes on the further bank. There was no sign of life in the meadows, and the woods were deep with peace.

Then she remembered Pelleas's horse. Going to the stable behind the manor, she found the beast stalled there, though Morgan's horses had been taken by the men in the barge. Igraine took hay from the rack, gave him a measure of oats in his manger, and watered him with water from the mere. Then she stood and combed his mane with her fingers as he fed. Some of the poppies she had plaited there were dead and drooping in the black hair. She thought as she unbound the withered things how nearly Pelleas's life had withered with theirs. She was very happy in her heart, and she sang softly the low tender songs women love when their thoughts are maying.

Igraine passed the whole morning in the garden, going every now and again to the porch to open the doors gently, and peep in upon the sleeper. She gathered a basket of fruit and a lapful of flowers. About noon she went in, and bringing jars from the triclinium, she filled them with water and garnished them with flowers. These jars she set in array about Pelleas's bed, one of tiger lilies and one of white lilies; a bowl of roses at his head, a jar of hollyhocks and one of thyme, and fragrant herbs at the foot. Moreover, she strewed the coverlet with pansies, and scattered rose leaves on his pillow. Then she went to the chapel to pray awhile, before sitting down to watch beside his bed.

Pelleas woke about an hour after noon had turned. At his first stirring, Igraine was hanging over him like a mother, with her hands on his. Pelleas looked up at her, saw the flowers about his bed, and, risking her menaces, spoke his first word.

"Igraine," he said.

She put her face down to his.

"I am much stronger," he said; "I can talk now."

"Perhaps a very little," she answered, with her eyes on his.

"Igraine!"

"Yes, Pelleas."

"You are very wonderful."

"Pelleas!" she said redly.

"I should have died without you, for I was witless, and coughing blood."

"I thought you would die," she said very softly, with her

eyes downcast. "I held you in my arms and, God helping me, staunched the flow from your wound. But tell me, Pelleas, who was it stabbed you?"

The man smiled at her.

"There, I am as ignorant as you," he said. "I woke with a fiery twinge in my side, and saw a man running out of the porch in the dark. I struggled to rise. Blood came into my mouth, and betwixt coughing and hard breathing I must have fainted. What of the others?"

Igraine knelt up from stooping over him, and thought.

"Morgan and her men," she said presently, "fled across the mere in the barge just after you had been stabbed. I saw them go in the moonlight. It was your cry that woke me in bed. I came and found you senseless in the corner, and the woman and her rascals making off in the boat. One of the men must have smitten you while you slept."

Pelleas kept silence for a while, as though he were thinking hard.

"Show me the knife," he said anon.

Igraine had washed away the stains, and laid it aside in a corner. She held it up now before Pelleas's eyes as he lay in bed. He took it from her with trembling hands, and handled it, his face darkening.

"This is my own poniard," he said, "the poniard I left in the heart of the man in Andredswold. Look, girl, look! Search and see, mayhap you may find a cross."

Igraine did his bidding, and searched the pavement, but found nothing. Then she came back to the bed, and began to turn the cushions up here and there, and to scan the tiled floor. Sure enough, under the foot of the bed, she found a small gold cross lying, smeared lightly with dried blood. She took it up and gave it to Pelleas. He caught and held it with a terse cry.

VIII

PELLEAS lay the afternoon through in a half dream of shifting thought. But for the tangible things about him there might have been elfin mischief in the air, for the last few days had passed with such flash of new feeling and desire that the man's mind was still in a daze.

He lay in bed, with jars of lilies round him, and a woman tending him with the grace of a Diana. It was all very strange, very pleasant, despite the ague in his ribs and his inordinate weakness. He was not so sure after all that he bore Morgan la Blanche any so fervent a piece of malice; fortune seemed to beckon him towards generosity, seeing that his condition was so truly picturesque. Uncouth feelings were swallowed up for the time being by a benignant stupor of contentment.

But the balance of human happiness is often very nice and subtle. Leaden reason tumbled into the scale of melancholy may even outscale the bowl of dreams. Love and law often dangle on either beam of a man's mind, or philosophy anchored to a rock may sky poor fancy into the clouds. So it was with Pelleas that day, wisdom being often enough a miserable nurse. When he thought of Igraine, reason as he would with himself, his soul began to shimmer like moon-rippled water. When she looked at him the very pillars of his manhood seemed to quake. When she passed, light-footed, from garden to porch, she seemed to come in like the sun, bringing streams of warmth into his wounded flesh. Of necessity, he soon met other cogitations less pleasant, and no less imperative. From legal quarters came that inevitable pedagogue blear-eyed Verity, paunched up with dogma and breathing ethical platitudes like garlic. "The woman's a nun," quoth Dom Verity, with a sneer. "Keep your fancy in leash, my good Pelleas, and forswear romance. Bar your thoughts from a child of the church or you will rue it. No man may serve a nun. The world has said."

What with his wound and his fractious meditations, Pelleas soon fell into a most dismal temper. Like most sick folk he had lost for the time that level sense of proportion that is the sure outcome of health. His thoughts began to gape at him, and to pull most melancholy grimaces. Even the dead man squatting in the great chair in the manor in Andredswold began to haunt him like an ogrish conscience. Hot and racked, he could stand his own company at last no longer. Calling Igraine to him, he began to unburden himself to her with regard to the man he had done to death in the forest.

The girl listened, mild as moonlight, and ready to swear away her soul to soothe him.

"I am troubled for the deed," he was saying, "though the man deserved death, twenty deaths, and though I served justice to the echo. His blood hangs on my hands, and makes me restless at heart."

"Tell me his sin, Pelleas."

"They were many, and too gross for ears such as thine."

"Then palpably he was too gross to live."

"No doubt, child."

"Then why trouble for his death, Pelleas; you would not shrink from treading out an adder's brains?"

"Ah, but there is the man's soul. I feel for him after my own down-bringing. What chance had he of penitence?"

"True," she said gravely, "but your mother, the Abbess Gratia, used to tell us that bad men repented only in legends and in the Bible; never in grim life. Besides, you prevented the man committing worse offences in the future, and getting deeper into the pit. Why, Pelleas, hundreds of good knights have lost life for a mere matter of love; why trouble for the life of a wretch who perhaps never knew what truth meant. You would not grieve for men slain in battle."

"In battle the blood is hot and the brain afire. This was a rank and reasonable stroke."

"And therefore the more deserved. Why trouble about

it, Pelleas? In faith, since your plight makes me tyrant, I forbid such brooding. It is but the evil fancy of a distraught mind, an incubus I must chase away. See, your hands are hot, and your forehead too. Will you sleep again, or shall I sing to you?"

"Presently," he said. "I have more to speak of yet."

Igraine knelt by him on her cushion, serene and tender.

"Say on, Pelleas," she said; "a woman loves a man's confidence. If I can give you comfort I will gladly listen here till midnight. You are not yourself, weak from loss of blood, and a gnat's sting is like a lance thrust to you. Tell me your other troubles."

Pelleas groaned, hesitated, looked up into her eyes, and recanted inwardly. He furbished up a minor woe to serve the occasion.

"It is my sword and shield," he said; "they were given me blessed and consecrated by my mother. It is in my thought that I had smirched them by this deed. What think you, girl?"

"I cannot think so," she said stoutly.

Then since his face was so wistful and troubled, she racked her fancy for some plan she thought might soothe him. A sudden purpose came to her like prophecy.

"Listen," she said. "I can do this for you. Give me your shield and sword, and let me lay them on the high altar under the cross with candles burning, and let me pray for them there. Will that comfort you, Pelleas?"

"Yes," he said, with a sudden sad smile; "pray for me, go and pray for me, Igraine."

It was the impulse of a moment. She bent down with a great thrill of wonder, and kissed the man's lips. It was soon done, soon sped. She saw Pelleas's blood stream to his face, saw something in his eyes that made her heart canter. Then she darted away, took up the great sword and the shield with its red face, and went to the chapel singing like a seraph. Her prayers were a strange jumble of worship and recollection. "Lord Jesu, cleanse his spirit," said her heart one moment; "truth, how he coloured and looked at me," it sang with more human refrain the next. "May he be a knight above knights," quoth devotion; "and may I be ever fair in his eyes," chimed love. Altogether, it was a most quaint prayer.

Now, a certain mundane matter had been troubling Igraine's thought that day. The barge, seized and put to use by Morgan and her men, lay amid the reeds on the nether shore, ready to give passage to any chance wayfarer, welcome or otherwise, who should choose to cross the mere. The boat, so fixed, floated as a constant peril to Pelleas and herself. She felt that peace would flout them so long as the barge lay ready to play ferry-boat to any casual intruder. Pelleas's wound might keep them cooped many days in the place. She vowed to herself that the boat should be regained, and blushed when the oath accused her.

At dusk, when the birds were piping, and there was a green hush over the world, she went back to Pelleas, a beautiful shameface, accompliced by the twilight.

"I have prayed," she said simply.

Pelleas touched her fingers.

"I feel happier," he said.

"That is well."

"Stay near me, Igraine. It grows dark fast."

"I shall be with you till you sleep," she said.

Igraine fed him with her own hands, talking little the while, but feeling very enamoured of her lot. She was thinking of her new surprise with some mischievous pleasure as she tended Pelleas. The man was silent, yet very placid and facile to her willing. When she had bathed his face and neck, and seen him well couched, she took the lute Morgan had handled, and began to sing to him softly—wistfully, as though the song was the song of a quiet wind through willows. It was a chant for the dusk, for the quiet gazing of the first fires of heaven. Pelleas heard it like the distant touching of strings over charmed water, and with the breath of lilies over him he fell asleep.

Igraine held by him still as a mouse in the dark, till she knew by his breathing that he was deep in slumber. Then she set the lute aside, put the lamp by the porch door, so that it should be ready to hand, and stole out into the garden.

The moon was just coming up above the distant trees. Igraine waited under the black-vaulted cedar till the great ring rode bleak above the fringe of the tops before she went down between laurels to the water's edge. There was a deep cedarn scent on the warm air, and everything seemed deathly still. Going to the landing stage, she stood there awhile looking at the water, dark and mysterious, with pale webs of light upon its agate surface. Then she began to bind her hair closely on her head, smiling to herself, and staring down at her vague image in the water.

Her hair in shackles, she turned to her task in earnest. Soon habit, shift, and sandals were lying in a heap, and she was standing clean, rare, gleamingly straight as a statue, with her arms folded upon her breast. For a moment she stood, making the night to swoon, before taking to the mere. Pearly white with an aureole of foam, she swam flankwise with an overhand stroke, one arm thrusting out like a silver sickle. Here and there, fretted by the willows, long moonbeams glinted on her round whiteness, as the maddened foam bubbled, and the water sighed and yearned amid the sedges. A fine glow had leapt through her body like wine, and the mere seemed to sway and sing as she swam for the main bank, where the willows stood blackly in a mist of phosphor glory. Soon she reached the shallows at a pleasant place where stretch of grassland tongued down into the mere. She climbed out, and stood like a water nymph, her body agleam and asparkle with its dew, her skin like rare silk, smooth as a star's glance. Down fell her hair like smoke. She stretched her arms to the moon, and laughed, aglow with the warmth gotten of her swim. Then she went to where the barge lay amid the reeds, and boarding it poled out into the deeps.

Standing on the poop she used an oar as a paddle, and so brought the cumbrous barge slowly under way. It stole out from the fretted shadows of the trees, and glided like a great ark over the mere in black silence, save for the dip of the blade and the drip of water. The voyage took Igraine longer than her swim. At last, with the boat moored at the stage, she dried her limbs and body with her hair, and took again to shift and habit. Then she stole back to the manor, listened a moment to Pelleas's breathing, and having lit her lamp she went to bed.

Next morning Igraine, with her deed locked up in her heart, was preparing Pelleas a meal. He had just stirred and roused himself from sleep with a little cry, and he was watching the girl with the mute reflective look of one just freed from the visions of the night.

"Igraine," he said.

She turned to him with a soft smile.

"I have been dreaming," he confessed gravely.

"Dreaming, Pelleas?"

"I thought," said he, "that I saw a great dragon of gold come over the meadows with a naked sword in his mouth, and a collar of rubies round his throat. And he came to the mere's edge, ramping and breathing fire. And lo! he entered into the barge there, and the barge went forth bearing him, while all the mere's water boiled and shone about the boat like flame. So he came to the island, and all greenness seemed to wither before him, and with the fear of him I awoke."

Igraine shook her head at the man.

"Your dreams are distraught," she said; "it is your wound, Pelleas. In faith we should need the great Merlin for such a vision."

"Ah," said he, "I can read you the riddle, Igraine. Our barge lies by the land bank ready for any foe. That is where the dream touches us."

Igraine brought him a bowl of crushed bread and fruit, and made as though to feed him.

"Never worry," she said; "the barge is moored safe at the stage."

Pelleas put the bowl aside with one hand, and stared at her from his pillows.

"Did the barge swim the mere of herself," quoth he, "and anchor for us so fairly?"

"No."

"Then —"

Igraine went red of a sudden, and looked at her knees.

"Sooth, Pelleas," she said, "I must have been the dragon of your dream; God pardon me."

"Igraine!"

"I never knew I seemed so fearful a creature."

"Honour and praise —"

He half rose on his pillows in his enthusiasm. Igraine put him gently back, and took up the bowl of bread and fruit.

"That will do, my dear Pelleas," she said; "now just lie still and have your breakfast."

What boots it to chronicle at length their sojourn in the island manor. Twelve days Igraine nursed the man there, giving all her heart for service, tending him from sunrise to the fall of night. She seemed to have no other joy than to sit and talk to him, to make music with voice and hand, to keep his couch posied round with flowers. On waking Pelleas would find her by him, fresh as the dawn and full of a golden tenderness; at night his eyes closed upon her gracious figure as she sat in the gloaming and sang. She was near to hear his voice, quick to see his needs and to remedy them with soft hands and softer looks. The very atmosphere about the man seemed touched and mellowed by her, and the hours seemed to trip to the measure of a golden rhyme.

Pelleas mended very rapidly under her care. His wound, sweet and innocent, gave him no trouble save some slight feverishness on the third day. The sixth morning found him so stalwart of temper that Igraine consented to his leaving bed for a morning provided he obeyed her to the letter. His first steps were taken in the atrium with Igraine's arm about his waist, and his upon her shoulders. So well did he bear himself that the girl led him to the chapel, and there side by side on the altar steps they winged up their devotion to heaven. Igraine's prayers, be it known, were all for love; Pelleas's for the threatening shadows over his own soul.

Daily after this innovation Igraine would make him a couch under the great cedar tree in the garden, where he could rest shaded from the sun, and there, morn, noon, and eve, they had much comradeship and speech together. They would talk of God, the saints, and the souls of men, of love and honour, and the needs of Britain. Pelleas would tell her of his own service with Aurelius, of all the fair pomp of Lesser Britain, where Conan had begun a goodly kingdom years ago, and where many British folk had taken refuge. He had been to Rome as a boy, and he described that vast city to her, or told her of the bloody fields he had seen when the steel of Christendom met the heathen. Fresh streams from either soul welled out, and mingled much during those summer days. Pelleas and Igraine looked deep each into the heart of the other, finding fine store of nobleness, of truth, and of things beautiful, till the heart of each had treasured everything for love and for love's desire. They were fair hours and very sweet to the two. The day seemed a casket of gold, and the night a bowl of ebony ablaze with stars.

About this time the man Pelleas began to go down into deep waters. Many days had passed with a flare of torches in the west; their sojourn was drawing to a close, and the night seemed near. The haler Pelleas grew in body, the more halt and hopeless waxed his soul. The whole world seemed to grow wounded to his eyes; the west was wistful at evening, and the starry sky a sob of pain. When Igraine harped and sang, each note flew like winged death into his heart. He had no joy that was not smitten through with anguish, no thought that was not crowned with thorns. It was a very simple matter indeed, but perverse to utter bitterness. Pelleas saw no hope for himself in the end. He would rock and toss, and think at night till the darkness seemed to crush him into a mere mass of misery. Above all there seemed to rise a great hand holding a cross of gold, and a voice that said, "Beware thy soul and death."

Not so was it with Igraine. To her life had no shroud, and love prophesied of love alone. She knew what she knew, and her heart was full of summer and the song of birds. Pelleas loved her; she would have staked her soul on it, though she did not realise the desperate turmoil passing in the man's clean heart. Knowing what she did, she was all for sun and moods of radiant thought and happiness. Each day she imagined that she would tell Pelleas of her secret; each day she gave the golden moment to the morrow. She knew how the man's face would flame up with the fulness of great wonder, and like a woman she hoarded anticipation in her heart and waited.

The day soon came when Pelleas declared himself hale enough to bear armour, though the admission was made with no great amount of satisfaction. To test his strength he armed himself with Igraine's help, harnessed his black horse, and rode round the island, first at a level pace with Igraine running beside him. Then he tried a gallop, handling spear and shield the while. Lastly, he took Igraine up to him, and rode with her as he had ridden through the wold. Suffering nothing from these ventures, and seeming sure in selle as ever, he declared with heavy heart that they should sally for Winchester on the morrow.

Pelleas and Igraine passed their last evening in the island under the great cedar in the garden. The place had deep memories for them, and very loth were they to leave it, so fair and kind a refuge had it proved to them in peril. Neither said much that evening, for their thoughts were busy. As for Pelleas, he was glum and heavy-browed as thunder, with a look in his deep eyes that spelt misery. It was as though he were leaving his very soul in the place to ride out like a corpse on a pilgrimage with despair. How much she might have eased him, perhaps Igraine never knew.

The west was already red and rosy, and there was a green hush over the meadows, and a canopy of pale porphyry in the east. All the soul of the world seemed to lift white hands to the night in a stupor of mutest woe. Yet the girl's mood tended towards mere sensitive regret, for the future was not dark to her imaginings.

"You are sad, Pelleas," she said.

"I am only thinking, Igraine."

"I am sorry to leave this place."

Pelleas sighed for answer. With a contradictory spirit, born of pain, he longed for night and the peace it would not bring. Something swore to him that he was more to the girl than man had ever been, and yet she seemed happy when he compared her humour with his own. The possibility that she could dream of broken vows was never in his thought. He could only believe that her heart was less deep than his, and the thought only added bitterness to his mead of sorrow.

"Igraine," he said anon.

She turned to him.

"You love life?"

"Truth, Pelleas, I do."

"Then love it not, girl."

"Ah!"

"'Tis a broken bowl."

"How so?" she said, thrilling.

Pelleas turned his face from her to hide the strife thereon. He felt as though death was in his heart, yet he spoke as quietly as though he were telling some mundane tale, and not words conjured up by a desperate wisdom.

"Igraine," he said, "I have lived and learnt something in

my time, and my words are honest. On earth what do we find — a lie on truth's lips, and anguish on the face of joy. The roses bloom and die, white hands shrivel, and harness rusts under the green grass. As for fame, it breeds hate and jealousy, and the curse of the proud. Music is broken by the laugh of the fool, nor can youth forget the crabbed noisomeness of age. Women sing and pass. A man marries one night and is tombed the next. And love, what of love? I tell you love lives only in the eyes of woe. It is all mockery, cold damned mockery. I have said."

IX

Pelleas and Igraine were stirring soon after dawn on the morning of their sally for Winchester. It was a summer dawn, still and stealthy; the meadows were full of a shimmering mist, the mere spirit-wrapped, and dappled here and there with gold.

Silent and distraught they made their last meal in the quiet manor. Everything seemed sad and solemn, as though the stones could grieve; the lilies by the impluvium seemed adroop, and the flowers about Pelleas's bed were withered. After the meal Pelleas armed himself, and went to harness his horse, while Igraine put up bread and foodstuff into a linen cloth for their journey. Before sallying they went all round the manor, into the chapel, where they prayed before the altar, into bower, parlour, and viridarium. The porch with its empty bed and withered flowers they took leave of last. There was such wistfulness there that even the dumb things seemed to cry out in pain.

Pelleas closed the gates with bowed head, and made the sign of the cross upon them with the pommel of his dagger. His throat seemed full of one great muffled sob. Together they wandered for the last time through the garden, while Igraine plucked some flowers for a keepsake. Pelleas felt that he loved every leaf in the place like his own soul.

Then they went down to the water's edge, and, getting the horse on board, they loosed the barge from the bank, and came slowly to the nether shore. It might have been the fury of death, so stark and solemn was Pelleas's face.

Before turning their backs and riding away, they stood and looked long at the place girdled with its quiet waters. The great cedar slept there with a hood of mist over his green poll. Like a dream island it seemed, plucked by magic from some southern sea, fair with all fairness. Anon, despite their grieving, the last strand cracked, and the wrench was done. They were holding over vapoury meadows with their faces to the west.

Pelleas was very stoical that morning. As a matter of fact he had been awake all night, couched with misery and with thoughts that wounded him. All night through the lagging hours he had tossed and turned, cursing his destiny in his heart — too bitter for any prayer. What mockery that he who had passed so long unscathed should fall into hopeless homage to a nun. Desperate, he left his bed in the dark, and made the garden a dim cloister until dawn. Yet in the rack of struggle a clear voice had come to touch and dominate his being, and day had found him steadfast. He would hold to the truth, he vowed, do his duty, and let God judge of the measure of his gratitude. He could obey, but not with humility; he could suffer, but not with resignation.

It was after such a night in the furnace of struggle that he forged his temper for the days to come. He had thought to meet love with a stark hardihood, to talk lightly, to go with unruffled brow while his heart hungered. Nothing should move him to any emotion. He would meet destiny like a rock, let surges beat and melt back to the sea. It was better thus, he thought, than to go moaning for the moon.

Such was the determination that met Igraine's lighter humour that morning. She could make nothing of the man as she rode before him. He was bleak, dismal, yet striving to seem contented with their lot, now conjuring up a withered smile, now lapsing into interminable silence. His eyes were stern in measure, but there was the old light in them when she looked deeply, and the staunch flame was there still. After all, Pelleas's quiet humour did not trouble her very vastly. She had her own reading of the riddle, and a word in her heart that could unlock his trouble. Moreover, she was more than inclined to put him to such a test as should bring his manhood to a splendid trial. Perhaps there was some imp of vanity deep down in her woman's heart. At all events, she suited herself to the occasion, and passed much of the time in thought.

A ride of some seventy miles lay before them before they should come to the gates of Winchester. Much of that region was wild forestland and moor, bleak wastes of scrub let into woods and gloom. Occasional meadows, and rare acres of glebe ringing some rude hamlet, broke the shadowy desolation of the land. Great oaks, gnarled, vast, and terrible, held giant sway amid the huddled masses of the lesser folk. Here the boar lurked, and the wolf hunted. But, for the most, it was dark and calamitous — a ghostly wilderness almost forsaken by man, and given over to the savagery of beasts.

Pelleas and Igraine came upon the occasional trail of the heathen as they went. A smoking villa, a burnt village with a dun mist hanging over it like a shroud, and once a naked man, bruised and bloody, bound to a tree, and shot through with arrows — such were the few sights that remembered to them their own need of caution. The wild country had been raided, and its sparse civilisation scattered to the woods. The crosses at the cross-roads had been thrown down and broken. A hermitage they came on in the woods had been sacked, and in it, to their pity, they found the body of a dead girl. They halted there to pray for her, and to give her burial. Pelleas dug a shallow grave under an oak, and they left her there, and went on their way with greater caution.

Not a soul did they meet, yet Pelleas kept under cover as much as possible for prudence' sake. He scanned well every valley or piece of open land before crossing it, and kept under the wooelshawe whenever the track ran near trees. Fear of the unknown, and the dear burden that he bore, kept him alert as a goshawk for possible peril. By noon, despite sundry halts and reconnoitrings, they had covered nearly twenty miles, and by the evening of the same day they had added another score, for Pelleas's horse was a powerful beast, and Igraine's weight cumbered him little.

Towards evening it began to rain, a heavy, summer, windless shower, that made moist rattle in the leaves, and flooded fragrant freshness into the air. Pelleas gave Igraine his cloak, and made her wear it, despite her excuses. As luck would have it, they came upon a little inn built in the grey shelter of a forsaken quarry. The inn folk were still there — an old woman, and a brat of a boy, her grandson. Seeing so great a knight, the beldam was ready enough to give them lodgings, and what welcome she could muster. She spread a supper of goat's milk, brown bread, and venison — not a bad table for such a hovel. The meal over, she pointed Pelleas with a leer to a little inner room that boasted a rough bed, a water-pot, and ewer.

"We will not disturb ye," she said; "my lad has foddered the horse. You would be stirring early?"

Pelleas gave the woman her orders, and sent Igraine into the inner room. He made himself a bed of dried bracken before her door, and laid himself there so that none could enter save over his body. The woman and the boy slept on straw in a corner. In this wise they passed the night.

On the morrow, after more goat's milk and brown bread, with some wild strawberries to smooth it, they sallied early, and held on their way to Winchester. The shower of the night had given place to fair weather, and a fresh breeze blowing from the west. Soon the sun was up in such strength that the green woods lost their dankness, and the leaves their dew. It was the very morning for a ride.

If possible, Pelleas was even more gloomy than on the day before. There was such a level air of dejection over his whole being that Igraine began to have grave qualms of conscience, and to suffer the reproaches of a pity that grew more clamorous hour by hour. None the less, maugre the man's sorry humour, there was a certain stealthy joy in it all, for Pelleas, by his very moodiness, flattered her tenderness for him not a little. She began to see, in very truth, how staunch the man was; how he meant to honour to the letter her imagined vows, though his love grieved like a winged merlion. His great strength became more and more apparent. A lighter spirit would have gone with the wind, or made great moan over the whole business. Pelleas, she saw, was striving to buckle his sorrow deep in his bosom, to save her the pain of knowing his distress. There was nothing little about the man. Palpably he had not succeeded eminently in his attempt to spur a wounded spirit into light courtliness and easy hypocrisy. Still, that was not his fault; it only said the more for his love.

It was not till noon had passed that Pelleas, with a heavy courage, constrained himself to speak calmly of their parting. Even then he was so eager to shape his speech into mere courtesies, that he overdid the thing, more than betraying himself to the girl's quick wit.

He had questioned her as to her friends in Winchester, and her purposes for the future. His rambling took somewhat of a didactic turn as he laboured at his mentorship.

"There is a fair abbey within the walls," he said; "I have heard it nobly spoken of both as to devoutness and comfort. Their rules are not of such iron caste as at some other holy houses; the library is good, and there is a well-planted garden. The abbess is a gracious and kindly woman, and of high family. I have often had speech with her myself, and can vouch for her courtliness and benevolence.

Assuredly you may find very safe and peaceful harbour there."

Igraine smiled to herself at the callous benignity of his counsel. He might have been her grandfather by his manner.

"You see," she said naively, "I do not like being caged; it spoils one's temper so. I have an uncle in the place — an uncle by marriage — a man not loved vastly by the proud folk of my own family. He is a goldsmith by trade, and is named Radamanth."

Pelleas's quick answer was not prophetic of great favour.

"Radamanth," he said — "a gentleman who weighs his religion by the pound, and is seen much at church. Pardon my frankness, I had this gold chain of him. He is rich as Rome, and has high rank among the merchants."

"So I had heard," she answered.

Pelleas looked into space with a most judicial air.

"You do not think of going to a secular house," he said.

Igraine smiled to herself, and halted a moment in her answer.

"Why not?" she said.

"You — a nun?"

"Pelleas, I do not see why it is necessary for holiness to be bricked up like a frog in a wall in order to escape corruption. Why, you are eating your own words."

"But you have vows," he said.

"I have; and doubts also."

"Doubts?" quoth the man, with a quick look, thrilling inwardly.

"Doubts, Pelleas, doubts."

She caught his eyes with hers, and gave him one long, deep stare that made him quake as though all that had been flame within him — that which he had sought to tread to ashes — had but spread redly into her bosom. There was no parrying such a message. It smote him blind in a moment. The spiritual bastions of his soul seemed to reel and rock as though some chaos had broken on their stones.

There was great outcry in his heart, as of a leaguer when guards and stormers are at grapple on the walls. "Cross! Holy Cross!" cried Conscience, in the moil. "Yield ye, yield ye, Pelleas," sang a voice more subtle, "yield ye, and let Love in!" He sat stiff in the saddle, and shut his eyes to the day, while the fight boiled on within him. Now Love had him heart and hand; now Honour, blind and bleeding, struggled in and stemmed the rout. He was won and lost, lost and won, a dozen times in a minute.

Recovered somewhat, he made bold to question Igraine yet further.

"Tell me your doubts, girl," he said.

"They are deep, Pelleas, deep as the sea."

"Whence came they, then?"

"Some great power put them in my heart, and they are steadfast as death."

Again the wild flush of liberty swept Pelleas like wind.

"Tell me, Igraine," he said, in a gasp.

She put her fingers gently on his lips. "Patience—patience," she said, "and perhaps I will tell them to you, Pelleas, ere long."

Thus much she suffered him to go, and no further. Her quick instinct had read him nearly to the "Explicit," and there she halted, content for an hour or a day. Her love was singing like a lark in the blue. She beamed on the man in spirit streams of pride and tumultuous tenderness. How she would comfort him in the end! He should carry her into Winchester on his horse, and she would lodge there, but not at the great inn that harboured souls for heaven. She would have the bow and the torch for her signs, and possibly the Church might serve her in other fashion. Like a lotus eater, she dallied with all these dreams in her heart.

With the sun low in the west, Pelleas and Igraine were still three leagues or so from Winchester. The day was passing gloriously, with the radiant acolytes of evening swinging their jasper censers in the sky. The two were riding on a pine-crowned ridge, and the stretch of wilderness beyond seemed wrapped in one mysterious blaze of smoking gold. Hills and woods were glittering shadows, like spirit things in a spirit atmosphere. The west was a great curtain of transcendent gold. Pelleas and Igraine could not look at it without great wonder.

Presently they came to a little glade, green and quiet, with a clear pool in it ringed round with rushes. A lush cushion of grass and moss swept from the water to the bases of the trees. It was as quaint and sweet a nook as they had passed that day. The place, with its solitude and stillness, pleased Igraine very greatly.

"What say you, Pelleas," she said, "let us off-saddle, and harbour here the night. This little refuge will serve us more kindly than a ride in the dark to Winchester."

Pelleas looked round about him, knelt for once without struggle to his own inmost wishes, and agreed with Igraine.

"Very good," he said. "I can build you a bower to sleep in. There are hazels yonder — just the stuff for a booth. The water in the pool there looks sweet enough to drink, and we have ample in the cloth for a supper."

Igraine gave him no more leisure to moralise on such trifles. She sprang down to the cushiony turf, and took his horse by the bridle.

"I will be master again for once, Pelleas," she said, "since, well of your wound, you have played the tyrant. At least you shall obey me to-night."

Pelleas, half in a stupor, gave up fighting his own heart for a while, and fell in with Igraine's humour. She was strangely full of smiles and quiet glances; her eyes would meet his, flash, thrill him, and then evade his soul with sudden mischief. She tethered his horse for him, and then, making him sit down under a tree, she began to unarm him, kneeling confidently by his side. Her fingers lingered over-long on the buckles. When she lifted off his helmet, her hands touched his face and forehead, and set him blushing like a boy. The very nearness of her — her breath, her dress, her lips and eyes so near to his — made him like so much wax — passive, obedient, yet red as fire.

When she had ended her task, she gave him his naked sword and her orders.

"Now you may cut me hazels for a bower, Pelleas," she said. "I will have it here under this tree where the moss is soft and dry. This summer night one could sleep under the stars and never feel the dew."

Pelleas rose up and did her bidding. The green boughs were ready to his great sword, as it gleamed and glimmered in the wizard light. He cut two forked stakes, and set them upright in the ground, with a pole between them. Then he built up branches about this centrepiece till the whole was roofed and walled with shelving green; he spread his red cloak therein for a carpet. Igraine sat and watched his labour. Life seemed to have rushed nearly to its zenith, and her thoughts were soaring in regions of gold.

The black moth night had come into the sky with his golden-spotted wings all spread. It was time for idyllic love, pure looks, and the touch of hands. The billowy bosoms of the trees rolled sombrously above, and the little pool was like a wizard's glass, black and deep with sheeny mysteries.

Igraine beckoned Pelleas to a seat on the grass bank at her feet when he had finished. There was a light on her face that the man had not seen before, a kind of quiet rapture, a veil of exultation, as though her maidenhood were flowering gold under a net of pinkest satin. She had loosened her hair in straight streams upon her shoulders, and her habit lay open to the very base of her shapely throat. She sat there and looked at him, with hands clasped in her lap, and her grey gown rising and falling markedly as she breathed. It seemed to Pelleas that there was nothing in the whole universe save twilight, two eyes, a stirring bosom, and two wistful lips.

They had been speaking of their ride, and of the many strange things that had befallen them during their adventures together. Igraine had waxed strangely tender in her talk, and had spoken subtle bodeful words that meant much at such a season. She was flinging bonds about Pelleas that made him exult and suffer. His heart seemed great within him and ready to break, for the blood that bubbled and yearned in it in glorious anguish.

"To-morrow," said the girl, "we enter Winchester, and I have known you, Pelleas, two weeks and some few hours more. You seem to have been in my life many years."

Words flooded into Pelleas's heart, and stifled all struggle for a moment. He was breathing like a hunted thing.

"Igraine," he said.

"Pelleas."

"I never lived till our lives were joined."

Igraine gave a little gasp, and bent over him suddenly, her eyes aglow, her hair falling down into his face.

"Kiss me, Pelleas," she said; "in the name of God, kiss me."

Pelleas gave a great groan.

"Girl, I dare not."

"You dare."

"Igraine?"

She bent herself till her lips were over his, and both their heads were clouded in her hair. Her eyes glimmered, her breath beat on his, he saw the whiteness of her teeth between her half-closed lips.

"Igraine," he said again, half in a groan.

She did not answer him, but simply took his face between her hands and looked into his eyes.

"Coward, Pelleas."

Power seemed to go from the man in a moment. He put his hands upon her shoulders and looked at her as in a splendid dream. Her face was beautifully peevish, and there lurked an infinite hunger on her lips. Then with a great woe in his heart he drew her face down to his and kissed her. There was such sweet pain in the grand despair of it all that he felt faint for strength of loving. Before he had gathered breath, Igraine had slipped away from him and was in the bower.

"Till dawn, Pelleas, till dawn," she said.

"Ah, Igraine!"

"Go and sleep, Pelleas; I will talk to you on the morrow."

X

WITH the girl's face lost behind the green eaves of the bower, Pelleas fell of a sudden into great darkness of soul. It was as though the moon had passed behind a cloud, and left him agrope in the woods without light and without guide. Igraine had bidden him to go and sleep. She might as well have told the sea to be still in the lap of the wind.

Going aside towards the mouth of the glade so that he might not disturb the girl, he began to tread the grass between brake and brake, while he held parley with his turbulent and seething thoughts. What was Igraine to be to him on the morrow? She had broken the back of his determination, and beaten down his strength in those grand moments of sudden passion. The rich June of her beauty was still on his sight. Her grace, her infinite tenderness, the purity of her, were all set about his soul like angels round a dreamer's bed. She was light and darkness, sound and silence; she had the round world in her red heart, and the stars seemed to go about her in companies of gold. Never had Pelleas thought idolatry so smooth and swift a sin. He had never believed that love in so brief a space could make such wrack of madness in a hale and healthy body.

As he walked under the giant limbs of the great trees he tried to grapple the thing with reason, to untangle this knot by natural logic. These were the bleak facts, and they stood up like white headstones in the night. He loved Igraine, and Igraine he knew loved him in turn; but Igraine was a nun despite her womanliness, and there lay the core of the whole matter. If he obeyed love he must disgrace the girl with broken vows, for like a staunchly taught Christian of somewhat stern and primitive mould he stood in honest awe of things spiritual and ecclesiastic. His very love for the girl made him fearful of in any way dishonouring her. If he held to the trite observations of a prompted conscience, then he must forswear love, and leave Igraine to the miserable celibacy of the Church, that chrysalid state that never burgeons into the fuller, fairer life of perfect womanhood. These were the two forces that held him shaken in the balance.

Long while he went east and west under the trees with the old gloom flooding back like thunder. His whole thought seemed warped into bitterness; the blatant mockery of it all grinned and screamed like a harpy. Again with clarion cry and rosy flush of banners love stormed in and held law at death's door for a season. Again came the inevitable repulse, the moaning lapse of desire, while the black banner of the Church flapped once more over him in dismal sanctity. Pelleas found no shred of peace wheresoever he looked. Who has not learnt that when anarchy is in the heart, the whole world seems out of gear?

As the night passed, love seemed to faint and wax pale before an ever-darkening visage that declared despair. A sense of inevitable gloom seemed to weigh down desire, and to drown hope in misery. Pelleas grew calmer at heart, though his thoughts were no less woeful. Love's voice, stifled and wistful, came like an elfin voice through woods, while the cry of conscience was like the thundering surge of the wind through trees. He grew less restless, more apathetic. Coming to a halt he leant against an oak's bossy trunk, and stood motionless as in a stupor for an hour or more. The blight of soul-sickness was on him, and he was like one dazed by a great fever.

Presently he went back slowly to Igraine's shelter of boughs, and stood near it — thinking. Then he dropped on his hands and knees, crept up close, and parting the leaves looked in on her as she slept, wrapped in his red cloak. He could see her face indistinctly white in a wealth of shadows; he could hear her breathing. Then he crept away again like a wounded thing, and lay for a time with his face in his arms, grieving without a sound.

Again, a second time, he crept to the bower, and listened there on his knees. Turning his face to the night he tried to pray, vainly indeed, for his heart seemed dumb. A corner of Igraine's gown lay near his hands at the entry; he went down on hands and knees and kissed it. Then he took the little gold cross from his bosom, the cross Morgan had held, and laid it on the grass at Igraine's feet. He also put a purse with a few gold coins in it beside the cross. When he had done this he crept away mutely, and began to arm in silence.

Once, as he was buckling on his casque, he thought he heard Igraine stirring. He kept very still, with a sudden, wild wish in his heart that she would wake and save him, but the sound proved nothing. He finished buckling on his harness, girded his sword, and hung his shield about his neck. Then he went to the little pool, and, kneeling down, dashed water in his face, and drank from his palms. He felt faint and bruised after the night's battle.

Once more he went and stood by the hazel shelter as though for a last leave-taking before the strong wrench came. The little pavilion of leaves seemed to hold all hope and human joy in its narrow compass. Pelleas stood and took long leave of the girl in his heart. He wished her all the fair fortune he could think of, prayed for her as well as he could in a broken, wounded way, and then with a great sob he turned and left her sleeping. His black horse was tethered not far away. As he went he staggered, and seemed blind for a moment. He soon had the girths tightened, and was in the saddle, riding away dry-eyed and broken-souled into the night.

Presently the dawn came, redly, gloriously, like a marriage pageant. Igraine, reft from dreams, woke with a little shiver of joy in her pavilion of green boughs. She lay still awhile, and let her thoughts dance like the motes in the shimmer of sunlight that stole in between the branches. The day seemed warm and glorious, for that morning was she not to tell Pelleas of the secret she had kept from him so many days, the words she had hoarded in her heart like love? It would be a fitting end, she thought, to the rare novitiate each had passed in the heart of the other.

Hearing no stir about her shelter, she thought Pelleas asleep, and peeped out presently between the boughs to bid him wake. Glade and pool lay peacefully in green and silver, but she saw no knight sleeping, no war-horse standing under the trees. Starting up, the gold cross glinting on the grass, with the purse beside it, appealed her with mute tragedy. She caught them up, trembling, and with sudden fear in her heart she went out into the glade and searched from brake to brake. It was barren as her joy. Pelleas had gone.

BOOK II

GORLOIS

I

Radamanth the goldsmith was held in no little honour and esteem by the townsfolk of Winchester. Even the market women and the tavern loungers stood aside for him in the street as he made his stately march in black robe and chain of gold. He was a man possessed of those outward virtues so well suited to commend a character to the favour of the world. He was venerable, rich, and much given to charity. His coffers were often open to infirmary and church; his house near the market square was as richly furnished as any noble's, and he gave good dinners. No man in Winchester had a finer aptitude for pleasing all classes. He was smooth and intelligent to the rich, bland and neighbourly to his equals, quite a father to the poor, and moreover he had no wife. Every Sabbath he went at the head of his household to the great basilica church in the chief square, worshipped and did alms as a rich merchant should.

Disinterestedness is a somewhat unique virtue, and it must not be supposed that Radamanth lived with his eye on eternity alone. It must be confessed that self-interest was often the dial of his philanthropy, and expediency to him the touchstone of action. Nothing furthers commerce better than a pious and merciful reputation, and Radamanth knew the inestimable value of a solid and goodly exterior. Wise in his generation, he nailed the Cross to his door, and plied his balances prosperously behind the counter.

Thus when the girl Igraine trudged sad-eyed into Winchester in her gown of grey, and appeared before him as a homeless child of the Church, he took her in like the good uncle of the fairy tale, and proffered her his house for home. Possibly he pitied her for her plight after the burning of Avangel, for she seemed much cast down in mind and very deserving of a kinsman's proper comfort. Then she was of noble family, a coincidence that no doubt weighed heavily in Radamanth's opinion. It was good to have so much breeding in the house, to be able to say with a smirk to his friends and neighbours, "My niece, the daughter of Malgo, Lord of the Redlands, slain and plundered of the heathen in Kent." Igraine brought quite a lustre into Radamanth's home. He beamed on her with sleek pride and satisfaction, gave her rich stuffs for dress, a goodly chamber, and a little Silurian maid to wait. Moreover, he gave his one child and daughter Lilith a grave lecture on sisterly companionship, advised her to study Igraine's gentle manners, and to profit by her aristocratic and educated influence. Luckily Lilith was a quiet girl, not given to jealousy or much self-trust, and Igraine found as warm a welcome as her unhappy heart could wish.

No few days had passed since that dawn on the hill above Winchester when Igraine had started up from under the green boughs to find Pelleas gone. They had been days of keen trouble to the girl. Often and often had she hated herself for her vain delay, her over-tender procrastination, that had brought misery in place of joy. The past was now a wounded dream to her, ripe and beautiful, yet fruited with such mute pain as only a woman's heart can feel. Igraine had conjured up love like some Eastern house of magic, only to see its domes faint goldly into a gloom of night. She felt as much for Pelleas as for herself, and there was a blight upon her that seemed as though it could never pass. She was not a woman given to tears. Her trouble seemed to live in her eyes with pride, and to stiffen her stately throat into a pillar of rebellious strength.

Not a word, not a sign had come to her of Pelleas. Taken into Radamanth's house, served, petted, flattered, she went drearily through its daily round, sat at its board, talked with the guestfolk, while hope waited wide-eyed in her heart and kept her brave. Pelleas had told her that he was for Winchester, and assuredly, she thought, she might find him and confess all. She often kept watch hour by hour at her window overlooking the street. In her walks she had a glance for almost every man who passed on foot or horseback, till she grew almost ashamed of herself, and feared for her modesty. Her eyes always hungered for a red shield and harness, a black horse, a face grieving in dark reserve and silence. At night she was often quite a child in herself. She would take the little gold cross from her bosom and brood over it. She even found herself whispering to the man as she lay in bed, and stretching out her arms to him in the dark as in pain. For all her pride and courage she was often bowed down and broken when no one was near to see.

It was not long before she found a confidant to befriend her in her distress of heart. Lilith, the goldsmith's daughter, had great brown eyes, soft and very gentle; her face was wistful and white under her straightly combed hair; she was a quiet girl, timid, but very thoughtful for others. The two appealed each other by contrast. Lilith had soon read trouble in Igraine's eyes, and had nestled to her in soul, ready with many little kindnesses that were like dew in a dry season. Igraine unbent to her, and suffered herself to be enfolded by the other's sympathy.

One day she told her the whole distressful tale. It was in the garden behind the house, a green and pleasant place opening on the river, and flanked with stone. The two were in an arbour framed of laurels, its floor mosaicked with quaint tiles. Igraine sat on the bench with Lilith on a stool at her feet. They were both sad, for Lilith was a girl whose heart answered strongly to any tale of unhappy mood. Igraine had made mere truth of the matter, neither justifying nor embellishing. Her clear bleak words were the more pathetic for their very simpleness. Lilith had been crying softly to herself. Her brown eyes were very misty when she turned her white face to Igraine's with a grievous little sigh.

"What can I say to you?" she said.

"Nothing," said Igraine, taking her hands and smiling through misery.

"I have never the words I wish for, and when I feel most I can say little."

"You understand; that is enough for me."

"Ah," said Lilith, with a fine blush and a shy look, "I think I can feel for you, Igraine, almost to the full, though I seem such an Agnes. I am woman enough to have learnt something that means all to a girl. I am very sad for your sake."

"Child."

"I will try to comfort you."

Igraine's eyes burned. She kissed Lilith on the lips and was mute. For a while they sat with their arms about each other, not daring to look into each other's eyes. Then the girl kissed Igraine's cheek, and touched her hair with her slim fingers.

"Perhaps I can help you," she said.

"Help me?"

Lilith flushed, and spoke very quickly.

"Yes — to find Pelleas. I tell you what I will do. I will send a friend of mine to question all the guards at the gates whether they have seen such a one as you have described ride in."

Igraine hugged the girl.

"And then you say this Pelleas was in the King's service. I have never heard of a knight so named; but there are so many, and I hear only gossip. I know a girl in the King's household. I will go and ask her whether she knows of a tall, dark knight whose colour is red, who rides a black horse, and is named Pelleas. You do not know how much I may not learn from her. I feel wise already."

Igraine plucked up heart and spirit. She felt sorry that she had not spoken of her trouble to Lilith before, for she had lost many days trusting to her own eyes and her little knowledge of the town. She kissed the girl again, and almost laughed. Then in a flash she remembered a speech of Pelleas's which she had forgotten till that moment.

"Fool that I am," she said; "the very chain he wore he had it from your father, and here in my bosom I have the little cross that nigh lost him his life. Surely this may help us in some measure."

Lilith looked at the cross that Igraine had taken from under her tunic, where it hung by a little chain about her neck.

"We will show it to my father," said the girl, "and ask him thereof. He may have record of such a chain, and to whom it was sold. Who knows? Come, Igraine, we will show it him after supper if you wish."

And again Igraine kissed her.

It was Radamanth's custom, after the business of the day had been capped by an honest supper, to sit in his parlour and drink wine with certain of his friends. He had a particular gossip, an old fellow named Eudol, who had been a merchant in his time, and had retired with some wealth. These two would spend many an evening together over their wine, taking enough to make their tongues wag, but never exceeding the decent warmth of moderation. Eudol was a lean old gentleman with a white beard and a most patriarchal manner. He was much of a woman's creature, and loved a pretty face and a plump figure, and he would father any wench who came in his way with a benignity that often made him odious. He had a soft voice, and a sleek, silken way with him that made folk think him the most tender-souled creature imaginable.

These two were at their wine together when Lilith and Igraine went in to them that evening. Radamanth since his spouse's death had grown as much a father as trade and the getting of gold permitted. In his selfish, matter-of-fact way he was fond of this timid, brown-eyed creature he called daughter. His affections boasted more of science than of sentiment. Lilith, unusually bold, went and sat on the arm of his chair, and patted his face in a half-shy, half-mischievous fashion. Eudol laughed, and shook his head with a critical look at Igraine.

"More begging," quoth he. "So, cousin Igraine, you look fresh as a yellow rose in the sun."

Igraine laughed, and sat down to talk to him, while Lilith questioned her father. The goldsmith bore his daughter's caresses with a sublime and patient resignation. She began to tell him about the chain, keeping Igraine and her tale wholly in the background. When she had said enough for the sake of explanation, she showed her father the cross, and waited his words.

Radamanth fingered it, turned it this way and that, and found his own mark thereon.

"I wrought and sold three such chains as you describe," he said; "but what is such a chain to you, child, and whence came this cross?"

Lilith flushed, hesitated, and glanced at Igraine.

"The cross is mine," quoth the latter.

Radamanth eyed her as though he were not a little desirous of questioning her further, but there was a very palpable coldness on his niece's face that forbade any such curiosity. He had a most hearty respect for the girl's pride, and never dreamt of any degree of tyranny that might seem vulgarly plebeian to her more noble notions. The remembrance of her parentage and estate had always a most emollient effect upon his mind.

"Well, well," he said, "I'll meddle discreetly, and go no further than I am asked."

Eudol winked at the company at large.

"Never ask a lady an uncomfortable question," quoth he.

Lilith beamed at him shyly.

"You are very wise," she said.

Radamanth rose from his chair, and going to a great press took a book from it. He set the book on the table, and after much turning of pages, discovered the record that he sought. Following the scrawling lines with his finger, he read aloud from the ledger:

"Gold chain of special weight, large links, two gold crosses pendant over either breast. Of such three were wrought and sold.

"The first to Bedivere, knight of the King's guard.

"*Nota bene* — unpaid for."

Eudol set up a sudden brisk cackle.

"The man, the very man, I'll swear."

Igraine gave him a look that made his mouth close like a trap and his body stiffen in his chair. Radamanth continued his reading.

"The second chain was sold to John of Glastonbury. The third to the most noble Uther, Prince of Britain."

Radamanth closed the book, and returned it to the press — orderly even in trifles. Lilith and Igraine had exchanged a mute look that meant everything. Slipping away without a word to either man, they went to Igraine's bedroom, a great chamber hung with heavy red hangings and richly garnished. A carved bed stood in the centre. The two girls sat on it and stared into each other's eyes. Igraine was breathing fast, and her face was pale.

"Know you Bedivere?" she said.

Lilith shook her head.

"Or John of Glastonbury?"

"No."

"Or Uther?"

Lilith's brown eyes brightened.

"Noble Uther I have often seen," she said, "riding through Winchester on a black horse. A dark man, and sad-looking. He would be much like your Pelleas."

Igraine was very white. There seemed a race of thoughts in her as she played the statue with her eyes at gaze, and her lips drawn into a line of red. Her hands hung limply over the edge of the bed, and she seemed stiffened into musings. Lilith sidled close to her, and put her warm arms round her neck, her soft cheek to Igraine's.

"We may learn yet," she said.

"Uther," said Igraine as in a dream.

"Can it be?"

Igraine drew a long breath and sighed like one waking.

"I must see him," was all she said.

Lilith kissed her.

"I will go to the King's house to-morrow," she said; "the girl may tell us something of use. I have heard it said that Uther has not been in Winchester for many a week. Ah, Igraine, if it should be he."

They looked deep in each other's eyes, and smiled as only women can smile when their hearts are fast in sympathy. Then they went to bed in Igraine's bed, and slept the night through in each other's arms.

Early next day they went together to the King's house that stood by the gardens and the river. At the kitchen quarters Lilith inquired for the girl who served as a maid in the household. Being constrained by a most polite lackey, she went in to see the woman, while Igraine kept her pride and herself in the porch, and watched the people go by in the street. Presently Lilith came out again with a frown on her mild face, and her brown eyes troubled. She took Igraine aside into the gardens that lined the great highway skirting the palace, and led her to where a fountain played in the sun, and stone seats ringed a quiet pool. White pigeons were there, coquetting and sweeping the ground with their spread tails, their low cooing mingling with the musical plashing of the water. An old beggar woman sat hunched in a corner, and three or four children were feeding the fish in the pool. All about them the gardens were thickly shadowed with great trees and glistening lusty laurels.

Igraine looked into Lilith's face.

"I see no news in your eyes," she said.

Lilith brooded at the pool and the children, and seemed disquieted, even angry.

"I have learnt little, Igraine," she said, "and am disappointed. I will tell you how it was. The old wretch who oversees the women found me talking with the girl Gwenith, read me a sermon on interfering with household work, scolded me for a young gossip, and had me packed off like a beggar."

"What a harridan!"

"I have learnt a little."

"Quick! — I thirst."

Lilith hurried on for sympathy.

"The girl has never heard of a knight named Pelleas," she said, "and there are so many dark men about Court that your description was little guide. As for Uther, no one knows where he is at present. Folk are not disquieted, for he seems to be ever riding away into the woods on adventure. So much gossip could read me."

Igraine's face clouded.

"Did you ask of Bedivere?" she said.

"Oh, yes; a silly, vain fellow, with a red beard and sandy hair."

"And John of Glastonbury?"

"Gwenith could tell me nothing of that man. Dame Martha caught us talking, and it was then she scolded — the ugly, red-faced old hen. She said" — and Lilith blushed — "that I was an idle, silly hussy to gad and gossip after Court gentlemen. Now that wasn't fair, was it, Igraine?"

"No, dear. I should like to have a talk with Dame Martha."

Lilith rose to the notion.

"She would never scold you, Igraine. You look far too stately."

"Simpleton! a scold would spatter Gabriel."

"Well, if I were Gabriel I know what I should do to Dame Martha."

"You quiet-faced thing — why, you are quite a vixen after all!"

"Ah, Igraine, was there ever a woman without a temper?"

"No, dear, and I wouldn't give a button for her either."

Suddenly, as they sat and talked, the beggar woman lifted up her head to listen, and the children turned from feeding the fish in querulous, childish wonder. There was something strange on the wind. Igraine and Lilith heard a gradual sound rising afar off over the city — a noise as of men shouting, a noise that waxed and waned like the roar of surges on a beach. It grew — rushed nearer like a storm through trees, — deep, sonorous, triumphant. The girls sat mute a moment, and looked at each other in conjecture.

"What can it be?"

"God knows!"

"The heathen?"

"Not that shout."

"Then — Uther."

Igraine caught a deep breath.

"Listen! it comes nearer. Come away, I must see."

Passing through the gardens they came again to the highway skirting the palace. Men, women, brats, monks, all Christendom, seemed swarming up from the city, and there was already a great throng in the street. The breeze of shouting came nearer each moment. Igraine climbed the pediment of a statue that rose above the balustrading of the gardens; the ledge gave room to both Lilith and herself. Together they stood and looked down on the crowd that began to swarm at their feet — soldiers, nobles, dirty craftsmen, courtezans, fat housewives, churchmen — their small prides lost in one common curiousness. The street seemed mosaicked with colour. The broken words and cries of the crowd were flung up to Igraine like so much foam.

"Gorlois, say you?"

"Noble Gorlois."

"A thousand heathen."

"What — all slain!"

"Where?"

"Under the walls of Anderida."

"Come to my house and I will give you red wine, and play to you on the cithern."

"Thank the Virgin."

"Great Gorlois."

"If it is true I'll burn twenty candles."

"Give over trampling me."

"A thousand heathen."

"Ho! there — some rogue's thieved my purse."

"They are coming."

"Let's shout for him."

"Great Gorlois."

Up between the stone fronts of the palace and the dwindling houses and the rolling green of the gardens came a blaze of gold and purple, of white, green, blue, and scarlet, a gross glare of steel thundered on with the tramp of men and the cry of many voices. A river of armour seemed to flow with a brazen magnificence between the innumerable heads of the crowd. Clarions were braying, banneroles adance. The sun flashed on helmet and shield, and made a brave blaze on the flanks of the great serpent of war as it swayed through the thundering street, arrogant, triumphant, glorious.

Well in the van rode a knight on a great white horse. His armour was all of gold, his trappings white with gold borders, and stars of gold scattered thereon. His baldric was set with jasper, his sword and scabbard marvellous with beryl and sardonyx. A coronet gemmed with one great ruby circled his casque, and shot red gleams at the archer sun.

Behind him came a veritable grove of spears, — lusty knights, their saddles weighed down with the spoil of battle, with torque, bracelet, sword, and axe. Further yet came pikemen, mass on mass, bearing each on his spear-point a heathen head, — pageant of leers, frowns, scowls of red wrath, wild eyes, blood, and blood-tangled hair.

The great knight on the white horse rode with a certain splendid arrogance, and his eyes were full of fire under the arch of his casque. It was easy to see that the noise and pomp were like wine to him, and that his pride blazed like a beacon in a wind.

"Gorlois, great Gorlois!" thundered the crowd.

By the palace there was such a press that the white horse came to a halt, hemmed in by a sea of vociferous faces. Igraine, in a gown of violet, was leaning from her statue, and looking at Gorlois. Her glance seemed to magnetise him, for he turned and stared full at the girl as she stood slightly above him in the glory of her beauty and her pride.

Long looked Gorlois, like a man smitten with a sudden charm. Then he wrenched the coronet from his casque, and spurring his horse through the crowd, rode close to the statue whose knees were clasped by Igraine's arm. It was the statue of Fame crowned by Love with a wreath of laurels. So, Gorlois, with head bowed, held up the coronet on the cross of his sword, and gave Igraine his glory.

II

Splendid in arms, magnificent in fortune, Gorlois of Cornwall held high place in the war lore and romances of the green isle of Britain. Ask any pikeman or gallowglass whose crest he would have advance in the van in the tough tussle of a charge home, and he would tell you of Gorlois or of Uther. Question any merchant as to the most prolific purse in the kingdom, and he would beam seraphically and talk to you of Gorlois. So much for the man's reputation.

Physically he was tall, big-chested, lean-limbed, with a square jaw and eyes that shone ever alert, as though watching a knife in an enemy's hand. You could read the swift, soaring, masterful spirit of him in the bleak lines of his handsome face, and the soldierly carriage of his head. He was quick as a hawk, supple and springy as a willow, keen and eager in his action as a born fighter should be. When you saw him move, the lean hard fibre of him seemed as tense and tough as the string of a five-foot bow. Though he might seem to the eye all impulse, there was a leopard reason in him that made him the more formidable. He was no mere fighting machine—rather a man of brain and sinew whose cunning went far to back his strength.

Meliograunt ruled in Cornwall in those days, Meliograunt who was to rear young Tristram for the plaguing of Mark, and the love of the fair Isoult. Gorlois was Meliograunt's nephew, holding many castles, woods, and wild coastlands towards Lyonesse, lording it also over other lands in Britain, houses in London and Winchester, and some mountainous regions in Gore, where Urience held sway. Mordaunt had been his father, a great knight who had done many brave deeds in his day. His grandsire, Gravaine, famed for his wisdom, had fought abroad and died in battle. Gorlois had ancestry enough to breed worship in him, and after Ambrosius and black Uther he held undoubted precedence of all knights in Britain.

Unblemished fortune is not always the nurse best suited to the dandling of a man's mind. It had been so with Gorlois. He was one of those beings whose life seemed to promise nothing but triumphal processions and perpetual bays of victory. Selfishness is such a glittering garment that it needs a great light to reveal its true texture to the wearer. Flattered, praised, obeyed, bent to, it became as natural for Gorlois to expect the homage of circumstance as to look for the obedience of his cook. There was much that was Greek about him in the worst sense, a certain sensuous brilliancy that aimed at making life a surfeit of rare sensations, with an infinite indifference for the hearts of others. Gorlois liked to see life swinging round him like a dance while he stood pedestalled in the centre, an earthly Jove.

The man had given Igraine his coronet on the cross of his great sword. That meant much for Gorlois. He was not a gentleman who had need to trouble his wits about women, for there were many enough ready to ogle their eyes out in his service. Yet in his keen way he had conceived a strong liking for the girl's face. A species of sudden admiration had leapt out on him, and brought him in some wonder to a realisation of the power of a pair of eyes. Igraine was such a one as would attract the man. In the first place she was very fair to look upon, a point of some importance. She was tall, big of body, and built for grace and strength, things pleasant to Gorlois's humour. Above all she was proud and implacable, no giggling franion hardly worth the kissing, and Gorlois had grown past the first blush of experiences of heart. He was sage enough to know that a woman lightly won is often soon lost, or not worth the winning. Let a man's soul sweat in the taming of her, and there is some chance of his making an honest bargain.

Moreover, like many a man of restless, soaring spirit, Gorlois ever hungered for romance, and the mysterious discomforts and satisfactions that hedge the way into a woman's bosom. Certain men are never happy unless they have the firebrand of love making red stir for them in heart and body. Of some such stuff was Gorlois. He had a soul that doted on nights spent at a window under the moon. All the thousand distractions, the infinite yet atomic cares, the logical sweats of reasoning were particularly pleasant to his fancy. He loved the colour, the exultation, the heroism, the desperate tenderness of it all. Battle, effort, ambition, lost half their sting for Gorlois when there was no woman in the coil.

Igraine's home was soon known to him, thanks to the apt vigilance of a certain page much in favour with Gorlois for mischief and cunning. The boy had Igraine's habits to perfection in a week or two. By making love to the girl who served her, he put himself into the way of getting almost any tidings he required. Every morning he would slip out early, meet Igraine's girl, Isolde, under the shadow of the garden-wall, and, under cover of a kiss, he would inquire what her mistress might be doing that day, pretending, of course, that his interest on such a subject merely arose from his desire to have Igraine out of the way, and her girl free. The lad quite enjoyed the game, Isolde being a giggling, black-eyed wench, who loved mischief. Of course he ended by falling in love with the reckless earnestness of a boy, but that kept him well to business. Betimes he would run home and tell his master where Igraine would probably be seen that day.

Gorlois's proud face began to come into the girl's life at every turn. Igraine would see him often from her window as he rode by on his white horse, looking up, and very eager to greet her. He would pass her in the aisles of the great basilica in the market, walking in gold and scarlet, amid silks and cloths from the East, vases, armour, skins of the tiger and camelopard, flowers, fruit, wine, and all manner of merchandise. On the river which ran by the end of Radamanth's garden his barge often swept past with the noise of oars and music, and a gleam of gold over the hurrying water. In the orchards without the walls his face would come suddenly upon her through a mist of green, and she would be conscious of his eyes and the nearness of his stride.

One Sunday morning she found him laving his hands in the labrum beside her before entering the long narthex porch of the church, and he was near her all through the service, watching her furtively, noting the graceful curves of her figure as she knelt, the profusion of her hair, a thousand little things that are much to a man. When the sacrament was given, he knelt close beside her, and touched the cup where her lips had been. Apparently Gorlois was content for a while with the rich delight of gazing. His bearing was courteous enough, and he never exposed her to any public rudeness that could warrant her in resenting his persistent, though distant, homage.

The great baths of Winchester stood in a little hollow near the southern gate of the city, a white pile of stone set about with quiet gardens. They had fallen into some decay and disrepute, but still in the summer-time girls and men of the richer classes went thither to bathe. On sunny mornings, in the great marble bath of the women, girls would flash their white limbs, and sport like Naiads in the laughing water. Afterwards they would have their hair dressed and perfumed, and then go to sun themselves in the rose-walks like eastern odalisques. The music of flute and citheon might often be heard in the grass-grown peristyles. The library attached to the place had once boasted many scrolls and tomes, but it had long ago been pillaged by the monks of the great abbey.

Lilith had taken Igraine there more than once. One morning Igraine had bathed, tied her hair, and had passed out into the garden alone. The place was of some size, boasting twenty acres or more, full of winding paths, grass glades, and knolls of bushy shrubs, where one might lose one's self as soon as think. Children often played hide-and-seek there, and idling up some green walk you might catch a giggling girl, with hair flying, bursting out of some thicket with a lad in full chase. Or in some shady lawn you might come upon a company of children dancing as solemnly as little elves to the sound of a pipe.

Nooks and grass walks were almost deserted at this hour, the gardens being most favoured towards evening, when the day was marked by a deepening discretion. Igraine had no purpose in the place. She knew that Lilith was somewhere within its bounds. She also knew that Lilith had no particular need of her that morning, and as the day was hot and slothful, Igraine's only ambition was to waste her time as pleasantly as possible till noon.

Turning round a holly hedge that hid a statue of Cupid, she came full upon a woman seated on the stone bench that ringed the statue's pedestal. The woman wore a light blue tunic, and a purple gown that ran all along the seat in curling masses. She was combing her fair hair as though she had only lately come from the bath. Her white glimmering arms were bare to the elbow, and she was humming a song to the sway of her hair, while many rings laughed on her slim white fingers. She had not heard Igraine's step upon the grass, but saw suddenly her shadow stealing along in the sun. Lifting her face, she stared, knew on the instant, and went red and grey by turns. Her comb halted, tangled in a strand of hair, and she was very quiet, and big about the eyes. Igraine remembered well enough where she had seen that would-be innocent stare, and that loose little mouth that seemed to bud for lawless kisses.

Morgan, with her face as white as her bosom, drew the comb from her hair, and flourished it uneasily betwixt her fingers. She was frightened as a mouse at the tall girl standing big and imperious so near, and her eyes were furtive for chance of flight. Igraine in her heart was in no less quandary than was dead Madan's wife. She could prove nothing against the woman, for Pelleas was lost and away, and even the man's name might be a myth likely to involve further mystery. She had as much to fear too from Morgan's tongue, as Morgan had from her knowledge of that night in the island manor.

Morgan, too flurried for sudden measures, sat biting her lips, while her blue eyes were fixed on Igraine with a restless caution. Neither woman said a word for fully a minute, but eyed each other like a couple of cats, each waiting for the other to move. The shrubs around were so still that you might imagine they were listening, while Cupid, poised on one foot, drew his bow very much at a venture.

"Good-morning, holy sister."

Igraine said never a word.

"I am glad to see you so improved in dress, that olive-green gown looks so well on you."

Still no retort.

"By the saints, sister, you are very silent. I hope you were not kept long on that island?"

Igraine arched her eyebrows and gave the girl a stare. She knew what a coward Morgan was, and guessed she was in a holy panic, despite her cool impudence and seeming ease of mind. Woman-like, she conceived a sudden strong desire to have Morgan whimpering and grovelling at her feet, for there is some satisfaction in terrorising an enemy, even if one can do no more.

"I presume, madame," she said, "you thought me safely packed away in that island, and likely to die of hunger, or be taken by heathen."

Morgan forced a smile, and began to bind her hair for the sake of having something to do in the full glare of Igraine's great eyes.

"You did not think I could swim."

"Madame, I could think anything of you. Nuns are so clever."

"After all, I am not a nun."

"Of course not. You could not be bothered with vows in summer-time. I turned nun myself once for a month, it being convenient."

Igraine began to fret and to lose patience.

"You are over venturesome, madame," she said, "in coming to Winchester."

"So!"

"I believe they hang folk here at times; they might even break your slim white neck."

Morgan's lips twitched, but she did not blench from the argument.

"You speak of hanging," she said, "and the inference is rather peculiar. Listen a moment, my good convent saint: your knight on the black horse would most certainly have needed the rope, if my man had not mended vengeance with that poniard."

"Pelleas and the gallows! You're a fool!"

Morgan smiled back at her very prettily.

"After all, your man did first murder," she said.

"On a traitor cur in Andredswold!"

"Madame, my husband."

The woman's contention was not so illogical when Igraine came to consider it in a less personal light. Morgan may have loved the man Madan for all she knew, and she could feel for her in such a matter. She looked at her with less scorn for the moment, and less injustice of thought.

"Perhaps you have grieved much," she said.

Morgan gave a blank stare.

"Grieved?"

"You loved your husband?"

"I did, while he lived."

"And no longer?"

"What is the use of wasting one's youth on a corpse?"

Igraine retracted her late sympathy, and returned to enmity. Morgan had risen, and was ruffling herself like a swan in her part of the great lady, and gathering her purple gown round her slim figure with infinite affectation.

"I cannot see that we have cause to quarrel further," she suggested.

"Indeed!"

"Seemingly we are quits, good Sister Morality. I have lost my man, you yours."

"You are very logical," said Igraine.

"Why should we women grieve?"

"Why indeed?"

"There are many more men in the world."

"Madame, I do not understand you."

Morgan gave a malicious little laugh that ended in a sneer. She touched her hair with her jewelled fingers, blew a kiss to Cupid, and again laughed in her sly mischief-making way. In a moment words were out of her lips that set Igraine's face ablaze, her heart at a canter, and mulled all further parley. Morgan saw trouble, dodged, and ran round the statue. Igraine was too quick for her, and winding her fingers into the woman's hair, gave her a cuff that would have set a helmet ringing. Morgan tripped and fell, dragging Igraine with her, and for a moment there was a struggle, green and purple mixed. Igraine, the heavier and stronger, came aloft on the other soon. Then a knife flashed out. Morgan got two quick strokes in, one on the girl's shoulder, a second in her left forearm. Igraine lost her grip, and fell aside in a stagger of surprise and pain, while Morgan, taking her chance, squirmed away, slipped up, and ran like a rabbit. She was out of sight and sound before Igraine had got back her reason.

Here was a pretty business. The girl's sleeve was already red and soaked, and the slit cloth showed a long red streak in the plump white of her flesh. Blood was welling up, and dripping fast to the grass at her feet. Despite the smart of her wounds and her temper, she saw it would be mere folly to chase Morgan. Following instinct, she ran for home, holding her right hand pressed over the gash in her shoulder.

In the main avenue who should she meet but Gorlois, carried in a litter, and looking out lazily from behind half-drawn curtains. His quick eyes caught sight of Igraine as she passed. He saw the blood and the girl's white face, and he was out of the litter like a stag from cover, and at her side, with spirited concern. Igraine was white and half dazed, her green gown soaked and stained. Her eyes trembled up at Gorlois as she showed him her gashed arm, with a smile and a little whimper that made him storm.

"Who did this?"

He had stripped his cloak off, and was tearing it into strips, while his jaw stiffened.

"An old foe of mine."

"Describe him."

"A woman, my lord."

"The damned vixen. Her dress?"

"Blue tunic, and gown of purple."

Gorlois turned to certain servants who stood round gaping at the girl in her blood-stained dress, and their lord tearing his cloak into bandages with characteristic furor.

"Search the gardens — a woman in blue and purple; have her caught. By my sword, I'll hang her."

He rent Igraine's sleeve to the shoulder, and wound the strips of his cloak about her arm with a strength that made her wince.

"Pardon," he said in his quick, fierce way; "this will serve a season; stern heart, good surgeon."

Igraine smiled, and made light of it, while he knotted the bandage. Some of his men had scattered among the shrubs and into the dark alleys of the place, for Igraine could hear them trampling and calling to each other. While she listened, and before she could hinder him, Gorlois had lifted her as though she had been but a sheaf of corn, and laid her in the litter. He drew the curtains. The bearers were at the poles, and setting off at a good stride they were soon in the town.

By the time they reached Radamanth's doorway Igraine, despite her spirit, was faint from loss of blood, and all atremble. Gorlois, tersely imperious, lifted her up as she lay half dazed and stupid, carried her in his arms into the house, and taking guidance from a white-faced maid, bore Igraine above to her chamber, and laid her on her bed. Then he kissed her hand, and leaving her to the women, hurried off to send skilled succour.

III

It was not long before Gildas, the court physician, a dear old scoundrel with a white beard and a portentous face, came down in state to attend on Igraine. He was an old gentleman of most solemn soul. His dignity was so tremendous a thing, that you might have imagined him a solitary Atlas holding the whole world's health upon his shoulders.

He soon dabbled his fingers in Igraine's wounds that morning, dropped in oil, and balmed them with myrrh and unguents under a dressing of clean cloth. He frowned all the time, as was his custom in the sick chamber, as though wisdom lay heavy on his soul, or at least as though he wished folk to think so. The only time you saw Gildas smile was when you payed him a fee or complimented him upon his knowledge. Tickle his pocket or his vanity, and he beamed on you. That morning he told Radamanth that his niece's wounds were serious, but that he trusted that they would heal innocently, treated as they had been by credited skill. Gildas always pulled a long face over a patient's possibilities; such discretion kept him from pitfalls, and enabled him to claim all the credit when matters turned out happily.

The streaks of scarlet in the white waste of skin soon died cleanly into mere bands of pink, and Igraine had little trouble from her wounds, thanks to the great Gildas. In fact, she was in bed but three days, while Lilith played nurse, chatted and sang to her, or leant at the open window to tell her of those who passed in the street. Master Gildas came and went morning and evening with the prodigious regularity of the sun. The girls aped him behind his back, and Igraine, with some ingratitude to science, made Lilith empty the ruby-coloured physic out of the window. It happened to spatter a lean booby of a man as he passed, who, looking up, flattered himself that Lilith must have sprinkled him with scented water by way of showing her affection. So much for Gildas's rose-water and flowers of dill.

The man of physic marched each day like a god into Gorlois's house to tell how the Lady Igraine fared at his hands. Such patronage was worth much to Gildas, and knowing how the wind blew, he puffed religiously upon the new-kindled fire. The girl's glamour had caught up Gorlois in a golden net. He had loved to look upon her and to dream, but now the perfume of her hair, the warm softness of her body, the very odour of her shed and scarlet blood were memories in him that would not fade.

One evening a posy of flowers came tumbling in at Igraine's window.

Lilith looked out, and saw Gorlois.

"For the Lady Igraine," were his words.

Lilith smiled down, and ventured to tell him that Igraine was much beholden to his courtesy and succour, and would thank him with her own lips when well of her wounds. She took the flowers to Igraine, who was listening in bed in the twilight.

"Shall I throw a flower back?" asked the girl.

"It would be courteous."

Lilith did so. The bloom struck Gorlois on the mouth like a blown kiss. The man put the thing in his bosom with a great smile, and went home to spend some hours like a star-gazer in his garden, while his musicians tuned their strings behind the bushes. At such a season Gorlois loved sound and colour. The voices, sweetly melancholic, thrilled up into the night—

"Her head is of brighter gold than the broom-flower,
Her breast like foam under her green tunic;
Like a summer sky at night are her glances;
Her fingers are as wood anemones in a daze of dew;
Of her lips,—who shall tell!
The gates of a sunset
Where love dies.
Her limbs are like May-blossoms
Bedded on a green couch:
The night sighs for her,
And for the touch of her hand."

Of course Morgan had escaped capture. Gorlois's men had hunted an hour or more, and had caught nothing, not even a glimpse of the purple gown for which they searched. Radamanth, who had had the affair from Gorlois's own lips, came and told Igraine, and began to ask her who this woman foe of hers was. Igraine put him off with a fable. She had no thought of letting him have knowledge of her love for

Pelleas, and she was glad in measure that Morgan had escaped capture, and so left her secret in oblivion. The woman might have proved troublesome if brought to bay, for she had as much right to claim the truth as had Igraine. Better let a snake go than take it by the tail.

In a week or so there was nothing left to mark the incident save the red lines in Igraine's white skin. Flowers and fruit came daily in from Gorlois, and every evening there was music under the window, till she began to consider these perpetual courtesies. She was woman enough to know whither they all tended. As for Radamanth, he was more kind to her than ever, seeing how the wind might blow favours into his ready lap. Gorlois was a great and noble gentleman, and the goldsmith had an intense respect for the nobility.

The very first day that Igraine walked abroad again after her seclusion, she fell in straight with Gorlois. By Gildas's advice, she had gone, presumably for her health's sake, to the baths with Lilith; and Gorlois, warned by the leech himself, followed alone, and overtook them near the porch. He was very gracious, very sympathetic, very splendid. He begged a meeting with Igraine after she had bathed, and since the girl had something in her heart that made her wish to speak with him, she consented, and left him in the laconicum, proposing to meet him in the rose-walk an hour later. Truth to tell, she intended questioning him as to Pelleas, whether Gorlois had heard of a knight so named; and also as to Uther, whether he had yet been heard of in any region of Britain. She knew Gorlois would take her consent as favour. Still, she imagined she could venture a little for her heart's sake without much prick of conscience.

An hour later, true to her word, she went alone into the rose-walk, a grassy pathway banked with yews, and hemmed with a rich tangle of red blooms. Gorlois was there waiting as for a tryst. He was full of smiles and staunch glances as he led her to a seat that was set back in an alcove, carved from the dense green of the yews, where they might talk at leisure, and out of sight. Igraine's hair lay loosened over her shoulders to dry in the sun. It had been perfumed, and the scent of it swept over Gorlois like a violet mist. He sat watching her for a while in silence, as she plied her comb with the sun-shaken masses pouring over her face like ruddy smoke.

"Lady Igraine," he said at length.

The girl's eyes glimmered at him slantwise from behind her hair.

"I knew your father, Malgo, before his death."

Igraine merely nodded.

"I am claiming to be the friend of his daughter, seeing that I have learnt the very colour of her several girdles, the number and pattern of her gowns since I rode into Winchester."

The venture in flattery was perhaps more suggestive than Igraine could have wished.

"You must waste much time, my lord."

"But little."

"I am sorry I have so poor a wardrobe, that you have fathomed the whole of it in less than a month. To tell the truth, when I came into Winchester, I had only one gown, and that rather ragged."

"They did not give you green and gold at Avangel?"

"No, the good women wore grey to typify the colour of their souls."

Gorlois laughed in his keen quiet fashion. The girl's eyes were wonderfully bright and subtle, and he had never seen such a splendour of hair. He longed to finger it, to let it run through his fingers like amber wine. Leaning one elbow on the stone back of the seat, and his head on his palm, he watched the silver comb rippling at its work, with a kind of dreamy complacency.

The girl's voice broke out suddenly upon him.

"My lord?"

Gorlois attended.

"You know many of the knights and gentlemen famed for arms in Britain?"

"I may so boast myself."

"I was once befriended, a piece of passing courtesy, yet I have always been curious to learn the character and estate of the man who did me this service. Have you heard of a knight named Pelleas?"

Gorlois fingered his sharp-peaked black beard, and looked blankly irresponsive.

"I have never known such a knight," he said.

"Strange."

"Never so. We men of the woods and moors often ride under false colours, sometimes to try our friends on the sly, sometimes to escape cognisance. The man who befriended you may have been Pelleas in your company."

Igraine cut in with a laugh.

"And Ambrosius at home," she said; "even Princes love masquerading in strange arms. Meadow-flower that I am, I have never seen the stately folk of the court — Ambrosius or Uther. I have heard Uther is an ugly man."

"If strength makes a man ugly, Uther may claim ugliness."

"Well?"

"Picture a dark man with black hair, eyes packed away under heavy brows, a straight mouth, and a great clean-shaven jaw that looks sullen as death."

"Not beautiful in words."

Gorlois stretched his shoulders, and half yawned behind his hand.

"Uther is a man with a conscience like a north wind," he said; "always lashing him into tremendous effort for the sake of duty. He has the head and neck of a lion, the grip of a bear. You have never known Uther till you have seen him in battle. Then he is like a mountain thundering down against a sea, a black flood plunging through a pine forest. A quaint, gentle, devilish, God-ridden madman; I can paint him no other way."

Igraine laughed softly to herself.

"A man worth seeing," she said.

"I should judge so."

"Tell me, is it true that Uther has gone into the wilds, and been seen of no man many days?"

"Uther left Winchester more than two months ago, and no word of him has come to Ambrosius."

"Curious."

"Madame, nothing is curious in Uther. If I were to hear some day that he had ridden down to Hades to fight a pitched battle with Satan, I should say, 'Poor Satan, I warrant he has a sore head.'"

"Indeed!" quoth Igraine.

She shook her hair, tilted her chin, and looked at Gorlois out of the corners of her eyes. She guessed her power, was young, and a woman. It tempted her to read this creature called "man" in his various forms and phases, and hold his heart in the hollow of her hand. Her interest in Gorlois was no discourtesy to her love for Pelleas. She had seen few men in her time; they seemed strange beings, strong yet weak, wise yet very foolish, sometimes heroic, yet utter children.

Gorlois, who had the sun in his eyes, beheld her as in an unusual mist. He was warming to life, for his brain seemed full of the sound of harping, and his blood blithe with summer. Stretching out a hand he touched Igraine's hair as it poured over her shoulders, for the red gold threads seemed magnetic to his fingers, and the glimmer of her eyes made his tough flesh creep.

"You have wonderful hair," he said.

"I learnt that long ago," drawing the strand away.

"The dawn of knowledge."

"It reaches not so very far from my feet."

Igraine hung out a flag, as it were, to try the man. She knew the look of Pelleas's eyes, and she wanted Gorlois for comparison. Standing up, she shook the glistening shroud about her while it seemed to drop perfumes and to spark out passion. The man's malady showed plainly enough on his face, but his eyes did not please Igraine. There was too much selfishness, not enough abasement. She knew Pelleas would have looked at her as though she was a saint in a church, and he but a lad from the brown ploughland. Igraine thought that she loved mute devotion far better than the bold impatient hunger on Gorlois's face.

The man leant back and tilted his beard at her, while his eyes were half shut for the sun.

"I have heard it told that women are ambitious. Is it truth?"

Igraine, all gravity again, with her tentative mischief banished, looked at her knees, and said she could not tell. Gorlois waxed subtle.

"Are you ambitious, Igraine?"

"Ambitious, my lord?"

"Have you never wished to stand out like a bright peak above the world?"

"No."

"Or to have the glory of your beauty filling the gate of fame like a scarlet sky?"

Igraine forced a titter.

"I suppose you are a poet, sir."

"Only a fool, madame."

"Ah!"

"All poets are fools."

"How do you contrive that?"

"Because they are for ever praising women."

"And yet you are a poet, my lord!"

"How could I be else, madame, since I am a man?"

Gorlois took a deep breath, and smiled at the dark yews, sombre and mysterious behind their belt of glowing roses. Igraine was watching his face in some uneasiness. It gave the profile of a strong, stark man, whose every feature spelt alert daring and great hardihood of mind. There was a keen, half-cruel look about the tight lips and impatient eyes. She was contrasting him with Pelleas in her heart, and the dark, brooding face of lion-like mould that so haunted her left little glory for Gorlois's lighter, leaner countenance.

They were both strong men, but she guessed instinctively which was the stronger.

Gorlois turned suavely again, with his courage strung like a steel bow.

"I am a queer fellow," he said.

Igraine began to bind her hair.

"If I ever loved a woman —"

"Well, my lord?"

"She could be ambitious to her heart's content. The more her pride flamed, the better I should like her."

Igraine frowned.

"She would be intolerable."

Gorlois arched his eyebrows, and covered his convictions with a laugh.

"Shall I tell how I should win her?"

"It would be a quaint tale."

"In the beginning, I should half-kill any man who braved it out that she was not the comeliest woman in Britain."

"Somewhat harsh, my lord, but emphatic."

"I should make her the envy of every lady, dame, and damoselle in the land."

"Not wise."

"Like a golden Helen should she rise in the east; blood should flow about her feet like water; I would tear down kingdoms to pile her up a throne. Such should be my wooing."

Igraine looked at her lap, and said never a word for a minute or more. All these heroics were rather hollow to her ear, though she did not doubt the man's sincerity towards himself, and his earnest mind to please her. Then she asked Gorlois a very simple question.

"Imagine, my lord, that the woman loved some other man?"

Gorlois's answer came swift off his tongue.

"I should meet him in open field, sword to sword, and shield to shield, and kill him."

Igraine started suddenly, grave and grey as any beadswoman. She did not think Pelleas would have taught any such doctrine.

"To you, that is love?" she asked.

"What else!"

Igraine thrust her silver bodkin into her hair with some vigour; there was no mirth or patience in her.

"I name it murder."

"Madame!"

"Stark, selfish murder."

Gorlois spread his hands and laughed.

"What is love?" he asked.

"Should I know!"

"Stark selfishness, — nothing more."

Igraine thought of Pelleas, and the way he had left her for knowledge of her imagined vows. Something in her heart told her that that was love indeed that had clasped thorns in the struggle to embrace truth. Therewith she wished Gorlois a very formal good-morning, refused his escort, and went straight home with the clear conviction that she had learnt something to her credit. Her talk with Gorlois had set a brighter halo about Pelleas's head.

Gorlois of Cornwall was nothing if not subtle. A selfish man of diplomatic mind may reach the very zenith of unselfishness to work his ends. Gorlois had so studied the expediencies and discretions of his purpose that even his love, headstrong though it may have been, was for the time being harnessed to the chariot of circumspection, whence intellect drove with steady hand. He had discovered for himself that Igraine was of sterner, prouder stuff than the general mob of women, and that he could not count much upon her vanity. She was to be won by honour, stark, unflinching honour, and by such alone, and Gorlois, thanks to the no mean wit that was in him, had judged that to his credit. He set about winning her at first with a consistency that was admirable, and a wisdom that would have honoured Nestor.

Naturally enough, Radamanth was amazed. Gorlois, one of the first men in Britain, sitting in a goldsmith's parlour and soliciting his patronage and countenance with a modest manliness! Radamanth stroked his beard, strove to appear at ease under so intense an obligation, struggled to wed servility with a new-found sense of importance. The whole business was most astonishing; not that Gorlois should love the daughter of Malgo of the Redlands, but that he should come frankly to a Winchester merchant and make such a Minos of him. Radamanth beamed, stuttered, excused himself, crept, condescended, in one breath. When Gorlois had gone, the good man sat down to think in a sweat of wonder. Probably he would find himself feasting with the king before long, and certainly it might prove excellent for trade.

After a cup of wine and a biscuit to restore his faculties, he sent for Igraine, who was in the garden, and prepared to parade his news with a most benevolent pleasure. He took a most solemn and serious mood, bowed her to a chair in magnificent fashion, and began in style.

"My dear niece, I have great honour to lay before you."

Igraine, who had heard nothing of Gorlois's visit, merely waited for Radamanth to unfold, with a mild and silent curiosity. The old man was big and benignant with the news he had, and when he began to speak he rolled his words with the sonorous satisfaction of a poet reading his verses to patrons in some Roman peristyle.

"Lady Igraine," he said, "honour is pleasant to an old man, and reverence welcome as savoury pottage. Yet, honour to those he loves is even sweeter to him than honour to himself. In honouring a kinswoman of mine, a certain noble gentleman has poured oil of delicious flattery on my grey head, and treated me to such an exhibition of grace, frankness, and courtesy, that my heart still warms to him. Perhaps, my dear niece, you can guess to whom I refer."

Igraine thrilled to a sudden thought — a thought of Pelleas. "I cannot tell," she said.

Radamanth could have winked, only in his present exalted frame of mind he remembered that such an expression was neither dignified nor courtly. If he were to become the associate of noble folk, it behoved him to raise up new ideals, and so he contented himself with a most ingenuous smile.

"Hear, then," he said, "that my noble visitor was the Count Gorlois."

"Gorlois!"

"Exactly."

Radamanth believed Igraine wholly overwhelmed. He waxed more and more patriarchal, till his very beard seemed to grow in dignity.

"Believe me, a most honourable man. Gentlemen of his position might well fancy other methods — well, never mind that. Count Gorlois came to me, like a man, to frankly crave my sanction for a betrothal."

Igraine stared, admired Gorlois's excellent plan for netting Faith, Hope, and Charity at one swoop, but said nothing. Radamanth prosed on.

"Count Gorlois besought me in most courtly and flattering fashion to countenance him in his claims. He would have everything done in the light, he said, in honourable, manly, and open fashion — no secret loitering after dark, or sly kisses under hedges. Mark the gentleman, dear niece."

The goldsmith idled over the words as though they were fat morsels of flattery, and Igraine had never seen him look so eminently happy before. She understood quite well that Gorlois's move had inspired him into complete and glowing partisanship, and that she was to have those sage words of advice that young folk love so much. Radamanth climbed down, meanwhile, to material things, and began to knock off Gorlois's possessions in practical fashion on his fingers.

"A grand match," he said. "There are the castles in Cornwall — Terabil and Tintagel; the lands in Gore and elsewhere; the palace in London; and the great house here by the river. In Logria he has lands, I have heard, — miles of fat pastures, woods, and many manors, lying towards the great oaks of Brederwode. The man is as rich as any in Britain, and if death took Ambrosius or Uther — "

Igraine cut in upon his verbosity.

"What did you tell him, uncle?"

Radamanth stared at her, with his fingers still figuring.

"Tell him, child?"

"Yes."

"What a thing to ask. Of course I promised to further his cause with you in every way possible. I said we should soon need the priest."

Igraine groaned in spirit.

"It is all useless," she said.

"What!"

"I have no scrap of love for this man."

Now Radamanth had never heard a word of Pelleas, for Igraine had cautioned Lilith never to speak to her father on the matter. Like many old people who have spent their lives in getting and possessing, he had lost that subtle something that men call "soul." Sentiment to him was a foolish and troublesome thing when it interfered with material advantage or profit, or barred out Mammon, with its rod twined with red roses. Consequently he was taken aback by Igraine's cool reception of so momentous a blessing. He sat bolt upright in his chair and stared at her.

"My dear niece."

There was such chagrin in his voice that Igraine, remembering his many kindnesses, hung her head and felt unhappy.

"Do not be angry," she said; "I do not wish you to speak of this more."

"But, my dear child, the honour, the fame, the noise of it!"

Igraine almost smiled at his palpable dismay, for she knew that her words must have flustered him not a little. Radamanth mopped his bald head, for the season was sultry.

"I am astounded," he said.

"Uncle!"

"Let me reason with you."

"Love is not reason."

"No, niece, it is prejudice. Yet I assure you Gorlois is a most noble soul."

"If he were a seraph, uncle, I could not love him."

"You women are all fancy. Why, you have hardly seen the colour of him. Come, now!"

"I do not need to see more of Gorlois."

"Why, bless my soul, my wife never loved me till we had been married a month, and she had learnt my fibre."

Igraine thought a moment. Then she asked Radamanth a question.

"Do you love Lilith?"

"Why, girl, what a question."

"Would you marry her to a man she did not love or trust, simply because it brought gold?"

Radamanth saw himself rounded in the argument like a rat in a corner. He sat stroking his beard, and striving to look pleased.

"Think over it, my dear," he said presently.

"There is no need."

"Gorlois will woo you like a hero."

"Let him. He will accomplish nothing."

"It would be a grand match."

Igraine jumped up, kissed him to show she bore no ill will, and ran away much troubled to find Lilith in the garden. She flung herself down beside the girl in the bower of laurels, and told her all that passed that morning in Radamanth's parlour. Lilith listened with her brown eyes deep with thought, and a quiet wonder. When Igraine had finished, Lilith took both her hands in hers, and, kneeling before her, looked up into her face.

"What will you do, Igraine?"

"Need you ask, dear?"
"Forgive me."
"Ah!"
"You love Pelleas."
Igraine put her arms round Lilith's neck, and kissed her.

IV

RADAMANTH'S words to the girl proved very true before many days had gone; his prophetic belief in Gorlois's mood found abundant justification in the event. Gorlois had the warm imagination of his race, an imagination that found extravagance and rich taste ready ministers to work his purpose. Igraine, met by all manner of devices on all possible occasions, began to realise the cares of those whom a purblind world insists on smothering with limitless favours.

Flowers were poured in upon her, worked into posies, garlands, shields, harps, crosses,—all bearing with them some mute plea for mercy. It might have been perpetual May-day in Radamanth's house, so flowered and scented was it. Flowers were followed by things more tangible, a pearl-set cithern, a great white hound, a gold girdle, a pair of doves in a cage of silver wire, a necklet of rich stones gotten from some Byzant mart. Gorlois seemed ready to send her all the finery in Winchester despite her messages and her words to him,—"My lord, I can suffer none of these things from you." Servants and slaves came down to Radamanth's house as though they had been sent from Sheba, while one of Radamanth's men went back from Igraine like an echo, bearing back the unaccepted baubles. It was a patient game, and rather foolish.

These were but small flutters in Gorlois's sweep for the sun. Had not Igraine been stabbed in the public gardens! Gorlois put the incident to use. He formed a bodyguard of certain of the noble youths who were under his patronage, and warned Igraine with all reverence that he had acted for her sanctity, and that a dozen gentlemen would follow near her when she walked abroad, or went to bath or church. Even her humblest stroll in the street began to partake of the nature of a triumphal progress. Children would gather to her in the gardens and throw flowers and laurel branches at her feet, or she would be followed by music and some sweet love ditty to the harp. A hundred quaint flatterers seemed to dog her from door to door, till she hardly dared to stir out of Radamanth's garden.

Naturally enough, her name was soon the one name in Winchester. The good folk with their Celtic beauty-loving souls spoke of her with quaint extravagance; her skin was like the apple-bloom in spring, and her lips like rich red May; her feet moved soft and swift as sunlight through swaying branches; her hair was a cloud of gold plucked from the sky at dawn. She was gaped at and pointed at in the street like a prodigy. When she went into church on Sunday half the folk turned to stare at her, and a clear circle was left about her where she sat in the nave. She was for the season the city's cynosure, its poem, its gossip. Aphrodite might have stepped out of mythology and taken lodging at Radamanth's, to judge by the curiosity displayed by the people, and doubtless many a comfortable piece of business came to Radamanth thereby.

Many women would have gloried for self's sake in such a pageant of flattery. It was not so with Igraine. She was a woman who mingled much warmth of heart with strength of will, and fair measure of innate wisdom; her feelings were too staunch and vivid to be swayed or weakened by any fresh circumstance, however strange and magnificent it might appear. Her love, once forged, could bend to no new craft. Her thoughts were all for Pelleas, and any glory her beauty received she kept it in her heart for him. Igraine was so eternally in love that even worldly prides seemed dead in her, and she had not vanity enough to be tempted by Gorlois's great homage.

The whole business troubled her not a little. There was a certain mockery in it that hurt her heart. It was as if she had panted in thirst for water, and some rude hand from heaven had thrown down gold. Gorlois had her in measure at his mercy. He seemed to take all her rebuffs with a sublime stoicism, and she had no one to whom she could appeal. She wished to bide in Winchester, for the city seemed to promise her the best chance of seeing Pelleas or Uther, and of learning if these twain were one.

One night there was music under her window. Flute, harp, and cithern with deep voices were pleading for Gorlois under the stars. Igraine listened, lying quiet, and thinking only of Pelleas.

Take then my heart,
My soul, my shield, my sword, —

sang the voices under the window. Igraine kissed the gold cross that hung at her bosom, and longed till her heart seemed fit to break for yearning. If only the song had come from Pelleas, how fair it would have sounded in the night. As it was, the whole business made her feel desperately weary.

Gorlois had begun by holding somewhat aloof. It was part of his purpose to work behind a glowing and fantastic screen, serving Igraine more at a distance, in a spirit of melancholy that should web him round with a mystery that was more splendid than truth. He bore Igraine's passive antagonism for a while with a spirit of enforced fortitude, going cheerfully by the old and somewhat foolish saying that a woman's looks lie against her heart, and that persistence wins entry in the end. To do credit to Gorlois's self-favour, he never considered the ultimate shipwreck of his enterprise as possible. He had fame, gold, bodily favour on his side, and what woman, he thought, could gainsay such a chorus. There are some men who never fail in anticipating success, and Gorlois possessed that quality of mind.

As the days went by, and the girl was still stone to him, he began to chafe and to look for stauncher measures. The gay gentlemen who served him suggested various expedients; one, a more passionate appeal; another, sly bribery of servants; a third, who was young in years, hinted at humble despair that might evoke pity. Gorlois laughed at them all, and swore he would win the girl, hook or by crook, in a month or less, or lose all the honour his sword had won. He was tired of mere courtesies that ran contrary to his more stormy spirit. He had a liking for insolent daring, for a snatch at love as at an enemy's banner in the full swing of a gallop on some bloody field. Mere mild homage was all very well for a season. Gorlois loved mastery, and believed there was no wine like success.

About this time a horde of heathen ships came from the east, sailed past Vectis, and began to pour their wild men into the country 'twixt Winchester and the sea. Hamlets and manors were burnt, peasant folk driven to the woods, the crops fired, the cattle slain. The noise of it came into Winchester with a rabble of frightened fugitives who had fled to the city for refuge. Ambrosius the king was in Caerleon, and Uther errant, so that the chance fell to Gorlois of driving the heathen into the sea.

No man could have been more heartily glad of this innovation. Igraine should see him swoop like a hawk in his strength; she should hear how he led men, and how his sword drank blood. In making war on the heathen he would boast himself before her eyes, and show her the merit of manhood, and the glory of a strong arm. Winchester bustled like a camp. Troops poured in from Sarum, and the sound of war went merrily through the streets. Folk boasted how Gorlois would harry the heathen. He rode out one night with picked men at his back, and held straight for the coast, while Eldol of Gloucester, a veteran knight, marched southward before dawn with five thousand footmen. It was Gorlois's plan to cut the heathen off from their ships, and crush them between his knights and the spearmen led by Eudol.

It was such a venture as Gorlois loved,— keen, shrill, and

full of hazards. Riding straight over hill and dale they saw the glimmer of waves as the sun rose, and knew they had touched the sea. Gorlois's scouts had located the main mass of the Jutes camped in a valley about a nunnery they had taken, and the British knights coming up through the woods saw smoke in the valley and men moving like ants about the reeking ruin of the holy house. Looking north they saw a beacon burning on a hill, — Eldol's signal that he had closed the woods, north, east, and west, with his footmen, and that he waited only for Gorlois to sweep up and drive the heathen on to the hidden spears.

Never was there a finer light in Gorlois's eyes than at such a season. He loved the dance and noise of steel, the plunging hustle of horses at the gallop, the grand rage of the shout that curled like the foam on an ocean billow. His courage sang with the wind as his knights rode down over the green slopes in a great half-moon of steel, a moving barrier that rolled the savage folk northwards, and rent them like a harrow of iron. By the blackened walls of the nunnery Gorlois caught sight of a line of mutilated bodies tied to posts, — dead nuns, stripped, and still bleeding. The sight roused the wolf in him. "Kill! kill!" were his words as they rode in upon the skin-clad horde. It was savage work, bloody and merciless. Eldol's men closed in on every quarter, and the heathen were cut down like corn in summer.

Very few went back to their ships that day. Scores lay dead with their fair hair drabbled in the blood about the ruins, and on the quiet slopes of the dale. As they had measured out violence to the peasant folk and women, so it was meted to them in turn, — vengeance, piled up, great measure, running over with blood. Some sixty maimed men were taken alive, but mere death was too mild for Gorlois when he remembered the slain nuns. He had certain of the captured burnt alive, others hacked limb from limb, the rest crucified near the river for the birds to feed upon. Then he buried the nuns, and made a great entry into Winchester, taking care to ride past Igraine's window with his white horse bloody to the saddle, and his armour splashed as he had come from the field. She should see his manhood, if she would not have his presents.

This single slaughter, however, did not end matters on the southern shores. Bands of Saxons were forraying from Kent, where they had established themselves, and Gorlois rode out again and again to crush and kill. There would be battles in the woods, bloody tussles in the deep shadows of Andredswold, wild flights over moor and waste, triumph cries at sunset. Three times Gorlois rode out at the head of his knights from Winchester; three times he came back victorious, hacked and war-stained, thundered in by the people, past Radamanth's house to the church in the market-square. Igraine sat at her window and watched him go by, lowering his spear to her with all his proud love ablaze on his face. Had he not driven the barbarians into the very heel of Kent, and left many a tall man from over the seas rotting in sun and rain?

It was customary year by year in Winchester to hold a water pageant on the river, depicting legendary and historic things that had passed within the shores of Britain. August was the pageant month, and in this particular year the display was made more elaborate in order to celebrate the rout of the heathen by Gorlois, and to please the common folk who had made him their idol. The pageant was of no little splendour. Great galleys, fittingly decorated, were rowed down the narrow stream amid a horde of smaller craft, each great barge bearing figures famed in British legend lore. The first barge portrayed Brute the Trojan voyaging for Britain; others, Locrine's death by the river Severn, Rudhudibras, mythical founder of Winchester, the reunion of Leyr and Cordelia, Porrex the fratricide done to death by damsels. One barge, draped in white and purple, moralised the reconciliation of Brennius and Belenus at the intercession of their mother. A great galley in red and white bore Joseph of Aramathy and the Holy Grail, and a choir of angels who sang of Christ's blood. Last of all came Alban the protomartyr, pictured as he knelt to meet his death by the sword.

The day was blue and quiet, with hardly the shimmer of a cloud over the intense gaze of the sky, while banners of rich cloth were hung over the balustrades of the river terraces, and the gardens themselves were full of gay folk who kept carnival, and watched the boats go by. The great pageant galleys had hardly passed, and the small craft that had kept the bank were swarming out into mid-stream, where a great barge with gilded bulwarks and a carved prow came sweeping down like a swan before the wind. It was driven by the broad backs of twenty rowers clad in scarlet and gold. In the stern sat Gorlois, holding the tiller, with a smile on his keen lips as a quavering clamour went up from the gardens and the boats that lined the shallows.

By Radamanth's house Gorlois held up a hand, and the blades foamed as the men backed water. The great barge lost weigh and lay motionless on the dappled silver of the stream. Slowly it was poled in to the steps that ran from the water's edge to the terrace of Radamanth's garden. A light gangway was thrown ashore, and a purple carpet spread upon the steps, while the men lined the stairway with their oars held spearwise as Gorlois went up to greet Igraine.

Clad in white and gold, with a rose over her ear, she was sitting between Radamanth and Lilith on a bench at the head of the stairway. There was an implacable irresponsive look on her face as Gorlois came up the steps and stood in front of her like a courtier before a queen's chair. Radamanth and the merchant folk present were on their feet, and uncovered; only Igraine kept her seat in the man's presence, and looked him over as though he had been a beggar.

They were left alone together on the terrace, Radamanth shepherding his merchant friends aside for the moment with the discreet desire to please the count. Gorlois stood by the stairhead and told Igraine the reason of his coming, as though she had not guessed it from the moment his barge had foamed up beside the steps. He told her frankly that he wished to speak to her alone, and that his barge gave her an opportunity of hearing him without his having the advantage of her in solitude, while the noise of oars would drown their words. Igraine listened to him with a solemn face. She began to feel that she must face her destiny and give the man the truth for good. Procrastination would avail nothing against such a man as Gorlois. Being so minded, she gave Gorlois her hand and hardened herself to satisfy him that day.

Away went the great barge before the strong sweep of the long oars. Igraine watched the water slide by — foaming like a mill race as the blades cut white furrows in the tide. The river gleamed with colour as innumerable galleys, skiffs, and coracles drifted in the shallows or darted aside to give passage to Gorlois's barge. Fair stone houses, gardened round with green, slid back on either side. They passed the spectacular galleys one by one, and the wooden wharfs packed with the mean folk of the city, and foaming on under the great water-gate, drew southward into the open country and the fields.

Igraine looked at Gorlois, and found his face impenetrable with thought. A fillet of gold bound his hair, and he was wearing his great sword, and an enamelled belt over his rich tunic. The cushions of the barge had been sprinkled with perfumes, and the floor covered ankle deep with flowers. Igraine groaned in spirit, and read the old extravagance that had persecuted her so long, and made a mockery of her love for Pelleas.

Gentle meads lapped greenly to the willows, giving place anon to woods that seemed to stride down and snatch the river for a silver girdle. The festival folk and their skiffs were out of sight and hearing, yet Gorlois's barge ran on, to plunge into emerald shadows, tunnels whose floors seemed of the blackest crystal webbed with nets of green and blue, whose vaultings were the dense groinings of the trees. Not a wind stirred. The great curving galleries in the woods were dark and mysterious, the water like glistening basalt, the trees dreaming over their own images in an ecstasy of silence. The foam from the oars was very white, and the moist swish of the blades made the silence more solemn by contrast, while the water seemed to catch a golden flicker from the flanks of the barge.

Igraine knew well enough what was in the man's heart as he sat handling the tiller, and watching her with his restless eyes. She was quite cold and undisturbed in spite of her being at his mercy, and the consciousness that in her heart she did not trust him vastly. Gorlois had spoken only of the town, and they were running on under dense foliage into the forest solitudes that edged the river. Yet Igraine had faith in her own wit, and believed herself a match for Gorlois, or any man, for that matter, save Pelleas. Gorlois passed the time by telling her of his battles in Andredswold, how he had driven the heathen into Thanet, and freed Andred's town from leaguer. Igraine began to wonder how long it would be before he would turn to matters nearer to his heart. She had marshalled up her courage for the argument, and this waiting under arms for the bugle-call did not please her.

The day had already slipped into evening, for the water pageant was ordered late, so that it might merge into a lantern frolic on the river after dusk. Igraine, seeing how the light lapsed, told Gorlois to have the barge turned for Winchester. She had hardly spoken when the boat ran out from the trees into open water. In the west the sky was already aflame, ridged tier above tier with burning clouds, while the blaze fainted zenithwards into gold and azure. A queer cry as from a man weary of torture came down from the west. On a low hill near the river, bleak against the sky, stood a black concourse of beams set upright in the ground, looking like the charred pillars of a burnt house. They were crosses, and the bodies of men crucified.

Gorlois pointed to them with the evening glow on his face, and taking a horn that hung at his belt, blew a loud call thereon. At the sound a vulture rose from a cross-beam, and went flapping heavenwards — a black blot against the scarlet frieze of the west. Others followed, like evil things driven from their food. Again the cry, the wail from one who had hung torn and wracked in the parching sun, came down from the darkening hill.

Igraine shuddered and felt cold at the sound, and watched the figures against the sky with a kind of awe.

"Who are these?" she said.

"Dogs from over the sea."

"Some are still alive."

"These pirates are hard; they die slowly, despite beak and claw. Such be the death of all who burn holy houses and homes, and put women and children to the sword."

"Take them down, or let them be killed outright."

"Never."

"At my prayer."

"What I have done, I have done."

"Cruelly."

"Cruelly, madame! You should have seen twenty dead nuns tied to stakes as I have seen, and you would gloat and be glad as I am. By God, little mercy had this offal at my hands in the glades of Andredswold. I burnt, and crucified, and tore with horses. Mere steel is too good for such as these."

"My lord!"

"What is hate unless it is hate? I can never brook an enemy to Britain."

Igraine had sudden insight into the core of Gorlois's nature. She understood, in a vague, swift way, what primæval instincts were hid in him ready at the beck of baser feelings such as jealousy or smitten pride. Woman-like, she recoiled from a man whose strength was so inflexible that it owned no pity or leavening kindness where malice or anger was concerned. She loved strength, and the natural wrath of a man, but she had no touch of the Semiramis about her, and her heart could not echo Gorlois's wolf-like cry.

The rowers had turned the barge, and they were soon back again under the shadows of the trees. It was dim and ghostly with the onrush of night, while a faint fire flickered through the trees from the west and touched the sullen water with a reddish flame. Gorlois's face was in the shadow. He was leaning over the tiller towards Igraine, and his eyes seemed to burn out upon her face and to make her heart beat faster. She sat as much away from him as the gunwale suffered, and looked ahead over the misty river, or up into the dense, black bosoms of the trees.

The foamy rush of the oars and the grind of the looms in the rowlocks half drowned Gorlois's words as he spoke to her.

"Igraine."

"My lord."

"You have read me to the heart."

Igraine turned and looked him full in the face. Now that the brunt had come, she was strong and ready to tell the man the truth, though it might be bleak and bitter to his pride. Gorlois was very near her, and she could see his white teeth between his lips, and the glint of his eyes as he leant towards her in the shadows.

"Are you ambitious, Igraine?"

"No, my lord."

"Not even a little?"

"My lord, I have no more ambition in me than one of those dead men hanging athwart the sunset."

"You are a queer woman."

"Pardon, I have a conscience."

Gorlois bit his lip, stared in her face, and set a hand upon her wrist.

"You can never shirk me," he said.

"I never shirk the truth."

"Come now, give me the word."

"My lord, may I save you pain in the telling of it! You can never come near my heart."

"Woman, never be so sure."

Gorlois drew back, and said never another word. Igraine watched him furtively as his keen profile hung near her in the dusk clear as marble. Now and again his eyes gleamed out upon her and made her fear the moment, while the oars swung out over the smiling stream, and the black woods started by like night.

Soon the lights of Winchester showed up against the northern sky, and far ahead over a straight stretch of water they could see the lanterns and torches of the folk who kept festival. A golden mist and the noise of music came down to them, as they surged under the great water-gate and ran on through the city amid a glimmering web of lights and laughter. Soon the barge found the shallows under white walls, and Igraine was standing on the steps leading to Radamanth's garden, with a starry sky sweeping like a wheel above the world.

Gorlois went slowly from her down the steps, with a face that was dark and brooding. Torchlight glimmered on the fillet of gold about his hair, on the splendid setting of his baldric, and the scabbard of his sword. At the water's edge he lifted up his face to her out of the night.

"It shall be life or death," he said.

Then he was swept away with a red flare of torches over the river, and Igraine went solemn-eyed to bed.

V

NOT a word of Uther yet, no sound of his name in Winchester, though Igraine lived on in Radamanth's house, and hoped for light in the dark.

Gorlois had had the truth, and she wondered what would come of it. Lulled by an ingenuous reasoning into the belief that she would be free of the man, she began to breathe again and to take liberty in her hand. She did not think Gorlois could plague her longer after the blunt answer she had given him. His pride would drag him aside, make further homage impossible, and there the matter would end.

If Igraine believed this, then she was in very gross error. Many men never show their true fibre till they are given the blunt lie, and Gorlois was never more himself than when baffled. There was much of the hawk about him, and Igraine had underrated his pride if she expected it to take league with her against its kinsman passion. Her measure only uncovered the darker side of the man's nature, and sounded the doom of a lighter, gayer chivalry. Gorlois's pride and self-love never dragged in the wind, but held him taut to the storm, as though determined to weather all the perversities of which a woman's heart is capable. In truth, Igraine had done the very thing least likely to free her from the man's thought; she had taunted his passion and thrown down a challenge to his pride.

Gorlois kept his own counsel, and frowned down the mischievous curiousness of his friends when they laughed at him and asked how the girl framed for a wife. He struck Brastias his squire to the ground for daring to jest sympathetically on the subject. Those who went about his house and hunted and diced with him soon found that he was in no temper for light raillery or the sly privileges of an intimate tongue. The fabric of a mere nice romance had stiffened into sterner, darker proportions. There was the look of a dry desire in the man's eyes, a lean hungry silence about him that made his men whisper. Some of them had seen Gorlois when he hunted down the heathen. They knew his temper, and the cast of his features when there was some lust of enterprise in his heart.

About that time a knight came from Wales thrusting a woman's beauty upon every man with the point of his spear. As had been his custom elsewhere, he set up a green pavilion outside the walls, and daily rode out armed to the sound of a trumpet to declare a certain Amoret of Caerleon the fairest gentlewoman in Christendom. He was a big man, red and burly, and had overthrown every like fanatic for love's sake on this particular adventure. Gorlois heard of the fellow with no little satisfaction. Every finger of him itched to spill blood, and he took the deed on him, vowing it should be the last peace-offering to Igraine.

Arming one morning, he rode down and fought the Green Knight in his meadow outside the walls. It took them an hour to settle the matter. At the end thereof the errant from Wales was lying impotent and bloody in his tent, and the name of Amoret aped the ineffectual moon. Afterwards Gorlois rode into the town, war-stained as he was, found Igraine at her window, and presented her the Green Knight's token on the point of his spear.

It was a woman's sleeve in green silk, and edged with pearls. Igraine saw a crowd of upturned faces about the man on the white horse. His bright arms seemed to burn in upon her, and to light a sudden impatience in her heart. She took the green sleeve from the spear, and looking Gorlois full in the face, in reckless mood she threw the thing down under his horse's hoofs.

There was a great hush all through the street at the deed, and Gorlois started red as a man struck across the face with a whip. His eyes seemed to grow large, like the eyes of an angry dog. Never had folk seen him look so black. He stared up a moment at Igraine, shook his spear, and trampling the green sleeve under the hoofs of his horse, rode away without a word through the glum and gaping crowd.

Igraine had thrown down the glove with a vengeance. It was a mad enough method of beating off the pride of a man such as Gorlois, whose temper grew with the blows given, and who knew no moderation in love or in hate. Gorlois had ridden home through the town that day to have his wounds dressed, and to spend half the night in a fury of cursing. Yet for all his bitterness he had the power of level thought, and of taking ground for the future. He would read this woman a lesson; that much he swore on the cross of his sword; and the early morning saw him again at Radamanth's, strenuous to speak his mind.

The goldsmith happened to know that Igraine was alone in the garden. Without noise or ceremony he sent Gorlois in to her, locked the door on them both, and went to watch from a narrow window on the stairs. He swore that Gorlois should have his own way, and not go balked for a woman's whim.

Igraine was sitting sewing in the arbour of laurels with the little gold cross hanging down over the bosom of her dress. A grass walk led to the arbour between beds of flowers. As she sat stitching she heard the sound of feet in the grass, and saw a shadow slanting across the entry. She expected Lilith, but looking up, found Gorlois.

He was white from his wounds of yesterday and the blood he had lost by the Green Knight's sword. His left arm lay in a sling of red silk. Igraine noted in her sudden half-fear how his eyes were very bright, and that his beard looked coal-black below his bloodless cheeks. There was something in his face too that made Igraine cautious.

She rose and folded her embroidery in the most unperturbed and quiet fashion, though she was thinking hard all the same. Gorlois watched her, and held back for her to speak, with a hollow fire creeping into his eyes, for the girl's passionless mood chafed him. He had no gentleness towards her for the moment; such love as he knew had been blown into a red beacon by starved and covetous desire.

"A word with you," he said.

The speech was rough and pertinent, showing the trend of the man's purpose. He had abandoned superficialities. Igraine, gathering up her silks, turned and faced him with the frankness of a full moon. Gorlois saw her lips tighten, and there was a temper swimming in her eyes that promised abundant spirit and no shirking. If he had launched out to rouse her from passive antagonism, he could not have chosen a better method.

Igraine made a step towards the house, but two strides put Gorlois in her path.

"Make way —"

"Not a foot till you have the truth out of me."

"Have a care, — I will be stormed at by no man."

"Woman, look at me."

Igraine was looking at him with all the temper she could summon. If Gorlois thought to ride straight over her courage, he was enormously mistaken. She would match him for all his hectoring.

"If you are not a fool," she said, "you will end this nonsense, and go."

"Am I a scullion?"

"You should know, my lord."

"I have not bled for nothing."

"As you will."

"What have you to say to me?"

Igraine lost all patience, tossed her embroidery aside, and simply flashed out at him with all her soul.

"Say!" she said; "I have somewhat to say, and that bitter; listen if you will. You, Gorlois of Cornwall, who bade you make my name a byword in Winchester? Listen to me, — hear the truth, and profit — you who pestered me with mad tricks till I hated it all and held it insolence. Who asked you to make me gossip for a city, did I? Who took your presents? Who told you the truth? Who threw your token under the hoofs of your horse to shame you? I have mocked you enough, now leave me in peace, or rue it."

"By God, madame —"

"Don't echo me. Go, get out of my sight; I hate you!"

Gorlois flushed to the temples in this wind of passion. The girl looked splendid to him in her great anger, her head thrown back and her eyes steady on him as stars. The scorn of her beauty leapt over him like crimson light, and he was more a sensation than a man. He had a great

"A SUDDEN MADNESS WHIRLED GORLOIS AWAY"

thirst in him to grip her with his hands, to bend her straight body as he would bend a bow, to strangle up the scorn in her throat with his own breath. He went near her, stooping and staring in her face.

"Igraine."

"Mark my words."

"You golden shrew, you temptation of tempers — "

"Hold off — "

"By God! I'll tame you, don't doubt me."

Igraine, very watchful, slipped past him suddenly like light, and walked for the house with a sweeping air that bade him keep his distance. Coming to the door of the house, she tried it but found the lock shot. The red badge of a new anger showed upon either cheek. She turned on Gorlois; her eyes blazed out at him.

"A pretty trick!"

"What now, madame?"

"You had this door locked."

"Never."

"You lie in your throat."

"Radamanth — "

"Open it."

"I have no key."

Igraine's figure seemed to dilate and grow taller, and her eyes shone well-nigh as bright in colour as her hair.

"Obey me."

"Not if I had the key."

"Obey me."

"I will be master before the sun is at noon."

"You dog!"

A sudden madness whirled Gorlois away. He went red from the neck, clutched at Igraine's wrist and held it. For a moment they stood rigid. The girl could not shake him off although he had but one hand to hold her. His breath was hot upon her face as he pressed her back against the wall, and held her there till his lips touched her neck. Igraine, breathing fast and straining from him with all her strength, set a hand on his face and thrust him away. She twisted her wrist free, and slipped from between him and the wall. Then the door opened, and Radamanth stood by them.

Igraine slipped away with a white face, and running above to her chamber threw herself down on the bed, and cried for Pelleas. She heard Gorlois stride through the house, heard the gate crash as he went out into the street. Shame and loneliness were on her like despair, and she was weak and shaken after her anger, and very hungry for love and comfort. The world seemed a dull blank about her, cold, irresponsive, and grey as a November evening. Every hand seemed against her. Even Radamanth, the man of serious years, had turned the key upon her, more kind to Gorlois than herself. Her thoughts were very bitter as she lay and brooded over it all.

Presently she heard some one coming up the stairs. Darting to the door, she bolted it, and went back to the bed, while a hand rapped out a somewhat diffident summons, and Radamanth's voice came in to her.

"My dear niece," it said.

Igraine made no answer.

"My dear niece, let me have a word with you."

Still no answer. Radamanth tried the door and found it fastened.

"Gorlois is gone," he said.

Igraine remained obdurate, with face drawn and sullen-eyed. She heard him shuffle down the stairs again, go into his parlour, and shut the door very gently, like a man who is ashamed. Then all was quiet save for casual footsteps in the street, and the garrulous chatter of a starling on the tiles.

Noon had come and gone a long while, and still Igraine lay in her room and moped. She felt sore and grieved to the heart, all her sanguine courage was at low ebb. Winchester seemed a prison-house where she was shut up with Gorlois. The man's greed and power of soul seemed to stare upon her till white honour folded its hands over its breast and turned to flee. Oh for Pelleas and the brave look of those honest eyes, the staunch touch of those great hands. He seemed to stand up above the world, above the selfishness, the lust, the violence, like a pine on some lonely hill. She could trust, she could believe. To find him would give her peace.

As she lay there that noontide a new purpose came to her, and lighted up hope. It was frail and flickering enough, but still, it burned. She would leave Radamanth's house and go afoot into the world to find a shadow. Anything was better than lying cooped in the place for dread of Gorlois. She had long contemplated such a measure, and that morning in Radamanth's garden gave her decision and made her strong.

She rose up from the bed and hunted out her old Avangel habit from a cupboard in the wall. Then she set to to doff the rich stuffs Radamanth had given her, the embroidered tunic, the coloured leather shoes, the goodly enamelled girdle. In their stead she stood again in the old grey gown, hood, and sandals, with a little thrill of delicious recollection. It was like stepping back into the dream of an enchanted past.

She had hardly ended the transformation when there came a shy tap at her door, and a mild voice calling to her from the landing. It was the girl Lilith. Igraine felt a sudden warmth at her heart as she let her in and barred the door again. Lilith stood and stared at her, her great brown eyes wide with astonishment.

"Why this old dress, Igraine?"

"I will tell you, dear."

"And you have been crying, for your eyes are red."

Igraine took the soft-voiced little woman to the window-seat and told her sadly enough all the doings of the morning. Even Lilith looked ashamed and showed her anger openly. Radamanth had confessed nothing of what had passed in the garden.

"I never loved my father less before," she said. "I

should never have thought this mean trick of him. I am ashamed, Igraine."

"Never trouble, dear, you are my joy in Winchester."

"And why this old nun's habit?"

"I am going to leave you, child."

Lilith clutched at her with both hands, her face suddenly white and almost piteous.

"Oh, no, no, Igraine!"

"I must, dear."

"Forgive —"

"It is not that alone. I cannot rest here longer. Gorlois and the city have crushed the heart out of me."

Lilith lifted up her child's face to her, and then began to sob unrestrained on Igraine's bosom.

"It seems cruel," she whimpered.

"No, no, it is best for me after all."

"But where will you go, Igraine?"

"Heaven knows, dear. I cannot rest here longer after this morning. I feel as if I should stifle."

"Don't go, Igraine."

"Hush, dear, don't weaken me. I am hard put as it is."

They were both weeping now. Lilith's slim body shook as she lifted up her face to Igraine's, and looked at her through her tears. She had learnt to love Igraine, and jealousy of her tall and splendid kinswoman had had no place in her heart. Lilith possessed to perfection the power of sympathy, and being a simple little soul who lived wholly for the present, she perhaps felt the more for that very reason. She could not say evil enough of Gorlois, nor put too much kindness into her kisses as she sat with her head on Igraine's shoulder.

"You cannot go out alone in the world," she said presently.

Igraine was silent.

"I know father would never forgive himself."

"There are convents, child. They would guard and give me harbour for a time."

"A convent — but you hate the life."

"If I could only hear of Uther, I would —"

"Yes, yes, I know. But will you go, Igraine?"

"My mind is made up; nothing can change it."

"Then let me come with you."

Igraine kissed her, but shook her head at the suggestion.

"I love you for the wish, dear, but I could never drag you into my own troubles, and it would be very wrong to Radamanth."

That afternoon they had many words together in Igraine's room, and dusk caught them still talking. Igraine had made Lilith promise that Radamanth should know nothing of her flight till the following morning. Lilith proved a little obstinate at first, but yielded in the end for fear of grieving Igraine. With the dusk she crept downstairs and brought up food. Igraine made a meal, while Lilith, with her tears still falling, put up food and a few trifles into a bundle, slipping in all the little store of money she had. Then she ran softly downstairs to see if the way were clear. Radamanth had gone to supper with a merchant friend, and the house seemed quiet and very lonely. In the passage-way the two girls took leave of each other, Lilith clinging to Igraine for a moment with all her heart. With sad eyes Igraine left her, and went out into the night.

VI

Igraine found lodging that night in the great abbey of St. Helena that Pelleas had spoken of on their ride from the island manor. Posing to the portress as one who had wandered long after her escape from Avangel, she was taken to the refectory, where supper was being spread by the juniors. The women of the place gathered round her, and Igraine inquired with some qualms for any chance news of Malt, Claudia, and the rest, but getting nothing she felt more confident. She told them her name was Meliboea, and she recounted at length the burning of Avangel and her subsequent wanderings, carefully purging the tale of all that might seem strange to their virgin ears, or set their tongues a-clacking. The women were very kind to her, partly for her own sake, and partly for the interesting gossip she had brought them.

At supper she sat next a young and merry nun who shared her misericords with her. The good women of the place were suffered to talk between vespers and complines, and Igraine, sly at heart, edged the talk to a tone for which she thirsted, and began to speak to her neighbours of Gratia, Abbess of Avangel.

"Did any of you know her?" she asked.

"Only by fame," said a fat nun opposite Igraine.

"I have heard she was near of kin to the King," said another, who drooped her lids in very modest fashion.

Igraine started in thought.

"Aurelius?" she said.

The nun nodded.

"How were they related?"

"I have heard Gratia was his aunt."

"And aunt to Uther also?"

"Of course, seeing they are brothers."

Igraine looked at her wooden platter, and pressed the little gold cross to her bosom with her hand. And now a strange thing happened. The old nun opposite Igraine, who was the Mistress of the Novices, brought out news that she had heard in the Abbess's parlour that very morning.

"Uther has been seen again," she said.

"Uther?"

The word snapped out like a bolt from a bow, and brought the nuns' eyes on Igraine across the table.

"The man comes and goes like a shadow. He is ever riding alone to do some great deed against the beasts, or against the heathen. A great soul is Uther."

Here were tidings dropped like dew out of heaven at the very hour she stood in need of them. Igraine felt the mist lighten appreciably in her brain. She popped an olive into her mouth and spoke almost carelessly.

"Where is Uther?"

"At Sarum town. He rode, they say, to the great camp there looking like a ghost, or as though he had been playing Simeon on a pillar."

Igraine merely nodded.

"Uther always looks a serious soul. Have you ever seen him, sister?"

"Never. A dark man?"

"With a face like a sun and a thunder-cloud rolled into one."

"A good man!"

"So they say; he has a clean look."

A little bell began to sound to call them away to complines. Igraine went with the rest into the solemn chapel, and let the chant sweep into her soul, and the prayers take her heart to heaven. Incense floated down, colours shone and glimmered on the walls, the dim lamps shivered like stars under the roof. Igraine felt her hollow heart warm as a rose in the full blaze of a golden noon. She said her prayers very fervently that night, for love was awake in her and glad of her new-blossomed hope. She would go to the great camp at Sarum and see this Uther for herself.

She had little comradeship with sleep in the great dormitory that night. When the matins bell rang she was up and ready for her flight like a young lark in the day. After chapel she begged a pittance from the cellaress and stowed it with her bundle in the little wallet Lilith had given her, excusing her early going on the plea that she had far to walk that day. She set out briskly from the grey shadows of the abbey. The place lay quite close by the western gate, so that she was soon beyond the walls and in the fields and orchards where all was goldly quiet at that early hour.

Winchester stood like a prison-house, void and fooled, in

the east. Igraine turned and looked down at it awhile huddled in its great girdle of stone, a medley of towers, roofs, and mist-wrapped trees. She shook her fist at it with a noiseless little laugh when she thought of Gorlois. Further yet to the east she could see the blue pine-smirched ridge where Pelleas had built her that little bower on the night he had left her sleeping. Her eyes grew deep with desire as she thought of it all, even as she had thought of it a thousand times since then. Pelleas's dark face was garlanded with green in her memory, and trouble, as it ever does, had made love take deeper root in her bosom.

Cheeriness comes with action. Igraine, fettered no longer, footed it along the road with snatches of song on her lips, and her eyes full of summer. A quiet wind came up from the west, and the clear morning air suited her courage. All the wide world seemed singing; the trees had an epithalamium on their whispering tongues, and the sky seemed strewn with white garlands. The tall corn in its occasional cohorts bowed down to her with murmuring acclaim as though it guessed her secret.

When she had gone a league or so she sat down under a tree and made a meal from the stuff in her wallet. Country folk went by on the road, for it was market-day in Winchester. One apple-cheeked lad seeing a nun sitting there came devoutly with his palms full of fruit taken from his ass's pannier, and made his offering with a shy smile and a bend of the knee. Igraine, touched, blessed him most piously, and gave him a kiss to cap it. The lad blushed and went away thinking he had never seen such a pretty nun before, and wondering if there were many like her in the great abbey. Igraine watched him towards Winchester, and wished some country girl joy of a good husband.

Presently she held on again in great spirits, nor had she gone very far when a tinkling of bells came up behind her with a merry clatter of hoofs. Turning aside to give passage, she looked back and saw an old gentleman riding comfortably on a white mule with two servants jogging along behind him on cobs. The old man's bridle was fringed with little silver bells that made a thin jingle as he rode; he was solidly gowned in plum-coloured cloth turned over with sable, and seemed of comfortable degree, judging by his trappings. Igraine looked up in his face as he passed by, while the old gentleman stared down to see what sort of womanhood lurked under a nun's hood. The man on the mule was Eudol, Radamanth's bosom gossip.

"Hey now, on my soul," said the little merchant, reining in with a will; "what have we here, my dear, gadding about nunwise on a high-road? My faith, I must hold a catechism."

Igraine, knowing the old man's vulnerability, answered with a smile.

"Ah, Master Eudol, you are a very lady's man, a gem of discretion."

"So, and truth," said the merchant, with a chuckle.

Igraine went close to him and patted the white mule's neck, while the serving men held at a wise distance.

"I am running away from Winchester," she said.

"Strange sport, my dear."

"Now you must not tell a soul, on your honour."

"Not a living soul, on my honour."

Igraine let her eyes flit a laughing look up at him.

"Why then, Master Eudol," she said, "if you will order one of your men to walk, I will get up and ride along with you for a league or two. There is trust for you."

Eudol appeared entranced with the suggestion. He ordered one of his fellows to dismount, to spread a cloak over the saddle, to shorten a stirrup leather and give Igraine his knee. The girl was soon mounted, seated side fashion with one sandalled foot in the stirrup and one hand on the pommel to steady her. She flanked Eudol's white mule, and they rode on side by side at a level tramp, with the henchmen some twenty paces in the rear.

Eudol soon waxed fatherly, as was his custom. He twitted Igraine on the temerity of her venture with the senile and pedantic jocosity of an old man. He said things that would have been impertinent on the tongue of a youngster, and exerted to the full that eccentric fad of age, the supposition that youth needs pleasant patronage and nothing more. Old men, holding young folk to be fools, reserve to their rusty brains the privilege of seeming wise. They are content to straddle the crawling, leather-jointed circumspection that they call knowledge. The bird flutters to his mate, sings, soars, and is taken before night by the fowler. The snail creeps his rheumy round covered with the slime and slobber of prudence, to rot in the end under a tree-stump, unless some good throstle cracks him prematurely on a stone. Eudol had something of the snail about him, but he assayed none the less to ape the soaring of youth with a very ragged pair of wings. That morning he flew with a senile eagerness for Igraine's favour, and thought himself a match for any young man in the matter of light chivalry.

"Come now, my dear," he said, "let us have a good look at you."

"Well, sir?"

"My word, you make a gorgeous nun. Who ever saw such eyes under a hood before! My dear, you are quite foolhardy to go pilgrimaging alone; men are such rogues, and you have such a pretty face."

There was a cringing tone about the old sinner that made Igraine thoroughly despise him. He seemed to combine elderly bravado with smooth servility, qualities peculiarly obnoxious to the girl's spirit. She had never liked or trusted Eudol overmuch in the past, but she was at pains to be civil to him now, seeing that he might serve her in sundry ways. She took his speeches with outward graciousness, and laughed at him hugely in her heart.

He began to lecture her in rather egotistical fashion.

"You must remember, my dear," he said, "that I am a man of the world, and one whose experience may be relied upon. I may tell you that my judgment is much valued by your good uncle Radamanth, a man of much sagacity, but yet one who lacks just that subtle insight into events that I may say has always been my special characteristic. I am so experienced that I may deserve the infinite honour of advising you if you care to tell me where you are going. I have had so much to do with the world, that I can tell you the best tavern in any town this side of the Thames where clean and honest lodging may be had. I can inform you as to tolls, prices, customs, bye-laws. Are you soon returning to Winchester?"

Igraine shook her head at him.

"Who have you been quarrelling with, my dear?"

"Myself most."

"To think of it, syrup quarrelling with honey! What will your Lord Gorlois do?"

Igraine stifled the question on the instant.

"Master Eudol, leave that name alone if you want more of my company."

"Pardon, my dear, pardon. I did not know it was so unpleasant a topic."

"I hate the very name of him."

"My dear, such a splendid fellow."

"Detestable boaster."

"Tut, tut,—a very popular nobleman; just the very man for you, and vastly rich. Now when I heard that he—that gentleman—"

"For God's sake, Master Eudol, leave your chatter."

The old merchant for the moment looked a little taken aback. Then he smiled, pulled his goat's beard, and grew epigrammatic.

"She who wears a gilded shoe," he said, "will find it pinch in the wearing. Stick to your sandals, my dear, and let your pretty white feet go brown in the sun. Better breathe in the open than freeze in a marble house. Just play the savage and let ambition go hang."

Igraine thanked him as though she held his counsel to be of the most inestimable value to herself. She was wise enough to know that to please an old man you must take his words in desperate earnest, and appear much caught by his supreme sagacity. Eudol smacked his lips and was comfortably warm within himself. He went on to tell the girl that he was riding to a little country manor that he owned some few leagues from Winchester. He informed her sentimentally that he was a very Virgil over his farm and garden. Igraine thought "Virgil" might well be Greek for "fool," but she hid her ignorance under her hood. Eudol ran on to dilate on the subtleties of husbandry, making a fine parade of expert phraseology in the doing of it.

"I see you do not follow me," he said presently. "Young folk are not fond of turning over the sods; they love grass for a scamper, not clay and dull loam. Shall we talk of petticoats or sarcenet that runs down a pretty figure like water? Eh, my dear? You set the tune, I'll follow."

Igraine contented herself with keeping him to his hobby.

"My father loved his violet beds," she said.

"Wise man — wise man. A garden makes thoughts sprout as though they would keep time to the leaves. You shall see my garden. Let me see, what road are you for following?"

"The road to fortune, Master Eudol."

"Truth, then, it must run near my doorway. The good woman who keeps house for me will make you most welcome. You must rest on your journey."

"You are very good."

"Not a bit of it, my dear. I shall call you St. Igraine — hee, hee! — and you will ripen all the apples in my orchard by looking at 'em. Faith, am I not a wag?"

"You ought to be at court, sir."

"Hee, hee!"

"You would make all the young squires red with envy."

"My dear, my dear!"

"Truth."

"To flatter an old man so — "

"But you are really such a courtier."

Eudol squirmed and chuckled in the grotesquest fashion.

"Assuredly we make very good friends," he said.

Eudol's manor nearly halved the mileage between Sarum and the royal town of Winchester, and Igraine found his suggestion quite a happy help to her plans. If needs be, she could bide the night there and make Sarum next day with but trivial trouble. She was glad in a way that she had fallen in with Eudol, for the ride had proved quite a charity to her, and his antique vanities had passed the time better than more modest characteristics could have done. Her only fear was lest he should cheat her, and send word to Radamanth. Accordingly she spoke to him again about her flight, and made him promise on the Cross that he would not betray her whereabouts. Eudol, silly soul, was ready enough by now to promise her almost anything.

About noon they halted and made a meal, with a flat stone lying under the shade of a tree for table. Eudol drank quite enough wine to quicken his failings, and to lull what common sense he had to sleep. He became so maudlin, so supremely sentimental, that Igraine had much ado to throttle her laughter. She quite feared for him when they had to get to horse again. His men had to hoist him into the saddle between them. Once there he seemed quite arrogantly confident of his seat, and being a hardy old gentleman at the pot he soon steadied down into comparative docility, managing his mule as though there had been no such luxury as dinner. He was more garrulous and fatherly than ever; now and again he had to quench a hiccough; otherwise he was only an exaggerated portrait of himself.

An hour's ride brought them to Eudol's own pastures. He pointed out his sheep to Igraine amid the clanking of their diverse bells, and told her the profits of the last shearing. Soon the house edged into view, a homely place set back an arrow's flight from the road, and ringed round with a score or so old trees. It was a green and quiet spot, mellow with the warm comfort of pastureland and wood. A pool twinkled in the meadows, through which ran a small stream.

There was no bridge over the brook; the track crossed

it by a shallow ford where the water gurgled over pebbles. The banks were loose and crumbling, and the trackway littered with stones. Eudol's mule went over sure-footed as a goat, but Igraine's horse, slipping on the slope, set a fore-hoof on a shifting stone, and rolled down with a crash. The girl did not avoid in time, and the brute's body pinned her ankle. She felt the sinews crack, and the stones bruise her flesh. For a moment she was in danger of the animal's plunges to rise, but one of the men came up and seized the bridle, while his fellow drew Igraine clear.

Eudol climbed down, splashed through the water, and came up puffing sympathy. Igraine tried to walk, but gave up with a wry face. The men helped her to the grass bank, where she sat down, with Eudol fussing round her like an old woman. He sent the men on to the manor to bring a bed; and seeing that Igraine had grown white from the wrench, he ran for the wine-flask at his saddle-bow and urged her to drink. The girl had more fear of a spoilt journey than a cracked bone, and feeling faint for the moment, she suffered Eudol, and took the wine. The old man was on his knees by her stroking her hand, his thin beard wagging, and his glazed eyes vinously sympathetic. When the men came back with the bed they laid Igraine thereon, and bore her through the meadows to the house, Eudol following like a spaniel at their heels.

VII

WHILE Igraine slept in the abbey dormitory and dreamt of Pelleas, the man Gorlois burnt on the grid of his own passions, and found no peace for his soul.

The night sky was not a whit more black than his spirit, and his sinister cogitations were chequered ever with palpitating points of fire. The restless fever of an unfed leopard seemed his, and he was in and out of his tumbled, sleepless bed ten times before dawn. Only a boar-hound kept him company, a savage red-eyed brute whose temper suited that of his master; the dog followed Gorlois as he wandered from bed-chamber to atrium, out from the peristyles to the garden, down walks of yew and cypress, between the beds of helicryse and asphodel, over the smooth lawns clear in the eye of the moon. There was an evil thing in Gorlois's thought, a thing fit for beggarly disrelish, yet very white and lovely to look upon. He stalked like a ghost in the night, biting his lips, looking into the dark with red and eager eyes. How often he reached out in naked thought and clasped only the air. He cursed himself and the woman, honoured and abused her in one breath, grew hot and cold like a live coal played upon by a fickle wind.

As soon as dawn came he had a plunge and a swim in a pool in the garden, and having suffered the ceremony of a state toilet, went out unattended into the town. It was the very hour when Igraine was shaking her fist at Winchester for thought of him, but Gorlois was spared the prick of self-knowledge and the frank truth of the girl's distaste. He thought her nothing more than a shrew, and the possessor of a splendid temper. His long legs and the heat at his heart soon took him down through the quiet streets and the market square to Radamanth's house.

Early as was the hour, the goldsmith had escaped sloth and was busy at his ledgers in his little counting-house behind the parlour. Gorlois came in in great state, with the serving wench who announced him feasting her curiosity on his face with a sheepish giggle. Radamanth, fetched from his figures, bowed very low, and made the gentleman a most obsequious welcome. He was wondering what Gorlois's humour might be after the repulse of yesterday. To tell the truth, Radamanth felt somewhat ashamed of the trick he had served Igraine, and he was none too eager to meet his niece, seeing that she still seemed determined to hide her anger in her room. His doubts as to Gorlois's mood were set at rest by that gentleman's somewhat saturnine opening.

"Radamanth!"

"Your honour's servant."

"I have come to make peace."

"Your lordship's magnanimity is phenomenal."

"Was I over hasty, goldsmith?"

"A young man's way, my lord; no fault at all. Many's the time I had my face smacked as a youngster, and was none the worse in favour. Take no serious view, sir, but press her the harder. She'll give in — my faith, yes, being young and full of bone. You are troubled, my lord, with too much conscience."

"Have you seen the woman since?"

Radamanth raised his eyebrows and shrugged.

"Well, no," he said. "I am afraid my niece has rather a hot spirit — breeding, my lord — proud blood in her."

"I know that part of her nobleness well enough."

Radamanth refrained a moment from a sense of discretion.

"My lord would see her?"

"I'll not budge till I have done so."

"You understand women?"

Gorlois smiled a peculiar smile.

"I have wit enough," he said. "I have my plan."

"If it please you, sir, to go into the garden, I will endeavour to send her to you."

"No more locking of doors, goldsmith."

"Sir, I contemn my late indiscretion in your service."

Gorlois passed out by a long passage into the gardens, with its green leaves shelving to the river, while Radamanth, half a coward at heart, went towards the stair that led to Igraine's chamber. Halfway up he met the girl Lilith coming down, very white and frightened looking, as though she dreaded her father's face. Radamanth kissed her, and asked for Igraine. Then her distraught look dawned on him in the twilight of the stairway, and made him suddenly suspicious.

"Is Igraine awake?"

Lilith hid her face in his sleeve.

"Speak, girl, what's amiss?"

"The room is empty."

"What!"

"Igraine has left us," said the girl with a stifled whimper.

Radamanth, sage and solemn soul, lapsed into the sin of blasphemy.

"When did you learn this, girl?"

"Father—"

"Quick now, don't lie."

He shook her by the shoulder.

"Father, be gentle with me."

"Quick, hussy."

"I can't, I can't."

Radamanth took her firmly by the wrist and brought her with no very considerate care into the parlour.

"Now," he said, thrusting her into a chair, "you atom of ingratitude, tell me what you know."

Lilith began to sob. She hid her face behind her fingers and dared not look at Radamanth. The goldsmith chafed and paced the room, hectoring her.

"Don't think to fool me," he said; "you know more yet; you would have answered before if there had been any truth in you."

Radamanth's harshness seemed certainly to calm the girl, and to conjure up some passing antagonism in her heart.

"The blame is yours, father."

"Impertinent child."

"Igraine was angry with you."

"Well, have I not treated her like a daughter?"

"She fled away last night."

"Where?"

"I don't know."

"You do."

"I don't, father; 'tis truth."

The girl's brown eyes appealed to him tearfully; she was honest enough, and Radamanth knew it. He took her sincerity for granted and proceeded to question her further.

"How was she clothed, child?"

Lilith looked at the floor and plucked at her gown with her fingers.

"Do you hear me?"

"Yes, father."

"Then answer at once."

"I can't."

"Upon my soul — "

"Igraine made me promise."

Radamanth lost his temper again and began to bluster like a March wind. Lilith's cheeks were wet with her tears; they ran down and dropped into her lap like little crystals. She shook and sobbed in her chair, but answered not a word, a martyr to her promises. Then Radamanth, man of money-bags and craft, found something wherewith to loose her tongue.

"Listen," he said; "a certain lad never enters this house again, and you never again have speech with him, unless you answer me this at once."

The mean measure triumphed. Lilith's tears never ceased, but she gave way at last, and hating herself, told Radamanth what he wanted. Then he left her there to whimper by herself, and went into the garden to speak with Gorlois.

The Count of Cornwall guessed from the merchant's face that matters had fallen out ill for him somewhere. He forestalled Radamanth's confession with an impatient gust of words.

"She is still in a deuce of a temper?"

"My lord, it is otherwise."

"Then why so glum — man, have I not uncovered ingots of gold for you if I wed?"

Radamanth held his hands up like a priest giving a blessing. Any one might have thought him grieved to death by the ingratitude of his niece's desertion. The goldsmith dealt in coarser sentiment.

"My lord, the girl has forsaken my house and fled."

Gorlois had half expected some such news. He said nothing, but merely stared at Radamanth with dark masterful eyes, while his fingers played with the tassels of his belt. His heart was already away over moor and dale chasing the gleam of a golden head of hair.

"When did you miss her, goldsmith?"

"She crept away at dusk yesterday."

"Whither?"

"Heaven knows, my lord."

"How dressed?"

"As a grey nun."

"Has she gone back to the Church?"

"She did not love such a life, my lord."

"By God, no."

Gorlois frowned a moment in thought. The scent of the girl's dress was still in his nostrils, and her eyes haunted him. Then he turned past Radamanth to go, hitching up his sword belt, a significant habit he had learnt long ago.

"I shall find her," he said.

"Good, my lord."

"I have your countenance."

"Be kind to the girl, sir."

"I could go to hell for her."

"My lord, why not try heaven?"

"A good jest."

"Men always go to hell for things," said the goldsmith.

There was life and stir enough in Gorlois's great house when its master came back that morning. Gorlois's orders were like a torch to tinder. Men went to every wind, some to the gates, some to the market, others to the religious houses and the inns, all bent on striking the trail of a nun's grey gown. The men knew their master's mood, and the measure of his pulse on such occasions. Gorlois bided quiet in his garden, more like a leopard than a lover. He had made up his mind to catch Igraine, and to win mastery of her, hook or by crook, since she chose to play the shrew and mar his wooing. It was not likely that one of the first men in Britain should be baffled by the temper of a goldsmith's niece.

About noon a certain slave who had gone out to net news came back with much elation and claimed his lord's ear. Brought in before Gorlois, he told how he had talked with a boy selling fruit in the market-place, and how the boy, when questioned, had told him of a nun he had seen sitting under a tree by the road to Sarum that very morning. The lad had described her as a very beautiful lady with large eyes, and a cloud of red-brown hair, and that she wore a grey nun's habit somewhat torn and travel-stained. Gorlois thought he recognised Igraine, and gave the slave fifty acres and his freedom on the instant. Waiting for further news, word was brought him that a grey nun had been marked by the guard going out of the western gate not very long after dawn. Later still Gorlois heard of such a nun, calling herself Melibœa, having lodged the night at the great abbey of St. Helena.

Gorlois held himself in leash no longer. He buckled on his richly gilt armour, and his great white horse was saddled and brought into the court. Not a knight would he have at his back, neither groom nor page. Getting to horse in the full welt of the afternoon sun, he rode out of Winchester alone by the western gate, watched of many people. Once clear of the town he pricked incontinently for Sarum, lusting much to catch Igraine upon the way.

About that very same hour Eudol was exerting himself in Igraine's service in the manor farm in the meadows.

The men had carried her up from the ford and set her at her own seeking in a shady place in the garden where she might lie at peace. It was a pleasant nook enough where they had set her bed, a patch of bright green grass with a bank of flowers on one hand and dense laurel hedge hiding it from the track to the house on the other. A vine trained upon poles raised a pleasant pavilion there. Autumn would soon be whispering in the woods, and already some few leaves were ribbed with gold and maroon.

Eudol played the physician and made a very critical examination of her ankle. He prided himself, among his other vanities, on having studied Galen, and since the healing craft is often a matter of phenomenal words and wise nothings, Eudol might have outphysicked Gildas at his own game. The art of medicine is the art of hypocrisy, and the sage apothecary is often a broken reed trembling in the wind of ignorance. Eudol, having no reputation at stake, pronounced Igraine's hurt to be a mere strain of the ankle-joint, and, as it happened, he was right. He swathed her foot in wet linen and set it on a pillow, while the woman who kept house for him, a red-cheeked piece of buxomness, brought wine and food-stuff on a tray. Seeing a nun's habit the good woman was comforted, and indulged Igraine with many smiles and much motherly care.

Eudol came and sat beside her with a great book on his knee, Virgil's Bucolics, as he told her, and writ most learnedly for the edification of the wise. Eudol read very little of the book that afternoon. The volume abode with him for effect, but he preferred rather to dwell upon the more Ovidian interest of the girl beside him, and to talk to her in his familiar and fatherly fashion. He made many sly attempts to get the purpose of her pilgrimage from her, but Igraine had enough wit to keep him discreetly mystified on the subject. She was wondering all the while how long her strained ankle would keep her to her bed.

Eudol smothered her with offers of hospitality.

"On my word you shall not be dull," he said, "though there is only an old man to entertain you. One day you shall ride out in a litter to my vineyards, another you shall be carried out a-hunting. I have a little wench here who can harp and sing like a mermaid. By the poets, I can make you quite a merry time."

Igraine made the best smile she could, and thanked him.

"You must not put yourself out for me."

"Nonsense."

"You are very good."

Eudol shook his finger with most earnest expression.

"My dear lady, it is duty, duty," he said.

They had not been so very long in the garden when Igraine's quick ear caught the sharp and rhythmic smite of hoofs on the stony track across the meadows. The sound disquieted her, for she was in the mood for dreads and suspicions. Listening to make sure that the sound approached, she appealed to Eudol and asked him to look and see who rode for the manor. There was a little wicket-gate some way down the laurel hedge carefully screened by shrubs. Eudol went to it, and scanned the meadows under his hand. He came back somewhat flustered to Igraine, and told her that a knight in gilded armour mounted on a white horse was riding up the track to the house.

Igraine started up on her bed with her eyes very big and suspicious.

"It is Gorlois," she said.

"Heavens, my dear!"

"You have not been lying to me?"

"On my soul — no."

Igraine touched her forehead with her hand, and looked askance at the sun.

"Master Eudol, if you would serve me, go and fool the man — send him away."

"My dear child —"

"He must not see the servants or have speech with them."

"But —"

"I command you, go and speak to him; he is very near."

Eudol looked at her with his lower lip a-droop. His grey-green eyes met Igraine's, gleamed, and faltered. He bent over the bed.

"I will do my best. Give me a kiss, my dear. By Augustus, I will get rid of Gorlois if I can."

He went out quickly by the wicket-gate, and closing it after him, waited for the knight to approach. There were no slaves about, and Eudol remembered with confidence that his men were in the corn fields, well away to the north. Gorlois came up with the splendid arrogance that so suited him, his rich armour glowing above the white flanks of his horse, his spear balanced on his thigh. Eudol went forward some paces to meet him, as though to learn his business. Igraine, listening behind the laurel hedge, heard their words as plainly as though the two men were but three paces away.

"Greeting, sir," said Eudol's thin voice.

Then she heard Gorlois's clear sharp tenor questioning him. She heard him ask whether a grey nun had called for food, or whether Eudol had seen or heard of such a person. She heard the old man's meandering negative, and Gorlois's retort that a grey nun had been seen riding beside a merchant on a white mule. Igraine's heart seemed to race and thunder. Eudol, rising to the event, suggested that the merchant might be a certain fabulous person from Aquæ Sulis; a man of means, he said, who often came by Sarum to Winchester in the fur trade. He hinted that the knight might overtake them on the road, or discover them at Sarum that evening. Gorlois fell to the suggestion. Igraine heard him inquire further of Eudol, speak to his horse, and ride away with a ringing clatter. She sat on her couch behind her laurel rampart and laughed.

Eudol came back to her, pleased as possible.

"How was that done, — sweeting?"

"Nobly," laughed Igraine.

"The Virgin pardon me; what perjury for a pair of lips."

VIII

NOTHING is more chafing to the patience than to lie abed crippled, knowing the while that coveted hours are slipping through one's fingers like grains of gold. To Igraine, her maimed ankle was a very thorn in the flesh. Her thoughts were tugging to be at Sarum, and she was in continual fear lest Radamanth or Gorlois should track her to her temporary refuge, and attempt to mar her freedom. She was not a woman who could take hindrance with perfect philosophy, comforting herself with the reflection that care never yet salved unrest. She chafed at delay, and even blamed Eudol with great unreason because he had obliged her with a horse not proof against stumbling.

The knowledge that Gorlois rode in search of her did not tend to the easing of her mind. She began to understand Gorlois to the full. He had betrayed so much of himself in Radamanth's garden that her dread grew nearly as great as her disrelish.

Eudol had made her comfortable enough in his manor, she had no need to find fault with his hospitality. She had her own room, a little girl to wait and sing to her, fruit and food of the best. She spent the greater part of each day in the garden, her bed being set under the vine leaves; two of Eudol's slaves would carry her down in the morning and bear her back again at night, so that she should not be too venturesome in trying her ankle. The old merchant kept his folk close on the farm and suffered none to go to Winchester or Salisbury, for fear lest the knowledge of Igraine's whereabouts should leak into interested channels.

The more the girl saw of Eudol the less she relished him in her heart. The lean look of him, his little green eyes, his thin goat-like beard, reminded her much of the picture of some old Satyr she had seen in the frescoes on the walls of the triclinium at Winchester. He grew more fatherly and kind to her, would smile like some old saint as he sat and read moralities to her from the lives of some of the Fathers. He was very fond of holding her hand and stroking it while he purred sentiment, and made her colour to hear his nonsense. He was quite wickedly delighted when he had fetched a blush to her face. He would sit and chuckle and hug himself, while his little eyes glistened and his beard shook. Igraine, though her cheeks often tingled, did her best to suffer him, knowing well enough that she was greatly dependent for her peace of mind upon his good-will. She would laugh, turn his senile flatteries into jest, and assume his humour as the most vapoury and fanciful piece of fun possible. She often hinted that Eudol must be neglecting his farm for her sake, though her suggestions were absolutely to no purpose, seeing that Eudol had forgotten all about such mundane matters as harvesting or the pressing of cider.

One afternoon they had a shrewd fright, and the incident led in its final development to Igraine's leaving the manor in the meadows. She was in the garden with Eudol when two horsemen wearing Gorlois's livery rode up to the gate and demanded entertainment with much froth and bombast. They were sturdy hot-tongued rogues, quick at liquor, quicker still at blasphemy. Eudol, much flustered, had them brought into the house and set loose upon a wine flask while he smuggled Igraine out of the garden. There was a barn standing on the other side of a little meadow near the house, and the building was screened by a fringe of pines and a thorn hedge. Eudol hurried Igraine to the barn, saw her couched on a pile of hay, closed the door on her, and scampered back to take great care of Gorlois's gentlemen.

Eudol proved a most obsequious and attentive host. He kept the men primed with wine, watched them like a lynx, forbade his slaves and servants the room so that there should be no chance of gossip. The fellows thought themselves well harboured. Eudol, hardy old tipster, kept them going with a will, till they swore he was the best old gentleman at his cups they had met this side of the Thames. He outdrank, out-yarned, out-jested the pair of them. Grown very mellow towards evening, they vowed by all the calendar that they loved him so much they would make a night of it, and not go to bed till they were carried. Eudol could have denied himself their great esteem, but there was nothing for it but to humour them.

He got rid of the fellows next morning, when they went away sadly, very glazed about the eyes, swearing they would pay him another visit at their very earliest opportunity. Eudol, when they were out of sight, went out to the barn and found Igraine comfortably couched there on a mass of hay. The little maid who served her had brought her supper on the sly the night before, and she had fared well enough in her new quarters.

As a matter of fact Eudol had had a parting cup with the men that morning, and had hardly outbreathed as yet the maudlin heritage gotten the previous night. He kissed Igraine's hand, mumbled his usual courtesies, excused his long absence with a warmth that nearly brought him to tears. He was somewhat flushed over the cheek bones; his eyes were bright, and his breath pregnant with the heavy scent of wine. Igraine wiped the hand he had kissed on her gown, looked at him with little love or gratitude, and told him that she had been trying to walk, and that her ankle bore her passably.

Eudol, edging near, proceeded to narrate at preposterous length how he had kept Gorlois's men employed, made them drunk as cobblers, and packed them off innocently to Winchester that morning. He was hugely sly over it all. He came and climbed up beside Igraine on the hay, and pinched her arm with his lean fingers as he talked. There was a gaunt, red, eager look about his face. It was quite twilight in the great barn, and a mingled smell of hay and pitch-pine filled the air, while dusty beams of light filtered through in steady streams.

Eudol's vinous and fatherly solicitude developed abruptly into an absurd revelation of his inner self. He had hold of Igraine's arm with one hand. Leaving go suddenly, he reached for her waist, poked his grey beard into her face, and made a clumsy dab at her cheek. In a moment the girl's arm had swept him backwards like an impotent bag of bones. She saw him overbalance and roll off the haycock on to the edge of a scythe. Without waiting for more, and with a glimpse of the old fool's slippers still in the air, she slipped down from the hay and out of the barn, and shutting the door, pegged the catch with a piece of wood. Then she went laughing half resentfully towards the house, and told Dame Phœbe that her master had gone to the fields to oversee his slaves.

The woman had taken a remarkable dislike to Igraine, being sulky-eyed and dumb-saucy in her presence as far as she dared. The grey nun told her that she was ending her sojourn at the farm that morning, and was going on foot for the west. The woman's face changed as suddenly as a spring sky. She was suave and smiling instanter, ready with queries as to Igraine's ankle, very eager to pack her wallet with stuff from Eudol's larder. Igraine, with an inward flush, saw how the wind blew. She was keen to be gone before Eudol should be loosed from the barn; even the woman's changed mood seemed a tacit insult in itself.

She was soon treading the meadows where the backs of Eudol's sheep stood out like white boulders on the solitary stretch of green. The country began to be as flat as a table, though there were still masses of woodland piled on either side the great white road. Igraine kept in among the trees with just a glimpse of the highway to keep her to her mark. Her grey gown passed almost unperceptibly among the mould-grown trunks as she went in the chequered light like a grey mouse through green corn. Her ankle bore her better than she had prophesied, and she made fair travelling at a modest pace. Later in the afternoon the strain began to tell in measure, and her ankle ached and felt hot, as though she had done enough. Sitting down on a fallen tree she watched the road, and waited for some one to pass.

A charcoal burner went by with a couple of asses panniered up with a comfortable load. Then came two soldiers and a couple of light wenches who haunted camp and castle and lived to the minute. Next, a great wain half ladened up with faggots came lumbering along, drawn by a pair of sleepy horses, and driven by a peasant in a green smock and leather breeches. Igraine took her choice, and going down from the trees, stood by the roadside, and begged of the man a lift.

Seeing a nun looking up at him the man reined in, climbed down cap in hand, and louted low to her. There was some clean straw spread over the boards at the bottom of the cart. The man helped her up on to the tail-board and raked the straw into a heap to make her a seat. Then they lumbered on again towards Sarum.

In due course she began to talk to the man as he sat on a couple of faggots and held the ropes. He was an honest, ignorant fellow, with a much whiskered face that wore a perpetual look of kindly stupidity. Igraine sought to know whether he was going as far as Sarum. The man shook his bushy head like an amiable ogre, and told her that he was for his lord's manor some two leagues distant, where he served as woodman and ranger, or soldier when there was need of steel. He commended his lord's house to her for lodging, with a solid faith in the generosity of its board. Questioned as to other habitations, he told her of a hermit's cell set in a little dale in the woods, a cell where wandering folk often found harbour for the night. Igraine made up her mind to choose the ascetic's bread and water, having had enough of the world's welcome. Possibly in some dim and distant way she began to realise the intense and engrained selfishness of the human heart.

The man of faggots, believing her a holy woman, soon began to relate his domestic troubles to her with a most touching reverence. He told her how his wife had been abed two months from her last childbirth, and how sad and dirty his little cabin was for lack of her hands. He asked Igraine to put the woman in her bede-role, a simple favour that she granted readily enough. Then the fellow with some stolid pathos went on to describe how his eldest lad, a boy of eight, had caught a fever through sleeping in the woods after rain, and how he had fallen sick.

"I went to a good monk," said the man, "and bought holy water and a pinch of dust from a saint's coffin. Pardy! but it cost me a year's savings. The good father bade me pour the water on the boy's head and shake the dust over his body. Glad I was, holy sister; I ran five miles home to cure the lad."

"And he is well?"

The man gave a doleful whistle.

"The boy died," said he with pathetic candour, and a short catch in his voice. "I didn't sleep two whole nights. Then I kissed my woman, mopped her eyes, and went and told the priest."

Igraine merely nodded.

"Ah, the dear father, he told me 'twas God's will, and that the blessed dust had drifted the lad straight to heaven, where he would be singing next King David like any lord. So he came and buried the boy, and there was an end on't."

Igraine for the moment felt heavy about the eyes.

"I should like to see him there in his little white stole," she said. "Do you know, goodman, why so many children die?"

"Faith, madame, I have no learning," said the fellow with a dumb stare.

"Because the great God loves to have children laughing for love of him in heaven."

"Is't so?"

"That is why he took your boy."

The man's face brightened with a new dignity.

"Little Rual was ever a gentle child," he said. "I must tell my woman; it will just make her happy."

"I will pray for her health."

"God bless you, holy lady, you have a wise, kind heart."

Igraine blushed, but said nothing.

Presently the man stopped his horses, and pointed her to a little path that led, he said, to the hermitage. He helped Igraine out of the cart, and knelt on the road for her to give him a blessing. Igraine had a Latin phrase or two from Avangel, and the benediction was earnest enough in spirit, though it lacked genuine authority. Then she took the path through trees, and left the man standing cap in hand by his waggon. Her brief ride with him had done her heart good.

A mile's walk through unkempt pastures and straggling thickets brought her to an open dale set beneath the shoulder of a wooded hill. On the grass slope over against her she saw the hermitage — a grey cell of unfaced stone standing in a garden in a grove of ancient thorns. By the rivulet that ran half hid by undergrowth a figure in a brown cassock was drawing water. Passing down over the water, Igraine overtook the recluse halfway up the slope to the hermitage garden. She remarked his bald head fringed with a mournful halo of hair, his stooping shoulders, his ungainly weak-kneed gait. Hearing her tread behind him he turned a tanned face to her, a face that brought forth a smile of brotherly greeting at sight of a nun. Igraine, by way of creating good feeling, took his water pot and carried it for him, pleading youth in extenuation of the service.

There was a keen yet kindly sapience about the old man's big-nosed face that caught her fancy. He was a bit of a cynic on the surface, but warm as good earth at heart. Igraine confessed her need of a lodging for the night, and the man retorted bluntly with the remark that the hermitage was not his house, — but only a refuge to bury strangers in. Pointing to a great slab of stone that stood near the little cell, he told her that the stone had been his bed, summer and winter, these fifteen years, and that dew, rain, frost, and snow had worked their will upon his body and found it leather. The confession, pithily — almost humorously — put, without a trace of rodomontade, set the girl smiling. She looked at the man's brown buckram skin and congratulated him, embodying her flattery in a little jest that seemed to catch the ascetic fancy. He commended it with a patriarchal twinkle, and throwing open the door of his cell surrendered her its shelter.

Igraine soon fathomed the shallow compass of the hermitage. It held two pallet beds, some rude furniture and crockery, and such things as were necessary to the old man's craft, namely a scourge, a calthrop set on the end of an iron chain, a coat made of furze, a garland of thorn twigs, and a pair of spiked sandals. Gardening tools were piled in a corner. Over the doorway hung a rusty suit of harness and a red crusted sword. Here in this narrow place the war tools of world and church were mingled.

Igraine turned back into the hermitage garden. It was a quiet spot, webbed with the faery tracery of flowers and flowering shrubs, golden with helichryse, full of the mist of unshorn grass, bright with the water of its little fish-pool, where the ferns grew thick. A low wattle fence, climbed about by late-seasoned roses of red, shut the whole within its rustic pale. Some of the herb beds were cut into symbols of holy things, and a bay tree had been laboriously pruned into the rude image of a cross. A number of doves peopled the place, flocking about the hermit as he worked, often lighting on his hands or shoulders, while an old hound dozed in the sun, or followed at his heels. Peace seemed over the little refuge like a tranquil sky.

The hermit handed Igraine a hoe, as a matter of custom, and set her to work on the weeds in a neglected corner, while he busied his hands with pruning some of his rose trees, and removing the clay and linen from his grafts. He was by no means the solemn, dismal soul or the kindly simpleton Igraine might have expected. He had a keen, world-wise air about him that made him seem a sort of Christian Diogenes, and it was plain that he had lived much among men. The mingled austerity and happiness of his habits, when set beside his inwardly sympathetic yet somewhat cynic humour, gave a strong interest to his personality that quite commanded Igraine's liking. Despite the vast responsibilities of man, as he himself put it, he was not above having a jest at life in general. "For," said he, as he pruned his rose bushes, "he who knows and obeys the truth can of all men afford to be merry."

Igraine, smiling through the boughs, agreed with him from her heart.

"There are no sour faces in heaven," she said.

"Assuredly not," said the hermit almost fiercely.

"Then why such mortifications of the flesh, father?"

Looking up from his pruning, he beamed over the world.

"I am a very human rogue."

"Human!"

"Well, you see, sister, *mea culpa*, I loved the world when I was in it like my own life, and even now if I did not gnash upon myself I should grow frivolous at times. When I have spent a night in the rain, or plied my scourge, it is marvellous how swiftly vain the fabrics of a vaunting pride become. 'I am dust, I am dust,' I cry, and am sound at heart again. I look upon bread and olives and a draught of river water as true godsends. Having endured exceeding discomfort of the flesh, I am as happy in the sun here among my flowers as a mortal could be."

Igraine rested on her hoe, and put her head back, while the evening light gave her hair a rare metallic lustre.

"You believe in a life of contrasts, father?"

The old man became suddenly more serious.

"To tell you the truth," he said, "I have found that by making myself fanatically uncomfortable so many hours a day, I can attain for the rest of it that simple, contented, and heaven-soaring mood that belongs to the honest Christian. Man's great peril is apathy, and my customs save me from sleepy ease. There is such a thing as living to pander to the flesh; it is the creed of the majority. In order to enjoy a truly spiritual end, I annihilate the appetites of the body, and *ecce homo*,— merry, conscience whole, clean."

Igraine resumed her harrowing of reprobate green-stuff.

"I suppose your doctrine is right for yourself," she said.

An answer came back to her leisurely over the rose bush.

"To the backbone, sister. Yet I am not one who would thrust my habits down other men's throats simply because the said habits happen to suit my soul. All religious methods are a matter of individual experiment. One man may feel more Christian if he drinks wine instead of water; if so — by all the prophets — let him have his wine. I hold doctrinal tyranny to be the greatest curse in Christendom."

Igraine agreed with him like a sister.

Soon the sun went down with a flood of gold over the trees, the little pool put off sheeny samite for black velvet, and the doves flew up to roost. The hermit in a genial mood went to his vesper meditations. Igraine saw him kneel down before the great stone with his scourge and crucifix beside him. She was still carnal enough to prefer the thin comfort of a pallet bed in the hermitage to stone or mother earth. When it had grown dark and very still she heard the swish of the steel scourge, and the man's mutterings mingled with the occasional baying of his dog. This phase of mind was, at her age, quite incomprehensible to her. She remembered to pray that night for the peasant's wife who had been sick in bed so long, and for the little lad who lay under the green grass. Then she went to sleep thinking of Pelleas.

IX

RADAMANTH the goldsmith had not wasted the hours since his niece had fled Winchester and his house in the dark. He was a man who did not let an enterprise slip into the limbo of the past till he had attempted honestly, and dishonestly, for that matter, to bring it to a successful issue. He had set his heart on getting Igraine married to one of the first lords in the island, and he also had skew ideas as to brimming up his own coffers. Taking it for granted that

Lilith and the girl had not been close friends for weeks together without sharing secrets, and being also strongly of the opinion that Igraine's perversity arose out of some previous affair, he laid methodical siege to his daughter's confidences, and cast a parental dyke about her that should compel her to open every gate and alley to his scrutiny.

Lilith, amiable, but weak as milk, was soon worn into surrender by her father's methods. He had an unfailing lash wherewith to quicken her apprehension, in that young Mark, the armourer's son, should be barred the house unless she bent to the parental edicts. Lilith soon brought herself to believe that after all there could not be so much disloyalty in telling certain of Igraine's adventures to her father. Radamanth, bit by bit, had the whole tale of the way from Avangel to Winchester. Seeing how often Igraine—woman-wise—had pictured her man to Lilith, the goldsmith won a clear perception of the strange knight's person, how he rode a black horse, wore red armour, bore a red dragon on a green shield, and was called Pelleas. Radamanth made a careful note of all these things, and laid the knowledge of them before Gorlois. Various subtleties resulted from these facts—subtleties carefully considered to catch Igraine.

To turn to Eudol. That lean old satyr had fallen gravely into error in the conviction that he had fooled Gorlois's men so cleverly over the wine-pot. The deceit had been deeper on the other side, and more effectual, seeing that there had been a kirtled traitor in the manor camp. If Eudol had been stirring just after daybreak on the morning after the carouse, he might have caught one of Gorlois's men coming down a little winding stair that led to a certain portion of the house. A little earlier still he would have found the fellow with his arm round Dame Phœbe's waist in a dark entry on the stairs. The woman did not love Igraine, nor did she want her in the house; moreover, Gorlois's man was young, and had fine eyes, and a most wicked tongue. Eudol, like most diplomats, was far from being infallible when there was a woman in the coil, and Dame Phœbe was very much a woman.

Gorlois's fellows had no sooner cleared the meadows that morning than they were away for Winchester at a dusty rattle. It was fast going over the clean, straight road, and the grey walls were not long in coming into view. The pair swung through the western gate, and went straight through the streets in a way that set the city folk staring and dodging for the pathway. At the gate of Gorlois's house the porter had a vexatious damping for the spirits of these fiery gentlemen. Gorlois had ridden out. The men swore, off-saddled, and made the best of the matter over a game of dice in the kitchen.

There was great bustle when Gorlois had heard the men's tale. They excused their not having taken Igraine on the plea that Gorlois had forbidden any to approach her save himself. The man was in a smiting mood, and he swore Eudol should rue giving him the lie and sending him a wild chase miles into the west. Getting to horse at once, and taking the two men with some ten more spears, he rode out and held for Sarum.

There was a swirl of dust before Eudol's gate, and a sharp scattering of shingle as Gorlois and his troop rode up. A slave, who had seen them from the garden, and had taken them for robbers, was prevented from closing the gate by a brisk youth wedging it with his foot. There was a short scuffle at the tottering door. Then Gorlois and his men burst it in, and cut down those slaves on the threshold who had tried to close the door. The women folk were herded screeching into the kitchen, and penned there like sheep. Out of a cupboard in an upper room they dragged the woman Phœbe, limp with fright, and hurried the truth out of her that Igraine had gone that very morning, and that Eudol was still in the fields. Gorlois, believing her a liar, had the house searched, beds overturned, cupboards torn open, every nook and cranny probed. Then they tried the garden and the stables, with like fortune. One of the fellows catching sight of the barn across the meadows, half-hidden by pines, they made a circle round it, closed in, and forced the door. A blinking, red-eyed face came up out of the shadows, its beard and thin thatch of hair whisped with hay.

Eudol, collared with little kindness, began to wonder after his drunken sleep who these rough folk could be. A word as to Igraine brought him to his senses. He saw Gorlois, a dark-bearded, black-eyed man, with a frown that he did not like the look of. He began to shake in his slippers, to excuse himself, and to deny all knowledge of the girl since the morning. Matters were against Eudol. Gorlois thought that he had plucked the old man from hiding, and that he was a liar to the bone; his shrift was short, measured out by the man's hard malice. They struck him down at the door of his own barn, covering his grey head with his hands, and screaming for mercy. His blood soaked the hay, and shot black streaks into the dusty floor. Then they cast back to the manor, and half-throttled the woman Phœbe, till Gorlois was satisfied that he had got all the truth from her he could. In half an hour they were at gallop again for Sarum.

Gorlois reined in cruelly more than once to fling hot questions at the folk they passed upon the road. His horse was all sweat and foam, and its mouth bloody with the heavy hand that played on the bridle. Wayfarer after wayfarer looked up half in awe at the iron-faced man towering above them in the stirrups. Their blank, irresponsive faces chafed Gorlois's patience to the bone. Not a word did he win of Igraine and her grey gown. Waxing sullen as granite, and very silent, he looked neither to right nor left, but plodded on like a baffled sleuth-hound with the rest of the pack trailing at his tail. The girl's hair seemed tossing over the edge of the world, like a golden hue from the west, and there was a passionate wind through the man's moody thought.

It was towards evening when Gorlois with his men — a bunch of spears — came upon the peasant in the green smock driving his wain-load of faggots slowly towards the setting sun. Gorlois drew up and hailed him, and began his catechism anew. The fellow pulled in his team, and eyeing the horseman with some caution, acknowledged curtly that he had carried in his cart a league or more such a woman as Gorlois had pictured. To further quick queries he proved stubborn and boorish. Gorlois had lost his temper long ago. "Speak up, you devil's dog!"

The man looked sullen. Gorlois's sword flashed out. He spurred close up, and held three feet of menacing steel over the peasant's head.

"Well, you be damned!" he said.

"What want you with the woman, lording?"

"Am I to argue with a clod of clay? The woman is marked for great honour, and must be taken. Will you spoil her fortune?"

The man fingered the reins, looking hard at Gorlois with his stupidly honest face. He guessed he was some great lord, by his harness and his following. It was not for him to gainsay such a gentleman, especially when he flourished a naked sword.

"I would do my best for the good nun, lording," he said.

"Then speak out."

"She promised to pray for my woman."

Gorlois gave a laugh, and scoffed at the notion.

"Let prayers be," he said; "tell me where she went."

The man told Gorlois of the hermitage in the dale where Igraine had gone for a night's lodging. He described how the path could be found, a mile or more nearer Winchester. Gorlois threw a gold piece into the cart, and let the man drive on. Then he sat still on his black horse with his sword over his shoulder, and looked into the wood with dark, glooming eyes. For a minute he sat like a statue, staring on nothing in keen thought. His men watched him, looking for some swift swoop from such a pinnacle of pondering; they knew his temper. His sword shot back into its scabbard, and he was keen as a wolf.

"Galleas of Camelford."

A man with a hooked nose and high cheek bones heeled his horse forward, and saluted.

"Ride hard, find the hermitage, be wary, watch at a distance for sight of the Lady Igraine. If she is at the hermitage, gallop back to Sarum before nightfall. I shall be in Sir Accolon's house. Attend me there."

The man saluted again, turned his horse instanter, and rode hard into the east. Gorlois, with a half smile on his lips, rode on with his troop for Sarum.

In Sarum town there was a queer house of stone, very dark and very saturnine. It was hid away behind high walls, and hedged so blackly with yews and hollies that it seemed to stand in the gloom of a perpetual twilight. After dark a sullen glow often hung above the trees; casements would blaze blood-red light into boughs creaking and clutching in the wind; or there would be a moony glimmer on the glass, and belated folk passing near might hear voices or elvish music about them as though dropped from the stars. It was the house of Merlin,—the man of dreams,—wrapped in the gloom of immemorial yews.

That night Gorlois sat in a room hung with black velvet, where a brazier held a dying fire, and a bowl thereon steamed up perfumes in a heavy vapour. A man with a face of marble and eyes like an eternal night was chaired before him, with his long, lean, restless fingers continually touching the cloud of hair that fell blackly over his ears. His fingers were packed with rings gemmed with all manner of stones—jasper, sardonyx, chrysolite, emerald, ruby, and the like. His gown was of black velvet, twined all about with serpent scrolls of white cloth. On his breast was brooched a great diamond that blazed and wavered back the glow from the fire.

Gorlois sat in his carved chair stiff as any image. His strenuous soul seemed mewed up by the psychic influence of the man before him. He spoke seldom, and then only at the other's motion—at a curious gesture of one of those long, lean hands. The room was as silent as the burial hall of a pyramid, and it had the air of being massed above by stupendous depths of stone.

Presently the man in the black robe began to speak with deliberate intent, holding his voice deep in his throat so that it sounded much like the voice of an oracle declaring itself in the noise of a wind.

"The woman is beautiful beyond other women."

"Like a golden May."

"And true."

"As a sapphire."

"Yet will not have you."

"Not a shred of me."

The man with the rings smiled out of his impenetrable eyes, and fingered the brooch on his breast.

"The woman has great destiny before her."

"Ah!"

"I have seen her star in the night. You dare take her fate on you?"

"Like ivy holds a tree."

"As a wife?"

Gorlois laughed.

"How else?"

"As a wife — by the church."

"Ah!"

"Or no help of my hand."

Again there was silence. A coal fell in the brazier, and seemed like a rock down a precipice. The black eyes that stared down Gorlois were full of light, and strangely scintillant. Gorlois listened, with his limbs asleep and his brain in thrall, while the man spoke like a very Michael out of a cloud. The clear glittering plot given out of Merlin's lips came like a dream vivid to the thought of the dreamer. If Gorlois obeyed he should have his desire, and catch Igraine to a white marriage-bed by law and her own willing. The fire died down in the brazier, and the bowl ceased to smoke perfumes. Gorlois saw the man gather his black robe with his glittering fingers, and move like a wraith round the room, to stand beckoning by the door. In another minute Gorlois was under the stars, with the house and its yews a black mound against the sky. Like a sleeper half wakened he took full breath of the night air, and stretched his arms up above his head. But it was not to sleep that he passed back through the void streets to the house of the knight Accolon.

To return to Igraine housed for the night in the little hermitage. At the first creep of dawn, when daffodils were thrown up against the eastern sky, she left her pallet bed in the cell and went out into the hermit's garden. The recluse was down at the brook drawing water, whither the dog and the doves had followed him. Igraine passed through the garden — spun over as it was with webs of dew. To her comfort she found her ankle scarcely troubling her, for she had feared pain or stiffness after the walk of yesterday. Going down the dale, she patted the old dog's head, and picked up the pitcher as the recluse gave her good-morning.

"You are an early soul, sister. My dog and I come down to the brook each morning as the sun peeps over the hill."

"You are not lonely," said Igraine.

The old man tightened his girdle, looked over the solemn piers of the woods, sniffed the air, and hailed an autumn savour.

"Not I," he said. "I have my dog and my doves, and folk often lodge here, and I have word of the world and how the Saxons vex us. The good people near bring me alms and pittances, or come to ask prayers for their souls, and" — with a twinkle — "for their bodies, too."

Igraine remembered the peasant's little son.

"Was it you," she said, "who gave a peasant fellow near here a saint's dust to scatter over a sick child?"

The old man shook his head and smiled enigmatically.

"I have no dealings in such marvels," he said.

"The boy died."

"Of course."

"They will sell your dust some day."

A keen look, cynical with beaming scorn, spread over the man's gaunt face.

"Much good may it do them," he said; "death is monstrous flatterer of mere clay. I may feed a rose bush with my bones; a better fate than the cheating of superstitious women."

He made a sign with his hand, and the birds went wheeling in circles above him. The dog crept up and thrust his snout into the old man's palm. The garden lay above them, ripe with an autumn mellowness; yet there was no regret though winter would soon be piping, and the man's hair was grey.

"What think you of life?" said Igraine.

"You should know, sister, as well as I."

"But you see, father, I am not a nun,—only a novice."

He stared at her a moment with a slight smile.

"Remain a novice," he said.

"You advise me so!"

"Why subordinate your soul to chains forged of men."

"These seem strange words."

He patted his dog's head, and, half stooping, looked at her with keen grey eyes.

"Have you ever loved a man?"

"Yes," she said, with a clear laugh and a slight colour.

"Is he worthy?"

"I believe him a noble soul."

"Naturally."

"He ran away and left me because he thought I was a nun."

The hermit applauded.

"That sounds like honour," he said critically.

"I am seeking him to tell him the truth."

"And I will pray that you may soon meet," said the old man, "for there is nothing like the love of a good man for a clean maid. If I had married a true woman, I should never have taken to the scourge or the stone bed. Marry wisely and you are halfway to Heaven."

They broke fast that morning in the garden, it being the man's custom to make his meals on the granite slab that served him as a bed. The little dale looked very green and gracious in the tranquil light, with its curling brook and dark barriers of trees. Igraine, as she sat on the great stone and ate the hermit's bread, followed the brook with her thoughts, wondering whether it became the stream that ran through Eudol's meadows. She was for Sarum that day, where she would throw off her grey habit and take some dress more likely to baffle Gorlois. She had enough money in her purse. Worldling again, she could give herself to winning sight of this Uther, and to learning whether he was the Pelleas she sought or no.

As she sat and fingered her bread, something she saw down the dale made her rigid and still as a priestess smitten with the vision of a god in some heathen oratory. Her eyes were very wide, her lips open and very white, her whole air as of one watching in a sudden stupor of awe. Another moment and she had broken from the mood like a torrent from a cavern. With eyes suddenly amber bright, she touched the hermit's hand and pointed down the dale, gave him a word or so, then left him and ran down the hill.

A man on a black horse had ridden out from the trees, and was pushing his horse over the brook at a shallow spot not far away. His red armour glowed in the sun with a metallic lustre. Even at that distance Igraine had seen the red dragon rampant on a shield of green. As she ran down the grass slope she called the man by name, thinking to see him turn and come to her. Pushing on sullenly as though he had not heard the cry that went after him like winged love, he drew up the further slope without wavering, and sank like a red streak into the dense green of the trees.

X

IGRAINE forded the brook and followed the man by the winding path that curled away into the wood.

She was ever a sanguine soul, and the mere sinister influences that might have discouraged her in her purpose that morning were impotent before the level convictions of her heart. She had seen Pelleas ride in amid the trees; she was sure as death as to his cognizance and his armour. Now Pelleas, she could vow, had not heard her call to him, and if he had heard he had not understood; if he had seen he had not recognised. Doubts could have no place in the argument before such a justification by faith.

It was not long before she caught sight of the red glint of armour going through the trees. It came and went, grew and disappeared, as the path folded it in its curves or thrust out a heavy screen of green to hide it like a heavy curtain. The man was going as he pleased, now a walk, now a casual jog, now a short burst of a canter over an open patch. One moment Igraine would see him clearly, then not at all. Sometimes she gained, sometimes lost ground, yet the knight of the red harness never seemed to come within lure of her voice.

In due course she reached the place where the path ended bluntly on the Winchester high-road, and where the way ran straight as a spear-shaft, so that she could see Pelleas riding for Winchester with a lead of a quarter of a mile. The distant ringing tramp of hoofs came up to her like a mocking chuckle. Putting her hands to her mouth, she hallooed with all the breath left her by her run through the wood; yet, as far as she might see, the man never so much as turned in the saddle, while the smite of hoofs died down and down into a well of silence.

Another halloo and no echo.

"He's asleep, or deaf in his helmet."

She forgot the distance and the din of hoofs that might

well have drowned the thin cry that could have reached the rider. Maugre her heat and her flushed face Igraine had no more thought of giving in than she had of marrying Gorlois. With Pelleas so near she had made her vow to follow him, and follow him she would like a comet's tail. If needs be she would wear her sandals to the flesh, but catch the man she must in the end.

A mile more on the high-road, with her feet and the hem of her gown dust-drenched, and she was still little nearer the man in the red harness for all her hurrying. She could have vowed more than once that he turned in his saddle and looked back at her as though to see how near she had come to him on the road. A mile from the hermitage path he turned his horse southwards from the track into a grass valley headed by a ruined tower and hedged densely on either hand by pine woods. Igraine, seeing from a slight rise in the road this change of course, cut away crosswise with the notion of getting near the man or of intercepting him before he should win clear law again. After all, the effort added only more vexation. She saw the black horse pressed to a canter and cross the point where she might have cut him off, while a great stretch of furze that rolled away to the black palisading of the pines came down and threw a promontory in her path. Pelleas was a mile to the good when she had skirted the furze and the bend of the wood, and taken a straight course southwards down the valley between the pines.

All that morning the sport of hunter and hunted went on between the novice in grey and the man on the black horse. For all her trouble Igraine won little upon him, lost little as the hours went by; while the rider in turn seemed in no wise desirous of being rid of her for good. They passed the pine woods with their midnight aisles, forded a stream, climbed up a heath, went over it amid the heather. From the last ridge of the heath Igraine saw the country sloping away into undulating grasslands, piled here and there with domes of thicketed trees. Far to the south a dense black mass rose like a rounded hill against the sky. The man in red was still about a mile in front of her, riding slowly, a red speck in a waste of green. Igraine, having him in view from her vantage point, lay down full length to rest and take some food. She was tired enough, but dogged at heart as ever. She vowed that if the man was playing with her she would tell him her mind, love or no love, when she came up with him in the end.

As the sun swam into the noontide arc she went on again downhill, and found in turn that the man had halted, for he had been hidden by trees, and getting view of him suddenly she saw him sitting on a stone with his horse tethered near. As soon as Igraine was within measurable distance she took advantage of a hollow, dropped on her hands and knees, and began to crawl like a cat after a bird. Edging round a thicket she came quite near the man, but could not see his face. His spear stood in the ground by his horse, and he had his shield slung about his neck, and a bare poniard in his hand. It was clear that he was watching for Igraine, for despite her craft he caught sight of her face peering white under the hem of a bush, and climbed quickly into the saddle. Igraine started up, made a dash across the open, calling to him as she ran. Perverse as hate his horse broke into a canter and left her far in the rear. The girl shook her fist at him with a sudden burst of temper. She was standing near the stone where the man had been sitting. Looking at its flat face she saw the reason of the naked poniard in his hand, for he had been carving out thin straggling letters in the stone.

"Sancta Igraine," she read—

"Ora pro nobis."

The screed dispelled the doubts in Igraine's mind on the instant. Palpably the man knew well enough who was following him, and was avoiding her of set purpose; but for what reason Igraine racked her wit to discover. She ran through many things in her heart, the possible testing of her devotion, a vacillating weakness on Pelleas's part that would not let him leave her altogether, a freakish wish to give her penance. Then, she knew that he was superstitious, and the thought flashed to her that he might think her a wraith, or some evil spirit that had taken her shape to have him in temptation. Maugre her vexation and her pride she held again on the trail, eating as she went some dried plums that she had in her wallet. The man had slackened down again and was less than half a mile away, now limned against the sky, now folded into a hollow or shut out by trees. Like a marsh-fire he tantalised her with a mystery of distance, holding steadily south at a level tramp, while Igraine plodded after him, her hair down and blowing out to the casual wind, her eyes at gaze on the red lure in the van.

So the mellower half of the day passed, and towards evening they neared the mount of trees Igraine had seen from the last ridge of the heath at noon. The black horse was heading straight for the cloudy mass in a way that set Igraine thinking and casting about for Pelleas's motive. Perhaps he had some quest in the solitary place that needed his single hand. Would he take to the wood and let her follow as before, or had he any purpose in leading her thither? Drowned in conjecture she gave up prophecy with a vicious sense of mystification, and accepted inevitable ignorance for the time being as to the man's moods and motives. She was no less obstinate to follow him to the death. If she only had a horse she would come near the man, pride or no pride, and tell him the truth.

Pressing on, with her strained ankle beginning to limp, she topped the round back of a grass rise and came full in view of the wood she had long seen in the distance. It looked very solemn in the declining light. The great trunks of giant beeches were packed pillar upon pillar into an impenetrable gloom. The foliage above, densely green, billowy, touched with red and gold, rolled upwards cloud on cloud as the ground ascended to the south and east.

A great bronze carpet of dead leaves swept away into the night of the trees. There was an eternal hush, a gross silence, over the glooming aisles that seemed to beckon to the soul, to draw the heart into the night of foliage as into a cavern. Over all was the glowing ægis of the setting sun.

Igraine saw the man on the forest's edge where an arch of gloom struck into the inner shadows. He was facing the west, motionless as stone on his black horse, with the slanting light plucking a dull red gleam from his harness. There was a mystery about him that seemed to harmonise with the stillness of the trees and the black yawn of the forest galleries. Igraine imagined that he might be in a mood at last to speak with her if he believed her human. At all events, if he took to the trees, and she did not lose him, she would have the vantage of him and his horse in such a barricaded place.

It began to grow dark very quickly as she passed down the gradual slope towards the forest. The trees towered above her, a black mass rising again towards the east. Keen to see the man's mood, she hurried on and found him still steadfast in the great arch, that seemed like the gate of the wilderness, ready to abide her. A hundred paces more and her heart began to beat the faster, and the moil of the day's march dwindled before the influx of a rosier idyl. Every step towards Pelleas seemed to take her higher up the turret stair of love till her lips should meet those that bent at last from the gloom to hers. Pride and vexation lay fallen far below, dropped incontinently like a ragged cloak; a more generous passion shone out like cloth of gold; she was no longer weary. Her eyes were very bright, her face full of a splendid wistfulness, as she neared the man under the trees, looking up to see his face.

Twilight lay deep violet under the wooelshawe, while horse and man were dim and impalpable, great shadows of themselves. Igraine could not see the man's face for the mask over the mezail of his helmet, and he was silent as death. She was quite close to him now and ready to speak his name, when he wheeled suddenly, looked back at her, and pointed into the wood with his long spear. She ran forward and would have taken hold of his bridle, but he waved her back and slanted his spear at her in mute warning. Igraine, heart-hungry, could hold herself no longer.

"Man — man, are you stone?"

He rode straight ahead into the night of the trees and said never a word. Igraine drew her breath.

"Pelleas."

"Ah, Igraine."

The voice that came to her was muffled like the voice of a mourner, yet the girl thought she caught the old deep tone of it like the low cry of the wind.

"Why do you vex me?"

"Follow!"

"Pelleas, Pelleas, I am no nun!"

"Follow!"

"I kept this truth from you too long."

"Follow!"

"Pelleas, would you hurt my heart more?"

"Follow; God shall make all plain and good."

She gave in with a half-sob, and bent quietly to the man's mood, though she had no notion what he purposed in his heart, or what his desires were in mystifying her thus. No doubt it would be well in the end if Pelleas bade her follow like a penitent and promised ultimate peace. At least he had not turned her away, and she trusted him to the death. He was a strong, deep-sensed soul, she knew, and her deceiving may have made him bitter in measure, and not easily appeased. In this queer trial of endurance, this tempting of her temper, she thought she read a penance laid upon her by the man for the way she had used his love.

They were soon far into the wood, with the western sky dwindling between the innumerable pillars of the trees. It began to be dark and utterly silent save for the rustle of the dead leaves as they went, and the shrilling chafe of bridle or scabbard, or the snort of the great horse. Wherever the eye turned the forest piers stood straight and solemn as the columns in a hypostyle hall in some Egyptian temple. The fretwork of boughs roofed them in with hardly a glimmering through of the darkening sky above. There was a pungent autumn scent on the air that seemed to rise like the incense of years that had fallen to decay on the brown flooring of the place, and there was no breath or vestige of a wind.

Presently as the day died the wood went black as the winter night, and Igraine kept close by the man, with his armour giving a dull gleam now and again to guide her. They were passing up what seemed to be a great arcade cut through the very heart of the wood, as though leading to some shrine or altar, relic of Druid days, or times yet more antique. The tunnel ran a curved course, bending deeper and deeper as it went into the dense horde of trees. So dark was the wood that it was possible to see but a few paces in advance, and Igraine wondered how the man kept the track. She was close at his stirrup now, with the dark mass of him and his horse rising above her like a statue in black basalt. Though he never spoke to her, and though she touched no part of him, his horse, or his harness, she felt content with the queer sense of trust and proximity that pervaded her. There was magic in the mere companionship. As she had humbled her will to Pelleas's the night when he had taken her from the beech tree in Andredswold, so now in like fashion she surrendered pride and liberty, and became a child.

Suddenly the trackway straightened out into a great colonnade that ran due south between trees of yet vaster girth. Igraine felt the man rein in and abide motionless beside her as she held to the stirrup and waited for what next should chance. Silence seemed like depths of black water over them, and they could hear each other take breath like the faint flux and reflux of a sea. Igraine saw the man lift his spear, a dim streak less black than the vault above, and hold it as a sign for her to listen. Her blood began to tingle a very little. There was something far away on the dead, stagnant air, a sort of swirl of sound, shrill and harmonious, like a wind playing through the strings of a harp. It was very gradual, very impalpable. As the volume of it grew it seemed to rush nearer like a wind, to swell into a swaying plaintive song smitten through with the wounded cry of flutes. It gave a notion of wood-fays dancing, of whirling wings and flitting gossamer moonbright in the shadows. Igraine's blood seemed to spin the faster, and her hand left the stirrup and touched the man's thigh. He gave never a word or sign in the dark. She spoke to him very softly, very meekly.

"What place is this, Pelleas?"

She saw him bend slightly in the saddle.

"It is called the Ghost Forest," he said.

"What are the sounds we hear?"

"Who can tell!"

Igraine had hardly heard him, when a streak of phosphor light flickered among the trees, coming and going incessantly as the great trunks intervened. It neared them in gradual fashion, and then blazed out sudden into the open aisle, a man in armour riding on a great white horse, his harness white as the moon, his face pale and wide-eyed, his hair like a mass of twisted silver wire. A misty glow haloed him round, and though he rode close there seemed no sound at all to mark his passing. As he had come, so he went, with streaks of flickering light that waxed less and less frequent till they died in the dark, and left the place empty as before. Igraine thought the air cold when he had gone.

She felt the black horse move beside her, and they went on as before into the night of the trees. The noise of flute and harp that had ceased awhile bubbled up again quite near, so that it was no longer the ghost of a sound, but noise more definite, more discrete. It had a queer way of dying to a sighing breath, and then gathering gradually into an ascending burst of windy melody. Igraine could almost fancy that she heard the sweep of wings, the soft thrill of silks trailing through the trees, yet the man on the horse said never a word as they went on like a pair of mutes to a grave.

The colonnade opened out abruptly on a great circular clearing in the wood shut in by crowded trunks, its open vault above cut by a dense ring of foliage. A grey light came down from the sky, showing great stones piled one upon another, others fallen and sunk deep in rank grass and brambles. The man halted his horse in the very centre of the clearing, with Igraine beside him, watchful for what should happen, and for the moment when Pelleas should unbend.

Hardly had she looked over the great cromlechs, black and sinister in that solitary wilderness, than the whole wood about them seemed dusted suddenly with points of fire. North, south, east, and west torches and cressets came jerking redly out of the night, flitting behind the trees in a wide circle, gathering nearer and nearer without a sound. They might have been great fireflies playing through the aisles and ways, or goblin lamps carried by fairy folk. Igraine drew very close to the man's horse for comfort, and looked up to see his face, but found it dark and hidden. Her hand crept up past the horse's neck, rested on the mane a moment, and ventured yet further to meet the man's hand, where it gripped the bridle. For a minute they abode thus without a sound, watching the weird torch-dance in the wood.

With a sudden gibber of laughter and a swirl of pipes the throng of lights seemed to seethe to the very margin of the clearing. Queer phantastic shapes showed amid the trees, and the great circle grew wide with light, and the grey cromlechs surprised in sleep by the glare and piping. At that very moment Igraine had a thought of some one looking deep into her eyes, of a will, a power, streaming in upon her like sunlight into a sleepy pool. Her desire went from the man on the black horse into the square shadow of the great central cromlech, where an indefinite influence seemed to lurk. Looking long under the roofing stone, she grew aware of a tall something standing there, of a pair of eyes like the eyes of a panther, of a lean white hand moving in the shadows.

The eyes under the cromlech seemed to follow Igraine like fire, and to burn in upon her a foreign influence. Rebellious and wondering, she stiffened herself against a spiritual combat that seemed moving upon her out of the dark. She could have smitten the eyes that stared her down, and yet the magnetic stupor of them kindled up things in her heart that were strange and newly sensuous. She felt her strength sway as though her soul were being lifted from her, and she was warmed from top to toe like one who has taken wine, and whose being swims into an idyllic glorification of the senses. Again her desire seemed turned to the man in red harness, yet when she looked the saddle was empty, and the horse held by an armed servant, who wore a wolf's head for covering. Still mute with fear, desire, and wonder, she saw a tall figure move into the full glare of the torches, a figure in red harness with a shield of green, and a red dragon thereon, and with head unhelmed. The armour was like the armour of Pelleas, but the face was the face of the man Gorlois.

And now the eyes under the shadow of the cromlech were full and strong upon Igraine. Breathing fast with a hand at her throat she stepped back from Gorlois—hesitated—stood still. She was very white, and her eyes were big and sightless like the eyes of one walking in a dream. For all her strength, her scorn, and the tricking of her heart, she was being swept like a cloud into the embraces of the sun. Reason, power, love, sank away and became as nothing. A shudder passed over her. Presently her hands dropped limp as broken wings, and her body began to sway like a tall lily in a breeze. A gradual stupor saw her cataleptic; she stood impotent, played upon by the promptings of another soul.

Gorlois went near to her with hands outstretched, stooping to look into her face. A sudden light kindled in her eyes, her lips parted, and new life flooded red into her cheeks as at the beck of love. She bent to Gorlois full of a gracious eagerness, a wistful desire that made her face golden as dawn. Her hand sought his, while the shadowy shape under the cromlech watched them with never-wavering eyes. Gorlois's arms were round her now all wreathed in her hair; her face was turned to his; her hands were clasped upon his neck. Another moment and he had touched her lips with his.

A sound of flutes, the tinkling of a bell, and a solemn company came threading from the trees, guests, acolytes, torch-bearers, in glittering cloth of gold, with a great crucifix to lead them. Gorlois and Igraine were hand in hand near the stone that hid the frame of Merlin. A priest in a gorgeous cape drew near, and began his patter. The vows were taken, the pact sealed, with the noise of a chant and music. Thus under the benedictions of the great trees, and the spell of Merlin, Gorlois and Igraine were made man and wife.

BOOK III

THE WAR IN WALES

I

Aurelius Ambrosius the king was dead, taken off in Winchester by the hand of a poisoner. He had been found stark and cold in his great carved bed, with an empty winecup beside him, and a tress of black hair and a tress of yellow laid twined together upon his lips. The signet-ring had gone from his finger, and by the bed had been discovered a woman's embroidered shoe dropped under the folds of the purple quilt. The truth, sinister enough in its bare suggestions, was glossed over by the court folk out of honour to Aurelius, and of love to Uther the king's brother. It was told to the country how an Irish monk sent by Pascentius, dead Vortigern's son, had gained audience of the king, and treacherously poisoned him as he drank wine at supper. The tale went out to the world, and was believed of many with a sincere and honest faith. Yet a certain child-eyed woman, wandering on the shores of Wales for sight of Irish ships, could have spoken more of the truth had she so dared.

Uther Pendragon had been hailed king at York before the bristling spears of a victorious host. But a week before he had marched against the heathen on the Humber, and overthrown them with such slaughter as had not been seen in Britain since the days when Boadicea smote the Romans. At the head of his men he had marched south in a snowstorm to be thundered into Winchester as king and conqueror. Twelve maidens of noble blood, clad in ermine and minever, had run before him with boughs of mistletoe and bay. Five hundred knights had walked bareheaded, with swords drawn, behind his horse. The city had glistened in a white web of frosted samite, sparkled over by the clear visage of a winter sun.

There were many great labours ready to the king's hand. Britain lay bruised by the onslaughts of the barbarians; her monks had been slain, her churches desecrated. The pirate ships swept the seas, and poured torch and sword along the sunny shores of the south. Andredswold, dark, saturnine, mysterious, alone waved them back with the sepulchral threatening of its trees. Yet, for all the burden of the kingdom upon his broad shoulders, Uther gave his first care to the honouring of the dead. Aurelius Ambrosius was buried with great pomp of churchmen and nobles at Stonehenge, and a royal mound raised above the tomb. At Christmastide, with snow upon the ground, a great gathering was made at Sarum of all the petty kings, princes, and nobles of the land. Hither came Meliograunt, king of Cornwall, and Urience of the land of Gore. Fealty was sworn with solemn ordinance to Uther Pendragon the king, and common league bonded against the heathen and the whelps of the north.

There were other perils brewing for Britain over the sea. Pascentius, dead Vortigern's son, had been an outcast and a wanderer since the days when the sons of Constantine had sailed from Armorica to save the land from the blind lust and treason of his father. He had been a drifting fire beyond the seas, an intriguer, a sower of sedition, a man dangerous alike to friend and foe. Beaten like a vulture from the coasts of Britain, he had turned with treasonable hope to Ireland and its king, Gilomannius the Black, a strenuous potentate, boasting little love for Ambrosius the king. Here, in Ireland, a kennel of sedition had arisen. Pascentius, keen, hungry plotter, had toiled at the task of piling enmity against those who had destroyed his father amid the flames of Genorium. A great league arose, a banding of the barbarians with the Irish princes, a union of the Saxons who ravaged Kent with the wild tribesmen over the northern border. Month by month a great host gathered on the Irish coast. Many ships came from the east and from the south. Mid-winter was past before Gilomannius embarked, and, setting sail with a fair wind, turned the beaks of his galleys for the shores of Wales.

Noise of the gathering storm had been brought to Uther as he journed through the southern coasts, rebuilding the churches, recovering abbey and hermitage from their desolate ashes. His zeal was great for God, and his love of Britain well-nigh as noble. Warned thus in due season, he marched for the west, calling the land to arms, assigning for the gathering of the host Caerleon upon Usk, that fair city bosomed in the fulness of its woods and pastures. Many a knight had answered to his call; many a city had sent out her companies; the high-roads rang with the cry of steel in the crisp winter weather.

Duke Gorlois had come from Cornwall from his castle of Tintagel, bringing many knights and men-at-arms by sea, and the Lady Igraine his wife, in a great galley whose bulwarks glistened with shields. In Caerleon Gorlois had a house built of white stone, set upon a little hill in the centre of the city. To Caerleon he brought this golden falcon of a woman, this untamable thing that he had kept prisoned in the high towers of Tintagel. He mewed her up like a nun in his house of white stone, so that no man should see the fairness of her face. She was wild as an eyas from the woods, fierce and unapproachable, and sharp of claw. Robbed of her liberty, had she not sought to take her own life with a sword, and to throw herself from the battlements of Tintagel? Gorlois had won little love by Merlin's subtlety, and he feared the woman's beauty and the spell of her large eyes.

It was the month of February and clear crisp weather. The white bellies of the Irish sails had shown up against the grey blue stretch of the sea, a white multitude of canvas that had sent the herdsmen hurrying their flocks to the mountains. Horsemen had galloped for Caerleon, and the cry of war went up over wood and water. Flames licked the night sky. From Caerleon to St. Davids, from St. Davids to Eryri, the red blaze of beacon-fires told of the ships at sea.

The cry of the storm arose in Caerleon, and the tramp of armed men sounded all day in her streets. The great host lodged about the city broke camp and streamed westwards along the high-road into Wales. Bugles blew, banners flapped, masses of sullen steel rolled away into purple of the winter woods. Bristling spears and lines of skin-clad shields vanished into the west like the waves of a solemn sea. On the walls of Caerleon stood many women and children watching the host march for the west, watching Uther the king ride out with his great company of knights and nobles.

At the casement of an upper room in Gorlois's house stood a woman looking out over Caerleon towards the sea. She was clad in a mantle of furs, and in a tunic of purple linked up with cord of gold. A tippet of white fur clasped with a brooch of amethysts circled her throat. Her hair was bound up in a net of fine silk, and there was a girdle of blue silk about her loins, and an enamelled cross upon her bosom. She stood with her elbows resting on the stone sill, and her peevish face clasped between her hands. Her eyes looked very large and lustrous as she stared out wistfully over the city.

In the great court below horses champed the bit and struck fire from the ringing flags. Men in armour clanged to and fro; rough voices cried questions and counter-questions; bridles jingled; spear-shafts clattered on the stones. Now a clarion blared as a troop of horse thundered by up the street, their armour gleaming dully past the courtyard gate. The growl of war hung heavy over Caerleon, a grim sullen sound that seemed in keeping with the restless chiding of the wind.

Igraine's face was hard as stone as she watched the men moving in the courtyard below. She looked older than of yore, whiter, thinner in cheek and neck, her great eyes staunch though sad under her netted hair. Her face showed melancholy mingled with a constant scorn that had rarely found expression with her in the old days, save within the walls of Avangel. She looked like one who had endured much, suffered much, yet lost no whit of pride in the trial. Though she may have been blemished like a Greek vase smitten by some barbaric sword, she was her self still, brave, headstrong, resolute as ever. The shame of the things she had suffered had perhaps wiped out the gentler outlines of her character and left her more stern, more wary, less honest, more deep in her endeavours. There was no passive humility or patience about her soul, and she was the falcon still, though caged and guarded beyond her liberty.

As she stood at the casement with the prophetic murmur of war in her ears, it seemed to her as though life surged to her feet and mocked her bondage like laughing water. The desire of liberty abode ever with her even to the welcoming of stagnant death. She thirsted for her freedom, plotted for it, dreamt of it with a zeal that was almost ferocious. Her life seemed a speculation, a perpetual aspiration after a state that still eluded her. In the Avangel days she had been wild and petulant. Then Pelleas had come through the green gloom of early summer to soften her soul and inspire all the best breath of the woman in her. Again, thanks to Gorlois, she had fallen with the usual reaction of circumstance upon evil times; the change had discovered the peevish discontent of the girl hardened into the strong wilfulness of the woman.

She hated Gorlois with a fanatical immensity of soul. When the man was near her she felt full of the creeping nausea of a great loathing, and she waxed faint with hate at the veriest touch of his hands. His breath seemed to her more unsavoury than the miasma of a gutter, and it needed but the sound of his voice to bring all her baser passions braying and yelping against him. He had driven the religious instinct out of her heart, and she was in revolt against heaven and the marriage pact forged by the authority of the Church. She had often vowed in her heart that she could do no sin against Gorlois, her husband. He had no claim upon her conscience. The bondage had been of his making; let God judge her if she scorned his honour.

Standing by the window watching the knights saddling for their lord's sally, she heard heavy footsteps mounting up the stairs, and the ring of steel-tipped shoes along the gallery. The footsteps were deliberate, and none too fast, as though the man walked under a burden of thought. A shadow seemed to pass over Igraine's face. She slipped from the window, ran across the room, shot the bolt of the door, and stood listening. A hand tried the latch. She knew well enough whose fist it was that rattled on the oaken panels. Her face hardened to a kind of cold malevolence, and she laughed noiselessly in her sleeve.

A terse summons came to her from the gallery.

"Wife, we ride at once."

The man could not have made a worse beginning. There was a suggestion of tyranny in a particular word that was hardly temperate. Igraine leant against the door; she was still smiling to herself, and her hands fingered the embroidered tassel of the latch.

"We are late on the road; I can make no tarrying."

The door quivered a moment as though shaken by a gusty wind. Everything was quiet again, and Igraine could hear the man breathing. Putting her mouth to the crack between post and hinge-board she laughed stridently as though in scorn.

"Igraine!"

The voice was half-imperative, half-appealing.

"My very dear lord!"

"Are you abed?"

"No, dear lord."

"Open to me; I would kiss your lips before I sally."

"You have never kissed me these many days."

"True, wife; is it fault of mine?"

"Nor shall again, dear lord, if I have strength."

She heard the man muttering to himself a moment, but this time there was no smiting of the door, no fume and tempest. His mood seemed more temperate, less masterful, as though he were half heavy at heart.

"Igraine — "

"Why do you whimper like a dog?" she said; "go, get you to war. What are you to me?"

"When will you learn reason?"

"When you are dead, sire."

"Perhaps I deserve all this."

"Are you so much a penitent?"

Her mockery seemed to lift Gorlois to a higher range of passion, and there was great bitterness in his voice as he tossed back words to her with a quick kindling of desire.

"Woman, I have been hard in the winning of you, but, God knows, you are something to me."

"God knows, Gorlois, I hate you."

His hand shook the door.

"Let me in, Igraine."

"Break down the door; you shall come at me no other way."

"Woman, woman, I am a fool; my heart smarts at leaving you."

"You sound almost saintly."

"I have left Brastias in charge of you."

"Thanks, lord, for a jailer."

Igraine drew back from the door and stood at her full height with her hands crossed upon her bosom. She quivered as she stood with the intense effort of her hate. Gorlois still waited without the door, though she could not hear him moving. The silence seemed like the deep hush that falls between the blustering stanzas of a storm.

"Igraine!"

It was a hoarse cry, quick and querulous. Igraine had both her fists to her chin in an attitude of inward effort, as though she racked herself to give utterance to the implacable temper of her scorn. Her face had a queer parched look. When she spoke, her voice was shrill like a piping wind.

"Gorlois."

"Wife."

"Would you have my blessing?"

"Give it me, Igraine."

"Go then, and look not to me for comfort. When you are in battle, and the swords cry on your shield, I shall pray on my knees that you may get your death."

Gorlois gave never a sound as he stood by the barred door with his hand over the mezail of his helmet. It seemed dark and gloomy in the gallery, and the staunch oak fronted him like fate. His eyes were full of a dull light as he turned and went clanging down the stairway with slow, heavy tread. His sounding footsteps died down into the din of arms that came from the great court. Igraine ran to the window and watched him and his men ride out, smiling a bleak smile as the last mailed figure gleamed out by the gate.

II

When Gorlois and his knights had gone, Igraine unbarred the door, and passed down the narrow stair to the state chamber of the house, where a fire was burning. It was a solemn room, shadowed with many arches, with vaults inlaid with marble, its walls painted green and gold, its glimmering casements lozenged with fine glass. Furs were spread upon the mosaic floor; painted urns held flowers that bloomed in the mock summer of the room.

Igraine stood and warmed herself before the fire. From an altar-like pillar near she took storax and galbanum from brazen bowls, and scattered the resinous tears upon the flames. A pungent fragrance rose up into her nostrils. The flicker of the fire played upon her face, and set a lustre in her eyes. It was winter weather, and the warmth was welcome.

The refrain of her talk with Gorlois still ran at fever heat like a wild song through her brain. She was stirred to the deeps of her strong soul. For Gorlois she had no measure of pity. He was a rotten tree to her, a slab of granite, anything but quick flesh and blood capable of aspiration and desire. She hated him more for his pleading than for his tyranny, fearing to be pleased by one she dreaded. He was strenuous and obstinate. She knew that it would be great joy to her if she saw his face no more, and if his body crumbled in the rain on some bleak coast in Wales.

As she stood by the fire and looked into it with pondering eyes she heard a curtain drawn and the sound of a footstep on the threshold. Turning briskly, like one accustomed to suspicions, she saw the man Brastias in the doorway looking at her half-furtively, as though none too proud of the office thrust upon him. He had great grey eyes and a calm face. Bending stiffly to Igraine with his hand over his heart, he turned aside to a cabinet by the wall, took therefrom an illumined scroll of legendary tales, and sat down on a bench to read, as though he had no other business in the room.

Igraine's long lip curled. She knew the meaning of the man's presence there shrewdly enough. Going to a window she opened the casement frame and looked out on the winter scene. Usk winding silver to the sea, the purple roll of the bleak bare woods, the far sea itself dying a sullen streak into a sullen sky. It was dreary enough, and yet it suited her; she could have welcomed thunder and the rend of forked fire above the woods. Thought was fierce in her with the wind crying about the house like a wistful voice, the voice of days long dead.

To be free of Gorlois!

To cast off her present self like a rotten cloak!

To adventure liberty, though the peril were shrill as the wind through the swaying pines on the hillside!

To deal with Brastias!

Now Brastias was a grave-faced knight, neither young nor old, but a very boy in the matter of the mock wisdom of the world. He was possessed of one of those generous natures that looks kindly on humanity with a simple optimism born of a contented conscience. He was a devout man, a soldier, and a gentleman. Moreover, he owned a holy reverence for women, a reverence that led him into a somewhat extravagant belief in the sincerity of their truth and virtue. He was blessed too in being nothing of a cynic in his conceptions of honour.

Gorlois knew the man to the heart, and trusted him, a fact well proven by the faith imposed upon him in his wardenship of the Lady Igraine. Brastias hated the task as much as he hated the telling of a lie. There are some men whose whole instinct is towards truth. They are golden souls, often too easily deceived with a gross dross that makes an outward show of kindred colour.

Brastias was no stranger to Igraine, for he had served her as one of the knights of the guard in the great castle of Tintagel. He was a man who could look into a woman's eyes and make her feel instinctively the clear honour of his soul. There was nothing of the flesh about Brastias. And it was in this chivalrous faith of his that Igraine discovered a credulity that might make him prone to believe a certain profession of faith that was taking sudden and subtle form within her mind. Months ago, she would have hesitated before the man's grey eyes. But feeling herself sinned against, and stirred by the shame of the past, she found ample justification for herself in the lie Gorlois had practised for her undoing.

She left the window, and went and stood by the fire, with her back to the man.

"Brastias," she said, quite softly.

The man looked up from the scroll, and seemed ill at ease.

"I trust your duty is pleasant to you?"

Brastias's eyelids flickered nervously, and he cleared his throat.

"May the Virgin witness," he said, "I have no love of the task."

"My Lord Gorlois trusts you?"

"He has said so, madame."

"And am I not his wife?"

Brastias put the scroll aside with a constrained deliberation. He felt himself wholly in the wrong, as he always did before a woman, and his wit ran clumsily on such occasions. It had needed but the observation of a child to mark the gulf between Gorlois and his wife. Gorlois had spoken few words on the matter, had given commands and nothing more. Brastias was not the man to tamper officiously with the confidences of others. He thought much, said little, and bided quiet for Igraine to speak.

She stood half-turned towards the fire, with her face in profile, and her hands hanging limply at her side. Looking for all the world like a penitent, she spoke with a certain unconscious pathos, as though she touched on a matter that was heavy upon her heart.

"Brastias, I may call you a friend?"

"I trust so, madame."

"Then there is no reason for me to be backward in speaking of the truth?"

The man bowed and said nothing.

"Come then, Brastias, tell me honestly, have I seemed to you like a woman who loved her husband?"

The girl's blue eyes were staring hard into the man's grey ones. There was little chance of prevarication before so blunt a question, and Brastias's courtesy, like Balaam's ass, refused to deny the scrutiny of truth. Igraine could read the man's face like a piece of blazened parchment.

"Never fear to be frank," she said; "your belief hangs on your face like an alphabet, and that shows me how much you know of a woman's heart."

"Pardon me, madame."

"Never blush, man, you would have said that I had as little love for Gorlois as for the dirtiest beggar in Caerleon?"

Brastias frowned mildly and agreed with her, remembering as he did a certain wild scene on the battlements of Tintagel.

"And doubtless you would say that it pained me not a whit to see Gorlois my lord ride out from Caerleon into the wilds of Wales?"

There was such reproach in her voice that Brastias fell into confusion before her eyes, reddened, and began to excuse himself.

"Your ladyship's behaviour," he said, with an ingenuous look and an intense striving after propitiation,—"your ladyship's behaviour would hardly warrant me in believing that my Lord Gorlois was vastly dear to you. And, pardon me, a woman does not seek to run away from her husband."

"You insinuate—"

Brastias felt himself in the mire, and groaned in spirit.

"Madame, I would say—"

"Yes, yes, I understand you."

"Give me leave—"

"Not another word."

Igraine smiled softly to herself, turned her back on Brastias and stared long into the fire. The man stood by, watching her with a humbled look, his fingers twisting restlessly at the broidery of his black tunic. Igraine traced out the mosaic patterns on the floor with the point of her shoe.

"I think you men are all fools," she said.

Brastias's silence might have suggested contradiction.

"Have you ever loved a woman?"

The man shifted, and went red under his straight fair hair. His eyes took a dreamy look.

"Yes," he said, as though half-ashamed.

Igraine hung her head and sighed.

"Perhaps," she said, growing suddenly shy and out of countenance, "perhaps you may have learnt the lesson of the froward heart, the heart that comes by love when it is in peril of great loss."

Brastias drew a quick, deep breath.

"By the Virgin, that's true," he said.

Igraine turned to the fire and hid her face from the man. There was a pathetic droop about her shoulders, a listless curving of her neck, that made Brastias picture her as burdened with some immoderate sorrow. He was an impressionable man, not in any amorous sense, but in the matter of sympathy towards his fellows. He thought he heard a catch in the girl's breathing that boded tears. Her hair looked very soft and lustrous as it curved over her ears and neck.

"Madame Igraine."

No answer. Brastias went a step nearer.

"Listen to me."

A slight turning of the head in response.

"What ails you, madame?"

"Never trouble."

"I beseech you, tell me."

The man was quite afire; his face looked bright and eager, and his eyes shone.

"Gorlois has gone to the war."

The words were jerked out one by one.

"Madame!"

"War — and death."

"Courage, madame, courage. On my soul, you are not going to say —"

"Brastias, you understand."

"Then?"

"Man, man, don't drag it out of me; don't you see? are you blind?"

Brastias invoked a certain saint by the name of Christopher, and straightway emphasised his words by falling down on his knees beside Igraine. She had contrived to conjure up tears as she bent over the fire. Brastias found one of her hands and held it.

"This will be my lord's salvation."

"Think you so?"

"On my soul, my dear lady, I thank our Lord Jesu from my heart. For I know my Lord Gorlois, and the bitterness that weighed him down, though he spoke little to me on this matter, being staunch to you, and to his courtesy. And by our Lord's Passion, madame, I love peace in a house, and quiet looks, and words like laughing water, for there is never a home where temper rules."

"Brastias, you shame me."

"God forbid, dear lady, there's no gospel vanity in my heart. I speak but out."

The man's quaint outburst of gladness touched Igraine's honesty to the core, but she had no thought of recantation, for all the pricking of her conscience. She passed back to the open window and leant against the mullion, while Brastias rose from his knees and followed her.

"I am faint," she said, "and the fresh wind comforts me."

"Courage, madame; Duke Gorlois fights for Britain and the Cross; what better blessing on his shield?"

Igraine was looking out toward the sea and the grey curtain of the sky cut in places by dark woods and the sweep of dull green hills. There was a wistful droop about her figure that made Brastias molten with intent to comfort, and dumb with words of sympathy that died inarticulate in his throat. He stood there, a man muzzled by his own sincerity, bankrupt of a syllable, though he commanded his wit to be nimble with stentorian cry of conscience. He felt hot in his skin and vastly stupid. By the time he had lumbered up some passable fancy, Igraine had turned from the window with a quick intelligence kindling in her eyes.

"Brastias."

"Madame."

"Listen to me, I have come by a plan."

A sudden flood of sunlight streamed through a rent in the grey canopy of clouds. The landscape took a warmer tinge, the purple of the woods deepened. Brastias saw the sudden gleam of light strike on Igraine's hair. Her head was thrown back upon her splendid neck, and her eyes seemed large with love.

"I will show Gorlois how I love him," she said.

Brastias's face was still hazed in conjecture.

"I will wipe out the past."

"Ah!"

"We will follow Gorlois to the war, you and I, Brastias, together. What say you to that?"

The man looked at her with clear grey eyes, and with a transient immobility of feature that changed swiftly to a glow of understanding. The words had gone home to him like a trumpet-cry; their courage warmed him, and he was carried with the wind.

"A great hazard—and a noble," he said, with a flush of colour; "the peril is on my neck, and yet—I'll bear it."

Igraine's face blazed.

"Brastias, you will go with me?"

"By my sword, to the death."

"Come hither, man; I must kiss your forehead."

Brastias knelt to her again with crossed hands. She looked into his grey eyes and touched his forehead with her lips.

"Thus I salute honour," she said.

"My lord's lady!"

"You have trusted me."

"Else had I been ashamed."

The man went away to arm, warm at heart as any boy. Igraine stood a moment looking into the fire with an enigmatic calm upon her face. For Brastias she felt a throttled pity, an impossible admiration that only troubled her. Her lust for liberty bore her like a storm-wind, and her hate of Gorlois made her iron at heart. She could dare anything to fling off the moral bondage that cramped and bound her like a net.

While Brastias was away arming and ordering horses, she went to a little armoury on the stairs and filched away a short hauberk and a sheathed poniard. She wore these under a gown of black velvet bound with a silver girdle, and a cloak of sables hooded and lined with sky-blue cloth. She had a strange joy of the knife at her girdle as she passed down the stairway to the court.

A few silent servants gaped at her as she passed from the house. Brastias came out to her in armour. In the court she heard the cry of steel bridles, the sparking of hoofs on the stones. They were soon mounted and away under the great gate and free of Caerleon in the decline of the day. The west had no colour, and a wind pined in the trees as they swept into the twining shadows of the woods, and saw the boughs clutch each other against the sullen sky. Soon night came in a black cowl, and with a winter wind that roamed the woods like the moan of a prophecy. Igraine, riding with her bridle linked in that of Brastias, pressed on for the west with a mood that echoed the roar of the trees.

III

A MAN in black armour, a lady in a cloak of sables, a pine forest under a winter sky.

Myriad trunks interminably pillared, grey-black below, changing to red beneath the canopy of boughs; patches of grey-blue sky between; a floor overgrown with whortleberry and heather, and streaked seldom by the sun. Through the tree-tops the veriest sighing of a wind, a sound that crept up the curling galleries like the softly-taken breath of a sleeping world. Away on every hand oblivious vistas black under multitudinous green spires.

The woman's face seemed white under the sweep of her sable hood. Its expression was very purposeful, its mouth firm and resolute, its air indicative of a deliberate will. Her eyes stared into the wood over her horse's head with a constant care, dropping now and again a quick side-glance at the man in black armour riding on her flank. She spoke seldom to him, and then with a certain assumption of authority that seemed to trouble his equanimity but little. Often she would lean forward in the saddle as though to listen, her eyes fixed, her mouth decisive, her hand hollowed at her ear to concavitate some sound other than the wind-song of the trees. It was evident that she was under the spell of some strong emotion, for she would smile and frown by turns as though vexed by perpetual alternatives of feeling.

The man at her side watched with his grey eyes the path curling uphill between the trees. Having his own inward exposition of the woman's mood, he contented himself wisely with silence, keeping his reflections to himself. He was not a man who blurted commonplaces when lacking the means of inspiration. And he was satisfied with the fancy that he understood completely the things that were passing through the woman's mind. He believed her troubled by those extreme anxieties of the heart that come with war and the handiwork of the sword. Perhaps he was fortunate in being ignorant of the truth.

The interminable trees seemed to vex the woman's spirit as their trunks crowded the winding track and shut the pair in as with a never-ending barrier. But for an occasional patch of heathland or scrub, no lengthy vista opened up before them. Tree-boles stood everywhere to baulk their vision, silent and stiff like sullen sentinels. The horses plodded on. Igraine's impatience could be read upon her face, and discovered in her slighter gestures. It was the impatience of a mind at war within itself, a mind prone through the chafe of trouble to be vexed with trifles; sore, sensitive, and hasty. Brastias watched her, pretending to be intent the while on the path that wandered away into the mazes of the wood. He was a considerate creature, and he suffered her petulance with a placid good-humour, and a certain benevolence that was the outcome of pity.

Igraine jerked her bridle, and eyed the trees as though they were the members of a mob thrusting themselves between her and her purpose. She was inclined to be unreasonable, as only a woman can be on occasions. Brastias, calm-faced and debonair, contented himself with sympathy, and refrained from reason as from the handling of a whip.

"That peasant fellow was a liar," he said, by way of being companionable.

"Yes, the whelp."

"I'll swear we've ridden two leagues, not one."

"The fellow should have a stripe for every furlong."

"Rough justice, madame."

Igraine laughed.

"If justice were done to liars," she said, "the world would be hideless, scourged raw."

Brastias edged his horse past an intruding tree and chuckled amiably.

"It would be a pity to spoil so much beauty."

"Eh!"

"The women would come off worst."

Igraine flashed a look at him.

"Balaam's ass spoke the truth," she said.

They had not gone another furlong when Brastias reined in suddenly and stood listening. He held up a hand to Igraine, looking at her with prophetic face, his black armour lustreless under the trees.

"Hark!"

Igraine stared into his eyes. Neither moved a muscle for fully a minute.

"A trumpet-cry!"

Brastias lowered his hand.

"From the host. And the 'advance,' by the sound on't."

"Then we shall be out of the woods soon."

"Go warily, madame; it would be poor wisdom to stumble on an Irish legion."

"Brastias, I would not miss the day for a year in heaven."

As they pushed uphill through the solemn shadows of the forest, a sound like the raging of a wind through a wood came down to them faintly from afar. It was a sullen sound, deep and mysterious as the hoarse babel of the sea, smitten through with the shrill scream of trumpets like the cry of gulls above a storm. In the alleys of the pine forest it was still as death, and calm beneath the beniscus of the tall trees.

Igraine and Brastias looked meaningly at each other as they rode. The sound needed no words to christen it. The two under the trees knew that they heard the roar of host breaking upon host, the cataractine thunder of a distant battle.

Pushing on as fast as the forest suffered, the din became more definite, more human, more sinister in detail. It stirred the blood, challenged the courage, racked conjecture with the infinite chaos it portended. Victory and despair were trammelled up together in its sullen roar; life and death seemed to swell it with the wind-sound of their wings; it was stupendous, sonorous, chaotic, a tempest-cry of steel and many voices merged into the grand underchant of war.

Igraine's face kindled to the sound like the face of a girl who hears her lover's lute at night under her window. Blood fled to her brain with the wild strength of the strain humming like a wind through the trees. She was in the mood for war; the tragedy of it solemnised her spirit, and made her look for the innumerable flash of arms, the rolling march of a multitude. For the moment it was life, and the glorious strength of it; death and the dust were hid from sight.

Yet another furlong and the red trunks dwindled, and the sombre boughs fringed great tracts of blue, and to the north mountains rose up dim and purple under an umbrage of clouds. To the west the sea appeared solemn and foamless, set with pine-spired aisles, and a great company of ships at anchor. Nigh the shore the grey pile of a walled town stood out upon green meadows. Igraine and the man pushed past the outlying thickets, and drew rein upon a slope that ran gradually down from them like the great swell of a sea.

Tented by the dome of the sky lay a natural amphitheatre, shelving towards the sea, but rising in the east by rolling slopes to a ridge that joined the mountains with the forest. The valley was a medley of waste land, scrub, gorse, and thicket, traversed by the white streak of a road, and closed on the west by the grey walls of the town rising up above the green. It was a wild spot enough. However still and solitary it may have seemed in its native desertedness, however much the haunt of the wolf and the boar, it seethed now like a cauldron with the boiling stir of battle. Men swarmed through scrub and thicket; masses of steel moved hither and thither, met, mingled, broke, and rallied. Wave rushed on wave. Bodies of horsemen smoked over the open with flashing of many colours and the glittering pomp of mail, to roll with clanging trumpets into some vortex of death. The whole scene was one shifting mass of steel and strife, dust and disorder, galloping squadrons, rolling spears, rank on rank of shields a-flicker in the sun. And from this whirlpool of humanity rose the dull grinding roar of war, fierce, stupendous, clamorous, grand.

To the trained eye of the soldier the chaos took orderly and intelligent meaning, and Brastias stood in his stirrups and pointed out to Igraine the main ordering of the hosts. Uther Pendragon held the eastern ridge with his knights and levies; Gilomannius and Pascentius thrust up at him from the sea; while the valley between held the wreck of the countercharges of either host, and formed debatable ground where troop ran against troop, and man against man.

The masses of Uther's army swept away along the ridge, their arms glittering over the green slopes, their banners and surcoats colouring the height into a terraced garden of war, the whole, a solemn streak of gold against the blue bosoms of the hills. To the north stood Meliograunt with his levies from Wales, and next him Duke Eldol and King Nentres headed the men of Flavia Cæsariensis. South of all the great banner of Tintagel showed where Gorlois and the southern levies reared up their spears like a larch-wood in winter. Brastias pointed them all out to the girl in turn, keeping keen watch the while on the shifting mob of mail in the valley.

Igraine, stirred by the scene, urged on from the forest, and the knight following her, they crossed some open scrubland, wound through a thicket of pines, and stood at gaze under the boughs. Igraine's eyes were all the while turned on the banner of Tintagel, and from the common mob of mailed figures she could isolate a knight in gilded harness on a white horse, Gorlois, her husband. The mere sight of him set her hate blazing in her heart, and seemed to pageant out all the ills she had suffered at his hands. Her feud against the man was a veritable insanity, a species of melancholia that wrapped all existence in the morbid twilight of self-centred bitterness. As she looked down upon the host there was a kind of overmastering madness of malice on her face, an emotion whose very intensity paled her to the lips, and made her eyes hard and scintillant as crystal. She was discreet for all her violence of soul. Turning to Brastias, who was scanning the valley under his hand, she pointed to the banner with a restless eagerness of manner that might have hinted at her solicitude for Gorlois, her lord.

"See yonder," she said, "is not that the Lord Gorlois on the white horse by yonder standard?"

Brastias turned his glance thither, considered for a moment, and then agreed decisively.

"Love is quick of eye," he said with a smile.

"Let us ride down nearer."

"I care not for the hazard, madame."

"Who fears at such a season?"

"By my sword, madame, not your servant; I am but careful of your safety."

"Fear for me, Brastias, when I fear for myself."

"Methinks, madame, that would be never."

"Brastias, I believe you."

Igraine's courage had risen to too high an imperiousness

for the moment to brook baffling or to endure restraint. She had been lifted out of herself, as it were, by the storm-cry of battle, and by the splendour of the scene spread out before her eyes. A furlong or more down the hillside a little hillock stood up amid a few wind-twisted thorns, proffering rare vantage for outlook over wood and dale. She was away like a flash, and several lengths ahead before Brastias had roused up, put spur to horse, and cantered after her. The man saw the glint of her horse's hinder hoofs spurning the sod, and though the wind whistled about his ears, he was left well in the rear for all his spurring. Igraine, with her hair agleam under her tossed-back hood, and her cheeks ruddied by the wind, headed for the rising ground at a gallop, gained it, and drew rein on the very verge of a small cliff that dropped sheer to the flat below. The hillock was like a natural pulpit, its front face a perpendicular some twenty feet high, while its hinder slope tailed off to merge into the hillside. Gorlois's mailed masses stood but a hundred paces away, and Igraine could see him clearly in his gilded harness under the banner of Tintagel.

Brastias galloped up to her with a mild bluster of expostulation.

"You court danger, madame."

"What if I do, Brastias, to be near my lord."

"Your sanctity lies upon my conscience."

"I take all such care from you."

"Madame, that is impossible; duty is duty both night and day, in battle and in peace; duty bids me fear for my lord's wife."

Igraine found certain logic invincible in the argument, and made good use of it; she meant to rule Brastias for her own ends.

"Fear," she said; "I forget fear when I am nigh Gorlois, my husband; and who can gainsay me the right of watching over him? I forget fear when I think of Britain, the king, and my lord, and had I a hundred lives I could cast them down to help to break the heathen, and serve my country."

"Amen," said Brastias, signing the cross upon his breast.

Sterner interests quashed any further polite bickerings that might have risen from Igraine's pride of purpose, for Brastias, with the instinct of a soldier, marked some large development in the struggle that had been passing in the valley below them. The scattered lines of horse and foot that had been thrown forward by Uther to try the strength and spirit of the Irish host, were falling back sullenly uphill before the masses of attack poured up from the flats by Gilomannius the king. The whole battle had shifted to the east. Bodies of horse were spurring uphill, driving in Uther's men, cutting down stragglers, harrowing the slopes for the solid march of the black columns of foot that were creeping up between the thickets, winding like giant dragons amid furze and scrub. It was a grand sight enough, the advance of a great host, a rocking sea of spears pouring up in the lull that had fallen over the valley as though the battle took breath and waited. Uther's men kept their ground upon the ridge, watching in silence the advance of Gilomannius's chivalry. Only a brief wild cry of trumpets betokened the gathering of the waves of war.

Even at this juncture Brastias racked his wit and courtesy to persuade Gorlois's lady to fall back and watch from the shelter of the woods. He pointed out her peril to Igraine, besought, argued, cajoled, threatened. All he gained was a blunt but half-smiling declaration from the woman that she would hold to her post on the hillock till the battle was over, or some mischance drove her from the place. Brastias caught her bridle, spurred round, and tried to drag her back by main force, but she was out of the saddle instanter, and obstinate as ever. In the end the man capitulated, and gave his concern to the fortunes of war.

The sudden uproar that sounded out along the hillside made mere individual need dull and impossible for the moment. The shock of the joining of the hosts had come like the fall of snow from a mountain — a sound sweeping down the valley, echoing among the silent fastnesses of the hills. Men had come pike to pike, shield to shield, upon the ridge. Mass rushed upon mass, billow upon billow. From the mountains to the forest the sweat and thunder of strife rolled up from the long line of leaping steel, from the living barrier, steady as a cliff. It was one of the many Marathons of the world where barbarism clawed at the antique fabric of the past.

Igraine's glance was stayed on Gorlois and the southern levies about the banner of Tintagel. Her hate surged up the green slope with the onrush of the Irish horde, and brandished on the charge in spirit towards the tall figure in the harness of gold. She saw Gorlois in the press smiting right and left with the long sweep of his sword. In her thirst for his destruction she grudged him strength, harness, sword, the very shield he bore. She was glad of his courage, for such would militate against him. Moment by moment her desire honoured him with death as she thought him doomed to fall beneath the surge of steel.

A sudden shout from Brastias brought her stare from this chaos of swords. The man was standing in his stirrups, and pointing to the west with his face dead white and his mouth agape.

"By God, look!"

Truth to tell, there was little need of the warning. A dull rumble of hoofs came up like thunder above the shriller din around. Igraine, looking to the west, saw a black mass of horsemen at the gallop, swaying, surging, rocking uphill full for Gorlois's flank. The sight numbed her reason for the moment. She was still as stone as the column swept past the very foot of the hillock — a flood of steel — and plunged headlong upon Gorlois's lines, hewing and trampling to the very banner of Tintagel. An oath from Brastias made her turn and look at him. He had his hand on his sword, and his face was twisted into a snarl of wrath and shame as he stood in his stirrups and watched the fight.

"My God!" he cried, "my God! they run."

It was palpable enough that the southern line was breaking and crumbling ominously before the rush of Gilomannius's knights. Little bunches of men were breaking away from the main mass like smoke, and falling back over the ridge. Igraine guessed at Brastias's pride and fury, saw her chance of liberty, and took it. She set up a shrill cry that stirred his courage like a trumpet-cry.

"My Lord, my Lord Gorlois, Brastias, what of him?"

The man's sword had flashed out.

"Send me to death, lady, only to strike a blow for Britain."

Igraine spread her hands to him like a Madonna, and made the sign of the cross in the air. Brastias lifted up his drawn sword, kissed it, and saluted her with the look of a hero. Then he wheeled his horse, plunged down from the hillock, and rode full gallop into the battle. Igraine soon lost sight of his black harness in the mêlée, and since he met his death there, she saw Brastias alive no more.

Despite the grim uproar of the overthrow, despite the taunts of a patriot pride, there was an under-current of gladness through her thought as she watched Gorlois's men giving ground upon the ridge. Her lord's shame was her gratification. To such a pitch of passion was she tuned that she could find laughter for the occasion, and a shrill cry of joy that startled even her own ears when the banner of Tintagel quivered and went down into the dust. Men were falling like leaves in autumn, and the southern wing of Uther's host seemed but a rabble — trampled, overridden, herded, and smitten over the ridge. Everywhere the swords and spears of Gilomannius's knights and gallowglasses spread rout and panic, while the wavering mass gave ground, rallied, gave again, and streamed away in flight over the hillside. She could see no sign of Gorlois, and with a whimper of hate the strong doubt of his escaping the slaughter took hold on her heart, and found ready welcome there. She was rid of Brastias — good fellow that he was — and though she honoured him, she loved liberty better. Liberty enough! Gorlois her lord had been slain. Such were her reflections for the moment.

Pendragon's host seemed threatened with overthrow. The southern wing had been driven off the field by a charge of horse; Gilomannius held the southern portion of the ridge, and pressed hard on Meliograunt, both flank and face. The imminent need of Britain was plain enough even to Igraine, yet a sense of calm and liberty had come upon her like the song of birds or the gush of green in springtide. Even her patriotism seemed dim and unreal for the moment before the treasonable gratitude that watched the overthrow of Gorlois's arms. She was alone at last, solitary among thousands, able after the bitterness of past months to pluck peace from the very carnage of battle. Trouble had so wrought upon her mind that it seemed a negation of all probable and natural sentiment, a contradiction of the ethical principles of sense.

The day was fast passing, and the grand fires of a winter sunset were rolling all the caverns of the west into a blaze of gold and scarlet. The pine forest, black and inscrutable as night, stood with its spines like ebony to the fringe of the west, while the slanting light lit the glimmering masses of steel on hill and valley with a web of gold. To the north the mountains towered in a mystery of purple, a gleam of amber transient on their peaks.

Sudden and shrill came a cry of trumpets from the hills, a sinister sound that seemed to issue in the climax of the last phase of a tragedy. Igraine's eyes were turned northwards to the green slopes of the higher ground where the great banner of the Golden Dragon had flapped over Uther the King. Here a great company of knights, the flower of the host, had stood inactive throughout the day. With a cry of trumpets this splendid company had moved down to charge the masses of Gilomannius's men, who now filled the shallow valley east of the ridge, and threatened King Meliograunt and the whole host with overthrow. Uther had ridden out to lead the charge with his own sword. It was one of those perilous hours when some great deed was needed to grapple victory from defeat.

The rest of the scene seemed blotted out as Igraine watched from her hillock the glittering mass rolling downhill with the evening sun striking flame from its thousand points of steel. On over the green slopes, past the pavilions of the camp, it gathered like a wave lifting its crest against a rock, on towards the swarm of men squandered in pursuit of Gorlois's broken line, on to where Gilomannius formed his knights for the charge. The green space dwindled and dwindled with the rush and roar of the nearing gallop. Igraine saw the rabble of Saxons, light-armed kerns and Irish gallowglasses, split and crack like a crumbling wall. For a short breath the black mass held, with Uther's storm of mail cleaving cracks and wedges in it — streaks of tawny colour like lava through the vineyards and gardens of a village. Then as by magic the whole mass seemed to deliquesce, to melt, to become as mist. All visible was a thunderstorm of horsemen tearing like wind through a film of rain with scattering fringes of cloud scudding swiftly to the west. The knights had passed the valley and were riding up the slope, hewing, trampling, crushing, as they came. Gilomannius's columns that had pushed Gorlois's men into rout had become a rabble in turn — wrecked, scattered to the wind, trodden down in blood and dust. They were streaming away in flight over the ridge, scampering for scrub and thicket, no lust in them save the lust of life. Igraine saw them racing past on every quarter, a blood-specked, dust-covered herd, their hairy faces panting for the west and the ships on the beach. Not a hundred paces away came the line of trampling hoofs and swinging swords, a demoniac whirlwind of iron wrath that hunted, slew, and gave no quarter.

Beyond the summit of the ridge, and all about the hillock where Igraine stood, the glittering horde of knights came to a halt with a great shout of triumph. Right beneath Igraine and the straight face of the hillock a man in red armour on a black horse, with a golden dragon on his helmet, stood out some paces before the ranks of the splendid company. A great cry rolled up, a forest of swords shook in the sun. The knight on the black horse stood in his stirrups, and with sword and helmet upstretched in either hand lifted his face to the red triumph fire of the west. Igraine knew him — Pelleas, Uther, the King.

IV

THE sun had rolled back between the pylons of the west. Night was in the sky, night in her winter austerity — keen, clear, aglitter with stars as though her robe were spangled with cosmic frost. The mountains' rugged heads were dark to the heavens, and the sea lay a faintly glimmering plain open to the beck of the moon.

The Irish host had broken and fled at sunset before Uther's charge and the streaming spears of Eldol and King Nentres. The green meadows, the wild scrubland, had been chequered over with the black swarm of the flying soldiery; the whole valley had surged with swords and the sound of the slaughter. By the grey walls of the town it had beleaguered, the driven host had turned and rallied in despair to stave off to the last the implacable doom that poured down from the hills. It was the vain effort of a desperate cause. Broken and scattered like dust along a highway, there had been no hope left them but their ships. The battle had ended in the very foam of the breaking waves. Crag and cliff, rock-citadel and yellow sand, had had their meed of blood and the shrill sound of the sword. The great ships had saved but a remnant, and had put out to sea in the dusk, their white sails like huge ghosts treading the swell of the twilight waters. Yet with night there had come no ceasing of the carnage. Despair had turned to front victory; Irish gallowglass and heathen churl, forsaken by their ships and hemmed in by sea and sword, had fought on to the end, finding and knowing no mercy. Gilomannius the King and Pascentius were dead, and the blood of invasion poured out like water.

Now it was night, and in the clear passionless light of the moon a figure in a cloak of sables moved towards the mound where Gorlois of Cornwall had flown his banner early in the day's battle. Everywhere the dead lay piled like sheaves in a cornfield, their harness glinting with a ghastly lustre to the moon — piled in all attitudes and postures, staring blankly with white faces to the sky, or prone with their lips in blood, contorted, twisted, clutching at throat and weapon, mouths agape or clenched into a grin, man piled on man, barbarian upon Briton. Dark quags chequered the grass with the sickly odour of shed blood, and sword and spear, shield and helmet, flickered impotently among the dead.

Igraine went among the bodies like a black monk seeking some still quick enough to be shriven before their souls took flight from the riven clay. Her cloak was gathered jealously about her as she threaded her way among the huddled figures, peering under helmets, scanning harness narrowly in her death-inspired quest. Casting hither and thither in the moonlight, she came to a tangled bank of furze, and beyond it a low hillock that seemed piled and paved with the bodies of the slain. Here had stood the banner of Tintagel, and here the prowess of Gorlois's household knights had fallen before the charge of Gilomannius's chivalry. Igraine saw the medley of mail, the dead horses, jumbled figures, wreck of shield and spear rising out above her in the moonlight, cloaked with a silence grim and irrefutable, as though Death himself sat sentinel on the pyramid of carnage. Half shuddering at the sight like an aspen, for all the intent that was in her heart, she drew near, determined and resolved to search the mound. Compelled to climb over the dead and to set her foot on the breasts and shoulders of the slain, her tread lighted more than once on a body that squirmed like a dying snake. Strong to do the uttermost after that day of revelation she struggled on, loathing the task, her shoes clammy with the blood-sweat of death. On the summit of the mound she came upon Gorlois's white horse lying dead by the wreathing folds of the fallen banner of his house.

A whimper of joy came up into Igraine's heart. Sinister as the sign seemed, she was soon searching the mound with an alert desire in her eyes that prophesied no vestige of pity for the thing for which she sought. Hunt as she would, and she was marvellously patient over the gruesome business, no glint of Gorlois's golden harness flattered her hate as she searched the mound. Many a good knight lay there, some that she had known at Tintagel, and hated because they served her husband, but of Gorlois she found no trace. As a last hope, she dragged aside the great standard and found a dead man there sheeted in its folds, a man in black armour with his face to the sky — Brastias, who had ridden with her from Caerleon.

She stood a moment looking down at him with a sudden feeling of awe such as had not come upon her through all that day. A white face lay turned to the sky, — a face that had looked kindly into hers with a level trust, — and smiled with a wealth of manly sympathy. It was a simple thing enough, nothing but one death among many thousands, but it touched Igraine to the core, and made her ashamed of the lies she had given him. She found herself wondering like a child whether Brastias was in heaven, and whether he watched her and her thoughts with his calm grey eyes. The notion disquieted her. She bent down, took his naked sword from his hand, and shrouded him again in the gorgeous blazonry of the flag for which he had died, and so left him with a sigh.

As she climbed back again from the mound, a gashed and clotted face heaved up and stared at her from a heap of slain. It was the face of a man who had struggled up on his hands to look at her with mouth agape, dazed after a sudden waking from the stupor of a swoon. For a moment in the moonlight she thought it was Gorlois by certain likeness of feature, but discovered her error when the man spoke to her in gibberish she did not understand. He began to crawl towards her with a certain air of menace that made her start back and rear up the sword she had taken from dead Brastias. The threat of steel proved needless enough, for the man dropped again with a wet groan, and seemed dead when she went and bent over him with thoughts of succour.

Passing back again to her hillock, she stood there brooding and looking out towards the west. A great bell in the town by the sea was pulsing heavily as though for the dead, and there were many cressets flaring on the walls, and torches going to and fro in the meadows. The sound of a triumph hymn chanted by hundreds of deep voices floated up like a prayer from the western meadows.

At the sound Igraine's eyes were strangely full of tears. By some strange echoing of the mind the idyls of past days woke like the song of birds after a storm of rain. Clear in the dusk she seemed to see the red figure on the black horse, his face lit like a god's by the slanting light from the west as he stretched his sword to heaven. Again the scene changed, and she saw him riding through the flowering meads of Andredswold, looking down on her with a grave and luminous pity. She was glad of him, glad of his great glory, glad that he had kissed her lips, and bewrayed the love to her that was in his heart. The scene and the occasion were strange enough for such broodings, yet her eyes were very dim as she stood in a half-dream and let the picture drift across her mind.

The revelation had come upon her with such suddenness that she had been for the moment like one dazed. She had watched Uther sweep on with his horde of knights, and had stood mute and impotent as one smitten dumb while the red harness and the golden dragon of Britain vanished again into the moil of war. Now her whole soul yearned out with a wistfulness born of infinite regret. If he had only come to her alone; if he had only come to her as Pelleas in some gloom of green, she could have fallen down before his horse's feet, kissed the scabbard of his sword, wept over his helmet, and burnished it with her hair. Sight of that dark sad face had made a beacon of her on the instant.

And Gorlois! If she had hated him yesterday, she hated him with a tenfold vigour since she had looked again upon Pelleas's face. Certainly her malice had grown with an Antæan strength with each humbling of her heart to the dust, and the very thought of Gorlois seemed blasphemy against her soul at such an hour.

With the memory of Gorlois a cloud dulled the clear mirror of her mind, and her mood of dreams melted into mist. The strong sense of bondage, of ineffectual treason, came back with a fuller force as though to menace her with the fateful realism of her lot. A hand seemed to sweep down and wave her back with a meaning so sinister that even her hate stood still a moment as in sudden fear; she had some such feeling as of standing on the brink of a mysterious sea whose waves sang to her a song of peril, of misery and desire cooped up together in the dim green twilight of some coral dungeon. The lure of the unknown beat upon her eyes, while love and hate, like attendant spirits, beckoned her over the yawn of an open grave.

For the moment the importunity of her immediate need drew her from meditations alike bitter and divine. A battlefield after dark, with all its lust and pillage, was no pleasant place for a woman. The lights of the town still showed up brightly in the west, but Igraine had little desire of the teeming streets where victory would be matching blood with wine, and where the revels of the soldiery would celebrate the day in primal fashion. She was content to be alone under the stars, and even the dead seemed more sympathetic than the living at such an hour.

A wind had risen, and she heard the hoarse "salvé" of the

forest in the night. The thousand voices of the trees seemed to call to her with a weird perpetual clamour. She saw their spectral hands jerking and clutching against the sky, and heard the creak and gibber of the criss-cross boughs swaying in the wind. Leaving the hillock, and still bearing Brastias's sword, she held across the open, seeing as she went the dark streaks that dotted the hillside — the bodies of men fallen in the flight. She gained the trees, and was soon deep among the crowded trunks, pondering on her lodging for the night.

Wandering hither and thither, looking for some more sheltered spot, her glance lighted on a dim swelling of the ground that proved to be an ancient mound or barrow. It had been opened in times past, probably in the search for buried treasure or for weapons. Brambles, weeds, and heather had roofed the shallow cutting into a little recess or cave that gave fair shelter from the wind, and Igraine, braving the notion of barrow ghost or spirit, claimed the place as a God-send, and took cover therein.

The last crumbs in her wallet finished, she sat with her face between her palms, brooding, big-eyed, in the night, like any Druidess wreathing spells in her forest solitude. The wind was crying through the trees, swaying them restlessly against the starry sky, making plaintive moan through all the myriad aisles. Igraine listened like one huddled among her thoughts to keep out the cold. Miserable as was her lodging, her mind seemed packed with the day's battle; the whirl and thunder of it were still moving in her brain, a wild scene towered over by a man bareheaded on a black horse, holding his helmet to the setting sun. Often and often she heard the roar of hoofs and saw the rush of the charge that had trampled the banner of Tintagel and hurled Gorlois and his men in rout from the ridge. Had it been death or life with the man? Was he with the King hearing holy mass and lifting up the wine cup to heaven under a flare of lights, or lying stiff and pinched under the mild eyes of night? It was this thought, holding hope and doubt in common yoke, that abode with her all the night in her refuge under the trees.

It was bleak enough, with a silvering of frost over the land, when darkness had rolled back over the western sea, uncovering the wreck of death that lay huddled on ridge and slope. Igraine was stirring early from the barrow. With the cold and her own thoughts she had slept but an hour, and at the first filtering of light through the branches she was glad and ready for the day. She wandered through the forest towards the open land that showed glimmering through the tree-boles, with no certain purpose moving in her mind. The future as yet was a blank to her, lacking possibilities, jealous of its secrets, saturnine as death itself. There shone one light above her that seemed to burn through the unknown; it had long led her from distant hills, yet even her red lamp of love beckoned her over a sepulchre.

Coming to the forest margin, she came full upon the incontestable handiwork of war. Under the sweep of a great pine lay the body of a knight in black harness, all blazoned with gold, while his grey horse was still standing with infinite patience by his side, nosing him gently from time to time. The man's helmet, a visored casque, somewhat gladiatorial in type, had fallen off, and a young beardless face was turned placidly up to the blue, a white oval pillowed upon a tuft of heather. There was no blood or sign of violence visible save a blue bruise on his left temple; it seemed more than probable that he had been pitched from the saddle and found death in the fall.

Igraine stood and looked at him in some pity while the horse snuffed at her, staring with great wistful eyes as though for help or sympathy. The man was young, with a certain nobility of early manhood on his face, and it seemed to her very pitiful that he should be cut off thus in life's spring. As she looked at him she noted that he was slim of figure, and not much above middle height. A sudden fancy took her on the instant. She tethered the horse, and kneeling down by the man her fingers were soon busy at the buckles and joints of his armour. Ungirding his sword, she drew it from the scabbard and set it upright at his head, sheathing Brastias's in its place. Having stripped off his armour and long surcoat she covered him reverently with her cloak, slung the horse's bridle round her wrist, and gathering up his arms and helmet went back to the barrow where she had passed the night.

The wood had received a woman in the dress of a woman; it gave in exchange a knight on a grey horse — a knight in black armour blazoned with gold under a surcoat of violet cloth. The brazen helmet, visored and hooded with mail over nape of neck and throat, gleamed and flashed under the green boughs. There were three lilies, snow-white, and a cloven heart upon the shield, and the horse trappings were bossed and enamelled gold and blue.

Igraine rode out from the trees with the pomp of a Launcelot. The grey horse's mane tossed in the wind, the furze rippled on the hillside, the cloud-ships sailed the blue with white sails spread. The girl was aglow with new life under her guise of steel. The essence of manhood seemed to have created itself within her as from the soul of the dead knight, and she suffered the glory of arms with a pride that was almost boyish.

Holding out from the trees at a solemn pace, she headed westward down the valley along the grass slopes that slid between scrub and thicket to the sea. On the road below her a company of spears trailed eastward uphill in a snake-like column that glittered through the green. Pushing on boldly across ground where the battle had raged hotly the night before, she reached the road as the head of the column swung up at a dull tramp on their march home for Caerleon. Gruffing her voice in her throat she hailed the knight who headed the troop for news of the battle of yesterday, posing as one late on the scene, and sore at having struck no blow for Britain.

The knight drew aside, and letting his men tramp by,

he gave tersely the tale of the fight as he had seen it from King Nentres's lines.

"St. Jude be blessed," said Igraine at the end thereof. "I am glad, friend, of these tidings. As for the field, it looks to have been as bloody a one as ever I set eyes on."

"Bloody enough," quoth the man, giving his moustache a twirl; "too bloody for Gilomannius and dead Vortigern's whelp."

"What of Uther?"

"Scarce a scratch."

"King Meliograunt?"

"Wounded, but drunk as the devil."

"And Gorlois of Cornwall?"

The man laughed as at a jest.

"Bedded in an abbey," said he, "with a split face; mere flesh, mere flesh, nothing deeper."

Igraine thanked him with her helm adroop, and turning her horse, rode back towards the forest heavy of heart.

V

THE King's house at Caerleon stood out above the Usk on a little hill whose slopes were set with shrubberies and gardens, the white pillars and broad façade glimmering above the filmy cloud of green that covered the place as with a garment. A great stairway ran to the river from the southern terrace that blazed in summer with flower-filled urns and stacks of roses that overspread the balustrade with crimson flame. It was a place of dawns and sunsets; of lights rising amber in the east over purple hills and amethystine waters; of quiet glows at evening in the west, with cypresses and yews carven in ebony against primrose skies; while in the burgeoning of the year birds made the thickets deep with melody; and all beyond, Caerleon's solemn towers, roofs, casements bowered in green, rested within the battlemented walls that touched the domes and leaf-spires of the woods.

It was noontide in Caerleon, and down the great stairway, with its rows of cypresses, its banks of yew and myrtle, a fair company was passing to the river, where many barges clustered round the water-gate like gilded beetles sunning their flanks in the shallows. Knights and churchmen in groups moved down from the palace talking together as they went. There had been a council of state in the King's hall, a great assembling of the noble folk and prelatry, to consider the need of Britain, the cry of the martyred and the homeless from Kentlands and the east. Anderida, that great city of the southern shores, had fallen in a tempest of fire and sword; no single soul had escaped from its smoking walls; the barbarian had entered in and made great silence over the whole city. Now it was told that more galleys had come bearing the fair-haired churls from the sand-dunes and pinewoods, the rude hamlets of that Angle land over the sea. Vectis had been overrun, Porchester burnt to the ground, even the noble city of Winchester threatened despite its walls. Beast and robber had sole rule in Andredswold; much of nether Britain was a wilderness, a wistful land given over to solitude and the wild creatures of the forest. Churches were crumbling; gillyflowers grew on the high altars, and ivy wrapped the tombs; sanctuary bells were silent, homes empty and still as death. Desolation threatened the south, while the valleys of Armorica oversea gave refuge to many who fled before the Saxon sword.

In the great hall of the palace Uther still sat in his chair of ivory under a gilded roof that mingled huge beams with banners, spears, and rust-rotted harness. The walls were frescoed with Homeric scenes — Helen meeting Paris in the house of Menelaus, Achilles slaying Hector, Ulysses and Calypso. Twelve painted pillars held the crossbeams of the hall, and from the fire on the great hearth a fragrant scent of burning cedar wood drifted upon the air. A long table covered with parchment, tablets, quills and inkhorns, and an array of empty benches testified to the number of noble folk who had assembled at the royal conclave. A single councillor remained before the King—Dubricius, Bishop of Caerleon, a tall spare man, whose white hair and sensitive ascetic face bore testimony to an inward delicacy of soul.

Uther was clad in a tunic of scarlet, with a dragon in gold thread blazoned upon his breast. No crown, coronet, or fillet was on his brow; on his finger he wore the signet of Ambrosius, and his sword was girded to him with a girdle of embroidered leather. His look was much the same as when he rode as Pelleas in Andredswold and was nursed of his wound by Igraine in the island manor. Possibly there were more lines upon his face, a deeper dignity of sadness in his eyes. Circumstance had put upon him the cherishing of an imperilled kingdom, and with the charge his natural stateliness of soul had risen into a heroism of benignant chivalry. No more kingly man could have taken a land under the strong sweep of his sword. With the grand simplicity of a great heart he had grappled the task as a thing given of God, bending ever in prayer like a child before the inscrutable wisdom of heaven.

There had been grave business on his mind that day, and his face was dark with a cloud of care as he talked with Dubricius on certain matters that lay near his heart. Uther, like the men of old time, was superstitious and ever prone to regard all phenomena as possessing certain testamentary authority from the Deity. In mediæval fashion he referred all human riddles to religious instinct for their solving, and searched in holy writ for guidance with a faith that was typical of his character. Wholly a Christian in a superstitious sense, he gained from the very fervour of his belief a strength that seemed to justify his very bigotry.

It was a certain experience, that to his mystic-loving instinct omened history still dark in the womb of the future, and kept him closeted with Dubricius that day after knight and churchman had filed out from the conclave. In the twilight of the hall, with its painted frescoes and glimmering shields, Dubricius listened to the King as he spoke of portents and visions of the night. Uther, with his elbow resting on the arm of his chair and his chin upon his palm, stared at the cedar wood burning pungently upon the hearth and catechised Dubricius on visionary belief. The old man looked keenly at the King under his arched white brows. He was as much a mystic in his creed as this son of Constantine, a believer in miracles and in manifestations in the heavens. Certainly unusual powers had been given to the early Church, and it was not for the atomic mind of man to deny their presence in any later age.

"My lord dreamed a dream," said Dubricius tentatively when he had heard the tale to the end.

Uther quashed the suggestion with the calm confidence of a man sure of his reason.

"Never a dream, Dubricius."

The old man's eyes were very bright, and his face seemed full of a luminous sanctity.

"A vision, then, my lord?"

"I am no woman, Dubricius; I must believe the thing a vision, or damn my senses."

"My lord, it is no mere woman's part to see visions; search holy writ where the chosen of God — the great ones — were miraculously blessed with portent and with dream."

Uther looked into the old man's face as though for succour.

"I am troubled to know what God would have me know," he said. "Dubricius, you are aged in the service of the Church!"

"My lord, I have no privilege from heaven in the rendering of dreams."

"Am I then a Pharaoh disappointed of mine own soothsayers?"

"Sire, what of Merlin?"

"Merlin — "

"The man has the gift of prophecy and can speak with

tongues. Send for him, my lord; he is a child of the Church, though a mage."

Uther warmed himself before the fire of cedar wood, his face motionless in contemplative calm. Presently he turned, and looked deep into Dubricius's vigil-hollowed eyes as though to read the thoughts therein.

"Merlin, the black-haired man who told Vortigern of the future!"

"He spoke the truth, my lord."

"Sad truth for Vortigern."

"Yet who should fear the truth?"

"Dubricius, to hear of death!"

"Death, my lord?"

"Remember Vortigern."

"My lord, he was a planet lurid with murder, and so damned to darkness. Need the sun fear light?"

Uther smiled sadly in the old man's face.

"You are too faithful a courtier, Dubricius."

"My lord, you are the pillar of a distraught land; God be merciful and spare you to us."

"I have done my duty."

"Amen, sire, to that."

Uther went and stood by the great window of the room with his arms folded upon his breast. His hollow eyes looked out over the city, and there was a gaunt grandeur of thought upon his face. He was not a man who galloped down destiny like a huntsman on the trail of a stag; deliberation entered into his motives, and he never foundered reason with over-use of the spur. Dubricius stood and watched him with the smile of a father, for he loved the man.

Presently Uther turned back towards the fire. Dubricius saw by his face that he had come by decision, and that his mind was steadfast.

"Merlin is at Sarum, my lord."

"I shall not play Saul at Endor."

"No, sire."

"The man shall come to me with no jugglery in dark corners."

"Wise forethought, my lord king."

"I remember me, Dubricius, that you have little leisure to hear of dreams. I have given you the names of the holy houses to be rebuilt and consecrated in the name of God. We will save Britain by the help of the cross. God speed you."

Alone in the half light of the hall Uther stood and stared into the fire, his eyes luminous in the glow, while the pungent scent of the burning wood swept up like a savour of eastern spices. There was intense feeling on his face, a kind of passionate calm, as he gazed into the red bosom of the fire. Presently, as though turning in thought from some enchantment of the past, he sighed wearily, put his black hair from his forehead with both hands, and looked at his image in a mirror of steel that hung from a painted pillar. There was a wistful look upon his strong face; he had a soul that remembered, a soul not numbed by time into mere painless recollection of the past. As in some mysterious temple, love, with solemn sound of flute and dulcimer, kept fire unquenched night and day upon the altar of his heart.

Rising up out of his mood of gloom, an earthly Hyperion whose face shone anew over Britain, he passed out, and calling to the guards lounging on the terrace, descended the stairway that sloped through gardens to the river. His state barge was in waiting at the gate, and entering in he was borne downstream towards the town whose white walls rose up amid the emerald mist of spring. Over all Uther cast his eye with a lustre look of love, a love that shone like the smile of a child at a mother's face. Caerleon was dear to him beyond all other cities; its white walls held his heart with the whispered conjure word of "home."

Landing at the great quay, where many ships and galleys lay moored, he passed up towards the market square with the files of his guard, smiling back on the reverences of the people, throwing here and there a coin, happy in the honour that echoed to him from every face. Before the walls of a pilastered house his guards halted with a fanfare of trumpets, a sound that rolled the gates wide and brought a mob of servants to line the outer court. Knights came down from the house with heads uncovered. It was the King's first entry into Gorlois's atrium since the disbanding of the host after the war in Wales.

A face scarred with red across cheek and chin, with nose askew, one lower lid turned down, came out to Uther from the doorway of an inner room. There was a drawn look upon the man's face, a sullen saturnine air about him as though he were vexed inwardly with the chafe of some perpetual pain. The pinched frown, the restless bloodshot eyes, the hunched shoulders, were all strange to Uther, who looked for Gorlois, the man of arrogant and imperial pride, whose splendour of person, carriage of head, and long lithe stride had marked him a stag royal from the herd of meaner men.

Uther, grave as a god, gripped the other's thin sinewy fingers, his eyes searching Gorlois's face with a large-minded scrutiny inspired by the natural sympathies of his heart. Gorlois, for his part, half crooked the knee, and drew a carved chair before the ill-tended fire. He had an Asmodean pride, and the look in Uther's eyes was more troublesome to him than a glare of hate. His face never lightened from the murk of reserve that covered it like a mask, and it was the King who spoke the first word over the flickering fire.

"What of your wounds?" he said.

Gorlois's black beard was down on his breast, and he looked only at the fire. He seemed like a man furtive beneath the consciousness of some inward shame, mocking his honour.

"My wounds are well, sire."

"You look like a man newly risen from a sick bed."

"If I look sick, sire, blame my physician; he has tinctured me to the level of perdition. Bodily I never felt in better fettle. I could hew down a horse, and .thrust my spear through a pine trunk. A man's face is a fallacy."

Uther saw the scars, the harsh smile, and caught the twinge in the seemingly careless voice. He could comprehend some humiliation in the marring of personal comeliness, but not the humiliation that seemed to lurk deep beneath Gorlois's pride. There was more here than the scarring of a cheek.

"There is some care upon you, Gorlois," he said.

"Sire, you have much observation."

"Your men have spoken of the change to you."

"They are too discreet, God save their skins."

"Pride, pride."

"Sire, you are right; my pride suffers the inquisitiveness of kings, not subjects. Eagle calls to eagle; men are mere magpies. Chatter maddens me."

"I grip your hand in spirit."

Both men were silent for a while, the fire crackling sluggishly at their feet. Gorlois's eyes were on the window and the scrap of green woodland in the distance; Uther's eyes were on Gorlois's face. The latter, with the sore sensitiveness of a diseased spirit, felt the look and chafed at it. His petulance was plain enough to Uther as he sat and watched him, and pondered the man's trouble in his heart.

"Gorlois."

"Sire."

"I am no gabbler."

"True, my lord."

"You are trouble ridden."

Gorlois's eyes flashed up to Uther's, faltered, and fell.

"What of that, sire?" he said curtly.

"You have a deadly pride."

"I own it."

Uther leant forward in his chair, and looked earnestly into the other's face.

"I too am a proud man in my trouble," he said, "buckling up unutterable things from the baseness of the world, jealous of my inward miseries. Yet when I see a strong man and a friend chained with the iron of a silent woe, I cannot keep my sympathy in leash, so tell him to unburden to a man whose pride feels for the pride of others."

The words seemed to stir Gorlois from his lethargy of reserve and silence. Uther's very largeness of soul, his stately faith and courtesy, were qualities that won largely upon the mind, lifting it above factious things to the serene level of his own soul. Gorlois, impulsive spirit, could not rebuff such a man as Uther. There was a certain calm disinterestedness in the King's nature that made trust imperative and condemned secretiveness as churlish. Gorlois was an obstinate man in the extreme rendering of the epithet. He had spoken to no one of his trouble, leaving his thoughts to be inferred. Yet staunch sympathy like Gige's ring has power over most hidden things of the heart, and Gorlois was very human.

"It is a woman, sire."

"Mine was a woman, too."

Gorlois scattered the half-dead embers with his foot.

"I married a wife," he said.

"I had never heard it."

"Few have."

"The woman's name?"

"Never ask it, sire; it will soon lie with her in the dust."

"These are grim words."

"Grim enough for the man of my own house,—my own familiar friend."

"Mother of Christ,—your friend!"

"My brother in arms, sire."

"The shedding of such blood seems like justice. Had I suffered thus—"

"Sire, you warm to my temper."

"It should be the sword."

"Mine yet waits white for blood."

Gorlois, implacable, grim as a werewolf, threw open the

door of a closet and led Uther within the narrow compass of its walls. It was a little oratory, dim and fantastic, with lamps hanging from the roof, and black curtains over the narrow casement. Two waxen candles burnt with steady, windless flames upon the altar, and beneath their light glimmered a great sword, naked, and a cup half filled with purple wine. Gorlois took up the sword and touched it with his lips.

"For the man," he said.

Then he set the sword down beneath its candle and touched the goblet with his fingers; his black eyes glittered.

"For the woman, sire."

"And the candles?"

"I burn them till I have crushed the life out of two souls; then I can pinch the wicks between my fingers, and snuff them out in smoke."

VI

It was spring at Caerleon, and a web of green had swept upon the empty purple of the woods and shut the naked casements to the sun. The meadowlands were plains of emerald that glimmered gold; the gorge blazed with its myriad lamps lighting the dark gateways of the pine forests, and covering all the hillsides as with a garment of yellow. In the woods the birds sang, and hyacinths and dog violets spread pools of blue beneath the infinite greenness of the boughs. In Caerleon's orchards the fruit trees stood like mounts of snow flecked with ethereal pink and a prophecy of green. Yew, cypress, cedar, reared their dark bosoms betwixt the gentler foliage, and many a bronze-leafed oak made mimic autumn with a mist of leaves.

In a forest glade that opened upon the high-road some three leagues eastward of Caerleon, an old man sat beside a shallow spring, whose waters lay a pool of tarnished silver within the low stone wall that compassed them. The old man by the pool was clad in a ragged cloak of coarse brown cloth lined with rabbit skin; he had sandals on his feet, a staff and wallet by his side, and under the shadow of his hood of fur a peaky white beard hung down like an icicle under the eaves of a house. His hands were thin and white, and he seemed decrepit as he sat hunched by the well with a crust of brown bread in his lap and a little bronze pannikin that served him as a cup.

It was late in the day, and the great oaks that reached out their arms over the well stood solemn and still in the evening calm, while the cloud masses bastioned overhead were radiant with the lustre of the hour. The road curled away right and left into the twilight of the woods; no folk passed to and from Caerleon to throw alms to the beggar who squatted there like any old goblin man out of a tomb. From time to time he would turn and look long into the pool as into a mirror, as though he watched the future glimmering dimly in a magic well. He had finished his crust of bread, and his head nodded over his lap as though sleep tempted him after a day's journey. Rabbits were scampering and feeding along the edge of the forest; a snake slid by in the grass like a streak of silver; far down the glade a herd of fallow deer browsed as though caring nothing for the huddled scrap of humanity by the well. The beggar man might have been dead, for all the heed he gave to the forest life that teemed so near.

Yet it was soon evidenced that his faculties were keenly alive to all that passed about him by a marvellous perception of sound, a perception that made itself plain before the sun had drifted much further down the west. The old man had heard something that had not stirred the fallow deer browsing in the glade. A thin metallic sound shimmered on the air, the clattering cadence of hoofs far away upon the high-road. The beggar by the pool had lifted his head, and was listening with his hooded face turned towards the west, his thin fingers picking unconsciously at his beard.

Presently the deer browsing in the glade reared up their heads to listen, snuffed the air, and swept back at a trot into the forest. Jays chattered away over the trees; rabbits stopped feeding and sat up with their long ears red in the sunlight. The indifferent suggestion of a sound had grown into a ringing tramp that came through the trees like a blunt challenge to the solitary spirit of the place. Through the indefinite and mazy screens of green a glitter of harness and a streaking of colour glimmered from the wizard amber glow of the west. Three horsemen were coming under the trees,—one in lurid arms before, and two abreast behind in black. The beggar by the pool pulled his cowl down over his face, and stood by the roadside with his bronze pannikin held in a shaky right hand to pray for alms.

The knights drew rein by the pool, and he in the red harness flung down money from his belt, and required tidings in return.

"The Lord Jesus have mercy on your soul in death," came the whine of gratitude; "what would your lordship learn from an old man?"

Uther considered him from the shadow of his casque. He had his suspicions, and was half wise in his conjectures. He could see nothing of the old man's face, and so elected to be innocent for the moment.

"Grandfather, have you heard in your days of Merlin the prophet?"

"Have I heard of the devil, lording!"

"Were he to ride here, should you know his face?"

"Sir, I have seen no man these three hours. Yet, in truth, I did but now smell a savour as of hell; and there was a raven here, a black villain of a bird that croaked 'Abracadabra to the letter.'"

Uther smiled.

"Are you from Caerleon?" he said.

"No, sire, it is Uther the King who comes from the City of Legions."

"Uther, say you? Put back that hood."

"My lord, lo! I bow myself; I have kept the tryst."

The cowl fell back, the cloak was unwrapped, the beard twitched from the smooth, strong chin. The bent figure, feeble and meagre, straightened and dilated to a stature and bulk beyond mere common mould. A man with hair black as a raven's wing, and great glistening eyes, stood with his moon-face turned up to Uther Pendragon. A smile played upon his lips. He was clad in a cloak of sombre purple, wreathed about with strange devices, and a leopard's skin covered his shoulders; his black hair was bound with a fillet of gold, and there were gold bracelets upon his wrists. It was Merlin who stood before Uther under the arch of the great trees.

"The benisons of all natural powers be upon you; the God of the stars and the spirit fires of the heavens keep you. Great is your heart, O King, and great your charity. Bid me but serve you, and the beggar's pence shall win you a blessing."

The man bowed himself even to the ground. Uther left his horse tethered to a tree, and faced Merlin over the pool. Both men were solemn as night in their looks.

"Merlin," said the King.

"Sire."

"I have a riddle from the stars."

"Speak it, O King."

"To your ear alone."

"Sire, pass with me into the forest."

"Blessed be thy head if thou canst read the testament of the heavens."

It was towards sunset, and the place was solemn and still as some vast church. In the white roadway the black knights stood motionless, with spear on thigh, their sable plumes sweeping like cloudlets under the dark vault of the foliage. Merlin, with the look of an eternity in his eyes, bowed down once more before Uther, and pointed with his hand into the dim cloister of the trees. Red and purple passed together from the pool, and melted slowly into an oblivion of leaves.

In a little glade under a great oak, whose roots gripped the ground like talons, Uther told to Merlin the vision that had come to him in the watches of the night. He had stood late at his window, looking over Caerleon shimmering white under the moon, and had seen a star of transcendent glory smite sudden through the blue vault of the heavens. A great ray had fallen from the star, and from the ray had risen a vapour, a golden mist that had shaped itself into a dragon of gold, and from the dragon's mouth had proceeded two smaller rays that had seemed to compass Britain between two streams of fire. Then, like smoke, both star and dragon had melted out of the heavens, and only the moon had looked down on Usk and the sleeping woods about Caerleon.

When Uther had spoken his whole soul in this mystery of the night, Merlin withdrew himself a little and looked long into the sky, his tall figure and strong face clear as chiselled stone in a slant gleam of the sun. For fully the third part of an hour he stood thus like a pillar of basalt, neither moving nor uttering a sound, while the sky fainted over the tree tops and flashed red fire from the armour of the King. Suddenly, as though he had caught inspiration from the heavens, prophecy came upon him like a wind at sunset. He stretched his hands to the sky. His body quivered; his eyes were as rubies in a mask of marble.

"I have seen, O King! I have looked into the palpitating web of the stars, into the glittering aisles of the infinite."

Uther strode out from the tree trunk where he had leant watching the man's cataleptic pose grow into the quick furor of prophecy.

"Say on," he said.

Merlin swept a hand towards him with a magnificence of gesture.

"Thou art the star, the dragon is thy son. He shall compass Britain with a band of steel, beat back the wolves of heathendom, and cast stupendous glory over Britain's realm. His name shall shine in history, sun-bright, magnificent, and pure; his name shall be Arthur. Thus, O King! Uther of the Dragon, read I this vision of the night."

Uther, a gradual lustre in his eyes, looked long at the sun behind the swart pillars of the forest. He seemed to gather vigour from the glow. Prophecy was in his thought, a prophecy that tempted the inmost dreamings of the heart, and linked up the past with promise of the future. To love, to be loved, to win the woman among women! To beget a son, a warrior, a king; to harden his body like to an oak, temper his heart like steel; to set the cross in his hands and send him forth against the beast and the barbarian like a god! Such, indeed, were the idyls of a King!

"Merlin, I have no wife, and you speak to me of a son," was his sole answer.

The retort echoed from the man.

"The King must wed."

"This is no mere choosing of a horse."

"Sire, you can learn to love. It is not so difficult a thing, no more than falling down upon a bed of roses."

The retort was in no wise suited to Uther's humour.

"I am no boy to be married on the moment to cap the reading of a vision."

"Sire!"

"Bring me the woman I may love, if you are magical enough, — then bid me wed."

"My lord, you mock me with a dream."

"Not so."

"She is dead then?"

"On my soul I know not."

"Then, sire —"

"All women are dead to me save one. Conjure her into my being, and I will give you the wiser half of myself, even my heart."

For an instant Merlin smiled — a smile like an afterglow in a winter sky, — clear, cold, and steely. He drew nearer

Uther, his purple robe with its fantastic scroll-work dim in the twilight, his black hair falling down about his face. His words were like silken things purring from his lips.

"My lord, tell me more."

"You are a prophet. Read my past."

"Sire, my vision fails at such a depth."

"But not thy flattery."

"Her name, sire?"

"I will read you a fable."

Uther, his eyes lit as with a lustre of recollection, turned from Merlin and the ken of his impenetrable face. He leant against a tree trunk, and looked far away into the dwindling vistas of the woods. His voice won emphasis from the absolute silence of the place, and he spoke with the level deliberation of one reading aloud from some antique book.

"A woman befriended a knight who was smitten of a dread wound. It was summer, and a sweet season full of the scent of flowers,—odours of grass knee deep in dreamy meadows. The woman had red-gold hair, and eyes like a summer night; her mouth was more wistful than an opening rose; her voice was like a flute over moonlit waters. And the knight lost his soul to the woman. But the woman was a nun, and so, to save his vows, he battled down his love and left her."

Merlin's eyes took a sudden glitter.

"A nun, sire?"

"A nun."

"With hair of red gold and eyes of amethyst. Her convent, sire?"

"Avangel. Burnt by the heathen on the southern shores."

"And the nun's name?"

"Igraine, Igraine."

Merlin gave a shrill, short cry; badges of colour had stolen into his cheeks, and he looked like a Bacchanal for the moment.

"Sire, sire, the woman is no nun."

Uther still leant against the tree, and looked into the distance with his hand shadowing his eyes. It might have seemed that he had not heard the words spoken by Merlin, or at least had not understood their meaning, so unmoved was his look, so motionless his figure. Unutterable thoughts were moving in his mind. There was a grandeur of self-suppression on his face as he turned and fronted Merlin with the quiet of a great strength.

"Man, what words are these?"

Merlin had recoiled suddenly within himself. He was silent again, subtle as steel, and very debonair.

"My lord, I swear she is no nun."

"Give me fact, not assertion."

"The woman is but a novice. I had the whole tale from one who knew her well at Radamanth's in Winchester, where she found a home. She had grieved, sire, for Pelleas."

"Pelleas—Igraine! My heart is great in me, Merlin; where saw you her last?"

"Wandering in a wood by Winchester."

"Alone?"

"Alone in heart."

"Where now?"

"My lord—I know not."

"O God!—to see her face again."

Merlin cast his leopard skin across his visage and stood like a statue, even his immense grandeur of reserve threatened for the moment with summary overthrow. In the taking of twenty breaths he had calmed himself again to stand with bare head and frank face before the King—a promise on his lips.

"My lord, give me a moon's season to stare into this mystery. On the cross I swear it—I will bring you good news at Caerleon."

"On the cross!"

"On the cross of your sword."

"Merlin, if this thing should come to be, if life returns to one whose hopes were dead, you of all men in Britain shall be next my heart. Behold — on the cross — I swear it."

A certain season of youth seemed to have come down upon Uther, and lighted up the solemn tenor of his mood. His face grew mellow with the calm of a great content; he was reasonable as to the future, not moved to any extravagant outburst of unrest; the constant overshadowing of the cross seemed to give his faith a tranquil greenness — a rain-refreshed calm that pervaded his being like moist quiet after a wind.

"Merlin, what of the night?"

"Sire, I am well provided; I have a pavilion near a brook where a damsel serves me."

"I go to Caerleon. You have conjured me back into the spring of life; my heart is beholden to you. Take my hand — and remember."

"Sire, I am your servant."

When Uther had passed, a streak of scarlet, into the blue twilight of the darkening wood; when the dull clatter of hoofs had dwindled into an ecstasy of silence, Merlin, white as the faint moon above, found again the pool under the trees by the high-road to Caerleon. Going on his knees by the brink he looked into its waters, black, sheeny, mysterious, webbed with a flickering west-light, sky mosaics dim and ethereal between swart-imaged trees. Still as a mirror was the pool, yet touched occasionally with light as from a rippling star-beam, or a dropped string from the moon's silver sandals. Merlin bent over it, his fateful face making a baleful image in the water. Long he looked, as though seeking some prophetic picture in the pool. When night had come he rose up with a transient smile, folded his cloak about him, and passed like a wraith into the forest.

VII

While Gorlois was lowering over an imagined shame, and Uther given to brooding on a vision, the Knight of the Cloven Heart wandered through wild Wales and endured sundry adventures that were hardly in concatenation with the distaff or the cradle.

In rough ages might was right, and every man's inclination law unto himself. To strike hard was to win crude justice; to ride a horse, to wear mail, to carry a sword, were characteristics that ensured considerable reverence from men less fortunate, by maintaining at least an outward arrogance of strength. Not only on these grounds alone did the Knight of the Cloven Heart hold at a disadvantage those folk of the wilderness who went — to speak metaphorically — naked. She made brave show enough, had a strong arm and a strong body, and could match any man in the mere matter of courage. The moral effect of her great horse, her shield and harness, and the sword at her side, carried her unchallenged through wood and valley where meaner wayfarers might have come to grief, or suffered a tumbling. The forest folk assumed her a knight under her helmet and her harness; a certain bold magnificence of bearing in no wise contradicted the assumption.

It would be wearisome to record the passage of two months or more, to construct an itinerary of her progress, to chronicle the events of a period that was solitary as the wilds through which she passed. She never slept a night under populous roof the whole time of these wanderings. Luckily it was fair weather, and a mild season; forest shade, such as it was, and the caves of the wilderness, a ruined villa, the forsaken hut of a charcoal burner, an empty hermitage,— such in turn gave her shelter from the placid light of the moon, or the black stare of a starless sky. She never ventured even among peasant folk unhelmeted. Her food was won from cottager or herdsman by such store of money as she had about her, though many she came across were eager to appease so formidable a person with milk, and pottage, and the little delicacies of the rude home. Often her fine carriage and youthful voice won wonders from the bosom of some peasant housewife. She had her liberty, and was free to roam; the life contented her instincts for a season, and at least she was saved the sight of Gorlois. Since war had failed to loose her from the man, she would essay her best to keep him at a distance.

If hate repelled, love drew with dreams. Yet had Igraine been asked of peace at heart, she would have smiled and sighed together. There are degrees of misery, and solitary suffering is preferable to that publicity which is very torture in itself, a galling whip to the tender flanks of pride. In being free of Gorlois she was happy; in thinking of Uther and in contemplation of the shadows of the unknown she was of all women most miserable. A mood of self-concentration was settling slowly upon her like an inevitable season upon the face of the earth. Day by day a dream prophetic of the future was pictured in the imagery of thought till it grew familiar as an often looked on landscape that awakes no wonder and no strange unrest. The ordinances of man had thrust on her a damnable tyranny, and she was more than weary of the restrictions of the world. The inevitable scorn of custom had long taken hold upon her being, and she had been driven to that state when the soul founds a republic within itself, and creates its ethics from the promptings of the heart.

Uther was at Caerleon; she had heard the truth from many a peasant tongue. Caerleon therefrom drew her with magic influence, as a lamp draws a golden moth from the gloom, or the light in the night sky wings on the wild-fowl with the prophecy of water. Caerleon became the bourn of all her holier thoughts; strange city of magic, it held love and hate for her, desire and obloquy; though its walls were as a luring net scintillant with spirit gossamer, her very reason lulled her fears to sleep, and turned her southwards towards Uskland and the sea.

It came to pass, on the very day that Uther spoke with Merlin in the forest, that Igraine rode over a stretch of hills by a sheep-track, and came down into a valley not many leagues from Caerleon. The place stood thick with woodland, ranged tier on tier with the peaked bosses of huge trees. That impenetrable mystery of solitude that abides where forests grow was deeply hallowed in this silent dale. The infinite majesty of nature had cast a spell there, and the vast oaks, like pyramids of gloom, caverned a silence that was utter and divine.

Glimmering beneath the huge, stupendous boughs, through darkling aisles and the colossal piers that held the innumerable roofing of the leaves, Igraine passed down through umbrage and still ecstasies of green, by colonnade and gallery,—interminable tunnels, where stray light struck slantwise on her armour, that it seemed a moving lustre in the solemn shade.

Deep in the woodland lay a valley, a pastureland girt round with trees, and where the meadows, painted thick with flowers, seemed all enamelled white and azure, green, purple, pink, and gold. A peace as from the sun shone over it like saffron mist. A pool gleamed there, tranquil and deep with shadows; all the trees that Britain knew seemed girdled round it—oak, beech and holly, yew, thorn and cedar, the elfin pine, the larch, whose delicate kirtle shames even broidery of silk. No sound save the cuckoo's cry, and the uncertain twittering of birds, disturbed the sanctuary of that forest solitude.

Igraine, halting on the brink of the meadowland, looked down over wood and water. The quiet of the place, the clear glint of the pool, the scent of the meadows, brought back the valley in Andredswold, and the manor in the mere. She loved the place on the instant. Even a blue plume of smoke rising straight to the sky, and the grey-brown backs of a few sheep in the meadows, evidencing as they did the proximity of man, failed to disenchant the solitary grandeur of the scene.

There is no stable perpetuation of peace in the world; care treads upon the heels of Mammon, and lust lies down by the side of love. Even in the quiet of the wilderness the hawk chases the lark's song out of the heavens, and wind scatters the bloom from the budding tree. Thus it was that Igraine, watching from under the woods, saw the sheep scampering suddenly in the meadows as though disturbed by something as yet invisible to her where she stood. Their bleating came up with a tinge of pathos, to be followed by a sound more sinister, the cry of one in whom pain and terror leapt into an ecstasy of anguish — a shrill, bird-like scream that seemed to cleave the silence like the white blade of a sword. Igraine's horse pricked its ears with a snort of wrath, as though recognising the wounded cry of some innocent thing. The girl's pulses stirred as she scanned the valley for explanation of this discord, sudden as the sweep of a falcon from the blue. Nor was she long at gaze. A flickering speck of colour appeared in the meadowlands, the figure of a woman running through the grass like a hunted rabbit, darting and doubling with a whimpering outcry. Near as a shadow a tall streak of brown followed at full stride, terrible even in miniature. Hunter and hunted passed before the eye like the figures of a dream, yet with a fierce realism that whelmed self in an objective pity.

Never did Britomart herself, with splendid soul, find fitter cause in faerie-land than did the Knight of the Cloven Heart in that woodland dale. Igraine rode down from the trees, a burning figure of chivalry that galloped through the green, and bore fast for the scudding forms, that skirted round the pool. Like a stag pressed to despair, the hunted one had taken to the water, and was already waist deep in ripples that seemed to catch the panic of the moment. Plunging on past tree and thicket, Igraine held on, while sheep scattered from her, to turn and stare with the stupidest of white faces at the horse thundering over the meadows. The pursuer had passed the water-weeds, and was to his knees in the pool when the Knight of the Cloven Heart came down to the bank and halted, like a mailed statue of succouring vengeance.

The white heat of the drama seemed cooled for the moment. Over the flickering scales of the little mere the girl's white face, tumbled hair, and blue smock showed, as she half-floated and half-paddled with her hands. Nearer still, the leather-jerkined, fur-breeched figure of the man bent like a baffled satyr baulked of evil. On the green slope of the bank the mailed splendour of chivalry waited like Justice to uphold the right.

The man in the mere wore the short Roman sword, or parazonium; any more effective weapon that he had possessed had been thrown aside in the heat of the chase and in the imagined security of his rough person. He had the face of a wolf. In girth and stature he seemed a young Goliath, a savage thing bred in savage times and savage places, and blessed with the instincts of mere barbarism. Igraine's disrelish equalled her heat as she looked at him, and slanted her great sword over her shoulder.

In another instant the scene revived, and ceased to be a mere picture. The girl in the pool had found a footing, and her half-bare shoulders showed above the water. The man, with his short sword held behind him, was splashing through the shallows with a grin on his hairy face that meant mischief. Igraine, every whit as hot as he, held her horse well in hand, and put her shield before her. Matters went briskly for a minute. The man made a rush; Igraine spurred up and sent him reeling with the charging shoulder of her horse; the short sword pecked at nothing, the long one struck home and drew blood. A second panther leap, a blow turned by the shield, a counter cut that made good carving of the fellow's skull. The shallows foamed and crackled crimson; hoofs stirred up the mire; a plunge; a noise of crossed steel; a last sweep of a sword, and then victory. Igraine's horse, neighing out the spirit of the moment, trampled the fallen body as it had been the carcase of a slaughtered dragon.

The girl in the pool waded back at the sight, her blue smock clinging about her, and showing an opulent grace of shoulder, arm, and bosom — a full figure swept by the damp tangle of her dark brown hair. She had full red lips, eyes of bright blue, a round and ruddy face, that told of a mind more for tangible pleasures than for spiritual aspiration. She came up out of the shallows like a water-nymph, her frightened face already all aglow with a smile of gratitude, mild shame, and infinite reverence. Going down on her knees amid the water-weeds and flags, she held up her playful hands as to a deliverer direct from heaven. "Grace, Lord, for thy servant."

With the peril past, Igraine could not forego the sly scrap of mischief that the occasion offered; her white teeth gleamed in a smile under her helmet, as she wiped her sword on the horse's mane, before sheathing it.

"Give Heaven thy thanks," she said, with a quaint sententiousness of gesture. "Be sure in thy heart that it was a mere providence of God that I heard thy screaming. As for yon clod of clay, we will bury it later, lest it should pollute so goodly a pool. For the rest, child, I am an old man, and hungry, and would taste bread."

The girl jumped up instantly, with a shallow and half-puzzled smile. The voice from the helmet was young, very young, and full of the free tone of youth; yet both manner and matter were sage, practical, leavened with a hoary-headedness of intention that seemed to baulk the inferences suggested by such panoply of arms. With a bob of a curtsey, she took the knight's bridle, and led the horse some fifty paces round the pool, where, under the imminent shoulder of a cedar tree, a little cabin nestled under a hood of ivy. It was built of rough timber from the forest, and thatched with reeds; honeysuckle clustered over its rude façade, and thrust fragrant tendrils into its reed-latticed windows, where an early rose or so shone like a red star against the russet-wood. A garden full of flowers lay before the rustic porch that arched the threshold; and an out-jutting of the pool brought a little fiord of dusky silver up to the very green of the path, a streak of silver blazoned with violet flags, golden marigolds of the marsh, and a lace-like fringe of snowy water-weed in bloom. All around, the great trees, those solemn senators, stood with their green shoulders bowed in a strong dream of deep eternal thought.

Igraine left the saddle and suffered the girl to tether her horse to a cedar bough. Her surcoat of violet and gold swept nearly to her ankles, and saved from any marring the infinite art of the anomaly that veiled her sex. Her man's garb seemed every whit as worthy of a woman, nor did it hinder that loving grace that made her beauty of body the more admirable and rare.

The girl came back with more bendings of the knee, and led Igraine amid the flowers to the porch of the forest dwelling. Once within, she drew a settle close to the doorway, spread a rug of skins thereon, and again bowed herself in homage.

"Let my lord be seated, and I will serve him."

"I am hungry, child; but first put off that wet smock of thine."

The girl crept behind the door of a great cupboard, with a blush of colour in her cheeks. Cloth rustled for a moment; a circle of blue and a slim pair of legs showed beneath the cupboard door; soon she was back again in a gown of apple green, fastening it with her fingers over the full swell of her bosom.

"What will my lord eat?"

"What you have, child."

"Bread and dried fruit, the flesh of a kid, new milk and cheese, a little cider."

"Give me milk, child, a mere flake of meat, some cheese and bread, and I ask nothing more. I will pay you for all I take."

"Lord, how should you pay me, when I owe more than life to your sword?"

The little shepherdess went about her business with a barefooted tread, soft as any cat's. The cottage proved a wonder of a place. The great cupboard disgorged a silver-rimmed horn, wooden platter, a napkin white as apple blossom, red fruit piled up in a brazen bowl. The girl set the things in order on the table, with an occasional curious look stolen at the figure in mail on the settle — splendid visitant in so humble a place. And what a rich voice the knight had, — how mellow, with its many modulations of tone. His hands too were wonderfully shapen, fingers long and tapering, with nails pink as sea-shells. There surely must be a face worth gazing at, for its very nobility, under that great brazen helmet that glinted in the half light of the room.

The meal was spread, but the guest still unprepared. The forest child dropped a curtsey, and a mild suggestion that the knight should make a beginning.

"Will not my lord unhelm?"

A rich, mischief-loving laugh startled her for answer.

"Child, take the thing off if you will."

The little shepherdess obeyed, and nearly dropped the helmet in the doing of it. A mass of gold fell rippling down over the violet surcoat; a pair of deep eyes looked up with a sparkling laugh; a satin upper lip and chin gave the lie to the nether part of the picture.

"Christ Jesu!" quoth the girl with the helmet, and again "Christ Jesu," as though she could get no further.

Igraine caught her smock and drew her nearer.

"Come, little sister, kiss me for — 'thank you.'"

With a contradictory impulse the girl fell down on her knees and began to cry, with her brown hair tumbled in Igraine's lap.

When persuasion and comforting had quieted her somewhat, she sat on the floor at Igraine's feet, her round eyes big with an unstinted wonder. Even Igraine's hunger and the devoir done upon the new milk could hardly persuade the girl that this being in armour was no saint, but a very real and warm-blooded woman. She even touched Igraine's fingers with her lips, to satisfy herself as to the warmth and solidity of the slim strong hand. She had never heard of such a marvel, a woman, and a very beautiful woman, riding out as a man, and doing man's bravest work with courage and cleverness. The girl made sure in her heart that Igraine was some princess at least, who had been blessed with miraculous power by reason of her maidenhood and the magic innocence of her mind.

Igraine talked to the girl and soon began to win her to less devotional attitude with that graciousness of manner that became her so well at such a season. She forgot herself for the time, in listening to this child of solitude. The girl's father — an old man — had died two winters ago, and she had buried him with her own hands, under a tree in the dale. Since his death, she had lived on in the cabin, alone, a forest child nurtured in forest law. Every Sabbath, Renan, a shepherd lad in a lord's service, would come over the hills and pass the day with her. They were betrothed, and the lord of those parts had promised Renan freedom next Christmastide; then Renan and Garlotte were to be married, and the cabin in the dale was to serve them as a home.

Garlotte was soon chattering like any child. She talked to Igraine of her sheep and goats, her little corn-field on a sunny slope, her garden, her wild strawberry beds and vine, her fruit trees, and her marigolds. The lad Renan, bronze-haired and brown-eyed, sprang in here and there with irresistible romance. He could run like a hound, swim like an otter, fish, shoot with the bow, and throw the javelin a great many paces. He had such eyes, too, and such gentle hands. Igraine's sympathies were quick and vivid on matters of the kind. The girl's head was resting against her knees before an hour had gone.

The evening was still and sultry and the sky overcast.

When Igraine went to the porch after supper, rain had begun to fall, and there was the moist murmur of a heavy, windless shower through all the valley. The sheep had huddled under the trees. Infinite freshness, unutterable peace, brooded over the green meadows and the breathless leaf-clouds of the woods. For all the sweet, dewy silence a bitter discontent lay heavy upon Igraine's heart, and woe made quiet moan in her inmost soul. Green summer swooned in the branches and breathed in the odours of honeysuckle, musk, and rose, yet for her there seemed no burgeoning, no bursting of the heart into song.

The girl Garlotte stood by and looked with a quaint awe into the proud, wistful face.

"What are you thinking of, lady?" she said.

Igraine's lips quivered.

"Of many things, child."

"Tell me of them."

"What should you know, child, of plagues and sorrow, of misery in high places, of despair coroneted with gold, of hearts that ache, and eyes that burn for the love of the world that never comes?"

"I am very ignorant, dear lady, but yet I think you are not happy."

"Is any woman happy on earth?"

"Yet you are so good and beautiful."

"Child, child, beauty brings more misery than joy; it is a bright fire that burns upon itself."

"Renan has told me I am beautiful."

"So you are, and to Renan."

"I never think of it, lady, save when Renan looks into my eyes and touches my mouth with his lips; then say in my heart, 'I am beautiful, and Renan loves me, God be thanked!'"

The words echoed into Igraine's soul. There was such pain in her great eyes that the girl was startled from the simple contemplation of her own affairs of heart.

"You are sad, lady."

"Child, I am tired to death."

"Bide with me and rest. See, I will feed your horse and give him water; he will do famously under the tree. There is my bed yonder in the corner; I spread a clean sheet on it this very morning. Shall I help you to unarm?"

"Thanks, child. How the rain hisses into the pool."

"I love the sound, and the soft rattle on the green leaves. All will be fresh and aglister to-morrow, and the flowers will smile, and the trees shake their heads and laugh. How clumsy my fingers are; I am so slow over the buckles; ah! there is the last. I will put the sword and the shield by the bed. Shall we say our prayers?"

"You pray, child; I have forgotten how to these many months."

VIII

THERE is a charm in simplicity of soul, and in sympathies green in the first rich burgeoning of the mind, unshrivelled and untainted by the miserable misanthropies of the world. The girl Garlotte was as ignorant as you will, but she loved God, had the heart of a thrush in spring-time, and was possessed naturally of a warm and delicate appreciation of the feelings of others that would have put to utter shame the majority of court ladies.

Women of a certain gilded class are prone to judge by superficialities. Living often in an artificial air of courtesy, the very life about them is a cultured, perfumed atmosphere unstirred by the deeper wind-throbs of true passion, or the solemn sweep of the more grand emotions. Hypocrisy, veneered with mannerisms, propped with etiquette, pegged up with gold, passes for culture and the badge-royal of fine breeding. Of such things the girl Garlotte was indeed flagrantly ignorant; she had lived in solitudes, and had learnt to comprehend dumb things — the cry of a sheep in pain. the mute look from the eyes of a sick lamb. Her life had made her quick to see, quick to discover. She had all the latent energy of a child, and her senses were the undebauched handmaids of an honest heart. She knew nothing of the trivial prides, the starched and petty arrogances, the small self-satisfactions, that build up the customs of the so-called cultured folk. She thought her thoughts, and they were generous ones, mark you, and spoke out on the instant without fear, as one whose words were in very truth the audible counterpart of the vibrations of her mind.

To Igraine at first there was some embarrassment in the ingenuous methods of this child of the forest. It was in measure disturbing to be confronted with a pair of blue eyes that looked at one like two pools of truth, and a pair of lips that naively remarked: "You seem pale, lady, and in pain; you slept little, and talked even when you slept. I am rosy and cheerful, and I sleep from dusk till dawn. What is there in your heart that is not in mine?" Still, with the abruptness once essayed, there was a refreshing sincerity in Garlotte's openness of heart. It was as the first plunge into a clear, cool pool—a gasp at the first moment, then infinite warmth, intense kindling of all the senses, with the clean ripples bubbling at the lips and the swinging water buoying up the bosom. Garlotte recalled Lilith—Radamanth's daughter—to Igraine, only that she had more penetration, more liberty of thought and character. The one was as a warm wind that lulled, the other a breeze blowing over open water—clean, invigorating, kind.

Igraine's mood of unrest found refuge in the valley, and in Garlotte's cottage. She won some measure of inward calmness in the simple life, the simple tasks, that kept the more sinister energies of the mind at bay. It contented her for a season with its companionship, its air of home, its green quiet and tranquil beauty. Garlotte's cheerfulness of soul, like some penetrating essence, suffused itself upon Igraine, despite the militant savour of things more turbulent. She fell into temporary contentment almost against her will, even as sleep enforces itself upon a brain extravagantly possessed by the delirium of fever.

For all the quiet of the place, circumstances were gathering and moving down upon her with that ghostly and inevitable fatefulness that constitutes true tragedy. No one could have seemed more hidden from the eye of fate than she in the deep umbrage of the trees, yet often when the heart imagines itself most secure from the factious meddling of the world, the far, faint cry of destiny smites on the ear like some sudden stirring of a wind at night.

It was late evening, on the fifth day of Igraine's sojourn in the valley. The day had been dull, grey, and colourless, wrapped in a blue haze of rain that had fallen heavily, drenching the woods and making monotonous music on the water. Towards evening the sky had melted to a serene azure; the air was a web of shimmering amber, the west streamed through a mist of gold, and every leaf glittered with dew. A luminous vapour hovered over the little mere, and there were rain pools in the meadows that burnt with a hundred sunsets like clear brass.

Garlotte and Igraine had been bathing in the mere. They had come up from the water to dry themselves upon a napkin of white cloth, the bronze-gold and brown hair of each meeting like twin clouds, while their linen lay like snow on the trailing branches of a tree near the pool. Their limbs and shoulders gleamed against the silver-black mirror spread by the mere; their voices made a mellow sound through the valley as they talked. Igraine had fastened her violet surcoat about her beneath her breasts; Garlotte's blue smock still hung from a branch above her head.

As they sat under the tree, drying their hair and looking over the pool to the forest realm beyond, Igraine told the girl much of the outer world as she had seen it; nor was her instruction unleavened by a certain measure of cynicism — a bitterness that surprised Garlotte not a little. The girl had great dreams of the glories of old cities, the splendour of court life, the zest of a mere material existence.

"You do not love the great world," she said.

"Once, child, I did. Everything outside a convent wall seemed good to me; I thought men heroes, and the world a faerie place; who has not! Thoughts change with time: that which I once hungered for, now I despise."

"I have never been into a great city, not even into Caerleon. My father loved the country and said it was God's pasture."

"I would rather have a dog for a friend than most men, child. Man is always thinking of his stomach, his strength, or his passion; he is vain, dull, and surly often; takes delight in slaying dumb things; drinks beer, and sleeps like a log save for his snoring."

"But Renan doesn't."

"There are some *men*, child, among the swine."

"And the women?"

"I have known good women."

"In the convent?"

"I suppose there they were good, just as stones that lie in the grass are good in that they do very little harm."

"But they served God!"

"Mere habit, just as you eat your dinner."

"A hard saying."

"Your sayings would be hard, child, if you had learnt what I have learnt of the world."

Garlotte pulled her blue smock from the tree and wrapped it round her shoulders.

"But you love God?" she said.

"What is God?"

"The Great Father who loves all things."

"Methinks then I am nothing."

"Nothing, Igraine?"

"You say God loves all men and women. Why, then, have I been cursed with perversities ever since I was born, tormented with contradictions, baffled, and mocked, till the eternal trivialities of life now make my soul sick in my body?"

"Sorrow is heaven sent to chasten, just as rain freshens the leaves."

"Old, old proverb. Rain comes from clouds; clouds hide the sun; how can sorrow be good, child, when it darkens the light of life, hides God from the heart, and makes the soul bitter?"

"That seems the wrong spirit, Igraine."

"So meek folk say; we are not all mild earth to be smitten and make no moan. There are sea-spirits that lash and foam, fire-spirits that leap and burn. My spirit is of the flame; am I to be cursed, then, because I was born with a soul of fire?"

"We cannot answer all this, Igraine."

"I hate to bow down blindly, to cast ashes on the head because a superstition bids us so."

"I have faith!"

"I cannot see with my heart."

"I would you could, Igraine."

"Perhaps you are right."

Garlotte put on her shift and frock with a sigh, and straightway went and kissed Igraine on the forehead. They sat close together under the tree and watched the valley grow dim as death, and the pool black and lustrous as a mirror turned to the twilight. Garlotte's warm heart was yearning to Igraine; her arm was close about her, and presently Igraine's head rested upon her shoulder. She began to tell the girl many things in a still, stifled voice; her bitterness gushed out like fermented wine, and for a season she was comforted — with no lasting balm indeed, for there was but one soul in the world that could give her that.

"Believe, Igraine, believe," said Garlotte very softly.

"Believe — child!"

"That there is good for every one in the world if we wait and watch in patience."

"I seem to have watched years go by, and life stretches out from me as a sea at night."

"Look not there, Igraine, but into your own heart and into the gold of faith."

"I have no heart to look to, child."

"Save into a man's. And it was a good heart."

"Good as a god's."

"Then look into it still."

"You speak like a mother."

They had talked on into the dusk of night, forgetful of time, hearing only the dripping from the leaves, seeing nothing but the short stretch of water and herbage at their feet. Yet an hour ago a figure in a palmer's cloak and cowl had come out from the western forest and stood leaning upon its staff, to stare out broodingly over the valley. The laurel green of the man's cloak harmonised so magically with the green of grass and tree that it was difficult to isolate his figure from the framing of wood and meadow.

The pilgrim had stood long in the shadows and watched the two white forms come up out of the waters of the pool. He had seen them sit and dry their hair under the tree as the dusk crept down. While they talked he had passed down towards the cottage, accompliced by the trees, slipping from trunk to trunk, to enter the cottage itself while the girls' faces were turned from it towards the pool. From one of the narrow casements his cowled face had looked out; he had marked Igraine's red gold shimmering hair; he had seen her face for a moment, also the shield hanging in the room with its cloven heart and white lilies, the sword and helmet, the harness of workmanship so subtle. When he had seen all this he had stolen out again into the gloaming, a thin gliding streak of green under the gnarled thorns and the night-bosomed cedars. The forest had taken him to its depths again and the unutterable silence of its shades. The girls by the pool had heard no sound, nor dreamt of the thing that had been so near, watching like a veritable ghost through the mist of the mere's twilight.

Caerleon slept under the moon, a dream city in a land of dreams. Its walls were like ivory in a dark gloom of green. The tower of the palace of the king caught a coronet from the stars, while in the window of an upper room a thin flame flickered like a yellow rose blown athwart the black foliage of the night. Within blood-red curtains breathed over the arched door; a little altar stood against the eastern wall, guarded above by angels haloed with gold, standing in a mist of lilies with wings of crimson and green. The silence of the hour seemed embalmed in silver — so pure, so still, so hallowed was it.

Uther knelt before the little altar in prayer; the light from the single lamp slanted down upon him, but left his face in the shadow. It was past midnight, yet the man's head was still bowed down in his devotion. He was in an ecstasy of spiritual ascent to heaven, a mood that made the world a Patmos, and his own soul a revelation to itself. At such a time his imagination could mount with a mystery of poetic rapture. Angels drumming on golden bells or bearing diamond chalices of purple wine seemed to gaze deep-eyed on him from a paradise of snow and amethyst. Above all shone the Eternal Face, that clear sun of Christendom shining with wounded love through the crimson transgressions of mankind.

Deliberate footfalls and the rustle of a drawn curtain intervened between solitude and devotion. The curtain fell again; footfalls echoed away to die down into a well of silence; a tall man wrapped in a cloak stood motionless in the oratory. Uther, still upon his knees, turned to the window and the moonlight, with big prayerful eyes that questioned the intruding figure.

"Merlin," he said, with a breath of prophecy.

"Even so, sire."

"I was praying but now for such a thing."

"Sire, pray no longer. I have kept my tryst."

Uther rose up straightway from before the altar and stood before the square of the casement. The moonlight made a halo of his hair, and lit his face with a whiteness that seemed almost supernatural. Strong as he was, his hands shook like aspen leaves; his lips were parted, and his eyes wide with the shadow of the night. Merlin stood in the dark angle of the room; his voice seemed to come as from a tomb; the single lamp flame shook and quivered in a fickle draught.

"Sire, the moon is not yet full."

"And Igraine?"

"Sire."

"Where?"

"Suffer me, sire, a moment."

"Speak quickly. God knows, I have prayed like a Samson."

Merlin cast his mantle from him, and stood out in the moonlight wrapped in the mystic symbolism of his robe. Sapphire and emerald, ruby and sardonyx, flashed with a ghostly gleam in the pale light, and caught the moonbeams in their folds. Merlin's thin hands quivered like a spray of May blossom waving in the night wind, and his eyes were like the eyes of a leopard.

"Sire, thou wert Pelleas once."

"I should remember it."

"Thou art Pelleas again."

"Again?"

"In thy red harness with thy painted shield, thy black horse; take them all."

"The past rushes back like dawn."

"Near Caerleon lies a valley."

"There are twenty valleys."

"Go north, sire, in thought. Pass the Cross on Beacon Hill, hold on for the Abbey of the Blessed Mary, take to the hills, go by a ruined tower, ford Usk, where there is a hermitage. Pass through a waste, cross more hills, go down into a valley that runs north and south."

"I follow."

"Go alone, sire."

"Alone."

"The valley is piled steep with forestland. Go down and fear not. In the valley's lap lie meadowlands, a pool, a cottage. In that cottage you shall find a knight; his armour is gilded gold, his horse a grey, his shield shows a cloven heart set amid white lilies. Speak with that knight."

"Yet more!"

"Speak with that knight, sire."

"In peace?"

"If you love your soul."

"And Igraine — Merlin, what of her?"

"That knight shall lead you to her. Sire, I have said."

IX

It was early and a clear dewy morning when Uther rode down alone from the palace by a narrow track that curled through the shrubberies clothing the palace hill. A generous sky piled its blue dome with mountainous clouds that billowed up above the horizon. The laurels in the shrubbery flickered their leaves like innumerable scales of silver in the sun; amber sun rays slanted through the dense branches of the yews, and flashed on the red harness that burnt down the winding track. The wind sang, the green larches tossed their 'kerchiefs, in the distance the sea glimmered to the white frescoes of the sky.

Uther — Pelleas once more — tossed his spear to the tall trees, and burst into the brave swing of a *chant d'amour*. With caracole and flapping mane his horse took his lord's humour. It was weather to live and love in, weather for red lips and the clouding down of perfumed hair. God and the Saints — what a grand thing to be strong, to have a clean heart to show to a woman's eyes! What were all the baser fevers of life balanced against the splendid madness of a great passion!

Down through Caerleon's streets he rode unknown of any on his tall black horse. It was pleasant to be unthroned for once, and to put a kingdom from off his shoulders. With what a swing the good beast carried him, how the towers and turrets danced in the sun, how bright were the eyes of the women who passed him by. All the world seemed greener, the sky bluer, the city merrier; the laughter of the children in the gutter echoed out of heaven; the old hag who sold golden lemons under a beech tree seemed almost a madonna — a being from a better world. Uther laughed in his heart, and blessed God and Merlin.

It is one of the rare reflections of philosophy dear to the contemplative mind, how joy jostles pain in the world, and pleasure in gold and scarlet elbows the grey-cloaked form of grief. Even innocent merriment may throw a rose in the face of one who mourns, innocent indeed of the desire to mock. The throstle sings in the tree while the beggar lies under it dying. So Uther the King flashed hate in the eyes of one who watched, knowing him only that morning as Pelleas the knight. In an old play the jealous man saw the devil ride by, and promptly followed him on the chance of finding his lost wife, deeming, indeed, the devil's guidance propitious for such a quest.

It was the shield that caught Gorlois's eye as he stood on a balcony of his house and looked out over Caerleon. The device smote him sudden as the lash of a whip. The red harness, the black horse, the painted shield, mingled a picture that burnt into his brain with a vividness that passed comprehension. He knew well enough to whom such arms should belong; had he not carried them fraudulently to his own doubtful profit? This knight must be that Pelleas whose past had worked such mischief with his own machinations, that Pelleas who had won Igraine the novice fresh from the shadow of her convent trees. Gorlois watched the man go by with a kind of superhuman envy twisting in him like a colic. The smart of it made him stiffen, go pale, gnaw his lip.

If this was the knight Pelleas, what then? Gorlois could not reason for the moment; his brain seemed a mass of molten metal in a bowl of iron. Convictions settled slowly, hardened and took form. Igraine had loved the man Pelleas; Igraine was his wife; he had lost her and Brastias also; poison and the sword waited to do their work. Supposing then this Pelleas was in quest of Igraine; supposing they had come to know each other again; supposing Brastias and Pelleas were one and the same man. Hell and furies — what a thought was this! It goaded Gorlois into action. He would ride after the man, hunt him, track him, in hope of some fragment of the truth. Hazard and hate, blood and battle, these were more welcome than chafing within walls as in a cage, or frying on a bed as on a gridiron.

Gorlois's voice rang through gallery and hall like a battle-cry.

"Ho, there! — my sword and harness."

There was a grimness in the sound that made those who came to arm him bustle for dear life. They knew his black, furious humour, the hand that struck like a mace, the tyranny that took blood for trifles. The stoutest of them were cowards before that marred and moody face. Be as brisk as they would, they were too slow for Gorlois's temper, a temper vicious as a wounded bear's.

"God and the Saints — was ever man served by such a pack of stiff-fingered fools! The devil take your fumbling. Go and gird up harlots, or hold cooking-pots. On with that helmet."

A fellow, very white about the mouth, clapped the casque on, and drew a quick breath when the angry eyes withered him no longer. Armlets, breastplates, greaves, cuishes, all were on. Gorlois seemed to emit fire like metal at white heat. He went clanging down stairway and through atrium to the courtyard, where a horseboy held a white charger. Gorlois cuffed the lad aside, mounted with a spring, took his spear from an esquire, and rode straight for the gate, his horse's hoofs sparking fire from the courtyard stones. Half an hour or more had gone since Pelleas had passed by on his black horse, and Gorlois spurred at a gallop through Caerleon, bent on catching sight of the red knight before he should have ridden into the covering masses of the woods.

Pelleas meanwhile rode on like a lad whose first quest led him into the infinite romance of the unknown. Woods and waters called; bare night and the blink of the stars summoned up that strangeness in life that is like wine to the heart of the strong and the brave. He was young again — young in the first glory of arms; the world shone glamoured as of old as he turned from the high-road to a bridle-track that led up through woods towards the north.

Holding on at a level pace he passed the woods and saw them rolling back like a green cataract towards the sea. Bare hills saluted him; the beacon height with its great wooden cross stood out against the sky; mile on mile of wooded land billowed out before him, clouded with a blue haze where the domes of the trees rose innumerably rank on rank. The Abbey of the Holy Mary lay low in meadows on his left, its fish pools shimmering in the sun, its orchards densely green about its walls. Two leagues or more of wood and wild, a climb over hills, a long descent, and Usk again shone out trailing distant in the hollows. A crumbling tower stood up above the trees. Pelleas passed close to it, giving antiquity due reverence as was his custom, looking up at its ivied walls, its crown of gillyflowers, its windows wistful as a blind man's eyes. Another mile and Usk ran at his feet. A hermitage stood by the ford. Pelleas gave the good man a piece of silver and besought his prayers before he rode down and splashed through the river to the further bank. Heathland and scrub rolled to the east, merging into the blue swell of a low line of hills. It was wild country enough, haunted by snipe and crested plover, an open solitude that swept into a purple streak against the northern sky.

It was noon before Pelleas had made an end of its shadeless glare and taken to the hills that rose gently towards the east. His red harness moving over the green was lost to Gorlois, who had missed the trail long ago in the woods beyond St. Mary's. It was dusk when the Cornishman came guided to the ford, and learnt from the hermit there that the chase lay across Usk and eastward over the heath. Gorlois gave the man no piece of silver, only a savage curse to gag his alms-seeking. Night came and caught him in the open, and rather than wander astray in the dark he spent the night under a whin bush, calming his incontinent temper as best he might.

An hour past noon Pelleas stood on the last hill slope and looked down upon the massed woodland at his feet. Here at last was Merlin's valley choked up with trees — a green lake of foliage that rippled from ridge to ridge. Pelleas, with the sun at his back, stood and looked down on it with a kind of quiet awe. So Godfrey and his knights looked down upon the holy city, so Dante saw Beatrice in his vision, and Cortez gazed at the Pacific in the west. Pelleas had taken his helmet from his head and hung it at his saddle-bow; there was a grand hunger on his face, a passionate calm, as he abode on the hill top with his tall spear a black streak against the sun.

Mystery waved him on to the great oaks whose tops rose like green flames to the blue of the sky. Could Igraine be in this valley? Would he set eyes on her that day, and see the bronze gloss of her hair go shimmering through some woodland gallery? It was nigh upon a year since he had seen her. It had been summer then, and it was summer now; his heart was singing as it had sung on that mere island when Igraine had looked into his eyes under the cedar tree. He had borne much, endured much, since then; time had hallowed memory and shed a crimson lustre over the past. Manwise, for the great love that was in him, he almost feared to look on her again lest she should have changed in face or in heart. Great God, what a thought was that! It had never smitten him before. Stiffened by his own strong constancy, he had dowered Igraine with equal loyalty of soul, nor had considered the lapse of time and the crumbling power of hours. The thought brought a dew of sweat to his forehead and made him cold even in the sun. No, honour to God, the girl had a heart to be trusted, or he had never loved her as he did!

Shaking the bridle, he rode down into the murk of the trees. He had to slant his spear and to bow his head often as the great boughs swooped to the ground. The dim glamour of the place had a sinister effect upon his mind; it solemnised him, touched the spiritual chords of his heart, uncovered the somewhat gloomy groundwork of philosophy that lay deep under the fabric of religious habit. Merlin had told a tale and nothing more. God's blessings were not man's blessings, God's ways not man's ways. Pelleas had learnt to look for what he might have called the contradictions of divine charity. We are smitten when we pray for a blessing, chided when desirous of comfort. Life would seem at times a gigantic tyranny for the creation of patience. Pelleas remembered the past, and kept his hopes and desires well in hand.

Betimes he judged himself not far from the bottom of the valley, for through gaps in the foliage overhead he could see the woods on the further slope towering up magnificently to touch the sky. Still further the long galleries of the wood arched out upon grassland gemmed with summer flowers. Showers of sunlight told of an open sky. He was soon out of the shadows and standing under the wooelshawe, with the dale Merlin had pictured stretching north and south before his eyes.

The scene smiled up at him from its bath of sunlight—the green meadows flecked white, blue, and gold, the diverse foliage of the trees, the little pool smooth as crystal, the solemn barriers of the surrounding woods. He looked first of all for the cottage built of timber, and could not see it for its overshadowing trees. None the less, by the pool a girl in a blue smock stood looking up towards him, her face showing oval white from her loosened hair. Pelleas held his breath for the moment, then saw well enough that it was not Igraine. Meanwhile the figure in blue had disappeared as though in fear of him; he could no longer see the girl from where he watched on the edge of the wood.

Riding out, he sallied down through the long grass with its haze of flowers, his eyes turned with a steadfast eagerness to the pool in the meadows. His impatience grew with every step, but he was outwardly cool as any veteran. First the brown thatch of the cottage came into view, then the blue smock of the girl who stood by the porch and watched. Last of all Pelleas saw a gleam of armour through the gloom of a cedar tree, heard the neigh of a horse, the jar of a swinging shield. The sight made his heart beat more briskly than ever ghost or goblin could have done. Pushing through the trees he came full upon a knight mounted on a grey horse, who was advancing towards him bearing on his shield the cognisance of a cloven heart.

The knight on the grey horse reined in and abode stone still in the meadows, the sunlight flashing on his helmet and such points of his harness uncovered by his surcoat. Pelleas as he rode down took stock of the stranger with an eagerness that was half jealous maugre his perspicuity of soul. What had this splendid gentleman to do with Igraine the novice? Truth to tell, Pelleas would rather have had some humbler person to serve as guide on such a quest.

The knight on the grey horse never budged a foot. Pelleas saw that he carried no spear and that his sword was safe in his scabbard. This looked like peace. Drawing up some three paces away, he scanned the strange knight over from head to foot, voted him a passable man, and admired his armour. And since his whole soul was set on a certain subject, he made no delay over courteous generalities, but came at once to the point at issue.

"Greeting, sir; I have ridden from Caerleon to speak with you."

The knight in the violet surcoat swayed in the saddle

as though shaken by a spear thrust on his painted shield. Pelleas noted that both his hands were tangled up in the grey horse's mane, though nothing could be seen of the face behind the fixed vizor of the helmet. A voice, husky, toneless, feeble, answered him after a moment's silence.

"What would you with me, knight of the red shield?"

"There is a lady whose name is Igraine; I seek her. I have been forewarned that a knight lodging in this valley has knowledge of her, and you, messire, seem to be that knight."

"That is the truth," quoth the cracked, husky voice from the helmet.

Pelleas considered a moment and held his peace. There was something strange about this knight, something tragical, something that touched the heart. Pelleas's instinct for superb miseries took hold of him with a queer, twisting grip that made him shudder. His dark eyes smouldered as he watched the strange knight, and gave voice to the grim thought that lay heavy on his mind.

"The lady is not dead?"

"No," said the husky voice with blunt brevity.

"And she is well fortuned?"

"Passably."

"Thank God," said Pelleas.

There was a dry sob in the brazen helmet, but Pelleas never heard the sound. He was staring into the woods with large, luminous eyes, and a half smile on his lips, as though his thoughts pleased him.

"Is the Lady Igraine far from hence?" he asked presently.

"If you will follow me, my lord, I can bring you to her in less than an hour."

Pelleas flushed red to the forehead, his dark eyes beamed. He looked a god of a man as he sat bareheaded on his black horse, his face aglow like the face of a martyr. The Knight of the Cloven Heart looked at him, flapped his bridle, and rode on.

Pelleas said never a word as they passed up the valley. There were deep thoughts in his heart, yearnings, and ecstasies of prayer that held him in a stupor of silence. His was a grandeur of mind that grew the grander for the majesty of passion. There was no blurting of questions, no gabbling of news, no chatter, no flurry. Like a mountain he was towering, sable-browed, impenetrable, while the thunder of suspense lasted. The knight on the grey horse watched him narrowly with a white look under his helmet that was infinitely plaintive.

At the northern end of the valley, on the very edge of the forest, stood a thicket of gnarled thorns still smothered with the snow of early summer. The Knight of the Cloven Heart drew rein in the long grass and pointed Pelleas to these white pavilions under the near umbrage of the oaks.

"Look yonder," said the voice.

Pelleas answered with a stare.

"Would you see your lady?"

"Be careful how you jest, my friend."

"I jest not, Uther Pendragon. Get you down and tether your horse; go in amid yon trees and look into the forest. I swear on the cross you shall see what you desire."

Pelleas gave the knight a long look, said nothing, dismounted, threw the bridle over a bough. Then he thrust his spear into the ground and went bareheaded in among the trees. Standing under the shadow of a great oak, he peered long into the glooms, saw nothing living but a rabbit feeding in the grass.

Suddenly a voice called to him.

"Pelleas, Pelleas."

It was a wondrous cry, clear and plaintive, yet tremulous with feeling. It rang through the woods like silver, bringing back the picture of a solemn beech wood under moonlight, and a girl tied naked to the trunk of a tree. A great lustre of awe swept over Pelleas's face; his eyes were big and luminous as the eyes of a blind man; he groped with his hands as he passed back under the May trees to the valley.

In the long grass stood a woman in armour, her helmet thrown aside, and her red gold hair pouring marvellous in the sunlight over her violet surcoat. Her head was thrown back so as to show the full sweep of her shapely throat; her face was very pale under her parted hair, while her lids drooped over eyes that seemed to swim with unshed tears. Her hands, slightly outstretched, quivered as with a shuddering impulse from her heart, and her half-parted lips looked as though they were moulded to breathe forth a moan.

Pelleas stood and stared at her as a dead man might look at God. He drew near step by step, his face white as Igraine's, his eyes as deep with desire as hers. Neither of them said a word, but stood and looked into each other's faces as into heaven — awed, solemnised, silenced. Above them towered the green woods; the meadows rippled from them with their broidery of flowers; the scent of the white May swept fragrant on the air. Solitude was with them, and the mild smile of Nature glimmered with the sunlight over the trees.

Igraine spoke first.

"Pelleas," was all she said.

The man gave a great sob, fell on his knees, and would have kissed her surcoat. Igraine bent down to him with eyes that shone like two deep wells of love. Both her hands were upon Pelleas's shoulders, his face was turned to hers.

"Kneel not to me."

"Igraine."

"Pelleas."

"Let me touch you."

"There, there, you have my hand."

"My God, my God!"

Igraine gave a low cry, half knelt, half fell before him. Pelleas's arms caught her, his face hung over hers, her hair fell down and trailed a golden pool upon the grass. She put her hands up and touched his hair, smiled wonderfully, and looked at him as though she were dying.

"Kiss me, Pelleas."

Pelleas drew a deep breath; his body seemed to quake; his whole soul was sucked up by the girl's lips.

"Igraine," was all he said.

Her face blazed, her hands clung about his neck.

"Again, again."

"My God, have I not prayed for this!"

His eyes were large and wonderful to look upon. There was such awe and love in them that an angel might have looked thus upon the Christ and have earned no reproach. Igraine kissed his lips, crept close into his bosom, hid her face, and wept.

X

WHEN Igraine had ended her tears, and grown calm and quiet, Pelleas took her hand and led her to a grass bank painted thick with flowers that sloped to the white boughs of a great May tree. He was radiant in his manhood, and his eyes burnt for her with such a splendour of pride and tenderness that she trembled in thought for the secret she had kept from him in her heart. He could know nothing of Gorlois, or he would not have come thus to her. The mocking face of fate leered at her like a satyr out of the shadows, yet with the joy of the moment she put the thoughts aside and lived on the man's lips and the great love that brimmed for her in his eyes.

Pelleas sat in the long grass at her feet and looked up at her as at a saint. Never had she seen such glory of happiness on human face, never such manhood deified by the holier instincts of the heart. The sheer strength of his devotion carried her above her cares and made her content to live for the present, and to gird time with the girdle of an hour.

"You are no nun, Igraine?"

She smiled at him and shook her head.

"No, no, Pelleas."

"Would to God you had told me that a year ago."

"Would to God I had."

"It would have saved much woe."

Igraine hung her head. The man's words were prophetic in their honest ignorance, and the whole tale had almost rushed from her that moment but for a certain selfishness that held her mute, a fear that overpowered her. She knew the fibre of Pelleas's soul. To tell him the truth would mean to call his honour to arms against his love, and she dreaded that thought as she dreaded death.

"I was a fool, Pelleas," she said, with a queer intensity of tone that made the man look quickly into her eyes.

"You did not know."

"Pardon, Pelleas, I knew your soul, how true and strong it was. God knows I tried you to the end, and bitter truth it proved to me. If you had only waited."

"Ah, Igraine."

"Only a night; you would have had the truth at dawn."

"I struggled for your soul and for mine, as I thought."

"Yes, yes, you chose the nobler part, thinking me a mere woman, a frail thing blown about by my own passion. I loved you, Pelleas, for the deed, though it nigh brought me to my death."

"God knows I honoured you, Igraine."

"Too well; it had been better for us both if you had been more human."

There was an anguish of regret in her voice, a plaintive accusation that made Pelleas wince to the core. He bent down and kissed her hand as it lay in her lap, then looked into her face with a mute appeal that brought her to the verge of tears.

"Courage, courage, dear heart."

"God bless you, Igraine."

"I am very glad of your love."

"Come now, tell me how the year has passed."

Igraine held his hand in hers and began to twist her hair about his wrist into a bracelet of gold. Her eyes faltered from his, and were hot and heavy with an inward misery of thought. The man's words wounded her at every turn, and in his innocence he shook her happiness as a wind shakes a tree.

"There is little I can tell you," she said.

"Every hour is as gold to me."

"Would I had them lying in my lap."

"We are young yet, Igraine."

There was a joyousness in his voice that sounded to the girl like a blow struck upon empty brass, or like the laugh of a child through a ruined house. His rich optimism mocked her to the echo.

"I took refuge in Winchester," she began, "with Radamanth my uncle, and lodged there many months. I watched for you and waited, but got no news of a knight named Pelleas. Week by week as my knowledge grew I began to think and think, to piece fragments together, to dream in my heart. I longed to see this Uther of whom all Britain talked. Ah, you remember the cross, Pelleas, which you left at my feet?"

Pelleas smiled. She put her hand into her bosom with a little blush of pride and looked into the man's eyes.

"I have it here still," she said, "where it has hung these many months. This scrap of gold first taught me to look for Uther."

"Ah, Igraine, am I a king!"

"My king, sire. And oh! how long it was before I could get news of you; yet in time tidings came. Then it was that I left Winchester, went on foot through the land, and hearing again of you I set out for Wales and Caerleon with rumours of war in my ears. Even from Caerleon I followed you, even to the western sea, where I saw the great battle with Gilomannius, and the noble deeds you did there for Britain."

Pelleas's dark eyes flashed up to hers. A man loves to be noble in deed before the face of the woman he serves, a species of divine vanity that begets heroes. The girl's staunch faith was a thing that proffered the superbest flattery.

"You are very wonderful, Igraine."

"It was all for my own heart; and what greater joy could I have than to see you a king before the thundering swords of your knights."

"You saw that, Igraine?"

"Do you remember a hillock by the pine forest on the ridge, where you reined in after the charge and uncovered your head to the sun?"

"As it were yesterday."

"I stood on that hillock, Pelleas, and saw your face after many months."

"Ah, Igraine, said I not you were very wonderful?"

"No, no, I am only a woman, only a woman."

"God give me such a wife."

The word was keen as the barb of a lance. Pelleas's head was bowed over the girl's hand as he pressed his lips to the gold circlet of hair, and he did not see the frown of pain upon her face. Wife! What a mockery, what bitterness! The sky seemed black for a moment, the valley bare with the blasts of winter and the moan of tortured trees. She half choked in her throat, and her heart seemed to fail within her like a bowl that is broken. Yet there was a smile on her face when Pelleas looked up from the circlet of her hair with the pride of love in his large eyes.

"What ails you, Igraine?"

"A mere thought of the past."

"Tell it me."

"No, no, it is a nothing, a mere vapour, and it has passed. How warm your lips are to my fingers. Tell me of yourself, Pelleas."

"But this armour, Igraine?"

"I took it from a dead knight, God rest his soul. I have

wandered long in Wales, yet ever drew to Caerleon where folk spoke your name, yet never might I come near you, lest — lest you were too great for me."

"Child, child!"

"Uther Pendragon, King of Britain!"

"Let the world die."

"And let us live; Pelleas, tell me of yourself."

The man looked long over the valley in silence. His face was very grave, and his eyes were deep with thought as though the past awed him with the recollection of its bitterness.

"May I never pass such another night," he said.

The words were curt and calm enough as though leaving infinite things unsaid. Igraine sat silent by him and still plaited her hair about his wrist.

"I went away in the dark, for I thought you were a nun, Igraine, and I would not break your vows. I was nearly blind for an hour. Twice my horse stumbled and fell with me in the woods, and once I was smitten out of the saddle by a tree. Dawn came, and how I cursed the sun. I seemed to see your face everywhere, and to hear your voice in every sound. Days came and went, and I hated the sight of man; as for my prayers, I could not say them, and I was dumb in my heart towards God. I rode north into the wilds, and into the fenlands of the east. Strange things befell me in many places. I fought often, beast and wild men and robber ruffians out of the woods. Fighting pleased me; it eased the wrath in my heart that seemed to rage up against the world, and against all things that drew breath. I wandered in the night of the forests, waded through swamps, took my food by the sword, and never blessed man or woman. I felt bitter and evil to the core."

Igraine bent down and touched his forehead with her lips.

"Brave heart," she said.

"You shall hear how I came by my own soul again."

"Ah, tell me that."

"It was as though a still voice came to me out of heaven.

I was riding in the northern wilds not far from rough coast-land and the sea, and riding, came upon a little house of timber all bowered round with trees. It was a peaceful spot, flowers grew around, and the sun was shining, and I drew near, moved in my heart to beg food and rest, for I was half starved and gaunt as a monk from an African desert. What did I see there? A dead man tied to a tree and gored with many wounds; a woman kneeling dead before his feet, thrust through with a sword; a little child lying near with its head crushed by a stone or a club. The sword was a Saxon sword, and I knew who had done the deed; but sight of the dead folk by their empty home seemed to smite my pity like the thought of the dead Christ. I had pitied but myself and you, Igraine, and had wandered through the land like a brute beast mad with the smart of my own wound. Here was woe enough, agony enough, to shame my heart. Straightway I went down on my knees and prayed, and came through penitence and fire to a knowledge of myself. 'Rise up,' said the voice in me, 'rise up and play the man. There is much sorrow in Britain, much shedding of innocent blood, much violence, and much brute wrath. Rise up and strike for woman and for babe, let your sword shine against the wolves from over the sea, let your shield hurl them from the ruined hearths of Britain, the smoking churches, and the children of the cross.' So I rose up strong again and comforted, and rode back into the world to do my duty."

When Pelleas had made an end of speaking, Igraine's eyes were full of tears. The simplicity of the man's words had awakened to the full all the pathos of the past in her, and she was as proud of him as when she saw him hurl Gilomannius and his host down the green slopes towards the sea. Her lips quivered as she spoke to him — looking into his face with her eyes dim and shadowy with tears.

"Forgive me all this."

"It has been good for me, Igraine, nor would I alter the days that are gone."

"No, no."

"We have found love again."

"Ah, Pelleas!"

"What more need we ask?"

"What more?"

Her voice was half a wail. Again it was winter, and the wind blew as though at midnight; the flowers and the green woods were blurred before the girl's eyes. Gorlois's hard face and the grey walls of Tintagel came betwixt her and the summer. And, though the mood lasted but for a moment, it seemed like the long agony of days crushed into the compass of a minute.

Evening stood calm-eyed in the east. A tranquil heat hung over wood and valley, a warm silence that seemed to bind the world into a golden swoon. Not a ripple stirred in the grass with its tapestries of flowers; every leaf was hushed upon the bough; nothing moved save the droning bee and the wings of the butterflies hovering colour-bright over the meadows. The sky was a mighty sapphire, the woods carved emeralds piled giantwise to the sun. There was no discord and no sound of man, as though the curse of Adam was not yet.

Igraine had drawn Pelleas's great sword from its sheath. She held it slantwise before her, and pressed her lips to the cold steel.

"Old friend," she said, "be ever true to me."

Pelleas laughed and touched her hair with his hand. A kind of exaltation came upon them, and the zest of life crept through the bodies like green sap in spring. Igraine had filled her brazen helmet to the brim with flowers, and she scattered them and sang as they roamed into the hoar shadows of the woods:—

"Dear love of mine,
Where art thou roaming?
The west is red,
My heart is calling."

Never had the vaults seemed greener, the half light more mysterious under the massive trees. The far world was out of ken; they alone lived and had their being; the toil of man was not even like the long sob of a moonlit sea, or the sound of rivers running in the night.

The infinite strangeness of beauty shone over them like a wizard light out of the west. Igraine's lips were very red, her face white in the shadows, her eyes deep with mute desire. Hand held hand, body touched body. Often she would lie out upon Pelleas's arm, her head upon his shoulder, her hair clouding over his red harness. They were content to be together, to forget the world save so much of it as came within the ken of their eyes, and the close grip of their twined fingers. They said little as they swayed together under the trees. Soul ebbed into soul upon their lips, and a deep ecstasy possessed them like the throbbing pathos of some song.

As the day deepened Pelleas and Igraine turned back into the valley, hand in hand. The west burnt gold above the tree tops, the gnarled trunks were pillars of agate bearing Byzant domes of breathless leaves. By the white May trees the two horses stood tethered, black and grey against the grass. Loosing them, and taking each a bridle, they passed down through flowers to the cottage and the pool.

Garlotte met them there with her brown hair pouring over her shoulders, and a clean white kerchief over her throat and bosom. She came to them through a little thicket of fox-gloves that were budding early, white and purple. Her blue eyes quivered for a moment over Pelleas's face as she made him a deep curtsey, and bent to kiss Igraine's hand. There was a vast measure of sympathy in Garlotte's heart, and yet for all her well-wishing she was troubled for the two, fearing for them instinctively with even her small knowledge of the world. She had learnt enough from Igraine to comprehend in measure that element of tragedy that had entered with Gorlois into her life. Her interest in the man Pelleas was no mere vulgar curiosity, rather an intense pity that permeated her warm innocence of spirit to the core.

She had spread supper on the table, a much meditated feast that had kept her eagerly busy since she had guessed the name of the strange knight who had ridden down out of the woods. She had the pride of a young housewife in her creamy milk, her bread. She had made a tansy cake, and there was a rich cream cheese ready in the cupboard, and a fat rabbit stewing by the fire. Yet for all her ingenuous pride she felt much troubled when it came to the test lest her fare should seem rude and meagre to the great knight in the red harness. Certainly he had a kind face and splendid eyes, but would he not smile at her humble supper, her horn cups, and her plates of hollywood? Her cares were empty enough, but they were very real to the sensitive child who feared to seem shamed before Igraine.

Half the happiness of life lies in the kindly sensibility of others to our desire for sympathy. A surly word, a trivial ungraciousness, a small deed passed over in thankless silence, how much these things mean to a sensitive heart! Garlotte, standing in her cottage door, half shy and timid, found her small fears mere little goblins of her own invention. Igraine, radiant as the evening, came and kissed her on the lips.

"Little sister, you have been very good to me."

The great knight too was smiling at her in quite a fatherly fashion. What a strong face he had, and what a noble look; she felt sure that he was a good man, and her heart went out to him like an opening flower. When he took her hand, and a lock of her hair and kissed it, she went red as one of her own roses, and was dumb with an impulsive gladness.

"Little sister, you have been very good to me."

"Good, my lord, to you!"

"Child, Igraine can tell you how."

"But the Lady Igraine, she saved my life!"

"Ah, I had not heard that. Tell me."

Garlotte found her ease in a moment. The whole tale came bubbling up like water out of a spring. Pelleas's strong face beamed; he touched Igraine's hair with his fingers and looked into her eyes as only a man in love can look. Garlotte saw that she was giving pleasure, and felt a glow from head to heart. Surely this great, grave-faced knight was a noble soul; how gentle he was, and how he looked into Igraine's eyes and bent over her like a tall elm over a slim cypress tree. She caught the happiness of the two, and from that moment her heart was singing and she had no more fear for herself and her poor cottage. Even the horn cups took a golden dignity, and her tansy cake and her cream seemed fit for a prince.

The three were soon at supper together round the wooden table, with honeysuckle and roses climbing close above their heads. Garlotte would have stood and waited on Pelleas and Igraine, but they would have none of it; so she was set smiling at the head of her little table, and constrained to play the lady under her own roof. It was a dull meal so far as mere words were concerned. Pelleas's eyes were on Igraine in the twilight, and he had no hunger save hunger of heart; yet that the supper was a success there was no doubt whatever. Garlotte watched them both with a quiet delight; young as she was she was wise in the simple love of love, and so she mothered the pair to her heart's content in her own imagination. If only Renan had been there to help her serve, and touch her hand under the table, what a perfect guest-hour it would have been.

When the meal was over she jumped up with a shy smile, took a rush basket from the wall, and went out into the garden. Igraine called her back.

"Where are you going, child?"

"Up the valley to the dead oak tree where herbs grow. I must make a stew to-morrow."

"It will soon be dark."

Garlotte swung her basket and laughed from her cloud of hair.

"You gathered herbs on Sunday, Igraine."

"You squirrel!"

"Renan was here; you came home after dusk; good-by, good-by."

They heard her go singing through the garden, a soft *chant a'amour* that would have gone wondrously to flute and cithern. It died away slowly amid the trees like an elf's song coming from woodlands in the moonlight. Pelleas drew a deep breath and listened in the shadow of the room with his hands clasped before him on the table. He looked as though he were praying. Igraine's eyes were glooms of violet mystery as she watched him, her hands folded over a breast that rose and fell as with the restless motion of a troubled sea. She called the man softly by name; her body bent to him like a bow, her hair bathed his face with dim ripples of gold as mouth touched mouth.

They went out into the garden together and stood under the cedar tree.

"Pelleas, my love, my own."

"Heart of mine."

"You will never leave me?"

"How should the sea put the earth from his bosom, or the moon pass from the arms of the night?"

"I am faint, Pelleas; hold me in your arms."

"They are strong, Igraine."

"There, let me rest so, for ever. Look, the stars are coming out, and there is the moon flooding silver over the trees. My lips burn, and I am faint."

"Courage, courage, dear heart."

"How close you hold me! I could die so."

"What is death to us, Igraine?"

"Or life?"

"God in heaven, and heaven on earth."

"Your words hurt me."

XI

How the birds sang that evening as a saffron afterglow fainted over the forest spires, and when all was still with the hush of night how the cry of a nightingale thrilled from a tree near the cottage!

The glamour of the day had passed, and now what mockery and bitterness came with the cold, calculating face of the moon. Igraine tossed and turned in her bed like one taken with a fever; her brain seemed afire, her hair like so much flame about her forehead. As she lay staring with wide, wakeful eyes, the birds' song mocked her to the echo, the scent of honeysuckle and rose floated in like a sad savour of death, and the moonlight seemed to watch her without a quaver of pity. Her heart panted in the darkness; she was torn by the thousand torments of a troubled conscience, wounded to tears, yet her eyes were dry and waterless as a desert. Gorlois's face seemed to glare down at her out of the idle gloom, and she could have cried out with the fear that lay like an icy hand over her bosom.

Pelleas slept under the cedar tree, wrapped in an old cloak, relic of Garlotte's father. How Igraine's heart wailed for the man, how she longed for the touch of his hand! God of heaven, she could not let him go again, and starve her soul with the old cursed life. His lips had touched hers, his arms had held her close, she had felt the warmth of his body and the beating of his heart. Was all this nothing—a dream, a splendid phantasm to be rent away like a crimson cloud? Was she to be Gorlois's wife and nothing more, a bitter flower growing under a gallows, sour wine frothing in a gilded cup?

God of heaven, no! What had the world done for her that she should obey its edicts and suffer for its tyrannies? Gorlois had cheated her of her liberty, let him pay the price to the fates; what honour, indeed, had she to preserve for him? If he was a brute piece of lust, a tyrant, a demagogue, so much the better, it would ease her conscience. She owed no fealty, no marriage vow, to Gorlois. Her body was no more his than was her soul, and a dozen priests and a dozen masses might as well marry granite to fire. How could a fool in a cape and frock by gabbling a service bind an irresponsible woman to a man she hated more than the foulest mud in the foulest alley? It was a stupendous piece of nonsense, to say the least of it. No God calling himself a just God could hold such a bargain holy.

And then — the truth! What a stumbling-block truth was on occasions! She knew Pelleas's intense love of honour, the fine sensibility of his conscience, the strong thirst for the highest good, that made him the victim of an ethical tyranny. If he had left her after Andredswold because he thought her a nun, what hope now had she of holding him if he knew her to be a wife? And yet for all her love she could not bring herself to keep him wholly from the truth. For all her passion and the fire in her rebellious heart she was not a woman who could fling reason to the winds, and stifle up her conscience with a kiss. Besides, she loved Pelleas to the very zenith of her soul. To have a lie understood upon her lips, to be shamed before the man's eyes, were things that scourged her in fancy even more than the thought of losing him. She trembled when she thought how he might look at her in later days if a passive lie were proven against her with open shame.

But to tell him of Gorlois, and the humiliation of that darkest hour of her life! Could such a man as Pelleas serve her longer after such a confession? He would become a king again, a stranger, a man set in high places far beyond the mere yearning of a woman's white face. And yet, it was possible that his love might prove stronger than his reason; it was possible that he might front the world and frown down the petty judgments of men. Glorious and transcendant sacrifice! She could face calumny beside him as a rock faces the froth of waves; she could look Gorlois in the eyes, and know neither shame nor pity.

Her mood that night was like the passage of a blown leaf, tossed up to heaven, whirled over the tree tops, driven down again into the mire. Strong woman that she was, her very strength made the struggle more indecisive and more racking. She could not renounce Pelleas for the great love she bore him, and yet she could not will to play a false part by reason of this same great love. Her soul, like a wanderer in the wilds, halted and wavered between two tracks that led forward into the unknown.

Garlotte was sleeping in the far corner of the cottage. The girl had given up her bed to Igraine, who envied her her quiet, restful breathing as she lay and listened. In her doubt she called and woke Garlotte from her sleep, hardly knowing indeed what she desired to say to her, yet half fearful of lying alone longer in the night with her own thoughts for company. Garlotte rose up and came across the room to the bigger bed. She knelt down; two warm arms crept under the coverlet, and a soft cheek touched Igraine's.

"Why are you awake, Igraine?"

The warmth of the girl's body, her quiet breathing, the sweep of her hair, seemed to bring a scent of peace and human sympathy into the moonlit room. Igraine put her arms about her, and drew her down to her side. Their white faces and clouding hair lay close together on the pillow.

"You are in trouble, Igraine?"

"How should I be in trouble?"

"You breathe like one in pain, and your voice is strange."

"Hush, Garlotte."

"Am I not right?"

"Pelleas must not hear us talking."

They were silent awhile, lying in each other's arms with no sound save that of their breathing. Igraine's misery burnt in her and cried out for sympathy; Garlotte, half wise by instinct, yearned to share a trouble which she did not wholly comprehend, to advise where she was partly ignorant. The girl felt a great stirring of her heart towards Igraine, but could say nothing for the moment. Having no better eloquence at command she raised her head and kissed the other's lips, a warm, impulsive kiss that seemed as rich in sympathy as a rose in scent.

Igraine's confidence woke at the touch of the girl's lips; she hungered even for this child's comfort, her simple guidance in this matter of life and love. It was easy enough to die, hard to exist as a mere spiritless Galatea devoid of soul.

"Garlotte!"

"Yes, Igraine."

"Imagine that you were married to a man you hated, and you loved Renan."

Garlotte raised herself in bed.

"And Renan loved you and knew nothing?"

"Yes."

"Would you tell Renan the truth?"

Garlotte remained motionless, propped on her two hands, and looking out of the window into the streaming moonlight. Her brown hair touched Igraine's face as she lay still and watched her. The room was very silent, not a breeze seemed stirring, the roses athwart the window were still as though carved in wood.

Garlotte spoke very softly, looking up with her face white and solemn in the moonlight.

"I should tell Renan," she said.

"Why?"

"Because I love him."

"Yes — go on."

"I should not love him rightly in God's eyes if I kept him from the truth."

The coverlet rose and fell over Igraine's bosom, and there was a queer twisting pain at her heart.

"But if you were never to see Renan again?" she said.

"If I told him the truth?"

"Yes, child."

Garlotte dared not look into Igraine's face; her lips were twitching, and her eyes were hot with tears.

"I do not know," she faltered.

"Think, child, think!"

"I should not tell him."

In half a breath she had contradicted herself with a little gasp.

"Yes, yes, I should tell him."

"The truth?"

"Because I should not be happy even with him if I were acting a lie."

Igraine gave a dry sob, and drew Garlotte down again to her side. They lay very close, almost mouth to mouth, their arms about each other's bodies.

"I love Pelleas."

"Yes, yes."

"I will tell him the truth."

"Ah, Igraine, it is best, it is best."

"But it will kill me if I lose him."

"Ah, Igraine, but he will love you all the more."

It was Garlotte who broke into tears, and hid her face in the other's bosom. Igraine's eyes were as dry as a blue sky parched with a summer sun, and her voice failed her like the slack string of a lute. The moonlight slanted down upon them both. Before dawn they had fallen asleep in each other's arms.

How many a heart trembles with the return of day; what fears rise with the first blush of light in an empty sky! The cloak of night is lifted from weary faces; the quiet balm of darkness is withdrawn from the moiling care of many a heart. To Igraine the dawn light came like a message of misery as she lay beside the sleeping Garlotte, and watched the gloom grow less and less in the little room. This dawn seemed a veritable symbol of the truth that she feared to look upon — and recognise. The night seemed kinder, less implacable, less grave of face. Day, like a pale justiciary, stalked up out of the east to call her to that assize where truth and the soul meet under the eye of heaven.

How different was it with Pelleas under the eaves of the great cedar. He had slept little that night for mere wakeful happiness; the moon had kept carnival for him above the world; at dawn the stars had crept back from the choir stalls into the chambers of the night. He had known no weariness, no abatement of his deep calm joy. His heart had answered blithely to the dawn-song of the birds as though he had risen fresh from a dreamless sleep. The day to him had no look of evil; the sky was never grey; the flush in the east recalled no flashing of torches over a funeral bier. He rose up in the glory of his clean manhood, the strong kindliness of his great love. His prayers went to heaven that morning with the lark, and the Spirit of God seemed like a wind moving softly in the green boughs above his head.

Very early before it was light he had taken a plunge and a swim in the pool, a swinging burst through the still water that had made him revel in his great strength. He had come up from the pool like a god refreshed, and had put on his red harness while the mists rose from the valley, and the birds chanted in the ghostly trees. When the day was fully awake he walked the grass-path in the garden like a watchman, with the scent of honeysuckle and thyme in his nostrils, and a blaze of flowers at his feet. As he paced up and down with his face turned to the sky, he sang in a mellow bass a song of Guyon's, the Court minstrel—

"When the dawn has come,
My heart sighs for thee and the gleam of thy hair;
Eyes deep as the night
When the summer sky arches the world."

So sang Pelleas as he paced the grass with his eyes wandering ever towards the doorway of the cottage.

Presently Igraine came out to him, and stood under the shadow of the porch. Her hair hung lustrous about a face that was white and drawn, despite a smile. Certainly a haze of red flushed her cheeks when Pelleas came up with a glory of love in his eyes, took her hands and kissed them, as though there was no such divine flesh in the whole wide world. How wonderful it was to be touched so, to have such eyes pouring out so strong a soul before her face, to know the presence of a great love, and to feel the echoing passion of it in her own heart!

After the barren months of winter, and the long bondage in Tintagel, it seemed an idyllic thing to be so served, so comforted. And was this faery time but for an hour, a day, and no longer? Was she but to see the man's face, to feel the touch of his hands, the grand calm of his love, before losing him, perhaps for life? Her heart fluttered in her like a smitten bird. And Pelleas, too, what a thrust lurked for the man, a blow to be given in the name of truth. How could she speak to him of Gorlois when he came and looked at her with those eyes of his?

Igraine had never felt such misery as this even in the gloomy galleries of Tintagel. It tried her courage to the death to face Pelleas's wistful gaiety, and the adoration that beamed on her from his eyes.

"Dear heart, it is dawn — it is dawn!"

Pelleas held her hands, and waited for her lips to be turned to his. Instead, he saw lowered lids and quivering lashes, lips that were plaintive, a face white beneath a wealth of hair.

"Ah, Igraine, you do not look at me."

Her eyes trembled up to his with a sudden infinite lustre.

"Pelleas!"

"Girl, girl!"

"Ah, I have hardly slept."

"Nor I, Igraine."

"I think I am worn out with thinking of you."

"Ha, little woman, you are extravagant; you will die like a flower even while I hold you in my bosom."

Garlotte came out from the cottage, and was kissed by Pelleas on the lips. The girl's eyes were red and heavy; she had been crying but a moment ago in the shadow of the cottage room, and she was timid and very solemn. Pelleas looked at her like a big brother.

"Come now, little sister," he said, with a rare smile; "methinks you must be in love too by your looks."

"Yes, lord."

"Said I not so? You women take things so to heart."

"Yes, lord."

"What a solemn face, little sister!"

Garlotte mastered herself for a moment, then burst into tears and ran back into the cottage. Pelleas coloured, looked troubled, glanced at Igraine, thinking he had hurt the girl's heart with his words. Igraine's face startled him as if the visage of death had risen up suddenly amid the flowers. He stood mute before her watching her starved lips, her drawn face, her eyes that stared beyond him with a kind of cold frenzy.

"Pelleas, Pelleas!"

It was like the wild cry of a woman over her dead love. The sound struck Pelleas with a vague sense of stupendous woe, a dim prophecy of evil like the noise of autumn in the woods. Before he could gather words, Igraine had turned and run from him as in great fear, skirting the pool and holding for the black yawn of the forest aisles. Pelleas started to follow her in a daze of wonder. Was the girl mad? Had love turned her brain? What was there hid in her heart that made her wing from him like a dove from a hawk?

By the trees Igraine slackened and turned breathless on the man as he came towards her through the long grass. Her eyes were dim and frightened, her lips twitching, and there was a bleak hunted look upon her face that made her seem white and old. Pelleas's blood ran cold in him like water; a vague dread sapped his manhood; he stared at Igraine and was speechless.

The girl put her arm before her eyes and shook as she stood. Pelleas fell on his knees with a cry, and reached for her hand.

"Igraine, Igraine!"

She snatched her arm away and would not look at him.

"My God, what is this, Igraine?"

"Don't touch me; I am Gorlois's wife!"

A vast silence seemed to fall sudden on the world. It might have been dead of night in winter, with deep snow upon the ground and no wind stirring in the forest. To Igraine, swaying in an agony with her arm over her face, the silence came like the hush that might fall on heaven before the damning of a lost soul to hell. She wondered what was in Pelleas's heart, and dared not look at him or meet his eyes. God in heaven! would the man never speak; would the silence crawl on into an eternity!

At last she did look, and nearly fell at the wrench of it. Pelleas was standing near her looking at her with his great solemn eyes as though she had given him his death. His face seemed to have gone grey and haggard in a moment.

"Gorlois's wife!" was all he said.

Igraine hung her head, shivered, and said nothing. Pelleas never stirred; he seemed like so much stone, a mere pillar of granite misery. Igraine could have writhed at his feet and caught him by the knees only to melt for a moment that white calm on his face that looked like the mask of death.

A voice that was almost strange to her startled her out of her stupor of despair.

"How long have you been wed, Igraine?"

"Nine months, Pelleas."

The man seemed to be struggling with himself as though he strove after the truth, yet could not confront it for all his strength. When he spoke his voice was like the voice of a man winded by hard running. He appeared to urge himself forward, to goad his courage to a task that he dreaded. There was great anguish on his face as he looked into the girl's eyes.

"I must speak what I know, Igraine."

The words seemed slow with effort. Igraine watched him in silence, full of a vague dread.

"Gorlois has spoken to me of his wife."

"Say on, Pelleas."

Pelleas hesitated.

"The truth — tell me the truth."

She was almost clamorous. Pelleas plunged on.

"Gorlois told me how his wife was faithless to him, how she had fled with Brastias, the knight who had ward over her at Caerleon. I never knew her name until this hour."

The words might have fallen like the strokes of a lash. Igraine stood and stared at the man, her open mouth a black circle, her eyes expressionless for the moment, like the eyes of one smitten blind. The full meaning of the words numbed her and hindered her understanding. A babel of shame sounded in her ears. The sinister intent of the man's accusation rose gradual before her reason like the distorted image of a dream. She felt cold to the core; a strange terror possessed her.

"Pelleas, what have you said to me?"

Her voice was a mere whisper. Pelleas hung his head and said never a word. His silence seemed to fling sudden fire into Igraine's eyes, and her face flamed like a sunset. It might have been Gorlois who stood and challenged the honour of her soul.

"Man, tell me what is in your heart."

Her voice was shrill — even imperious. Pelleas hung his head.

"Gorlois keeps poison for his wife," were his words.

Igraine's lips curled.

"A sword for Brastias."

"Generous man."

Pelleas was watching her as a prisoner watches a judge. He had a great yearning to believe. Fear, anguish, anger, were in Igraine's heart, but she showed none of the three as she stood forward and looked into the man's eyes with a steadfastness no honour could gainsay.

"Pelleas!" she said.

"Girl!"

"Look into my eyes."

He did so without flinching. Igraine took his sword and gave it naked into his hand.

"Listen! Gorlois told you a lie."

"Igraine!"

"Do you believe me, Pelleas? If not, strike with the sword, for I will live no longer."

The man gave a sudden cry, like one who leaps over a precipice, threw the sword far away into the grass, and falling on his knees, buried his face in his hands.

XII

IGRAINE stood and watched Pelleas as he knelt in the grass at her feet with his face hidden from her by his hands. She saw the curve of his strong neck, the sweep of his great shoulders. She even counted the steel plates in his shoulder pieces, and marked the tinge of grey in his coronal of hair.

Calm had come upon her with the trust won by the confessional of the sword. She felt sure of the man in her heart, and eased of a double burden since she had told him the truth and brought him to a declaration of his faith. She knew well from instinct that her honour stood sure in Pelleas's heart.

Going to him, she bent and touched his head with her hand.

"Pelleas," she said very softly.

The man groaned and would not look at her.

"Mea culpa, mea culpa!" was his cry.

Igraine smiled like a young mother as she put his hands

from his face with a gradual insistence. It was right that he should kneel to her, but it was also right that she should forgive and forget like a woman. Yet as she stood and held his hands in hers, Pelleas hung his head and would not so much as look into her face. He was convicted in his own heart, and contrite according to the deep measure of his manhood.

Igraine touched his hair softly with her fingers, and there was a great light in her eyes as she bent over him.

"Come, Pelleas, and sit by me under the trees, and I will tell you the whole tale."

Never had she seemed so stately or so superb in Pelleas's eyes as she stood before him that morning, strong and sorrowful with the burden of her past. He knelt and looked up at her, knowing himself pardoned, humbled to see love in the ascendent so soon upon her face as she looked down at him from her golden aureole of hair.

"I am forgiven?" he said.

"Ah, Pelleas!"

"You have shamed me; I am a broken man."

He rose up half wearily and stood looking at her as though some mysterious influence had parted them suddenly asunder. So expressive were his eyes, that Igraine read a distant anguish in them on the instant, and fathomed his thoughts, to the troubling of her own heart.

"Look not so," she said, "as though a gulf lay deep between us here."

"How else should I look at you, Igraine, when you are wife to Gorlois?"

"Never in my soul."

"How can that help us?"

Igraine winced at the words and took refuge in silence. She went and seated herself at the foot of a gnarled oak. Pelleas followed her and lay down more than a sword's length away, leaving a stretch of green turf between, a thing insignificant in itself, yet full of meaning to the girl's instinctive watchfulness. The man's face too was turned from her towards the valley, and she could only see the curve of his cheek and chin as she began to speak to him of that which was in her heart.

"You know the man Gorlois?" she said.

Pelleas nodded.

"In Winchester Gorlois saw my face and straightway pestered me as he had been turned into my shadow. By chance he had rendered me service, and from the favour casually conferred plucked the right of thrusting his perpetual homage upon me. I trusted Gorlois little from the beginning, and trusted him less as the weeks went by. His eyes frightened me, and his mouth made my soul shiver; the more importunate he grew the more I began to fear him."

Pelleas shifted his sword and said nothing.

"A day came when the man Gorlois grew tired of courtesies, and would be gainsaid no longer. It was in Radamanth's garden; we quarrelled, and the man laid hands upon me and crushed me against the wall to thieve a kiss. In my anger I broke from him and ran into my uncle's house. The same night I fled to an abbey, the abbey of St. Helena, and left Winchester in my dress at dawn."

Igraine could see the muscles of Pelleas's jaw standing out contracted as though his teeth were clenched in an access of anger. He was breathing deeply through his nostrils, and his hands plucked at the grass with a terse snapping sound. These things pleased Igraine, and she went on forthwith.

"I left Winchester on foot at dawn and travelled towards Sarum, for I heard that Uther the King was there, and it was greatly in my mind, sire, to see his face. An old merchant friend of Radamanth's overtook me on the road; at a ford the horse he had lent me fell and twisted my ankle. I was carried to Eudol's house, and lay abed there many days, learning little to my comfort that Gorlois had ridden out and was hunting me through the countryside. Recovered of my strain, and fearful of Gorlois's trackers, I held on for Sarum through the woods, and lodged the same night in a hermitage in a little valley. Here the first piece of craft overtook me, for early in the morning outside the hermitage I saw a knight ride by on a black horse, bearing red harness, and armed at all points like to you."

Pelleas turned his head for the first time and looked at her as though with some sudden suspicion of what was to follow. Igraine saw something in his dark eyes that made her heart hurry. His face was like the face of a man who fronts a storm of wind and rain with brows furrowed and eyes half-closed. There was much that was threatening in his look, a subdued ominous wrath like a storm nursed in the bosom of a cloud.

Igraine told the whole quaint tale, how she followed Gorlois in faith, how she was led into the forest, bewitched there, and made a wife, mesmerised into a false affection for the man by Merlin's craft. It was a grim tale, with a clear contour of truth, and credible by reason of its very strangeness. It was sufficient to manifest to Pelleas how Igraine's strong love for him had lost her her liberty and made her the victim of a man's lust.

When she had ended the tale Pelleas left the grass at her feet and began to pace under the trees like a sentinel on a wall. His scabbard clanged occasionally against his greaves. Masses of young bracken covered the ground between the trees with a rich carpet of green, and his armour shone like red wrath under the wreathing arcs of foliage. His face was dark and moody with the turmoil of thought, but there was no visible agitation upon him; nothing of the aspen, more of the unbending oak. Igraine leant against her tree and watched him with a curious care, wondering what would be the outcome of all this silence. Down in the valley the pool glistened, and she could see Garlotte walking in the cottage garden. How different was this child's lot to hers. With what warm philosophy could she have changed Pelleas into a shepherd, and taken the part of Garlotte to herself.

Presently Pelleas stayed in his stride through the bracken, and came and stood before her, looking not into her face but beyond her into the deeps of the wood.

"Tell me more, Igraine."

"What more would you hear from me?"

"That which is bitterest of all."

"God, must I tell you that!"

"Let us both drink it to the dregs."

Igraine's face and neck coloured rich as one of Garlotte's red roses, and she seemed to shrink from the man's eyes behind the quivering sunlight of her hair. She put her hands to her breast and stood in a strain of thought, of struggle against the infinite unfitness of the past.

Pelleas saw her trouble, and his strong face softened on the instant. He had forgotton milder things in his grappling of the truth. Igraine's red and troubled look revived the finer instincts of his manhood.

"Never trouble, child," he said; "I know enough of Gorlois to read the rest."

But Igraine, as by inspiration, had come by other reasons for telling out the whole to the last pang. She was at pains to justify herself to Pelleas, nor was she undesirous of inflaming him against Gorlois, her lord. She had wit enough to grasp the fact that Pelleas's wrath might be roused into insurrection against custom and the edicts of the Church. A volcanic outburst might throw down the barriers of man and leave her at liberty to choose her lot. Moreover, her hate of Gorlois, an iconoclastic passion, had crushed the reverence of things existing out of her heart. A contemplation of her evil fortune had brought her to the conviction that she was exiled from the sympathies of men, a spiritual bandit driven to compass the instincts of a rebellious soul. In her hot impulse for liberty and the justification of her faith, she did not halt from making Pelleas feel the full malignity of truth. She neither embellished nor emphasised, but portrayed incidents simply in their glaring nakedness in a fashion that promised to inflame the man to the very top of her desire.

Igraine's cheeks kindled, and she could not look at the man for the words upon her lips. Pelleas's face was like the face of man in torture. The woman's words entered into him like iron; his wrath whistled like a wind, and the very air seemed tainted in his mouth. What a purgatory of passion was let loose into the calm precincts of the place! This burning vault of blue, was it the same as roofed the world of yesterday? The feathery mounts of green dappled with amber, and these flowers, had they not changed with the noon lust of the sun? There was a rank savour of fleshliness over the whole earth, and all life seemed impious, passionate, and unclean.

"My God, my God!"

The man's cry shook Igraine from her rage for truth. In her confessional she had been carried like a bird with the wind. Looking into Pelleas's face she saw that he was in torment, and that her words had smitten him in a fashion other than she had foreseen. It was not wrath that burnt in his eyes, only a deep grieving, a frenzy of shame and anguish that seemed to cry out against her soul. A sudden stupor made her mute. With a great void in her heart she fell down amid the bracken with a sense of ignominy and abasement overwhelming her like a deluge.

Pelleas stood and shut his eyes to the sun. A red glare smote into his brain; love seemed numb in him and his blood stagnant. Prayer eluded him like a vapour. Looking out again over wood and valley, the golden haze, the torpor of the trees mocked him with a lethargy that smiled at the impotence of man.

And Igraine! He saw her prone beneath the green mist of the fern fronds, lying with her face pillowed on her arms, her hair spread like a golden net over the brown wreckage of the bygone year. To what a pass had their love come! Better, he thought, to have lived a king solitary on a throne than to have wandered into youth again to give and win such dolor.

His face was dark as he stood and looked at the woman's violet surcoat gleaming low under the bracken. How symbolical this attitude seemed of all that had fallen upon his heart — love cast down upon dead leaves! Igraine had feared his honour. Pelleas feared for it in another sense as he looked at the woman, and felt his pity clamouring for life. He could have given his soul to comfort her if no shame could have come upon her name thereby. As it was, some spiritual hand seemed at his throat stifling aught of love that found impulse on his lips. A superhuman sincerity chilled him into silence, and held him in bondage to the truth.

A face stared up from the bracken, wan, tearless, and tragic. The wistfulness of the face made him quail within his harness. He knew too well what was in Igraine's heart, and the look that questioned him like the look of a wounded hare. Her eyes searched his face as though to read her doom thereon. There was no whimpering, no noise, no passionate rhetoric. A great quiet seemed to take its temper from the silence of the woods.

"Pelleas."

"Yes, Igraine."

"Tell me what is in your heart."

Pelleas hung his head; he could not look at her for all his courage. She was kneeling in the bracken with her hands crossed over her breast and her face turned to his with the white wistfulness of a full moon. Pelleas felt death in his heart, and he could not speak nor look into her eyes.

"Pelleas."

"Child."

"You do not look at me."

"Great God, would I were blind!"

The truth came crying to her like the wild cry of a bird taken by a weasel in the woods. A great sobbing shook her; she fell down and caught Pelleas by the knees.

"Pelleas, Pelleas!"

"My God, Igraine, I stifle!"

"Don't leave me, don't send me away."

"What can I say to you?"

"Only look into my eyes again."

Pelleas put his fists before his face; the girl felt him quiver, and he seemed to twist in an agony like a man dangling on a rope. Igraine's hands crept to his shoulders; she drew herself by his body as by a pillar till her face met his and she lay heavy upon his breast.

"Pelleas!"

Her breath was on his lips, and her hair flooded over his hands like golden wine.

"Pelleas, Pelleas!"

The words came with a windless whisper.

"Have pity, Igraine."

"I will never leave you."

"Gorlois's wife!"

"Never, never!"

"My God!"

"I am not his. Pelleas, take me body and soul; take me and let me be your wife."

"How can I sin against your soul, Igraine?"

"Is it sin, then, to love me?"

"You are Gorlois's wife before God."

"There is no God."

"Igraine!"

"I will have no God but you, Pelleas."

The man took his hands from his face and looked into Igraine's eyes. A strong shudder passed over him, and he seemed like a great ship smitten by a wave, till every fibre groaned and quivered in his massive frame.

A green calm covered the valley, and the whole world seemed to faint in the golden bosom of the day. Not the twitter of a bird broke the vast hush of the forest. The sunlit aisles climbed into a shadowland of mysterious silence, and an azure quiet hung above the trees. As for Pelleas and Igraine, their two lives seemed knotted up with a cord of gold. They had mingled breath, and taken the savour of each other's souls. Yet for all the glory of the moment it was but autumn with them — a pomp of passion, a red splendour dying while it blazed into the grey ruin of a winter day.

Igraine read her doom in the man's face. It was the face of a martyr, pale, resolute, yet inspired. A dry sob died in her throat, and her hands dropped from the man's shoulders. Pelleas stood back and looked at her with a warm light in his dark eyes, the green woods rising behind him like a bank of clouds.

"Igraine."

She nodded, felt miserable, and said nothing.

"I cannot love you easily."

Igraine's eyes stared at him with a mute bitterness. She was a woman, and thought like a woman; mere saintly philosophy was beyond her.

"You are too good a man, Pelleas," she said.

"I would hold my love in my heart like a great pearl in a casket of gold."

"What comfort is there in mere splendid misery, and in such words?"

"How should I love you best?"

"Ah, Pelleas, ask your own heart."

The man was an impossible being for mere mortal argument. He seemed to bear spiritual pinions that tantalised the intelligence of the heart. Igraine felt herself adrift and beaten, and she was hopeless of him to the core.

"Think you I shall be a saint, Pelleas," she said, "when you have given me back to myself?"

"I shall pray for you."

"And for a devil!"

She gave a shrill laugh, and twined her hair about her wrist.

"Ah, Pelleas! you know not what you do."

"Too well, Igraine."

"You are too strong for me, and yet—and yet—I should not have loved you so well if you had not been strong."

"That is how I think of you, Igraine."

"You love me more by leaving me."

"I love you more by keeping you pure before my soul."

A great calm had come upon Igraine. She was very pale and firm about the lips, and her eyes were staunch as steel. Her voice was as clear and level as though she spoke of trivial things.

"I shall not go back to Gorlois," she said.

"Beware of the man."

"Doubtless you would speak to me of a convent."

Pelleas fell into thought, with his dark eyes fixed upon her face.

"As a novice."

Igraine almost smiled at him.

"And not a nun?"

For answer he spoke three simple words.

"Gorlois might die."

The stillness of the woods seemed like the hush of a listening multitude. A blue haze of heat hung over the rolling domes of the western trees, and never a wind-wave stirred the long grass. Mountainous clouds sailed radiant over ridge and spur, and it might have been Elysium where souls wandered through meads of asphodel.

Igraine looked long over the valley with its stately trees, its flowering grass and quiet pool in the meadows. She was vastly calm, though her eyes were full of a woe that seemed to well up like water out of her soul. She still twisted and untwisted a strand of her hair about her wrist, but for all else she was as quiet as one of the trees that stood near and overshadowed her.

"Pelleas," she said.

The man came two steps nearer.

"Go quickly."

"Igraine!"

"Man, man, how long will you torture me? I am only a little strong."

The calm of tragedy seemed to dissolve away on the instant. Pelleas thrust his hands into the air like a swimmer sinking to his death. His heart answered Igraine's exceeding bitter cry.

"Would we had never come to this!"

"I cannot say that, though my heart breaks."

Pelleas fell down and clasped her with his arms about the knees. His face was hidden in the folds of her surcoat. Presently he loosed his hold, looked up, took a ring from his hand and thrust it into her palm.

"The signet of a king," he said; "keep it for need, Igraine. Have you money?"

"I have money, Pelleas."

"God guard you!"

Igraine was white to the lips, but she never wavered.

"Heaven keep you!" she said.

Her voice was hoarse in her throat, and she began to shiver as though chilled by a sleety wind.

"Go quickly, Pelleas; for God's sake hide your face from me!"

"It is death; it is death!"

He sprang up and left her without a look. Igraine saw him go through the long grass with his hand over his eyes, staggering like one sword-smitten to the brain. He never stared back at her, but held straight for the cottage and the cedar tree where his black horse was tethered under the shade. She watched him mount and gallop for the forest, nor did she move till his red harness had died into the gloom of the trees.

XIII

Down through the woods that morning rode Gorlois on his great white horse, with helmet clanging at saddle-bow, shield hung at his left shoulder, spear trailing under the trees. He was hot, thirsty, and in a most evil temper. His bronzed face glistened with sweat, and the chequered webs of light flickering through the leaves flashed fitfully upon his golden harness. Since dawn he had ridden the hills in the glare of the sun till his armour blazed like an oven; it was June weather, and hot at that; his tongue felt like wood rubbing against leather; it was a damnable month for bearing harness.

Casting about over the hills he had come upon Garlotte's valley, and seeing it green and shadowy, had plunged down to profit by the shade. Since the Red Knight was lost to him, it was immaterial whether he rode by wood or hill. On this account, too, Gorlois's temper was as hot as his skin. He hated a baulking above all things; he was moved to be furious with trifles, and like the savage who gnashes at the stone that bruises his foot, he cursed creation and felt thoroughly at war with the world. A grim unreason had possession of him, such a mood as makes murder a mere impulse of the hand, and malice the prime instinct of the heart.

As he rode with loose rein the trees thinned suddenly, and the forest gloom rolled back over his head. Gorlois halted mechanically under the wooelshawe, and scanned the valley spread before him under the brown hollow of his hand. He had expected no such open land in this waste of wood — open land with water, a cottage, sheep feeding, and horses tethered under the trees. One of the horses tethered there was a black. The coincidence livened Gorlois's torpid, sunburnt face with a cool gleam of intelligence. He sat motionless in the saddle and took the length and breadth of the valley under the keen ken of his black eyes.

The man swore a little oath into his peaked black beard. His face grew suddenly rapacious as he stared out under the hollow of his hand. He had seen a streak of red strike through the green wall far up the eastern slope that fronted him, a scrap of colour metallic with the hint of armour.

It went to and fro under the distant trees like a torch past the windows of a church. Gorlois's hand tightened on the bridle. He watched the thing as a hawk watches a young rabbit in the grass.

Betimes he gave a queer little chuckle, and turned his horse into the deeper shade of the trees. He began to make a circuit round the valley, holding northwards to compass the meadows. He cast long, wary glances into the wood as he went; tried his sword to see that it was loose in the scabbard; took his helmet from the saddle-bow, and let down the cheek-pieces from the crown. Before long he kicked his stirrups away, rolled out of the saddle, and tied his horse to an oak sapling in a little dell. Going silently on foot over the mossy grass, stopping often to stare into the sunny vistas of the forest, moving more or less from tree to tree, he worked his way southwards along the eastern slope. Streaks of meadowland and the glint of water showed below him, and he heard the bleat of sheep far away, and the tinkling of a bell.

Presently the murmur of voices came to him through the woods. He ventured on another fifty paces, then stopped behind a tree to listen. There were two voices, he was sure of that: one was a woman's, and the other had the sonorous vibration of a man's bass. Gorlois's eyes took a queer, far-away look, and his strong teeth showed between his lips.

He worked his way on through the trees with the cautious and deliberate instinct of a hunter. The two voices gained in timbre, character, and expression. Their talk was no jays' chatter; Gorlois could tell that from the emphasis of sound, and a certain dramatic melody that ran through the whole. Soon the voices were very near. Going on his belly, with his sword held in his left hand, he crawled like a gilt dragon through a forest of springing fern. He crawled on till he was quite near the two who stood and talked under the trees. Lying flat, never venturing to lift his head, he crouched, breathing hard through his nostrils and holding his scabbarded sword crosswise beneath his chin.

Gorlois's face, scarred and drawn as it was, seemed as he listened a clear mirror for the portrayal of human passion. His black moustachios twitched above his angular jaw; his eyes took a rapacious and glazed look, and a shadow seemed to cover his face. He turned and twisted as he lay, and dug the points of his iron-shod shoes into the soft ground as though in the crisis of some pain. It was the woman's voice that did all this for him. Every word seemed like the wrench of a hook in his flesh, as he cursed and twisted under the bracken.

Presently he lay still again, as though to listen the better. He could hear something of what was said to the man in the red harness, but the main drift of their talk was beyond him. Pelleas! Pelleas! He squirmed like a crushed snake at each sounding of the name. The bracken hardly swayed as he crawled on some twenty paces and again lay still, with his cheek resting upon the scabbard of his sword.

"Gorlois might die."

Gorlois heard the words as plainly as though they had been spoken into his ear. A vast silence hung like thunder over the forest. Gorlois lay as though stunned with a stone, his dry mouth pressed to the cold steel of the sword. His eyes took a stubborn stare under the sweep of his casque. With gradual labour he raised himself upon his elbows, drew his knees up under his body, and lifted his head slowly above the sweep of green.

The ground fell away slightly from where Gorlois knelt in the bracken, and he could look down on the two who stood under the trees, while the fern fronds hid his harness. He saw a woman in violet and gold, her hair falling straight on either side of her face, and her arms folded crosswise over her breast. He saw also the knight in red harness, with his locked hands twisting above his head as in an agony, while his face was hidden by his arm. A passionate whisper of words passed between the two. Even when Gorlois

"LIFTED HIS HEAD SLOWLY ABOVE THE SWEEP OF GREEN"

watched, the man in the red harness jerked round and fell on his knees at the woman's feet. Gorlois suddenly saw his face; it was the face of Uther the King.

Gorlois dropped back under the bracken as though smitten through with a sword. He lay there a long while with his head upon his arms. A sudden breeze came up the valley, sounding through the trees, swaying the green fronds above the man's harness, calling a gradual clamour from the woods. The overmastering image of the King seemed to frown down Gorlois for the moment, and he crouched like a dog—with the courage crushed out of his soul.

Betimes Gorlois's reason revived from the stroke that had stunned it for a season. Like Jonah's gourd a quick purpose sprang up and shadowed him from the too hasty heat of his own passions. He was a virile man, capable of great wrath and great resentment. Yet he was no mere firebrand. His malice, strangely enough, was one-handed and reached out only against the woman. For Uther he conceived a superhuman envy, a passion that rose above mere bloody expiation by the sword. Gorlois had the wit to remember the finer cruelties of a spiritual vengeance, the gain of wounding the soul rather than the flesh. His malice was a thing fanatical in itself, yet taken from the forge to be cooled and tempered like steel.

When he lifted his head again above the bracken, Uther had gone, and Igraine stood alone under the trees. She stood straight and motionless as some tall flower, her hair falling like quiet sunlight, unshaken by a wind. Her great beauty leapt out into Gorlois's blood and maddened him. As she looked out over the valley, Gorlois, straining his neck above the bracken, could see that she watched Uther as he went down from her towards the pool. Even to Gorlois there was something tragic about the solitary figure under the trees, a stiff, grievous look as though woe had transformed her into a pillar of stone. To him the affair seemed a mere assignation, a hazardous passage of romance. Measuring the souls of others by his own morality, he guessed nothing of the deeper throes that surged through the tale like the long moan of a night wind.

Gorlois saw Uther and his black horse disappear into the opposing bank of woodland. Viciously satisfied, he lay in the bracken and watched Igraine, coming by a queer pleasure in considering her beauty, and in the knowledge that her very life was poised on the point of his sword. How little she thought of the man-dragon lying in his gilded scales under the green of the feathery fronds. Gorlois felt a kind of arrogance of ownership boasting itself in his heart. Certainly he held a means more sinister than the sword wherewith to perfect his vengeance and to preserve his honour. A very purgatory, bolgia upon bolgia, stretched out in prospect for the souls of the two who had done him this great evil. Gorlois made much of it, with a joy that was hard and durable as iron.

Igraine stirred at last from her stupor of immobility. Walking unsteadily, as though faint in the heat, she passed out from the trees with their mingling of sun and shadow, and went down through the long grass towards the pool and the cottage. Gorlois knelt in the bracken, and watched her with a smile. There was little chance of her escaping, and he could be as deliberate as he pleased over the matter. He inferred with reason that the cottage served her as a lodging in this woodland solitude, where she lay hid from all the world save from Uther, whose courtezan she was. Gorlois laughed—a keen, biting laugh—at the thought of it all. At least he would go back for his horse and spear, and make a fitting entry before the woman who was his wife.

Igraine, walking as though in her sleep, came into the cottage, and almost fell into Garlotte's arms. The girl looked frightened, and very white about the lips. She could find nothing in her heart to say to Igraine; she helped her to the bed, and ran to the cupboard to get wine.

"Drink it," she said, the cup rocking to and fro in her hand.

Igraine did her best, but spilt much of the stuff upon her

bosom, where it made a stain like blood. She sat on the edge of the bed, and looked into the distance with expressionless eyes. Her hands were very cold. Garlotte chafed them between her own, murmured a word or two, but could not bring herself to look into Igraine's face. From the valley the bleating of sheep came up with a sudden wind, and the red roses flung their faces across the latticed casement.

Igraine was looking through the window into the deep green of the woods. She could see the place where Pelleas had left her, even the tree under which she had stood when she had pleaded with him without avail. How utterly quiet everything seemed. Surely June was an evil month for her; had it not brought double misery—and well-nigh broken her heart? And the end of it all was that she was to go back to a convent, to grey walls, vigils, and the sounding of a bell. Even that was better than being Gorlois's wife.

Suddenly, as she sat and stared out of the casement, her body grew tense and eager as a bent bow. Her eyes hardened, lost their dreamy look; the hands that had rested in Garlotte's gripped the girl's wrists with a force that made her wince.

"Saddle the horse."

The words came in a hard whisper. Garlotte stared at her, and did not stir.

"Child, never question me; be quick, on your life."

Igraine, a different woman in a moment, had started up and taken her shield and helmet from the wall. Her sword was girded to her. Quick as thought, she gathered up her trailing hair, thrust on the casque, strapped it to the neck-plate under her surcoat. Garlotte, vastly puzzled, but inspired by Igraine's earnestness, had hurried out with saddle and bridle over her shoulder. As she ran through the garden, she looked up to the woods and saw the reason of Igraine's flurry. A knight had come out from the forest on a white horse, his armour flashing and blazing in the noonday sun. He had halted motionless at the edge of the woodland, as though to mark what was passing beneath him in the valley.

Garlotte found Igraine armed beside her, as she stood by the grey horse under the cedar, and tugged with trembling fingers at the saddle straps. Bit and bridle were quickly in place. Igraine, moved by a hurried tenderness, gripped Garlotte to her with both arms.

"God guard you, little sister."

"Where are you going, Igraine?"

"God knows!"

"Who is yonder knight?"

"Gorlois, my husband."

Igraine climbed into the saddle from the girl's knee. She dashed in the spurs and went at a gallop over the meadows towards the south. Gorlois's white horse was coming at full stride through the feathery grass. The man was riding crosswise over the valley, bent on cutting off Igraine from the southern stretch of meadows, and driving her back upon the woods. It was Igraine's hope to overtake Pelleas, and to put herself behind the barrier of his shield. Gorlois, guessing her desire, drove home the spurs, and hunted her in earnest.

Igraine headed the man and won a lead in the first half mile. Her grey horse plunged like a galley in a rough sea, and she held to the pommel of her saddle to keep her seat. Gorlois thundered at full gallop in her wake, the long grass flying before his horse's hoofs like foam. He had thrown away his spear, and his eyes were set in a long stare on the galloping horse ahead. The zest of the chase had hold of him, and he used the spurs with heavy heel.

The green woods rolled down on them as the valley narrowed to its southern end. Igraine had never wandered so far from Garlotte's cottage, and the ground was strange to her, nor did she know how the country promised. Riding at full gallop, she saw with a shudder of fear a barrier of rock running serrate across her path and closing the narrow valley like a wall. Gorlois saw it too, and sent up a shout that made Igraine's hate flame up into a kind of rapture. To have turned right or left up the steep grass slope towards the woods, would have given back to Gorlois the little start she had of him. With a numb chill at her heart she abandoned all hope of Pelleas, and turned to face the inevitable, and Gorlois her lord.

The man came up like a wind through the grass, and drew rein roughly some ten paces away. He laughed as he stared at Igraine, an uncouth, angering laugh like the yapping of a dog. He looked big and burly in the saddle, and the muscles stood out in his neck as he tilted his square jaw and stared down at his wife. Igraine had not looked upon his face since he had been smitten in battle. Its ugliness seemed to match his soul.

Gorlois lifted up his voice and mocked her.

"Ha, my brave, you are trapped, are you? Mother of God, but you make a good figure of a man. These many months I have missed you, wife in arms. And you have served in the pay of my lord the King. Good service and good pay, I warrant, and plenty of plunder. I will have that harness of yours hung over my bed."

Igraine suffered him not so much as a word. She was furious, and in no mood to be scoffed down and cowed by mere insolent strength. She looked into Gorlois's libidinous face from behind the vizor of her helmet, and thought her thoughts. Gorlois ran on in his mocking fashion. His bronzed face gleamed with sweat, and a rough lascivious smile showed up his strong white teeth to her.

"Ha, now, madame! deliver, and let us have sight of you. The King loves your lips, eh! They are red, and your arms are soft. I warrant he found your bosom a good pillow. Uther was ever such a solemn soul, such a monk, such a father. It is good for the heart to hear of him knotted up in a woman's hair."

Igraine shook with the immensity of her hate.

"You were ever a foul-tongued hound," she said.

"Am I your echo?"

"I wish you were dead."

"So said the King."

"So you spied on us?"

Gorlois set up a scoffing laugh, showing his red throat like a hungry bird.

"And saw my wife the King's courtezan; ha, what a jest! Come, madame, let us be going; your honest home waits for you. I will chatter to you of moralities by the way."

He had hardly delivered himself of the saying, when Igraine's hand clutched at the handle of her sword. She jerked the spurs in with her heels. Her grey horse started forward like a bolt; blundered into Gorlois; caught him cross-counter, and rolled his white stallion down into the grass. Igraine had lashed out at the shock. Her sword caught Gorlois's arm, and cut through sleeve and arm-guard to the bone. As he rolled with his horse in the grass, she wheeled round, and clapping in the spurs, rode hard uphill for the forest.

Gorlois, hot as a furnace, scrambled tc his feet, and dragged his horse up by the bridle. Half off the saddle, with empty stirrups dangling, he went at a canter for the yawn of the wood. His slashed arm burnt as though it had been touched with a branding-iron; blood dripped down upon his horse's white shoulder. He was soon steady in the saddle and galloping full pelt after Igraine, the ground slipping under his horse's hoofs like water, the long grass flying like spray.

Igraine's horse lost ground up the slope; he had less heart than Gorlois's beast, and was weaker in the haunches. By the time they reached the trees, Igraine had twenty yards to her credit and no more. She saw her chance gone, and heard Gorlois close in her wake, caught sideways a glimpse of plunging hoofs and angry harness. Drawing aside suddenly with all her strength, she let Gorlois sweep up on her flank and pass her by some yards. Before he could turn, she rode into him as fast as she could gather; her sword clattered on his helmet, — sparks flew.

Gorlois wrenched round and put his shield above his head.

"By God,—hold off,—would you have me fight a woman?"

A swinging cut rattled on his shoulder-plate for answer.

Gorlois rapped out an oath and drew his sword.

"Hold off!"

His roar seemed to shake the trees. To Igraine it was the mere meaningless threatening of a sea. She struck home again and again while Gorlois foined with her; more than once she reached his flesh.

Gorlois's grim patience gave way at last; a clean cut drew spurting blood from his shoulder.

"God curse you!—take it then."

He swung his sword with a great downward sweep, a streak of steel that struck crackling fire from the burnished casque. Igraine's arm dropped like a broken bough; for half a breath she sat straight in the saddle, swayed, sank slantwise, and slid down into the long grass. Her horse stood still at her side, looking at her with mild blue eyes.

Gorlois gave a queer short laugh. He looked frightened for the moment; the flush of anger had passed and left him pale. He dismounted, bent over Igraine, unstrapped her helmet. She was only dazed by the blow; blood trickled red amid her hair, and her blue eyes stared him in the face.

She lifted up a hand with a bitter cry of defiance.

"Strike, strike, and make an end."

Gorlois's grimness came back, and his eyes hardened.

"That were too good for you."

"Devil!"

"By God, I shall tame you—never fear!"

BOOK IV

TINTAGEL

I

THE castle of Tintagel stood out above the sea on a headland that rose bluffly above the white foam that girdled it. The waves swinging in from the west seemed to lift ever a hoarse chant about the place with their perpetual grumbling against the cliff. Colour shifted upon the bosom of the sea. Blue, green, and grey it would sweep into the west, netted gold with the sun, banded with foam, or spread with purple beneath the drifting shadow of a cloud. Hills rose in the east. Between these crags and the sea rolled a wilderness cloven by green valleys and a casual stream. Tintagel seemed to crown a region grand and calamitous as the sea itself.

The sun was going down over the waters, watched by a flaxen-haired lad squatting on the wall of an outstanding turret. His legs dangled over the battlements, and his heels smote against the weathered stone. There was a premature look of age upon his face, a certain wistful wisdom as though he had completed his novitiate early in the world. His blue eyes, large and sensitive as a dog's, stared away over the golden edge of the sea.

This was Jehan the bastard, a pathetic shred of humanity, thin and motherless, blessed with nothing save a dreamy nature that stood him in poor stead in such a hold as Tintagel. Like any mongrel owned of none, he was given over largely to the cuffs and curses of the community. Men called him a fool, and treated him accordingly. He was scullion, horse-boy, pot-bearer, by turns. The men of the garrison could make nothing of a lad who wept at a word, never showed fight, but crept away to mope and snivel in a corner. He had earned epithets enough, but little else; and the rude Philistines of the place, beings of beer and bone, knew little of those finer instincts with which Nature chooses on occasion to endow a soul.

At times Jehan would creep away up this turret stair to live and breathe for a season with no friend save the ever-complaining sea. He would perch himself on the battlements with the salt wind blowing through his hair, the rocks beneath him boiling foam from the waves that swept in from the west. The perch was perilous enough, but the lad had no fear of the windy height, or of the waves breaking against the pediment of the cliff. To him man alone was terrible. There appeared to be a confident understanding between Nature and himself, a sense of good fellowship with his surroundings, such as the chamois may feel for its mountain pinnacle, and the bird for the tree that bears its nest.

Jehan's thin face was turned often towards the central tower of the castle, a square campanile that stood in the centre of the main court, forming a species of citadel or keep. High up in the wall there was a window, a streak of gloom that showed nothing of the room within. Over Jehan this window possessed a peculiar influence. It was the casement-royal of romance. Day by day, ever since Gorlois had come south again, the lad had watched for the white oval of a face that would look out momentarily from the shadow. Sometimes he saw a woman's hand, a golden head glimmering in the sun. Jehan had seen Gorlois's wife brought a second time into Tintagel. Her staring grief had taken strange hold upon his heart. Ever since, with the kindled chivalry of a boy, he had done great deeds in dreams, handled a sword, taken strong men by the throat. The imagined event had fired the soul in him, and made him the disciple of these sad and wistful eyes.

A bell smote in the court below. Its iron clapper dinned the fancies out of Jehan's head, calling him to the menial realities of life. It was the supper hour, and the men of the guard would be strenuously inclined over the steaming pot, the wine-jar, and the twisting spit. Jehan left his turret with the pathetic cynicism of an autumn twilight. Little drudge that he was, he yet had the inward independence to despise the folk who fed like swine, and terrorised him with pure blatant barbarism. He could listen to their blasphemy, their ribald songs, and breathe the moral garlic of their tongues with a disrelish that never wavered. He had none of the innate impudence of youth. Had he been of coarser fibre the men would soon have made a lewd and insolent imp of him, but he was spared such a fate by a certain spiritual instinct that recoiled from the vapouring brutality of it all.

There seemed more ribaldry abroad in the guard-room that night than was customary even in so pious a place. The company, much like a pack of hounds, hunted jest after jest from cover, and gave tongue royally with a zest that would have been admirable in any other cause. Lamps swirled ill-smelling smoke about the room. There was a lavish scattering of armour along the benches, and the floor was dirtier than the floor of any tavern.

Jehan's ears tingled as he went among the men, climbing over sprawling legs, edging between stools and benches. The air reeked of mead, and the miasma of loose talk rising from twenty throats. A woman's name was tossed from tongue to tongue, bandied about with a familiar insolence that made him blush for her like a brother. His heart burnt with the bestial impudence, the sweat, the foul breath of it all. Yet before these red-bearded faces, these vociferous mouths, he was a coward, hating himself for his fear, hating the men for the sheer tyranny of the flesh that awed him.

To hear in this den such things spoken of a woman, and of such a woman! That she was true his quick instinct could aver in the very maw of the world. There was the silver calm of the full moon in her face, and she had for him the steadfastness, the incomprehensible eloquence, of the stars. Were these men blind, that the staring grief, the divine scorn, that had smitten him from the first with a vague awe, were invisible to them? Their coarse cynicism was brutally incomprehensible to Jehan. Having a soul, he could not see with the eyes of the sot or the adulterer, nor had he learnt to mistrust the intelligence of his own heart.

As he laboured from man to man with his jug of mead to keep the brown horns brimming, he thought of the golden head that had glimmered in the criss-cross light of the yews in the castle garden. The woman had been faithless, to put popular report mildly; and Gorlois was a hard man; he would see her dead before he pitied her. Jehan was so far gone in dreams for the moment that he tripped over an outstretched pair of legs, and shattered his stone jar on the floor.

A "God curse you," and lavish largesse in the way of kicks, recompensed the dreamer for this contempt of office. Jehan, bruised, spattered with mead, crawled away under the benches, and took refuge in a dark corner, where he could recover his wits behind the piled pikes of the gentlemen who cursed him. Such incidents were the trivialities of a menial existence. Jehan wiped his face on his sleeve, choked down his sobs with a dirty fist, and devoutly hoped to be forgotten.

Meanwhile a broad figure had stood framed in the doorway, and drawn the attention of the company from the boy squirming like an eel along the floor. Jehan, peeping round the pile of pikes, saw a woman in a scarlet gown standing under a lamp that flared on the threshold. The woman was of unusual girth and height. Her black hair streamed about her sensual red face like clouds about a winter sun. Her neck was like the neck of a bull, and her bare arms would have shamed the arms of a smith. Jehan watched her as he would have watched a natural enemy, a thing whose destiny was to be brutish and to destroy.

Men called her Malmain, the evil-handed. She was a cub of the forest, strong as a bear, cruel as any wolf. Years ago she had been caught as a child in the woods, tracked down to a rocky hole, a whelp that clawed and bit, and knew nothing of the speech of men. She had been brought to

Tintagel and bred in the place, the pet of the soldiery, who had taught her the use of arms and the smack of wine. In ten years she had grown to her full strength, a creature wise in all the uncomely things of life, coarse, bold, and violent. Last of all, Gorlois, with a genius for vengeance, had given her charge of Igraine, his wife.

The woman was good to look upon in a large, florid fashion. She came in and sat herself down on a stool at the end of one long wooden table, and stared round with her hard brown eyes. One man passed her a cup, another the wine jar. She tossed the former aside with an air of scorn, and buried her face in the mouth of the jar. When she had taken her pull she spat on the floor with a certain quaint deliberation, and wiped her mouth on the back of her bare arm.

A wicked innuendo came from a man grinning at her elbow. Malmain laughed and pulled at her lip. Her presence conferred no leavening influence upon the place, and her sex made no claim for decorum. She was more than capable of caring for herself in the company of these gentlemen of the guard, for she could take her laugh and liquor with the best of them, and claim a solid respect for a fist that could smite like a mace.

She flustered up a sigh that ended in a hiccough. "I am tired," she said, stretching her arms and showing the breadth and depth of her great chest.

"Go to bed, fragile one, and shake the castle."

"Little chance of that; who says I snore?"

"Gildas the trumpeter."

"Curse him; how should he know?"

The man questioned grinned, and shrugged his shoulders.

"I meddle no further," he said. "How is the lord's wife?"

Malmain licked her lips and reached for the pot. She tilted it with such gusto that the liquor overflowed and ran down her chin. After more cat's-pawing and a snivel she waxed communicative with a matter-of-fact coarseness, and like an old hound soon had the rest tonguing in her track.

"Gorlois will break her yet," quoth one.

"Or bury her."

"A fit fellow, too, — and a gentleman; why can't she knuckle to him and play the lady?"

"The woman's worth three of that chit with the white face; a fine brat ought to come of it."

Malmain showed her strong white teeth.

"Somehow," she said, "there's no more cross-grained creature than a woman with a grievance, especially when she has been baulked of her man. Let a woman speak for a woman, though I break the spirit of her with a whip. There's less fighting now; by Jesus, you should see her bones staring through her skin."

Jehan had listened to their talk behind the pile of pikes in the corner. The blatant cynicism of it all chilled him like a March wind. He thought of the sad, strong face, the patient scorn, the youth, the prophetic May of her of whom they spoke. There was a certain terrible realism here that tore the tender bosom of his dreams.

The room stifled him with its smoke and stew. Crawling round by the wall on all fours, he gained the door and crept out unnoticed into the dark. In the sky above the stars were shining. The world seemed big with peace, and the face of the heavens shone mild and clear as the face of God.

Jehan stood under the shadow of the wall and looked at the window high up in the tower. It was black and lustreless, and only the dust of the stars shone up in the vast canopy of gloom. Jehan shook his fist at the dark pile of stone. Then he went up to the roof of the little turret and watched the sea foaming dimly on the rocks below.

II

"I WOULD have you know, madame, that every woman is pleasing to man, — saving his own wife."

"Who in turn is pleasing to his friend,—even if he chance to be a king."

The woman on the couch tossed her slipper from her small foot, and struck a series of snapping chords from the guitar that she held in her bosom. There was a certain rich insolence in her look,—a sensuous wickedness that was wholly poetic. The man bent forward from his stool, lifted the slipper, and kissed the foot whence it had fallen. He won a smile from the face bowered up in cushions, a smile like sunlight on a brazen mirror, brilliant, clear, metallic. There was a fine flush on her face, and the star on her bosom rose and fell as her breathing seemed to quicken and deepen for the moment. Her fingers plucked waywardly at the strings as she looked out from the window towards the sea.

"I love life," she said.

"Surely."

"The pomp, the pride, the glory of being great. I have a future for you."

A kind of spiritual echo burnt in the man's eyes.

"And my wife?"

"You are still something of a madman."

"So you say."

"I—indeed!"

He bent forward with a sudden eruption of passion and kissed her foot again, till she drew it away under the folds of her dress.

"Ah, you are still a little mad," she said, turning and smiling at him with her quick eyes; "bide so, my dear lord; I can suffer it."

"And yet—"

"I hate her! I hate her! I hate her!"

"Bah!—she cannot harm you."

"I hate her for being a martyr, for being strong, for thinking herself a saint. Pah!—how I could scratch her proud, big face. She humiliates me because of her misery, because she is contented to suffer. It is impossible to trample such a woman underfoot."

The man gave a queer laugh.

"You are still envious."

"I envious, — I!"

"Because she is never humbled, never asks mercy."

"Curse her, let her die! Come and fan me, I am sleepy."

On the southern side of the central tower, between it and the State quarters of the castle, lay the garden of Tintagel. It was a lustrous nook, barriered by grey walls, sheltered from the sea wind, and open to the full stare of the sun. Sombre cypresses lifted their spires above flower-beds mosaicked red, gold, and blue. The paths were tiled with coloured stones, and bordered with helichryse. In the centre of all a pool glimmered from a square of bright green grass.

The window in the tower that had so seized upon the lad Jehan's heart looked out upon this square of colour that shone beneath the extreme blue of the summer sky. The casement was an open mihrab whence tragedy could look out upon the world. The glory of the sea, the sky, the cliffs, contrasted with the twilight tint of the prison room.

Gorlois's wife sat in the window-seat and watched the waves and the horizon with vacant eyes. She was clad in a tattered gown of grey. Her hair had been shorn close, leaving but a golden aureole over neck, ears, and forehead. One hand was wrapped in a blood-stained cloth, and there were marks left by a whip upon her face. Her gown reached hardly to her ankles, showing bare feet and wheals, where the scourge had been. She was very frail, very worn, very spiritual.

Her face was the face of one who looks into the solemn sadness of the past. Her lips were pressed together as in pain, and a certain divine despair dwelt in her deep eyes like light reflected from some twilight pool. The muscles stood limned in her neck like cords, and the fingers of one hand were hooked in the neck-band of her gown.

Many days had passed since the life in Garlotte's valley. They had taught Igraine the deeds that might result from the stirring of the passions of such a man as Gorlois. It was a strenuous age, and men's souls were cast in large mould either to the image of good or evil. Even Boethius could not escape the malice of a great king. Attila had scourged the nations with a scourge of steel. Old things were passing amid disruption and despair. Gorlois had caught the Titanic, violent spirit of the age. His personality had won a lurid emphasis from tragedies that shook the world.

Igraine had suffered many things, shame, torture, famine, since she had fallen again into his power. The man had shown no pity, only a fine fecundity in his devices for the breaking of her spirit. He could be barbarous as any Hun, and though she had guessed his fibre, it was not till these latter days that she learnt to know him more fully to her own distress. It was not the physical alone that oppressed her; Gorlois had imagination, ingenuity; he made her moral sufferings keener than the lash, and subordinated the flesh to the spirit. Igraine withstood him through it all. She felt in her heart that she was going to die.

As she sat at the window, the sound of laughter came up suddenly from the garden, glowing in the sunlight. Mere mockery might have been its inspiration, so light, so merry, and so mellow was it. Igraine heard it, and leant forward over the sill to gain a broader view of the tiled walks and flower-beds below. She saw a woman dart out of a doorway in the wall opposite, and run in very dainty fashion, holding her skirts gathered in one hand, the other flourishing a posy of red roses. As she ran she laughed with an unrestrained extravagance that had in it something sensual and alluring.

Igraine watched her with a badge of colour in her cheeks. The woman in the garden was clad in a tunic of sky-blue silk that ran down her body like flowing water. The tunic was cut low at the neck so as to show her white breast, whereon shone a little cross of gold. Her hair shimmered loose about her in the sunlight like an amber veil. Her lips were tinctured with vermilion; her face seemed white as apple blossom, and shadows had been painted under her lids. She moved with a graceful, sinuous air, her blue gown rippling about her, her small feet, slippered with silver embroidery, flashing glibly over the stones.

A man was following her among the cypresses, and Igraine saw that it was Gorlois, sunburnt and strong, with ruddy arms, and the strenuous zest of manhood. There was something unpleasing in the muscular movement of his mood. He was Græcian and antique, a Mars striding with the red face of no godly love; sheer bovine vigour in the curves of his strong throat.

Igraine saw the woman run round the garden, laughing as she went, her hair blowing behind her in the sunlight. She turned up the central path that led to the pool, with its little lawn closed by a balustrade of carved stone. Morgan la Blanche stood by the water and watched Gorlois abjuring the paths and striding towards her, knee-deep in blue and purple. He leapt the balustrade, and stood looking at the woman laughing at him through her hair.

The red roses were thrust into Gorlois's face as he came to closer quarters. There was a short scuffle before the girl abandoned herself to him with a kind of sensuous languor. Igraine saw her body wrapped up in the man's brown arms.

It was a minute or more before the two became aware of the face at the window overhead. Igraine found them staring up at her, Gorlois's swarthy face close to the woman's light aureole of hair as she stood buttressed against his broad chest. By instinct Igraine drew back into the room, till pride conquered this shrinking impulse. She leant forward upon her hands and stared down at the two, allegorical as Truth shaming Falsehood.

The woman, meanwhile, had drawn aside from Gorlois's arms. She was pulling the roses to pieces, and scattering the red petals on the water, and there was a peevish sneer upon her lips.

"Ever this white death," she said.

Igraine saw the impatient gesturing of Morgan's hands, the tap of the embroidered slipper on the grass. The woman's words seemed to trouble Gorlois; he stood aside, and did not look at her, even when she edged away, watching him over her shoulder. It was a conflict of dishonourable sensations. Morgan jerked a quick look from her large blue eyes at the window overhead. There was nothing but rampant egotism upon her face, and it was evident that she trusted on Gorlois to follow her. He was staring swarthily into the water as though he watched the fish moving in the shallow basin. He hardly heeded Morgan as she picked up her pride and left him. Other thoughts seemed to have strong hold upon his mind, and he stood at gaze till the blue gown disappeared under the arch of the door it had so lately quitted.

Gorlois leant against the balustrade and pulled his moustachios. His eyes had no very spiritual look, and his red lower lip drooped like an unfurled scroll. More than once he cast a quick, restless glance at the window in the tower. Irresolution seemed to run largely through his mood, and it was some while before he gathered his manhood and passed up an avenue of cypresses towards the tower. At the foot of the stairway he stood pulling his lip, and staring at the stones, oppressed by a certain dubiousness of thought.

Climbing the stairs, he found the woman Malmain in an alcove, asleep on a settle. Her head had fallen back against the wall, her mouth was agape, and she was snoring with her black hair tumbled over her face. Gorlois woke her with his foot.

The woman started up with the growl of a watch-dog, stared, and stood silent. Gorlois, curt as a man burdened with a purpose, spoke few words to her. She opened a door by a certain mechanical catch, went in, and closed it after her.

Half an hour passed.

The door rolled again on its hinges. Malmain came out and stood before Gorlois on the threshold. She was breathing hard, and sweat stood on her face. Gorlois gave her a look and a word, passed in, and slammed the door after him. Malmain sat down on the settle, wiped her face, and listened.

For a minute or more she heard nothing. An indefinite sound broke the silence, like the moving of branches in a wind at night. There was the sound of hard breathing, and the creaking of wood. Something clattered to the floor.

"God judge between you and me."

The voice was half-stifled as with the choking bitterness of great shame. Malmain grinned in her corner, and leant her head against the door to listen the better.

"What of God!" said the man's voice with a certain hot scorn; "what is God?"

"Take your knife and end it."

"Madame wife, there is good in you yet."

There was silence again, like a lull betwixt ecstasies of rain. Presently the woman's voice was heard, low, sullen, shamed.

"Man — man, let me die!"

"Own me master."

"You — you! How can I lie in my throat!"

"Is truth so new a thing?"

"You have taught me to love death."

Malmain heard Gorlois's hand upon the door. She opened it forthwith; he came out upon the threshold. His hands were trembling, and his face seemed dull, his eyes passionless.

"I shall tame you yet," he said.

"You can kill me!" came the retort from the room.

III

There was in Tintagel a certain man named Mark, a legionary of the guard. The castle had known him two months or less, when he had come south into Cornwall with Gorlois's troop from Caerleon. He was an olive-skinned mercenary, black of beard and black of eye. In the guard-room he had become vastly popular; he could harp, tell a tale, hurl the bar, with any man in the garrison. He was strong and agile as a panther, and as ready with his tongue as he was with his sword. His comrades thought him a merry rapscallion enough, a good fellow whose life was rounded comfortably by the needs of the flesh. He could drink and jest, eat, sleep, and be happy.

Women have quick instinct for a man of mettle, one whose capabilities for pleasing are somewhat of a perilous kind. Malmain of the Forest had taken note of Mark's black eyes, his olive skin, the immense self-control that seemed to bridle him. He had a fine leg, and a most gentlemanly hand. Moreover, his inimitable impudence, his supple wit, took her fancy, seeing that he was a man who professed a superb scorn for petticoats, and posed as being wise beyond his generation. There was a certain insolent independence about him that seemed to make of him a philosopher, a person pleased with the puerilities of others.

It came about that Malmain — clumsy, lumbering creature — took to heaving stupendous sighs under the very nose of Mark of the guard. She had not been bred to reservations. If she liked a man, she told him the truth, with a certain admirable frankness. If she hated him, he could always rely upon her fist. Any ethical principle was like a book to her — very curious, no doubt, but absolutely beyond her understanding.

Now the man Mark was a person of intelligence and discretion. He needed the woman's friendship for diplomatic reasons snared up in his own long skull, and since such partisanship could be won by a look and a word, he soon had Malmain very much at his service. Shrewd and cunning wench that she was in the course of nature, she was somewhat easily fooled by the man's suave impudence. She haunted Mark like a shadow when off her duty, — a very substantial shadow, be it noted, — and made it extravagantly plain that she was blessed after all with some of the sentiments of a woman.

One evening, being in the mood, she caught him in a bye-passage as he came off guard. He was in armour, and carried a spear slanted over his shoulder. His burnished casque seemed to give a fine setting to his strong, sallow face.

Malmain, generous creature, filled the passage like a gate. Her face matched her scarlet smock, and she was grinning like some grotesque head from the antique. Mark came to a halt, and leaning on his spear, looked at her in the most bland manner possible. He did not trust women overmuch, and he mistrusted Malmain in particular. Moreover, she smacked of the wine-cask.

The woman edged close, and shook a fist in his face with a certain bluff enthusiasm.

"A bargain! a bargain!"

The passage was open to the west, and a glare of sunlight shimmered into Mark's eyes. He could only see the woman as a great blurr, a mass of trailing hair, a loose, exuberant smock haloed with gold.

"Ha! my cherub, you seem in fettle."

The fist still flickered in his face.

"A bargain! a bargain!"

"Mother of mercy! you are in such a devil of a hurry."

"A kiss for what's in my hand."

"A buffet — big one — a rush-ring, or a garter?"

"That tongue of yours; look and see, look and see!"

Malmain spread her fingers. The man saw a ring of gold carved in the form of a dragon, with rubies for eyes, and a collar of emeralds about its throat. Lying in the woman's moist, fat palm, it glimmered in the slant light of the sun. Mark's eyes glittered as he looked at it.

"I had the thing from the woman above," quoth Malmain, jerking her thumb over her shoulder.

"A bribe?"

"Who'd bribe me? Not a woman!"

"Honest soul."

"'That ring looks well on your finger,' said I. 'I shall have it.' 'Never!' said she. 'That's too big a word,' said I. So I forced it off, for all her temper, and broke her finger in the doing of it."

A transient shadow seemed to pass across the man's face, the wraith of a ghost-wrath insensible to the world.

"Close the bargain, cherub."

"A buss for it."

"Twenty kisses in a week, and my mug of supper beer." He had the ring.

Malmain did not stand alone in her devotion to Mark of the guard. The man had come by another friend in Tintagel, a friend without influence, it is true, but one, at least, who possessed abundant individuality, and the charm of an ingenuous nature. Mark was no mere bravo when he turned partisan to the lad Jehan, and took him within the pale of his mothering wit. He had a profound knowledge of men, and a philosophic insight into character that had not been gained solely on the march or in the ale-house. By profession he appeared a devil-may-care gentleman of the sword, a man of bone and muscle, the possessor of a vigorous stomach. These attributes were mere stage properties, so to speak, necessary to him for the occasion. For the rest, he knew what he knew.

Mark had seen more than cowardice in the sensitive face of the lad. He had discovered the soul beneath the surface, the warmer, bolder personality behind the deceit of the flesh. Jehan appealed to him as a friendless thing, a vial of glass jostled in the stream of life by rough potsherds and sounding bowls. Mark took the lad in hand and made a disciple of him in less than a week. He humoured the lad, encouraged him, treated him like a comrade, drew the soul out of his limp, starved body. Jehan had never fallen upon such a friend before. He was bewitched by the man's personality. This Mark with the strong face and the falcon's eye seemed to see deep into the finer sentiments of life, to think as he thought, to conceive as he conceived. Jehan, unconscious little idealist that he was, bubbled over into innumerable confidences and confessions of feeling. This dark-eyed man, who never laughed at him, whose voice was never blatant and threatening, seemed to exert a magnetic influence upon his spirit. Jehan throned him a species of demigod, and idolised him as he had idolised few living things on earth before.

There was more method in Mark's friendship than his comrades of the guard ever dreamt of in their thick noddles. They had many a laugh at Malmain and many a jest at her expense, but their wit never worked beyond vulgar banality. As for Jehan, his existence certainly seemed to better itself so far as they were concerned, though what the man Mark could see worth patronising in the lad, they were at a loss to discover. Jehan grew less servile, less diffident, more open of countenance. He hided a cook-boy of his own age in a casual scuffle. Mark had used a strong arm and a stronger wit for him on occasion, and the little bastard was no longer cuffed at the random pleasure of every gentleman of Gorlois's guard.

Jehan often spoke to Mark of the lady of the tower whose hair was like the red-gold cloak of autumn. The man seemed ready to hear of her beauty and her distress, and all the multitudinous tales concerning her given from the guard-room. He kindled to the romantic possibilities of the affair, and was as full of sentiment as Jehan himself could wish. Saying little at first, he watched the lad with keen, discerning eyes, as though tracing out the trend, depth, and sincerity of his sympathies; nor was he long ignorant of the strain of chivalry that was sounding in the lad's heart. The more generous sentiments leapt out in a look, a word, a colouring of the cheek. Given inspiration, it was possible to make a fanatic of the boy, a hero in the higher rendering of the term.

In due course the man grew more communicative, less of a listener. Jehan heard of Avangel, of the island manor in Andredswold, of Pelleas, and of the days in Winchester. The whole tragedy was spread before him like a legend, some mighty passion throe of the past. He listened open-mouthed, with blue eyes that searched the man's face. Mark had taken to himself of a sudden an air of mystery and peril. Jehan knew by intuition that these matters were to be kept secret as the grave. Great pride rose in him at being held worthy of such trust. He felt even aggrieved when Mark spoke to him of discretion, with a finger on his lip. Such a secret was like a hoard of gold to the lad. It pleased him with a sense of responsibility and of faith, and Jehan loved honour, for all his novitiate amid the morals of the guard-room.

He had drunk deep of old songs, and of the heroics of the harp. Such things were like moonlight to him, touching his soul with a lustre of idyllic truth. He began to dream dreams, and to speculate extravagantly as to the things that were yet hid from his knowledge. It was borne in upon his mind that Mark was this Pelleas in disguise, come to save Igraine from Gorlois and the towers of Tintagel. The notion took his heart by storm, and his sympathies hovered over the woman like so many scarlet-winged moths. He desired greatly to speak to Mark of that which was in his heart, but feared to seem mischievous and lacking in discretion.

Some three days after Malmain had given Mark the Lady Igraine's ring, Gorlois rode hunting with Morgan la Blanche and a train of knights and damsels. Half the castle turned out to see them sally with their ten couple of hounds in leash, and a goodly company of prickers and beaters. Gareth the minstrel rode with the company on a white horse and sang to the harp a hunting song, and then a *chant d'amour.* Morgan's laugh was as clear as a bell pealing over water as she rode at Gorlois's side in the sunlight, her silks and samites and gold-green tissues fluttering in the wind.

Jehan ran over the bridge to see them go down into the valley. The dogs tugged at the thongs, the boar spears glittered, the dresses threaded the maze of green as roses thread a briar. Jehan climbed a rock, exulting in the life, the spirit, the colour of it all. Gareth's strong voice came up from the valley as he sang of love and of the fairness of women. Jehan envied him his harp and the honour that it won him. It was his own hope to sing of the beauty of the world, the green ecstasy of spring, of autumn forests flaming to the sky, the eternal sorrow of the tortured sea. He came by this same desire in later years when he sang to Arthur and Guinevere and Launcelot of the Lake in the gardens of Caerleon.

A hand plucked him by the heel as he lay curled on the rock watching the cavalcade flickering away into the green. Looking down, he saw the strong face of Mark of the guard. There was a smile on the man's lips, and to Jehan there seemed something prophetic in his eyes. He climbed down and stood looking into the other's face, the mute, trusting look of a dog.

Mark took him by the shoulder.

"The sea is blue and gold, and the 'Priest's Pool' like a violet well."

"There is time for a swim."

"We will watch for a sail from the cliffs."

"And you will tell me more of Pelleas and Igraine."

Mark was in a visionary mood; he used his spear as a staff and talked little. A sleepy sea bubbled a line of foam along the shore. Bleak slopes rolled greenly against an azure sky, and landwards crag and woodland stood steeped in a mist of sunlight. Jehan, sedulous and reverent, watched the passionless calm of thought upon the man's face. His eyes were turned constantly towards the sea with the hope of one waiting for a white sail from the underworld.

When they had gone a mile or more along the cliffs, they came to a path leading to a bay whose lunette of sand shone red gold above the foam. It was a place of crags and headlands, poised sea billows, purple waters pressing from the west. Jehan sat on a stone and waited. Mark took his cloak and bound it to the staff of his spear. Jehan watched him as he stood at his full height like a tall pine on the edge of the cliff and lifted his spear at arm's length above his head. Seawards, dim and distant like a pearl over the purple sea, Jehan saw a sail strike out of the vague west. Mark still held the cloak upon his spear. Jehan understood something of all this. His mind, packed with plots and subtleties, shone with the silvery aureole of romance.

The sail grew against the sky, and a ship loomed gradual out of the west. Mark shook the cloak from his spear, and climbed down the path that curled from the cliff with Jehan at his heels. Below, the waves swirled in amid the rocks and ran ripple on ripple up the yellow sand. The whole place seemed filled with the hoarse underchant of the sea.

In a narrow part of the track Mark stopped suddenly, and stood leaning on his spear. Jehan nearly blundered into him, but saved himself by the help of a tuft of grass. The man's face was on a level with the lad's, and his eyes seemed to look into Jehan's soul.

He pointed to the distant headland, where the towers of Tintagel rose against the sky.

"Death waits yonder," he said.

"For whom?"

"Igraine, — Gorlois's wife."

Jehan looked at him with all his soul. The man was no longer the quaint, vapouring soldier, but a being of different mould, keen, solemn, even magnificent. Jehan felt himself on the verge of romance; the man's face seemed to stare down fear.

"And Pelleas!" he said.

"Pelleas?"

"Art thou not Pelleas?"

Mark smiled in his eyes.

"Your dreams fly too fast," he said.

"And yet —"

"You would see some one play the hero. Who knows but that a bastard may save a kingdom."

Mark moved on down the path, stopping now and again to watch the ship at sea; Jehan followed at his heels. They reached the beach, and saw the waves rolling in on them from the west, with the white belly of a sail showing over the water. Mark made no further tarrying in the matter. Standing on a stretch of sand levelled smooth by the water, he traced a cross thereon with the point of his spear.

"Swear by the cross."

Jehan's face was turned to the man's, eager and enquiring.

"To whom shall I swear troth?" he said.

"To Gorlois's wife."

"Ah!"

"And to the King."

"The King!"

Jehan crossed himself with great good-will.

"By the blood of the Lord Jesu, I swear troth."

They went down close to the waste of waters, and let the spume sweep almost to their feet. A vast blue bank of clouds mountained the far west; the sea seemed deep in colour as an amethyst. Gulls were winging and wailing about the cliffs. Tintagel stood out in its strength against the sky, and they could see the waves white upon its rocks.

Mark took the ring Malmain had given him from a pouch at his belt, and held the gold circle before the lad's eyes.

"From the hand of Gorlois's wife," he said.

Jehan nodded.

"This ring was given her by that Pelleas."

"Yes."

"Who is Uther Pendragon, the King."

Jehan's blue eyes seemed to dilate till they looked strangely large in his thin white face.

"The King!" he said, in a kind of whisper.

Mark made all plain to him in a few words.

"The Lady Igraine loved Pelleas, as well she might, not knowing him to be Ambrosius's brother. It was this same great love that brought her in peril of Gorlois's sword. It is this same love that draws her down to her death — there in Tintagel. Uther Pendragon is at Caerleon; her hope is with him. You, Jehan, shall carry word of this to the King."

The lad's heart was beating like the heart of a giant. The world seemed to expand about him, to grow luminous with the glory of great deeds; he had the braying of a hundred trumpets in his ears. He heard swords ring, saw banners blow, and towers topple like smitten trees.

"I am the King's servant," he said.

"You have sworn troth; so be it. You shall go to the King, to Uther Pendragon, at Caerleon. Tell him you had this ring from a soldier, bribed to deliver it by the Lady Igraine. Tell him the evil that is done to her in the castle of Tintagel. Tell him all — withhold nothing."

Jehan flushed to the temples; his lips moved, but no words came from them. He stood stiff and erect, looking out to sea, following with his eyes the sweep of Mark's spear.

"I am the King's servant," he said.

The ship had drawn in towards the shore. She was lying to with her sails put aback, her black hull rising and falling morosely against the tumultuous purple of the clouds. Nearer still a small galley came heading for the shore with a gush of foam at her prow as the men in her bent to the oars. The galley came swinging in on the broad backs of the sluggish waves, and shooting the surf, grounded on the sands, the men in her leaping out and dragging her beyond the reach of the sea.

There was a more mellow light on Mark's face as he

pointed Jehan to the boat, and the ship swaying on the sun-gilded waves.

"They will carry you to Caerleon," he said.

"And you, sire?"

"There is need of me at Tintagel."

"I have sworn troth."

Jehan stood and looked into the west at the clouds gold-ribbed, domed, snow, and purple. His face might have been lit by the warm glow of a lamp, so clear and radiant was it. He had thrust the King's ring into his bosom.

"The Lord Jesu speed me," he said; "through the Lady Igraine's face I am no longer a coward. God speed me to save her!"

Mark kissed him on the forehead.

"You have a soul in you," he said.

The man stood on the strand under the black cliffs and watched the boat climb the waves. He saw the galley hoisted up, the sails flapping in the wind as the ship sheered out and ran for the open sea. Her sails gleamed white against the tumultuous west, and the ridged waters hid her hull. Overhead, the gulls screamed and circled. Mark, shouldering his spear, turned back and climbed the cliff, with his face towards the towers of Tintagel.

IV

A GALLEY came up the Usk towards dawn, towards dawn when the woods were hung with mist, and a vast quiet brooded over the world. The river made a moist murmur through reeds and sedge, seeming to chant of golden meads as it ran to wed the sea. All the eastern casements of Caerleon glimmered gold as the dawn struck over wood and hill; the city's walls smiled out of the night; her vanes and towers were noosed as with fire. The galley drew to the great quay, and poled to the steps as the city awoke.

A lad, with his russet mantle turned up over his girdle,

passed up from the galley and the quay towards the southern gate of the city of Caerleon. His step was sanguine, his face deep with dreams. He seemed to personate "Youth" entering that city of woeful magic that poets and painters name "Romance."

Within the walls the stir of life had been sounded in by the clarions of the dawn. Seafaring men went down to the river and their ships. At the gate arms rang, tumbrils rumbled. Slim girls passed out into the orchards and the fields, under the trees all heavily grained, russet and green and gold. Women drew water at the wells. The merchant folk in the market square spread their stalls for the day—fruit, flesh, fish, cloth, and the fabrics of the East, armour and brazen jars, vases of strange device.

The city pleased the lad as he passed through its stirring streets, and took the vigour of it, the human symbolism, into his soul. His idealism shed a glamour over the place; how red and white were its maidens; how fair its stately houses; how splendid the clashing armour of its guards. In the market square he asked a wizened apple-seller concerning the palace, and was pointed to the wooded hill where white walls rose above the green. Jehan solaced himself with a couple of ruddy apples from the stall. It was early yet for the palace, so the seller said, and Jehan sat down by a fountain where doves flew, and thought of his errand as he watched the folk go by.

The sun was high before he came to the great gate leading to the gardens of the King. It chanced to be a great day at Caerleon, a day of public appeal, when Uther played patriarch to his people, and sat to hear the prayers of the wronged or the oppressed. Hence it followed that Jehan, pressing in at the gate, found himself one among many, one of a herd, a boy among his elders. In the antechamber of the palace he was edged into a corner, elbowed and kept there by stouter clients who, as a mere matter of course, shouldered a boy to the wall. Argument availed nothing. Men were used to plausible tales for winning precedence, and each considered his especial matter the most pressing in the eyes of justice. The crowd overawed him. The doorkeepers thrust him back with their staves when he waxed importunate and attempted to parley. Often he bethought him of the ring, but, being quick to suspect theft in such a mob, he kept the talisman tight in his tunic, and trusted to time and the powers of patience.

What with giving way to women whose sex commended them, and men whose strength and egotism seemed vested in their elbows, Jehan was fended far from the door all day. A squabbling, querulous crowd filled the place; women with grievances, merchants who had been plundered on the road; peasants, priests, soldiers; beggars and adventurers; a Jew banker whom some Christian had taken by the beard; a farmer whose wife had taken a fancy to a gentleman's bed. It was a stew of envy, discontent, and misfortune. Jehan, whose none too sumptuous clothing did him little service, was shouldered casually into the background. "Take second place to a brat of a boy! God forbid such an indignity!" The vexed folk believed vigorously in the premiership of years.

It was well towards evening when Jehan, who had gone fasting save for a rye-cake, found himself the last to claim audience of the King. A fat pensioner, yawning phenomenally and dreaming of supper, eyed him with little favour from the top step of the stair. The day had been a crowded one, and the savoury scent of roast flesh assailed the senses of the gentleman of the "white wand." Jehan braved the occasion with heart thumping, produced the ring, and held it as a charm under the doorkeeper's nose.

There was an abrupt revulsion in the methods of this domestic demigod. Doors opened as by a magic word; servants went to and fro; bells sounded. A grey-bearded Pharisee appeared, scanned the lad over with an aristocratic contempt, beckoned him to follow. The man with the white wand refrained for a moment from yawning over the paltriness of the world at large.

Jehan, taken by galleries and curtained doors, and disenchanted somewhat with the palatial régime, found himself in a chapel casemented towards the west. Lamps burnt upon the altar, and a priest knelt upon the steps as in prayer. Sacramental vessels glimmered at the feet of the frescoed saints. A fragrant scent of musk and lavender lay heavy on the air.

Jehan saw a man standing by a window, a man girded with a sword, and garbed in no light and joyous fashion. The man's face possessed a kind of sorrowful grandeur, a solemn kindliness that struck home into the lad's heart. The eyes that met his were eyes such as women and children trust. Jehan guessed speedily enough that this was the King.

There was a certain intuition big in him, prophesying of the pain that burdened his message. He faltered for the moment, knelt down, looked into the man's eyes, and took courage. There was a questioning calm in them that quieted him like the dew of prayer. He took the ring and gave it into the King's hand.

"From the Lady Igraine," was his plea.

Now Jehan, though he looked no higher than Uther's knees, saw him rock and sway like some great poplar in a storm. A strange lull seemed to fall sudden upon the world. The lad listened to the beating of his own heart, and wondered. He had soul enough to imagine the large utterance of those few words of his.

A deep voice startled him.

"Your message."

He knelt there and told his tale, simply, and without clamour.

"It is the truth, sire," he said at the end thereof, "so may I drink again of the Lord's blood, and eat his bread at the holy table."

"My God, what truth!"

The man's voice swept the chapel like a wind, deep, sonorous, and terrible. The large face, the broad forehead, the deep-set eyes were turned to the casement and the west. The face was like the face of one who looks into hell. Jehan, on his knees, looked up and shivered. He had told the truth, and the storm awed him like a miracle. It seemed almost impious to be witness of a wrath that was as the righteous passion of a god.

"Gorlois tortures her?"

"To her death, sire."

"The whole — spare nothing."

"She is starved and scourged, and harlots mock her."

"God!"

"They drag her soul in the mire."

It was sunset, and all the sky burnt gold and crimson in the west. Every lozenge of glass in the casement shone red as with fire. Beyond Caerleon a mysterious gloom of trees rolled blackly against the chaos of the decline. The whole world seemed glamoured and steeped in a ghostly quiet. Usk, a band of shadowy gold, ran with vague glimmerings to the sea.

The King spread his arms to the west, and under his black brows his eyes smouldered.

"Am I Uther of Britain — and a King?"

And again in a deep half-heard whisper —

"Igraine! Igraine! thou art true unto death."

From the terrace below came sudden the sound of harping. It was Rivalin, the Court minstrel, singing as the sun went down —

"Quenched be all the bitter pain,
When the roses bloom again
Eyes shall smile through glimmering tears."

The face of the King was like the face of a man who sees a vision. All the glow of the hills seemed in his eyes. His hands shook as he stretched them to the west, the west that was a chasm of torrential gold.

"Igraine," he said, as in a dream.

And again —

"Tintagel will I hurl into the sea."

Jehan knelt and looked mutely at the King. The gloom of the roof seemed to cover him like a canopy, and the frescoes glimmered through the blue shadows. Uther wore a small crucifix about his neck. Jehan, full of a sense of tragedy, saw him tear the crucifix from its chain, and cast it at his feet. The priest at the altar, haloed by the glowing of his lamps, looked at the King, white and wondering. It was an exultant voice that made the chalice quiver.

"Hitherto I have served a God," it said; "now I will serve my own soul!"

V

THE woman's face, haloed by the gloom of the casement, still looked out from Tintagel over the solitary grandeur of sea and cliff. Igraine saw ships pass seldom athwart the west, but they brought no hope for her, for she thought herself alone, and served of none. How should Uther the King know that she was mewed in Tintagel at Gorlois's pleasure! Had he not commended her to the calm orchards and cloisters of a nunnery? Even the ring he had given her had been stolen by sheer force. Days came and went, dawn flooded the eastern woods with gold, and evening tossed her torches in the west. To Igraine they were as alike as the gulls that wheeled and winged white over the blue waters.

There are few men of such despicable fibre that they are wholly ruled by the egotism of the flesh. Your complete villain is no frequent prodigy, being more the denizen of the regions of romance than of the common, trafficking, trivial world. There are bad men enough, but few Neros. Give a human being passions, pride, and intense egotism, and his potential energy for evil is unbounded. Virtue is often a mere matter of habit or circumstance. Joseph might have ended otherwise if Potiphar's wife had had more wit; and as for Judas, he was unfortunate in being made banker to a God.

Gorlois of Cornwall was beholden to his own strenuous, north-winded nature for any trouble he might incur in his madness against Igraine. However much he braved it out to his own conscience, he knew well enough whether he was content or no. He was a strong man, and selfish, resentful, and very human. He was no Oriental monster, no mere Herod. What magnanimity he possessed towards his wife had been frozen into a wolfish scorn by the things that had passed in Garlotte's valley in Wales. Moreover, he had a bad woman at his elbow. Like many a vexed and restless man, he had turned to ambition, and the darker features of his character were being developed thereby. A king had wronged him; it was easy for a great noble to lay plots against a king. War and the clamour of war became like the prophetic sound of a storm from afar in his ears.

Little comment had followed upon the disappearance of the lad Jehan on the day when Gorlois and his knights had ridden hunting. No one cared for the lad; no one missed him materially. Casual gossip arose thereon in the guard-room. The lad had risked the halter or the branding-iron, and sundry threats were launched after him at random. Mark of the guard shrugged his shoulders and laughed.

"There's pluck in the lad," he said, "for all your bullying. By my faith, I guess he grew tired of kicks and leavings, and of being cursed by so many sons of the pot. Bastard or no bastard, the lad's no fool."

The guard-room scoffed complacently at the notion. Jehan do anything in the world but snivel! Not he! These gentlemen judged of a man's worth by the animal propensities of the creature. They weighed a man as they would weigh an ox — for flesh, and the breed in him. Mark, making a show of warming to his wine, enlightened his men further as to Jehan's disappearance.

"The lad and I went to bathe," he said; "there was a ship in the offing, and sailors had come ashore to get water by St. Isidore's spring. They wanted a lad for cabin service, so I took two gold pieces, and told them to kidnap Jehan."

A laugh hailed the confession, a laugh that changed to a cheer when Mark won accomplices by casting largesse for a scramble on the guard-room floor.

"I wish them luck of him," said the captain, pocketing silver; "devil of a spark could I ever knock out of the lad."

"May be you hit too hard."

"May be not. I'll lay my fist against a rope's-end for education."

"Mark takes his wine like a gentleman," quoth one.

"May he get drunk on pay day."

"And sell another Joseph into Egypt."

The woman Malmain came in to join them, corpulent and thirsty. Superabundant and colossal, she impressed a strenuous and didactic mood upon the company, grumbling like a volcano, emitting a smoke of mighty unfeminine gossip. Her black eyes wandered continually towards Mark of the guard. She watched him with a certain air of possession amid all her sweat and jabber, laughing when he laughed, making herself a coarse echo to his will.

Some one spoke of Gorlois's wife. So personal a subject moved Malmain to mystery on the instant. She tapped her forehead with her finger; shook her head with a significance that was sufficient for the occasion.

"Mad!" said the captain of the guard.

Malmain sucked her lips and yawned with her great chasm of a mouth.

"She was always that," she said with a hiccough.

"Paradise, eh?"

"And golden harps!"

"And, damme, no beer!"

There was a certain flavour in the last remark that made the men roar.

"I wonder where they'll bury her," said the captain.

"Throw her into the sea."

"Gorlois's little wench won't weep her eyes out."

Malmain smote a stupendous hip, and tumbled to the notion. The settle shook and creaked under her as though in protest.

"We'll all get married," she said; "Mark, my man, don't blush."

Babylon was compassed round! The same evening a soldier on the walls of Tintagel saw a dim throng of sails rise whitely out of the west. The streaks of canvas stood above the sea touched by the light of the setting sun. There was something ominous in these gleaming sails sweeping in a wide half-circle out of the unknown. A motley throng of castle folk gathered on the walls. Men spoke of the barbarians and of Ireland as they watched the ships rising solemn and silent from the west. Gorlois himself climbed up into a tower and gazed long at these sails whose haven was as yet unknown. He learnt little by the scrutiny. The ships had hardly risen above the purple twilight when night came and shrouded the whole in vague and impenetrable gloom.

Gorlois ordered the castle into a state of siege, and with the night an atmosphere of suspense gathered about Tintagel.

About midnight some dozen points of fire burst out redly on the hills. Sudden and sinister they shone like beacon fires, but by whom lit the castle folks could not tell. Men idled on the walls, shoulder to shoulder, talking in undertones, with now and again a bluff oath to invoke courage. The black infinite, above, around, seemed to hem the place as eternity hems the soul. War and death lurked in the dark, and on the rocks the sea kept up a perpetual moan.

Gorlois walked the walls with several of his knights. He was restless, and in no Christian temper, for the dark muzzled him. Not that he feared the unknown, or the perils that might lurk on hill or sea. He had the soul of a soldier, loved danger for its own sake, and took a hazard as he would take wine. Yet there are certain thoughts that haunt a man for all his hardihood, thoughts that may not weaken him though they may chafe his temper. Such to Gorlois was the memory of a starved face looking out at him scornfully from the gloom, the face of Igraine, his wife.

That night Gorlois's mind was prophetic in dual measure. Like a good captain he scanned the human horizon for snares and enmities, old feuds and the vengeances of men. The dark sky seemed to hold out two scrolls to him tersely illumined as to the near future. To Gorlois they read —

THE BARBARIANS,

OR

THE KING!

Forewarned thus in spirit, he kept to the walls till dawn. The sea sang for him stern epics of tumult and despair. Large projects were moving in his mind like waters that bubble up darkly in a well. He was in a mood for great deeds, alarms and plottings, lusts, gnashings, and the splendid agonies of war.

When the grey veil rose from the world many faces looked out east and west from Tintagel for sign of legions or of ships at sea. Strange truth! not a sail showed upon the ocean, not a spear or shield glimmered on the eastern hills. The threatenings of the night seemed to have cleared like the leaden cloudscape of a stormy sky.

Gorlois, scarred, brooding, sinister, appealed his knights as to the event.

"Not a ship, not a shield," he said, "yet I'll swear we saw watchfires on the hills. Were we scared for nothing?"

"Devil's beacons," quoth one.

"I have heard sailors tell of the phantom fleet of the Phœnicians."

"Have a care," said Sir Isumbras of the wrinkled face; "I remember me of the taking of Genorium; given the chance of an ambuscado, the good captain — "

Gorlois cut in upon his prosings.

"Scour the country, well and good," he said, "send out

your riders; we will see whether there is a Saxon betwixt Tintagel and Glastonbury."

Gorlois had hardly delivered himself, and the company was passing from the battlements, when a trumpet-cry thrilled the solitary morning air. Gorlois and his knights halted at the head of the turret-stair, and looked out from the walls towards the east. A single figure on horseback was moving along the ridge leading to the headland. The rider was clad in black, and his horse-trappings were of sable. He carried neither spear nor shield, but only a herald's long trumpet balanced upon his thigh. He rode very much at his leisure, as though the whole world could abide his business.

Gorlois eyed him blackly under his hand.

"I was wrong, sirs," he said.

Old Isumbras's wrinkles deepened. He tapped the walls with the scabbard of his sword, and waxed oracular after an old man's fashion. Gorlois turned his broad back on him.

"There is trouble in yonder gentleman's wallet," he said.

They passed with clashing arms down the black well of the stairway to the court. Gates were rumbling on their hinges. The herald had ridden over the bridge, and the guards had given him passage. He was brought into the court where Gorlois stood in the centre of a half-circle of knights. The herald wore a cap of crimson velvet and a mask over his face. He walked with a certain stately swagger; it was palpable that he was no common fellow.

There was no parley on either part. Those who watched saw that this emissary carried a case of scarlet cloth and a naked poniard. He gave the case into Gorlois's hands, but threw the poniard on the stones at his feet. A fine insolence burnt in his stride and gesturing. Gorlois's scar seemed to show up duskily upon his cheek, and he looked as though tempted to tear the mask from the stranger's face. An incomprehensible dignity waved him back, and while he dallied with his wrath, the man turned his back on him and marched unconcernedly for the gate. The court bristled with steel, but none hindered or molested him. They heard the gate roll to, and the rattle of hoofs on the bridge. The sound died rapidly away, leaving Tintagel silent as a ruin.

Gorlois picked up the poniard, for none of his men stirred, and cut the woven band that held the lappets of the case. The white corner of a waxen tablet came to light. Gorlois drew the tablet out, held it at arm's length, and read the inscription thereon. His face grew hard and vigilant as he read, and he seemed to spell the thing over to himself several times before satisfied to the letter. He stood awhile in thought, and then leaving his knights to their conjectures, walked away to that quarter of the castle where Morgan la Blanche had her lodging.

He found the woman couched by the window that looked out towards the sea. Though dawn had but lately come, she was awake, and sat combing her hair, while a kitten slept on the blue coverlet covering her lap. Wine and fruit stood on the table near the bed, with scented water, a rouge-pot, and a bowl of flowers. Morgan was smothered in fine white linen, banded at neck and wrists with sky-blue silk. A kerchief of gold gossamer work covered her shoulders.

Gorlois touched her lips, and let her hair run through his fingers like water.

"Minion, you are awake early."

Morgan's face shone white, and her eyes looked tired and faded. She had heard rumours and had watched the night through, being tender-conscienced as to her own skin. Adversity, even in its meaner forms, was a thing insufferably insolent, a cloud in the absolute gold of a sensuous existence. Being quick to mark any shadowing of the horizon, she was undeceived by Gorlois's mere smile. She caught his hand and stared up at him.

"Well!"

"What troubles you?"

"Is it to be a siege?"

Gorlois stretched his strong neck, laughed, and eschewed

subtlety. It interested him to see this worldling ruffled, Morgan, whose chief care was how the world might serve her.

"Read," he said, putting the tablet into her hands.

Morgan sat up in bed with her fair hair streaming over her shoulders. She traced out the words hurriedly with a white finger-tip. Her eyes seemed to grow large as she read; her hands trembled a very little. At the end thereof she dropped the tablet into her lap and looked at Gorlois with a certain petulant dread.

"How did the man hear of all this?"

"God knows!"

"Treachery!"

Gorlois jerked his belt and said nothing.

The woman Morgan sat and hugged her knees. She looked out to sea with a frown on her face, and the blue coverlet dragged in tight folds about her waist. The kitten woke up and began to play with Morgan's hair as it trailed down upon the bed. She cuffed the little beast aside, and looked at Gorlois. Her eyes now were steely and clear, and very blue under her white forehead.

"Obviously, he has learnt all," she said.

Gorlois nodded morosely.

"And this matter is to be between you alone?"

"I have his word."

"And he is a fool for truth."

Silence held them both awhile, and Morgan seemed to dally with her thoughts. Her lips worked loosely as though moving with her mind. The kitten clawed its way up the coverlet and rubbed its glossy flank against the woman's arm.

"What of an ambush?" she suggested mildly.

Gorlois darted a look at her and shook his head.

"No; it shall be fair between us."

"Honour!"—with a sneer.

"I am a soldier."

"By the prophet, that is the strange part of it all. You go out to kill a man, and yet trouble about the method."

"There honour enters."

"You kill him, all the same."

Morgan tossed the quilt aside, thrust a pair of glimmering feet out of the bed, and stood at Gorlois's elbow. She took the tablet of wax and held it over a lamp that was burning till the wax softened and suffered the lettering to be effaced. Gorlois's great sword hung from the carved bedpost. Morgan took it and buckled it to the man with her plump, worldly little hands.

"Let it not fail," she said.

Gorlois kissed her lips.

"There will be no King; and the heir—well, you are a great soldier, and men fear your name."

She kept him with her awhile and then bade him farewell. The sun was high in the heavens when Gorlois, in glittering harness, rode out alone from Tintagel, and passed away into the wilds.

VI

THERE was a preternatural brightness over sea and cliff that day. Headland and height stood limned with a luminous grandeur; the sea was a vast opal; mountainous clouds sailed solemn and stupendous over the world. Towards evening it grew still and sultry, and storms threatened. A vapoury leviathan lowered black out of the east, devouring the blue, with scudding mists spray-like about his belly. The sky changed to a sable cavern. In the west the sun still blazed through mighty crevices, candescent gold; the world seemed a chaos of glory and shadow. Sea-birds came screaming to the cliffs. The walls of Tintagel burnt athwart the west.

Presently out of the blue bosom of an unearthly twilight a vague wind rose. Gusts came, clamoured, and died into nothingness. The world seemed to shudder. The dry bracken and grass on the hillsides hissed as the wind came seldom and tumultuous. The roadway smoked. In the valleys the trees moaned, shivered, and stood still.

Mark of the guard stood in the garden leaning on his spear, watching the storm gathering above. It was his guard that night over the stairway leading to Igraine's room, and he stood under the shadow of the tower.

A red sword flashed sudden out of the east, and smote the hills. Thunder followed, growling over the world. Then rain came, and a whirlwind seemed to fly from the face of the storm. In the west a burning crater still poured gold upon a restless and afflicted sea.

It grew dark very rapidly, and a thundering canopy soon overarched Tintagel. Now and again flaming cracks of fire ran athwart the dome of the night, lighting battlements and sky with a weird momentary splendour. Rain rattled on the stones and drifted whirling against door and casement. Small torrents formed along the walks; every spout and gully gushed and gurgled. Like an underchant came the hoarse cry of the sea.

Mark had withdrawn under the arch of the tower's entry. A cresset flamed and spluttered higher up the stairway, throwing down an ineffectual gleam upon the man's armour as he stood and looked into the night. The storm fires lit his face, making it start out of the dark white and spiritual, with largely luminous eyes. He held motionless at his post like a Roman soldier watching the downfall of Pompeii.

Solitude possessed garden, court, and battlement, for no one stirred on such a night. The knights of the garrison were making merry in the great hall, and the men of the guard, unpestered by their superiors, had gathered a great company in the guard-room to emulate their officers. The scullion knaves and wenches had fled the kitchen; the sentinels had sneaked from the walls. There was no fear now of a leaguer. Had not Duke Gorlois declared as much before his sally?

Mark alone stood to his post, listening to the laughter that reached him between the stanzas of the storm. His face was like the face of a statue, yet alert and eager for all its calm. More than once he went out through the storm of rain to the great gate and stood there listening while the wind howled overhead. About midnight the noise of gaming and revelling seemed suddenly to cease, as when folk hear the tolling of a bell for prayer. Only the wind kept up its hooting over the walls.

Mark stood a long while by the guard-room door with his ear to the planking. Seldom a quavering cry came out to him, and the place grew empty of human sound. All Tintagel seemed asleep, though many casements still shone out yellow against the gloom. Mark slipped to the main gate. There was a postern in it for service after dark. He drew back the bolts and loosed the chain from the staple, and leaving the small door ajar, passed back to the tower's entry.

Thunder went rolling over the sea. Mark left his spear by the porch and went up the first few steps of the stairway. He took the cresset from its bracket, carried it down, and tossed it into the court, where the flames spluttered out in the rain. Darkness accomplished, he went up the stairway to the short gallery leading to Igraine's room. At the top he stood and listened. He heard the sound of breathing, and knew that it came from the woman Malmain who slept in the alcove before the door.

Mark smote the wall a ringing blow with the handle of his poniard. A bench creaked; some one yawned and began to grumble. It was so dark that the very walls were part of the prevailing gloom.

"Who's there?"

Mark stood aside.

"The cresset's out on the stairs."

Two arms came groping along the wall.

"You've been asleep, cherub."

"Mark!"

"You were forgetting our tryst."

A thick sensual laugh sounded from the stairhead. Something opaque moved in the dark; a pair of arms felt along the passage; a hand touched Mark's face. Malmain's arms wrapped the man's body; she lifted him to her with her great strength, and kissed his lips.

"Rogue!"

Once, twice, a streaking shadow rose and fell with the faintest glinting of steel. There was a staggering sound, a wet cough, a sharp-drawn breath, and then silence. Malmain fell against the wall with her hands to her side, held rigid a moment, and then slid into a heap. Mark bent over the woman and gripped her wrist.

In a short while he left the body lying there and moved to the door. Sliding his long fingers over the panels, he found the spring that marked the catch. Light streamed through into the gallery and fell upon Malmain as she lay huddled against the wall, her hair trailing along the floor like rills of blood.

A lamp burnt in the room, showering a thin silvery lustre from its pedestal, leaving the angles in dull brown shadow. The room was bare and bleak as a beggar's attic. The one window had been shuttered up against the rain, and the crazy lattice shook in the wind. The whole tower seemed to quake, pressed upon by the broad shoulders of the storm.

Gorlois's wife lay asleep on a rough bed in the centre of the room. Mark went forward and stood over her. The light fell upon Igraine's face and haloed it with a quiet radiance. Her hands were folded over her breast, and the man looking upon her face saw it drawn and haggard even in sleep. It had a kind of tragic fairness, a stained beauty like the wistful strangeness of an autumnal garden. It was pale, piteous, thin, and spiritual. The flesh shone like white wax; the short hair glimmered like a net of gold.

So changed, so ethereal, was the face of the sleeper, that the man stood and looked at her with gradual awe. Passed indeed was the blood-red rose of life, green summer with its ecstasy of song. Autumn's rich tapestries of bronze and gold were falling before the wind of winter and the shrill sword of death. The woman on the bed looked like some pale princess slumbering out her doom in some baleful tower.

Igraine's sleep was shallow and ineffectual, a restless stupor impressed upon a troubled mind. The storm seemed to figure in her dreams. A kind of splendid misery played upon her face, such misery as floods forth from some old legend, strange and sad. Her hands tossed to and fro over the coverlet like fallen flowers stirred by a wind. Her lids drooped over half-opened eyes.

A sudden gust broke the catch of the casement, and swung the frame into the room. All the boisterous laughter of the storm seemed to sweep in with the wind. With the racket Igraine woke and started up in bed upon her elbow. The lamp flame, draught-slanted over the rim, gave but a feeble light; the room was filled with wavering darkness.

Mark stood back from the bed. There was blood upon his tunic. For a moment he was speechless like a man caught in a theft.

In the dim light and to the half-awakened senses of the sleeper, the intruder stood for Gorlois, beard, face, and figure. A moment's hesitancy lost Mark the lead. The door stood wide. What ensued came crowded into the compass of a few seconds.

Igraine, quick to conceive, jerked the coverlet from the bed. Before Mark could prevent her, she had thrown it over the lamp and smothered the flame. The room sank into instant darkness and confusion. Mark's voice sounded above the storm. Then came the slamming of a door, and silence save for the blustering of the wind.

Igraine stood on the threshold in the dark, and drew her breath fast. She had shut the man in the room, and the door opened only from without by a spring catch. Mark of the guard was trapped.

And Malmain!

Igraine remembered the woman, and heeding nothing of the voice that called to her from the room, groped her way to the stairhead, expecting at every step to hear the woman's challenge start out of the gloom. At the end of the gallery she nearly tripped and fell over some inanimate thing. Reaching down out of curiosity she drew her hand back with a half cry, her fingers fouled with a thick warm ooze. An indefinite terror seized her in the dark. She went reeling down the stairway, clutching at the walls, grasping the air. A faint outcry still followed her from the room above.

In the garden rain still rattled, and scud blew from the pools. Igraine stood motionless under the shadow of a cypress, with her face turned to the sky. Her ragged gown blew about her bare ankles, and the wind whirled rain into her face. She drew deep breaths and stretched out her hands to the night, for there was the kiss of liberty in this cold, shrill shower.

Anon the old fear urged her on, companioned now by a reawakened courage. She was weak and starved, but what of that! The storm seemed to enter into her soul with its blustery vigour, crying to her with the multitudinous echoes of the night. What was the mere peril of the flesh to one who had faced spiritual torture more keen than death!

Creeping round under the shadow of the wall with quick glances darted into the dark she made her way round the court to the great gate. The gate-house was dark as the sky, and there was no tramping of sentinels from wall to wall. Igraine crept into the yawn of the archway, brushing along the stones. With each step she listened for the rattle of a spear, and looked for the armed figure that should clash out on her from the gloom. She won the gate and leant against it, breathless from mere suspense. Her fingers groped over the great beams, touched an outstanding edge, and tugged at it. The edge moved; a door came open and let in the wind.

Igraine stood a moment and pondered this mystery in her heart. She had chanced on nothing in the whole castle save one man and a corpse. Some strange doom might have fallen upon the place like the doom that smote the Assyrians in their sleep.

Plain before her stood the open gate and liberty. The hint was sufficient for the occasion. Igraine, leaving Tintagel to the unknown, gathered her rags round her and passed out into the night.

VII

A ROLLING country spread with moor, wood, and crag. A storm creeping black out of the east over the tops of a forest of pines. On the slope of a hill covered with a mauve mist of nodding scabei and bronzed tracts of bracken, two horsemen motionless in armour. Far away, the glimmer of a distant sea.

Uther the King wheeled his horse and pointed northwards towards the pine woods with his sword. The challenge came plainly in the gesture. There was no need for vapouring or for heroics; a quick stare—eye for eye—said everything a soldier could desire.

Uther, on his black horse, rode with loose bridle, looking straight ahead into the darkness of the woods. He carried his naked sword slanted over his shoulder. Frequent streams of sunlight flashed down upon his harness and made it burn under the boughs, leaving his face calm and solemn under the shadow of his helm. Gorlois held some paces away, stiff and arrogant, watching the man on his flank with restless, smouldering eyes. It was a silent pilgrimage for them both, a pilgrimage to a shrine whence, for one of them, there might be no return.

A shimmering curtain of sunlight spread itself suddenly before them among the pines. The two men rode out into an oval glade palisaded by the innumerable pillars of the wood, bowered in by rolling heights of dusky green. On all sides the spires made a jagged circle of the sky. A pool, black as obsidian, slept in the sun. Heather bloomed there, girdling the confines of wood and water with a blaze of purple.

Uther dismounted and tied his horse to a tree. His deliberation in no way pandered to Gorlois's self-esteem; there was to be no flurry or bombast in the event. No one was to witness this judgment of the sword; chivalry and malice alike were to be locked up in the heart of the forest. A smooth circle of grass lay on the northern side of the pool, promising well to the two who moved thither with nothing more eloquent than an exchange of gestures.

The heather swept away, a purple dirge to the black sounding of the pines, and a whorl of storm-laden clouds swam towards the sun. Uther, with a face strong as a god's, swung his sword from his shoulder and grounded the point in the sod. His destiny waxed great in him in that hour. There was something inevitable in the quiet of his eyes.

"You are ready," he said very simply.

Gorlois jerked a quick glance at him, and licked his lips. He, too, was in no mood for words or matters ethical. Temporal lusts ran strong in his blood.

"For a woman's honour!"

"As you will, sire," with a shrug.

"We have no need of courtesies."

"Over a harlot!"

"Guard, and God pardon you."

Both swords flickered up hotly in the sunlight. Gorlois, sinewy and full of fettle, gave a half-shout and sprang to engage. He had vast faith in himself, having come scatheless out of many such tussles; nor had he ever been humbled by man or beast. Vigorous as a March morning he launched the first blow, a grim cut laid in with both hands, a cut that rattled home half-parried on the other's shoulder. Uther, quick for all his calmness, gave the point in retort, a lunge that slid under the Cornishman's sword and made the muscles gape in Gorlois's neck. There was blood to both.

The swords began to leap and sing in the sunlight, and the forest echoed to the clangour of arms. Both men fought without shields, and for a season well within themselves, and there was much craft on either part. Cut and counter-cut rang through the pine alleys like the cry of axes whirled by woodmen's hands. As yet there was no bustle, no wild smiting. Every stroke came clean and true, lashed home with the weight of arms and body.

Hate overset mere swordsmanship anon, and reason grew less and less as the men waxed warm. Gorlois, running in with a swinging buffet, stumbled over a heather tuft and caught a counter full in the face. The smart of it and a split lip quickened him immeasurably. The blades began to whirl with more malice, less precision. Matters grew tumultuous as leaves in a whirlwind. For some minutes there seemed nothing but a tangle of swords in the sun, a staggering chaos of red and gold.

Such fighting burnt itself to a standstill in less than three minutes. Uther drew back like a boar pressed by hounds. There was no whit of weakening in his mood, only a re-assertive reason that would trust nothing to the fortune of a moment. The muscles stood out in his strong throat, blood ran from his slashed tunic, and he was breathing hard; but his manhood burnt strong and true. Gorlois, with mouth awry, eyed him with sword half up, and drew back in turn. His face streamed. He spat blood upon the heather.

"God! what work."

It was Gorlois's testimony, wrung from him by the stress of sheer hard fighting. The storm-cloud crept across the sun and overcharged the world with gloom. The pool grew more black in its purple bed; the forest began to weave the twilight into its columned halls.

"You lack breath, sire."

"I wait for you," Uther said.

But the man of Tintagel was in a sinister mood for the moment. Genius moved his sweating brain. He dropped into philosophic brevities as he spat blood from his bruised lips.

"All for a woman," he said thickly.

"True."

"Are you much in love, sire?"

Uther answered him nothing, but waited with his sword over his shoulder.

"She made fuss enough."

Still silence.

"I never knew a woman so obstinate in making an end. And we buried her in the sand, where the waves roll at flood. Now, you and I lose our brains over a corpse."

Uther's sword shone again.

"Guard," he said quietly.

A sudden gust came clamouring through the wood. The darkening boughs tossed and jerked against the sky, breathing out a multitudinous moan, a hoarse cry as of a smitten host. The east piled thunder over the world. It was the same storm that swept the battlements of Tintagel.

By the pool swords rang; red and gold strove and staggered over the heather. It was the death tussle and a sharp one at that. Destiny or not, matters were going all against Gorlois; his blows were out of luck; he was rent time on end and gave little in return. Rabid, dazed, he began making blind rushes that boded ill for him. More than once he stumbled, and was mired to the knees in the pool.

The end came suddenly enough as the light failed. Both men smote together; both swords met with a sound that seemed to shake the woods. Gorlois's blade snapped at the hilt.

He stood still a moment, then plucked out his poniard and made a spring. A merciless down-cut beat him back. The fine courage, the strenuous self-trust, seemed to ebb from him on a sudden as though the blow had broken his soul. He fell on his knees and held his hands up with a thick, choking cry.

"Mercy! God's mercy!"

"Curse you! Had you pity on the woman?"

"Sire, sire!"

Thunder rolled overhead, and the girdles of the sky were loosed. A torrent of rain beat upon the man's streaming face; he tottered on his knees, and still held his hands to the heavens.

"I lied," he said. "God witness, I lied."

"Ah—!"

"The woman lives—is at Tintagel."

"Man—"

"Give me life, sire, give me life; you shall have her."

Uther looked at him and heaved up his sword. Gorlois saw the King's face, gave a great cry, and cowered behind his hands. It was all ended in a moment. The rain washed his gilded harness as he lay with his blood soaking into the heather.

VIII

As the world grew grey with waking light Uther the King came from the woods, and heard the noise of the sea in the hush that breathed in the dawn. The storm had passed over the ocean, and a vast quiet hung upon the lips of the day. In the east a green streak shone above the hills. The sky was still aglitter with sparse stars, and an immensity of gloom brooded over the sea.

Gaunt, wounded, triumphant, he rode up beneath the banners of the dawn, eager yet fearful, inspired and strong of purpose. Wood and hill slept in a haze of mist; the birds were only beginning in the thickets, like the souls of children yet unborn calling to eternity. Beyond, on the cliffs, Tintagel, wrapped round with night, stood silent and sombre athwart the west.

Uther climbed from the valley as the day came with splendour, a glow as of molten gold streaming from the east. Wood and hillside glimmered in a smoking mist, dew-brilliant, wonderful. As the sun rose the sea stretched sudden into the arch of the west — a great pavement of gold. A mysterious lustre hovered over the cliffs; waves of light beat like saffron spray upon Tintagel.

The dawn-light found an echo on Uther's face. He came that morning the ransomer, the champion, a King indeed; Spring bursting the thongs of Winter; Day thrusting back the Night. His manhood smote in him like the deep-throated cry of a great bell, voluminous and solemn. The towers on the cliff were haloed with magic hues. Life, glory, joy, lay locked in the grey stone walls. His heart sang in him, and his eyes were afire.

As he walked his horse with a hollow thunder of hoofs over the bridge, he took his horn and blew a blast thereon. There was a quiet, a lifelessness, about the place that smote his senses, bodying forth mystery. The walls were void against the sky. At the sound of the horn there came no stirring of armed men, no answering fanfare, no glimmering of faces at the casements. Only the gulls circled from the cliffs, and the sea made its moan along the strand.

Uther sat in the saddle and looked from tower to battlement, from battlement to gate. There was something tragic about the place, the silence of a sacked town, the ghostliness of a ship sailing the seas with a dead crew upon her deck. Uther's glance rested on the open postern, an empty streak in the great gate. His face darkened somewhat; his eyes lost their sanguine glow. There was something betwixt death and treachery in all this quiet.

He dismounted and left his horse on the bridge. The postern beckoned him. He went in like a man nerved for peril, with sword drawn and shield above his head, ready for blows in dark corners. Again he blew his horn. The blast rang and resounded under the arch of the gate. No man came to answer or avenge it.

The guard-room door stood ajar; Uther thrust it open with the point of his sword and looked in. A grey light filtered through the narrow windows. The place was like the cave of the Seven Sleepers. Men, women, guards, servants, were huddled on the benches and on the floor. Some lay fallen across the settles; others sat with their heads fallen forwards upon the table; a few had crawled towards the door. They were cast in every posture, every attitude, bleak, stiff, and motionless. Some had froth upon their lips, glistening eyes, clenched fingers. The shadow of death was over the whole.

The King's face was as grey as the faces of the dead. He had looked for human throes, perils, strong hands, and the vehemence of man. There was something here, a calm horror, a mystery that hurled back the warm courage of the heart. Prophecy lurked open-mouthed in the shadows. Uther shouldered his sword, passed out, and drew to the door.

In the great court he looked round him like a traveller who has stumbled upon a city wrapped in a magic sleep. Urged on by manifold forebodings, and knowing the place of old, he went first to the State quarters and hunted the rooms through and through. The same silence met him everywhere. In the great hall he came upon a ring of corpses round a table, a ring of men in armour, stiff and rigid as stone, with wine and fruit mocking their staring eyes. In the lodging of the women he found a lady laid on a couch by an open window. Her fair hair swept the pillow; her eyes were wide and glazed; an open casket lay on the bed, and strings of jewels were scattered on the coverlet. The woman's face was white as apple blossom; she had a half-eaten pomegranate in her hand.

Uther passed from the death-chamber of Morgan la Blanche to the garden. The shadows of the place, the staring faces, the stiff hands clawing at things inanimate, were like phantasms of the night. He took the sea air into his nostrils, and looked into the blue realism of the sky.

All about him the garden glistened in the dawn, the cypresses shimmered with dew, the pool was like a steel buckler on cloth of green. Here was the placid life of flowers making very death the more apparent to his soul.

As he stood in deep thought, half dreading what he still half knew, a voice called to him, breaking suddenly the ponderous silence of the place. A face showed overhead at the upper window in the tower; a hand beckoned and pointed towards the tower's entry. Here at last was something quick and tangible in the flesh, something that could speak of the handicraft of death. Uther climbed the stairs and found Malmain's body by the well. When he had looked at the woman's face and seen blood he paid no more heed to her. She was only one among many.

Guided by a voice, Uther unlatched the door and passed in with sword drawn. A man met him on the threshold, a man with the face of a Dante, and shaven lip and chin. It was the face of Merlin.

IX

WITHOUT the gate of Tintagel stood Uther the King looking out towards the eastern hills clear against the calm of the sky. He stood bare-headed, like one in prayer; his face was strong, yet wistful and patient as a sick child's. At his elbow waited Merlin, silent and inscrutable. Much had passed between them in that upper room, that room more hallowed to Uther than the rock tomb of the Christ.

"Ever, ever night," he said, stretching out his hands as to an eternal void.

Merlin's eyes seemed to look leagues away over moor, hill, and valley. A strange tenderness played upon his lips, and there was a radiance upon his face impossible to describe. It was like the face of a lover, a dreamer of dreams.

"A man is a mystery to himself," he said.

"But to God?"

"I know no God, save the god my own soul. Let me live and die, nothing more. Why curse one's life with a 'to be'?"

Uther sighed heavily.

"It is a kind of fate to me," he said, "inevitable as the setting of the sun, natural as sleep. Not for myself do I fear it."

"Let Jehovah follow Jupiter into the chaos of fable. Sire, look yonder."

Merlin's eyes had caught life on the distant hillsides, life surging from the valleys, life, and the glory of it. Harness, helm, and shield shone in the sun. Gold, azure, silver, scarlet, were creeping from the bronzed green of the wilds. Silent and solemn the host rolled gradual into the full splendour of the day.

Uther's eyes beheld them through a mist of tears.

"King Nentres, King Urience, and the host," he said.

"Even so, sire."

"They were bidden to follow."

"Loyal to their king."

Uther watched them with a great pride stealing into his eyes; he smiled and held his head high.

"All these are mine," he said.

Merlin's face had kindled.

"Grapple the days to come," he said; "let Scripture and old ethics rot. You have a thousand knights; let them ride by stream and forest, moor and mere. Let them ride out and sunder like the wind."

"The quest of a King's heart!"

"Sire, like a golden dawn shall she rise out of the past. Blow thy horn. Let us not tarry."

X

Six days had passed. Once more the sun had tossed night from the sky, and kindled hope in the hymning east. The bleak wilderness barriered by sea and crag had mellowed into the golden silence of autumnal woods. The very trees seemed tongued with prophetic flame. The world like a young lover leapt radiant out of the dawn.

Through the reddened woods rode Uther the King with Merlin silent at his side. Gloom still reigned on the gaunt, strong face, and there was no lustre in the eyes that challenged ever the lurking shade of death. Six nights and six days had the quest been baffled. Near and far armour glimmered in the reddened sanctuaries of the woods. Not a trumpet brayed, though the host had scattered in search of a woman's face.

At the seventh dawn the trees drew back before the King, where the shimmering waters of a river streaked the meads. Peace dwelt there, and a calm eternal, as of the Spirit that heals the throes of men. Rare and golden lay the dawn-light on the valley. The song of birds came glad and multitudinous as in the burgeoning dawn of a glorious May.

Uther had halted under a great oak. His head was bare in the sun-steeped shadows; his face was as the face of one weary with long watching under the voiceless stars. Hope, like a dewless rose, drooped shaken and thirsty with desire. Great dread possessed him. He dared not question his own soul.

A horn sounded in the woods, wild, clamorous and exultant. It was as the voice of a prophet cleaving the despair of a godless world. Even the trees stood listening. Far below in the green shadows of the valley a horseman moved brilliant as a star that portents the conception of a king.

Uther's eyes were on the horseman in the valley.

"I am even as a child," he said.

Merlin's lips quivered.

"The dawn breaks, sire, the night is past. Tidings come to us. Let us ride on."

Uther seemed sunk in thought; he bowed his head, and looked long into the valley.

"Am I he who slew Gorlois?"

"Courage, sire."

"My blood is as water, my heart as wax. Death and destiny are over my head."

"Speak not of destiny, sire, and look not to the skies. In himself is man's power. Thou hast broken the crucifix. Now trust thine own soul. So long as thou didst serve a superstition, thou didst lose thy true heaven."

"And yet —"

"Thou hast played the god, sire, and the Father in heaven must love thee for thy strength. God loves the strong. He will let thee rule destiny, and so prosper."

"Strange words!"

"But true. Were I God, should I love the priest puling prayers in a den? Nay, that man should be mine who moved godlike in the world, and strangled fate with the grip of truth. Great deeds are better than prayers. See! it is young Tristan who comes."

The horseman in the valley had swept at a gallop through a sea of sun-bronzed fern. He was a young knight on a black horse, caparisoned in green and gold. A halo of glistening curls aureoled his boyish face; his eyes were full of a restless radiance, the eyes of a man whose heart was troubled. He sprang from the saddle, and leading his horse by the bridle, kissed the scabbard of Uther's sword.

"Tidings, sire."

"Tristan, I listen."

The knight looked for a moment into the King's face, but dared not abide the trial. There was such a stare of desperate calm in the dark eyes, that the lad's courage whimpered, and quailed from the truth. He hung his head, and stood mute.

"Tristan, I listen."

"Sire — "

"My God, man, speak out!"

"Sire — "

"The truth."

"She lives, sire!"

A great silence fell within the hearts of the three, an ecstasy of silence such as comes after the wail of a storm. Merlin stroked his lip, and smiled, the smile of one who dreams. The King's face was as the face of one who thrusts back hope out of his soul. He sat rigid on his horse, a scarlet image fronting Fate, grim-eyed and steadfast. There were tears in the eyes of Tristan the knight.

"What more?"

Tristan leant against his horse, his arm hooked over the brute's neck.

"In the valley, sire, is a sanctuary; you can see it yonder by the ford. Two holy women dwell therein. To them, sire, I commend you."

"You know more!"

"Sire, spare me. The words are for women's lips, not for mine."

"So be it."

The three rode on in silence; Merlin and Tristan together, looking mutely in each other's faces. Uther's chin was bowed on his breast. The reins lay loose on his horse's neck.

A grey cell of unfaced stone showed amid the green boughs beyond the water. At its door stood a woman in a black mantle. A cross hung from her neck, and a white kerchief bound her hair. She stood motionless, half in the shadow, watching the horsemen as they rode down to the rippling ford.

Autumn had touched the sanctuary garden, and the King's eyes beheld ruin as he climbed the slope. The woman had come from the cell, and now stood at the wicket-gate, with her hands folded as in prayer. Tristan took Uther's bridle. The King went on foot alone to speak with the anchoress.

"Sire," she said, kneeling at his feet, "God save and comfort you."

The man's brow was twisted into furrows. His right hand clasped his left wrist. He looked over the woman's head into the woods, and breathed fast through clenched teeth.

"Speak," he said.

"Sire, the woman lives."

"I can bear the truth."

The anchoress made the sign of the cross.

"She came to us, sire, here in this valley, a tall lady, with golden hair loose upon her neck. Her feet were bare and bleeding, her robe rent with thorns. And as she came, she sang wild snatches, such as tell of love. We took her, sire, and gave her meat and drink, bathed her torn feet, and gave her raiment. So, she abode with us, gentle and lovely, yet speaking like one who had suffered, even to death. And yet, even as we slept, she stole away from us last night, and now is gone."

The woman had never so much as lifted her eyes to the man's face. Her hands held her crucifix, and she was pale as new-hewn stone.

"And is this all?"

The man's voice trembled in his throat; his face shone in the sun.

"Not all, sire."

"Say on."

The anchoress had buried her face in her black mantle; her voice was husky as with tears.

"Sire, you seek one bereft of reason."

"Mad!"

"Alas!"

"My God, this then is the end!"

XI

AN indefinite melancholy overshadowed the world. Autumn breathed in the wind; the year was rushing red-bosomed to its doom.

On the summit of a wood-crowned hill, rising like a pyramid above moor and forest, two men stood silent under the shadow of an oak. In the distance the sea glimmered; and by a rock upon the hillside, armed knights, a knot of spears, shone like spirit sentinels athwart the west. Mists were creeping up the valleys as the sun went down into the sea. A few stars, dim and comfortless, gleamed out like souls still tortured by the platitudes of Time. An inevitable pessimism seemed to challenge the universe, taking for its parable the weird afterglow in the west.

Deep in the woods a voice was singing, wild and solitary in the gathering gloom. Like the cry of a ghost, it seemed to set the silence quivering, the leaves quaking with a windless awe. The men who looked towards the sea heard it, a song that echoed in the heart like woe.

"Sire, there is yet hope."

"Life grows dim, and dreams elapse in fire."

Merlin pointed into the darkening woods. His eyes shone crystal bright, and there was a great radiance upon his face.

"Sire, trust thine own heart, and the god in thee. Through superstition thou hast been brought nigh unto death and to despair. Trust not in priestcraft, grapple God unto thy soul. The laws of men are carven upon stone, the laws of heaven upon the heart. Be strong. From henceforth scorn mere words. Trample custom in the dust. Trust thyself, and the god in thy heart."

The distant voice had sunk into silence. Uther listened for it with hand aloft.

"Yonder — heaven calls," he said.

"Go, sire."

"I must be near her—through the night."

"And lo!—the moon stands full upon the hills. You shall bless me yet."

Dim were the woods that autumn evening, dim and deep with an ecstasy of gloom. Stars flickered in the heavens; the moon came, and broidered the trees with silver flame. A primæval calm lay heavy upon the bosom of the night. The spectral branches of the trees were rigid and prayerful towards the sky.

Uther had left Merlin gazing out upon the shimmering sea. The voice called him from the woods with plaintive peals of song. The man followed, holding to a grass-grown track that curled purposeless into the gloom. Moonlight and shadow were alternate upon his armour. Hope and despair were mimicked upon his face. His soul leapt voiceless and inarticulate into the darkened shrine of prayer.

The voice came to him clearer in the forest calm. The gulf had narrowed; the words flew as over the waters of death. They were pure, yet reasonless, passionate, yet void, words barbed with an utter pathos that wounded desire.

For an hour the King followed in the woods, drawing ever nearer, waxing great with prayer. Anon the voice failed him by a little stream that quivered dimly through the grass. A stillness that was ghostly held the woods. The moonlight seemed to shudder on the trees. A stupendous stupor weighed upon the world.

A hollow glade opened sudden in the woods, a white gulf in the forest's gloom. Water shone there, a mere, rush-ringed, and full of mysterious shadows, girded by the bronzed foliage of stately beeches. Moss grew thick about the roots; dead leaves covered the grass.

The man knelt in a patch of bracken, and looked out over the glade. A figure went to and fro by the water's brim, a figure pale in the moonlight, with a glimmering flash of unloosed hair. The man kneeling in the bracken pressed his hands over his breast; his face seemed to start out of the gloom like the face of one who struggles in the sea, submerged, yet desperate.

Uther saw the woman halt beside the mere. He saw her bend, take water in her palms, and dash it in her face. Standing in the moonlight she smoothed her hair between her fingers, her hands shining white against the dark bosom of her dress. She seemed to murmur to herself the while, words wistful and full of woe. Once she thrust her hands to the sky and cried, "Pelleas! Pelleas!" The man kneeling in the shadow quivered like a wind-shaken reed.

The moon climbed higher, and the woman by the mere spread her cloak upon a patch of heather, and laid herself thereon. Not a sound ravaged the silence; the woods were mute, the air rippleless as the steel-surfaced water. An hour passed. The figure on the heather lay still as an effigy upon a tomb. The man in the bracken cast one look at the stars, crossed himself, and crept out into the moonlight.

Holding the scabbard of his sword, he skirted the mere with shimmering armour, went down upon his knees, and crawled slowly over the grass. Hours seemed to elapse before the black patch of heather spread crisp and dry beneath his hands. Breathing through dilating nostrils, he trembled like a craven who creeps to stab a sleeping friend. The moonlight showered vivid as with a supernatural glory. Tense anguish crowded the night with sound.

Two more paces, and he was close at the woman's side. The heather crackled beneath his knees. He held his breath, crept nearer, and knelt so near that he could have kissed the woman's face. Her head lay pillowed on her arm, her hair spread in a golden sheet beneath it. Her bosom moved with the rhythmic calm of dreamless sleep. Her lips were parted in a smile. One hand was hid in the dark folds of her robe.

Uther knelt with upturned face, his eyes shut to the sky. He seemed like one faint with pain; his lips moved as in

"'SHALL I NOT BE YOUR WIFE?'"

prayer. A hundred inarticulate pleadings surged heavenwards from his heart.

Again he bowed himself and watched the woman as she slept. A strange calm fell for a season upon his face; his eyes never wavered from the white arm and the glimmering hair. Vast awe possessed him. He was like a child who broods tearless and amazed over the calm face of a dead mother.

Hours passed, and the man found no sustenance save in prayer. The unuttered yearnings of a world seemed molten in his soul. The moon waned; the stars grew dim. Sounds oracular were moving in the forest, the mysterious breathing of a thousand trees. Life ebbed and flowed with the sigh of a moon-stupored sea. Visions blazed in the night sky. The portals of heaven were open; the sound of harping fell like silver rain out of the clouds; the faces of saints shone radiant through purple gloom.

Hours passed, and neither sleeper nor watcher stirred. The night grew faint, the water flickered in the mere. The very stars seemed to gaze upon the destinies of two wearied souls. Death hid his countenance. Christ walked the earth.

A sudden sound of light, and the stirring of a wind. Far and faint came the quaver of a bird's note. Grey and mysterious stood the forest's spires. Light! Spears of amber darting in the east. A shudder seemed to shake the universe. The vault kindled. The sky grew great with gold.

It was the dawn.

Even as the light increased the man knelt and lifted up his face unto the heavens. Hope, glorious, seemed to fall sudden out of the east, a radiant faith begotten of spirit power. Banners of gold were streaming in the sky. The gloom elapsed. A vast expectancy hung solemn upon the red lips of the day.

Igraine sighed in her sleep. Her mouth quivered, her hair stirred sudden in the heather, tendrils of gold that shivered in the sun. Uther, kneeling, lifted up his hands with one long look to heaven. Prayer burnt upon his face. He strove, Jacob-like, with God.

A second sigh, and the long lashes quivered. The lips moved, the eyes opened.

"Igraine! Igraine!"

Sudden silence followed, a vast hush as of hope. The woman's eyes were searching silently the man's face. He bent and cowered over her like one who weeps. His hands touched her body, yet she did not stir.

"Igraine! Igraine!"

It was a hoarse, passionate cry that broke the golden stupor of the dawn. Sudden light leapt lustrous in the woman's eyes; her face shone radiant amid her hair.

"Pelleas!"

The man's arms circled her. She half crouched in his bosom, her face peering into his.

"Pelleas!"

"At last!"

A great shudder passed through her; her eyes grew big with fear.

"Speak!"

"Igraine."

"Gorlois?"

"Gorlois is dead."

Great silence held for a moment. The woman's head sank down upon the man's shoulder; madness had passed; her eyes were fixed on his with a wonderful earnestness, a splendid calm.

"Is this a dream?"

"It is the truth."

Presently she gave a great sigh, and looked strangely at the sun. Her voice came soft as music over water.

"I have dreamed a dream," she said, "and all was dark and fearful. Death seemed near, and shadows, and things from hell. I knew not what I did, nor where I wandered, nor what strange stupor held my soul. All was dark about me, horrible midnight peopled with foul forms. It has passed; now, I behold the dawn."

The man lifted up his voice and wept.

"My God! my God! out of hell hast thou brought my soul. Never again shall my vile lips blaspheme."

And Igraine comforted him.

"Shall I not be your wife?" she said.

THE END

CPSIA information can be obtained at www.ICGtesting.com
Printed in the USA
BVOW041509261212

309120BV00001B/204/P

9 781434 465726